WITHDRAWN

Billy Lynn's Long Halftime Walk

Billy Lynn's Long Halftime Walk

Ben Fountain

W F HOWES LTD

This large print edition published in 2013 by
W F Howes Ltd
Unit 4, Rearsby Business Park, Gaddesby Lane,
Rearsby, Leicester LE7 4YH

1 3 5 7 9 10 8 6 4 2

First published in the United Kingdom in 2012
by Canongate Books

A CIP catalogue record for this book is available
from the British Library

ISBN 978 1 47123 978 6

Typeset by Palimpsest Book Production Limited,
Falkirk, Stirlingshire
Printed and bound by
CPI Group (UK) Ltd, Croydon, CR0 4YY

MIX
Paper from
responsible sources
FSC
www.fsc.org   FSC® C013604

For my parents

THE THING BEGINS

The men of Bravo are not cold. It's a chilly and windwhipped Thanksgiving Day with sleet and freezing rain forecast for late afternoon, but Bravo is nicely blazed on Jack and Cokes thanks to the epic crawl of game-day traffic and the limo's minibar. Five drinks in forty minutes is probably pushing it, but Billy needs some refreshment after the hotel lobby, where over-caffeinated tag teams of grateful citizens trampolined right down the middle of his hangover. There was one man in particular who attached himself to Billy, a pale, spongy Twinkie of a human being crammed into starched blue jeans and fancy cowboy boots. 'Was never in the military myself,' the man confided, swaying, gesturing with his giant Starbucks, 'but my granddaddy was at Pearl, he told me all the stories,' and the man embarked on a rambling speech about war and God and country as Billy let go, let the words whirl and tumble around his brain

1

                    terrRist

                                freedom

        evil

                          nina leven

                    nina leven

                                nina leven

        troops

                    currj

              support

                                sacrifice

                        Bush

        values

God

Thanks to asswipe luck Billy will have the aisle seat at Texas Stadium, which means he will bear the brunt of these encounters for most of the afternoon. His neck hurts. He slept but poorly last night. Each of those five Jack and Cokes puts him deeper in the hole, but the sight of the stretch limo pulling up to the hotel aroused a bundle of nervous cravings in him, this boat of a snow-white Hummer with six doors to a side and black-tinted windows for maximum privacy. 'What I'm talking a-*bout*!' cried Sergeant Dime as he pounced on the bar, everyone whooping over all the pimp finery, but after destroying all hopes for a quick recovery Billy subsides into a gnarled, secret funk.

'Billy,' says Dime, 'you're flaking on me.'

'No, Sergeant,' Billy says at once. 'I'm just thinking about the Dallas Cowboys cheerleaders.'

'Good man.' Dime raises his glass, then conversationally remarks to no one in particular, 'Major Mac is gay.'

Holliday yelps. 'Damn, Dime, the man sitting right here!'

And indeed, Major McLaurin is seated on the rear banquette, watching Dime with all the emotion of a flounder on ice.

'He can't hear a damn word I say,' Dime laughs. He turns to Major Mac and slows down his rate of speech to moron speed. 'MAY-JURH, MACK-LAAAUUURIN, SIR! SAR-JINT, HOLLI-DAY, HERE, SAYS, YOU'RE, GAY.'

'Aw fuck,' Holliday moans, but the major's eyes merely take on a needling glint, then he holds out his fist to show his wedding band. Everyone howls.

There are ten of them in the limo's plush passenger bay, the eight remaining soldiers of Bravo squad, their PA escort Major Mac, and the movie producer Albert Ratner, who at the moment is hunkered down in BlackBerry position. Counting poor dead Shroom and the grievously wounded Lake there are two Silver Stars and eight Bronze among them, all ten of which defy coherent explanation. 'What were you thinking during the battle?' the pretty TV reporter in Tulsa asked, and Billy tried. God knows he tried, he never *stops* trying,

3

but it keeps slipping and sliding, corkscrewing away, the *thing* of it, the *it,* the ineffable whatever.

'I'm not sure,' he answered. 'Mainly it was just this sort of road rage feeling. Everything was blowing up and they were shooting our guys and I just went for it, I really wasn't thinking at all.'

His chief fear up to the moment the shooting started being that of fucking up. Life in the Army is miserable that way. You fuck up, they scream at you, you fuck up some more and they scream some more, but overlying all the small, petty, stupid, basically foreordained fuckups looms the ever-present prospect of the life-fucking fuckup, a fuckup so profound and all-encompassing as to crush all hope of redemption. A couple of days after the battle he was walking down the gravel path to chow and there it was, this sense of reprieve or release, of a terrible burden eased, and all with no more effort on Billy's part than the exhalation of a normal breath. This feeling of *ahhhhh,* like there was hope for him? Like maybe he wasn't completely expendable. By then the Fox News footage was viraling through the culture and there were rumors that Bravo was going home, the kind of suicidally hopeful talk no soldier in his right mind would dare credit, and then, lo, they were QT'ed to Baghdad on two hours' notice and thence across the ocean for their *Victory Tour.*

One nation, two weeks, eight American heroes, though technically there is no such thing as Bravo

4

squad. They are Bravo Company, second platoon, first squad, said squad being comprised of teams alpha and bravo, but the Fox embed christened them Bravo squad and thus they were presented to the world. Now, here at the tour's end, feeling soft, sated, bleary, under-rested and overproduced, Billy grows sad and nostalgic for the beginning. They were hustled onto a C-130 in the middle of night and took off from Baghdad in a hard spiraling scrooge. Shroom was with them, in a flag-draped coffin at the back. For the entire flight to Ramstein a couple of the Bravos were always sitting with him, but it's the others who Billy thinks of now, the twenty or so civilians of various shades and accents who joined them for the ride. Not spooks – they were too plump for that, their smiles too heedless of the woes of the world, and as soon as the plane was airborne those guys were partying hard. Good whiskey, music blasting from a dozen boom boxes, a forest of Cuban cigars set ablaze – the fuselage quickly filled with a witches' brew of smoke. It turned out that they were gourmet chefs. For who? The men just smiled. 'The coalition.' They were French, Romanian, Swedish, German, Iranian, Greek, Spanish, Billy could discern no pattern or meaning in their nationalities, but to a man they were friendly and more than generous, eager to share their booze and smokes with soldiers. Evidently they'd made a lot of money in Iraq. One of the Swedes opened his calfskin attaché case and showed Billy the gold stash he'd acquired in Baghdad, several pounds' worth of chains and ropes and coins, of such purity that they glowed more orange than gold. There amid the cigar smoke and rollicking laughs Billy had lifted one of the chains, testing it for heft. He was nineteen years old and had no idea that his war contained such things, and what a damn shame for him and the rest of Bravo that it has not been won in the two weeks since.

'Yes,' Albert is saying into his cell, which he bought special in Japan, which is two years ahead of everyone else in the race for cell phone superiority. 'Tell her that, you can tell her this picture will maul. But it will also reward.' He's silent for a moment. 'Carl, what can I say? It's a war picture – not everybody gets out alive.' Meanwhile Crack is reading aloud from the sports pages of the *Dallas Morning News*, reciting the odds from America's Line so Holliday and A-bort can get their bets down. There are more than two hundred ways to bet on the game, including whether the coin toss will be heads or tails, which song Destiny's Child will open with at halftime, and which quarter will the network broadcast make its first reference to President Bush.

Crack speaks as if reading from a recipe. 'Drew Henson's first pass of the game will be, complete, minus two hundred; incomplete, plus a hundred and fifty; an interception, plus a thousand.'

'Incomplete,' says Holliday, making a note in his little book.

'Incomplete,' A-bort agrees, marking his little book.

'How about quarter where Beyoncé sits on my face,' Sykes says.

'Fucking never,' Holliday says, not missing a beat.

'In a million years,' A-bort adds, similarly deadpan. Sykes is saying hell yes he'll take those odds as Albert snaps his cell phone shut.

'All right, guys, it looks like Hilary Swank is officially interested.'

Whanh, whoa, *who*? 'Hilary Swank a *bitch*,' Lodis sputters. 'Why she talking to us?'

'Bee-*cause*,' Albert answers, punching it, knowing the rise this will get from Bravo, 'she wants to play *him*,' and he points at Billy. Bravo erupts in hoots and cheers.

'Wait. Wait a second.' Billy is laughing along with everyone else, but he's troubled too, already he senses the potential here for humiliation on a global scale. 'If she's a girl then I don't see how—'

'Actually,' Albert says, 'she's floating the idea of playing Billy *and* Dime. We'd fold both parts into one role and she'd play that as the lead.'

More hoots, this time directed at Dime, who merely nods as if well satisfied. 'I still don't see . . .' Billy murmurs.

'Just because she's a woman doesn't mean she can't do it,' Albert tells them. 'Meg Ryan was the lead in that chopper flick, the one she did with Denzel a couple years ago. Or she could play it as a guy, hell, Hilary won a goddamn Oscar playing

7

a guy. Well, playing a girl playing a guy, but whatever. The point is she's not just another pretty face.'

Others who Albert is in talks with: Oliver Stone, Brian Grazer, Mark Wahlberg, George Clooney. It is a heroic tale, not without tragedy. A tale of heroism ennobled by tragedy. Movies about Iraq have 'underperformed' at the box office, and that's a problem, according to Albert, but not Bravo's problem. The war might be up to its ass in moral ambiguity, but Bravo's triumph busts through all that. The Bravo story is a rescue story, with all the potent psychology of the rescue plot. People respond deeply to such stories, Albert has told them. Everyone worries, everyone feels at least a little bit doomed basically all the time, even the richest, most successful, most secure among us live in perpetually anxious states of barely hanging on. Desperation's just part of being human, so when relief comes in whatever form, as knights in shining armor, say, or digitized eagles swooping down on the flaming slopes of Mordor, or the U.S. cavalry charging out of yonder blue, that's a powerful trigger in the human psyche. Validation, redemption, life snatched from the jaws of death, all very powerful stuff. Powerful. 'What you guys did out there,' Albert has assured them, 'that's the happiest possible result of the human condition. It gives us hope, we're allowed to feel hopeful about our lives. There's not a person on the planet who wouldn't pay to see that movie.'

Albert is in his late fifties, a big-boned, fleshy

man with an unruly cloud of mostly gray hair and thick, wiry hedgerows of midlength sideburns. He wears black-frame glasses with round lenses. He chews gum. His hands are large and knuckly, and dark clumps of jungle growth sprout from his ears. Today he's wearing a white dress shirt with the collar open, a navy blazer with a lining of brilliant scarlet, a black cashmere overcoat and cashmere scarf, and sleek, dainty loafers that appear to be made of pliable chocolate bars. This crossfire of dishevelment and suavity provides no end of fascination for Billy, and from it he infers a worldliness that could eat Bravo for breakfast and swallow the bones. This is a man who direct-dials the likes of Al Gore and Tommy Lee Jones and whose movies have featured such money stars as Ben Affleck, Cameron Diaz, Bill Murray, Owen Wilson, two of the four Baldwin brothers and so on, all of whom unfortunately have prior commitments or aren't interested in a profile-leveling ensemble piece.

'We're gonna *Platoon* it,' Albert says on his next phone call. 'Ensemble plus star, hell yes it works. Hilary's extremely interested.'

The Bravos listen for a minute. Ho'Wood talk. It is its own tribal dialect, rich in tonal permutations of put-down, bitch-slap, call-out, and gaff.

'No way. I'd rather sleep with Mother Teresa than make a movie with that guy.'

Bravo smirks.

'Oh sure. Like having an enema when you've got a catheter shoved up your cock.'

The Bravos' eyes bug out, they chortle snot through their noses.

'*Only* one battle? Larry, come on, *Black Hawk Down* was *only* one battle. Look, I know it's a war movie, but I need a director who can bring some human empathy to the story.'

Pause.

'Enemas I can handle, it's the catheter I can't take.'

More nasal chortles. Lodis would fall off his seat if he wasn't strapped in.

'Listen, Larry, we're talking two days. My boys ship out in two days and access becomes extremely problematic after that. Unless your lawyers feel like parachuting into a war zone.'

'Hooo-kay,' Crack resumes, rattling the paper. 'Will Drew Henson throw an interception – yes, minus a hundred and twenty, versus no, plus a hundred and five.'

'Yes,' Holliday says.

'No,' says A-bort.

'Will Beyoncé show me her tits while sitting on my face,' Sykes offers, then starts singing in a screechy black-girl falsetto, *I need a soldjah, soldjah, need me a soldjah soldjah boy . . .*

'Quiet,' Dime woofs, 'Albert's on the phone,' which the rest of the Bravos take as their cue to scream at Sykes. *Shut up, fuckhead, Albert's on the phone! Quiet, shitbag, Albert's trying to talk!* Meanwhile an SUV has drawn even in the next lane, and women, actual females, are hanging out the windows and yelling at the Hummer, college girls, maybe a couple of years older, and they are fine prime examples of that buxom talent pool of all-American booty that runs amok every night on reality TV.

'Hey,' they cry as traffic crawls along, 'roll down your windows! Hey you, whoever you are, got any Grey Poupon? Woooo-hoooo, go Cowboys! Roll down your window!'

Oh Lord, beauties they are and amped as all fuck, bellowing, whipping their hair around like proud war banners, they are the girls gone wild of Bravo's fondest dreams. Sykes and A-bort futz with the windows on that side and are roundly cursed for their incompetence, then they realize the damn things have been childproofed and everybody screams toward the front, finally the driver flips a switch and the windows go down and you can just see those girls deflate. Oh, soldiers. *Jarheads,* they're probably thinking, because it's all the same to them. Not rock stars, not highly paid professional athletes, nobody from the movies or the tabloid-worthy world, just grunts riding on some millionaire's dime, some lame support-the-troops charity case. Bravo tries, but the girls are just being polite now. *We're famous!* A-bort cries. *They're gonna make a movie about us!* The girls smile, nod, look up and down the freeway as if scouting better prospects. Sykes flops his entire torso out the window and yells, 'Hell yes I'm drunk baby and I'm married too! But I'll still

11

love you ugly in the morning!' This gets the girls laughing and for a moment there's hope, but Billy can see the light already dimming in their eyes.

He sits back and pulls out his cell; they were probably never serious anyway. *Ten hut!* reads the text from his sister Kathryn,

keep it in yr holster kid

Then from Pete, his other sister's roughneck husband,

Bang a cheerldr

Then this from Pastor Rick, who won't leave him alone,

He who honors me, I will honor

And that's it, no more texts, no calls, nothing. Fuck, doesn't he know. *anybody*? He is sort of famous after all, at least that's what people keep telling him, so you would think. Traffic is moving and they've lost the wild girls, but now the stadium appears on the horizon, rising from the sweep of suburban prairie like an engorged and wart-spattered three-quarter moon. They are supposed to appear today on national TV, details pending, no one knows the actual drill. They might have lines to speak. They might be interviewed. There's talk that they'll take part in the halftime show, which raises hopes of personally meeting Destiny's Child, but equally if not more plausible is the possibility that they'll be coaxed, cajoled, steam-rolled, or otherwise harassed into doing something incredibly embarrassing and lame. Local TV has already been bad enough – in Omaha there was footage of a very stiff Bravo 'interacting' with the zoo's new monkey habitat, and in Phoenix they were taken to a skateboard park, where Mango did an ass-plant for the evening news. Humiliation always stalks the common man when he ventures onto the tube, and Billy is determined it won't happen to him, not today, not on nationwide TV, no sir, thank you sir, I respectfully refuse to act like a moron, *sir*!

The possibilities set off a whinge in his gut like air escaping through a pinhole wound. He wants to be on TV, and he doesn't. He wants to be on TV as long as he doesn't screw up and it might help get him laid, but watching the stadium swell outside his window to Death Star proportions he wonders if he's truly up to the day. Self-confidence has been a struggle these past two weeks, this sense of treading water way over his head. He's too young. He doesn't know enough. Not counting the small-time drag races his father used to emcee, he's never been to a professional sporting event. In fact he's managed to grow up in Stovall, a mere eighty miles west, without ever setting eyes on fabled Texas Stadium save through the expurgating medium of TV, and this first sighting feels historic, or at least strives to be. Billy studies it at length, with real care and attention, taking the measure of its size and lack of humor, its stark and irremediable ugliness. Years and years of carefully posed TV shots have imbued the place with intimations of mystery and romance, dollops of state and national pride, hints of pharaonic afterlife such as always inhere in large-scale public architecture, all of which render the stadium of Billy's mind as the conduit or portal, a direct tap-in, to a ready-made species of mass transcendence, and so the real-life shabbiness is a nasty comedown. Give bigness all its due, sure, but the place looks like a half-assed backyard job. The roof is a homely quilting of mismatched tiles. There's a slumpiness, a middle-aged sag to the thing that suggests soft paunches and mushy prostates, gravity-slugged masses of beached whaleness. Billy tries to imagine how it looked brand-new, its fresh gleam and promise back in the day – thirty years ago? Forty? The past is always a shaky proposition for him, but there's a backdoor link between the way he feels now, looking at the stadium, and the feelings he gets when he thinks about his family. That same heaviness, the same torpor and melancholy, a kind of sickly-sweet emo funk that's almost pleasurable, in the sense that it hints at something real. As if sorrow is the true reality? Without ever exactly putting his mind to it, he's come to believe that loss is the standard trajectory. Something new appears in the world – a baby, say, or a car or a house, or an individual shows some special talent – with luck and huge expenditures of soul and effort you might keep the project stoked for a while, but eventually, ultimately, it's going down. This is a truth so brutally self-evident that he can't fathom why it's not more widely perceived, hence his contempt for the usual public shock and outrage when a particular situation goes to hell. The war is fucked? Well, duh. Nine-eleven? Slow train coming. They hate our freedoms? Yo, they hate our actual guts! Billy suspects his fellow Americans secretly know better, but something in the land is stuck on teenage drama, on extravagant theatrics of ravaged innocence and soothing mud wallows of self-justifying pity.

'Shit,' someone murmurs, a speed bump in the silence – their first burst of enthusiasm on sighting the stadium has flatlined into verbal arrest. Maybe it's the weather that brings them down, all this early-winter gloom, or maybe performance anxiety or just plain weariness, the burden of knowing much will be required of them today. Bravo doesn't do so well with silence anyway. Guff and bullshit are more their working style, but the spell of intro-spective dread concludes with the appearance of a large, carefully rendered homemade sign affixed to a roadside utility pole. *STOP ANAL RAPE IN IRAQ!* the sign reads, below which someone has scrawled, *heavens to betsey*. Bravo howls.

A PRIVATE IN THE INFANTRY

They arrive two hours before kickoff and no one seems to know what to do with them, so they're parked in their seats for the time being, forty-yard line, home side, seventh row. Sykes and Lodis immediately start debating the retail value of such totally sick seats and how much they would bring on eBay, $400, $600, up and up they go, their analysis based on nothing more than air and wishful thinking. It's a fuckwit conversation and Billy tries not to listen. He's got the aisle seat with Mango on his left, and they talk a little bit about last night and how awesome it is to be here instead of spitting sand out their ears at FOB Viper. Hebert known as A-bort is sitting to Mango's left, then Holliday known as Day, then Lodis a.k.a. Cum Load, Pant Load, or just plain Load, then Sykes who will never be anything other than Sucks, then Koch as in coke which makes him Crack and *Crack kills!*, especially when he squats and shows a slice of his ass, then Sergeant Dime, then Albert's empty seat, then that infinite enigma known as Major Mac. Everyone says it's cold, but Billy doesn't feel it. The forecast calls for sleet and freezing rain by late afternoon, and through the stadium's open dome they can watch the weather going to hell, the cloud deck bristling like a giant Brillo pad. The half-empty stands – it's early yet – give off the low hum of a floor buffer or oscillating fan.

'Load!' barks Sergeant Dime. 'How long is a football field?'

Lodis snorts; too *easy*. At least ten times a day he has to prove that certitude is the hallmark of the true moron.

'A hunrud yards, Sergeant.'

'Wrong, dumbshit. Billy, how long is a football field?'

'A hundred twenty yards,' Billy answers, trying to keep it low-key, but Dime leads the rest of Bravo in whooping applause.

Hooah, Billy, get some. He's leery of this roll Dime's on for singling him out for favors and praise and doing it in so frontal a manner, as if daring the other Bravos to call him on it. It's like a punishment, whose Billy hasn't figured out, but instructional aggression is a specialty of Dime's. *NO* he's bellowing now at Sykes, who's begging permission to place a couple of small bets. Ever since he maxed out his credit cards on porn, Dime has had him on a vicious budget.

'Sergeant, just fifty bucks.'

'No.'

'I've been saving up—'

'No.'

'I'll send every penny to my wife—'

'Damn right you will, but you aren't betting.'

'Please, Sergeant—'

'Sucks, have you not had your morning glass of shut up?' With that Dime is stepping over the seat below and sidling down the vacant row at Bravo's front. 'Gentlemen, what it do?' he says on reaching the end of the row.

'Just chillin',' says Mango.

'You get any chiller, we're gonna put you on a stick and sell mango Blow Pops. Lodis still says the football field's a hundred yards long.'

'Is!' Lodis calls from down the row. 'Since when anybody count the end zone, yo.'

'Sergeant,' Sykes wails, 'just please this once—'

'Shut!' Dime barks, the stalk of his neck twisting around as if he means to pop his head off by self-induced torque, then his eyes alight on Billy and there it is, The Look, the fixed fire of Dime's gaze bearing down on Billy's humble self. This has happened a lot lately and it's freaking Billy out, the concentrated calm of Dime's gray eyes with that sense of mad energy swirling at the edges, like finding yourself at the center of a hurricane.

'Billy.'

'Sergeant.'

'Your thoughts on the Hilary Swank deal.'

'I don't know, Sergeant. It seems sort of weird, having a girl play a guy.'

'But Billy, haven't you heard, weird is the new normal.' Dime is buzzing with game-day energy,

18

arms swinging, hips juking little half-feints and slants. 'But maybe she'd play it as a girl, you heard Albert. They'd turn you into a chick, how about that? So for the rest of your life people'll be like, "Look, there goes ol' Billy Lynn. He let them turn him into a girl for that movie they made."'

'She wants to play you too, Sergeant. Would you do it?'

Dime gives a lippy sort of laugh. 'I tell you what, maybe. If she'd let me be her boyfriend for a couple of weeks, I could be persuaded.'

Now he laughs for real, cackling with the wicked innocence of the bright and easily bored. Staff Sergeant David Dime is a twenty-four-year-old college dropout from North Carolina who subscribes to the *Wall Street Journal,* the *New York Times, Maxim,Wired,Harper's,Fortune,* and *DicE Magazine,* all of which he reads in addition to three or four books a week, mostly used textbooks on history and politics that his insanely hot sister sends from Chapel Hill. There are stories that he went to college on a golf scholarship, which he denies. That he was a star quarterback in high school, which he claims not to remember, though one day a football surfaced at FOB Viper, and Dime, caught up in the moment, perhaps, nostalgia triggering some long-dormant muscle memory, uncorked a sixty-yard spiral that sailed over Day's head into the base motor pool. He has a Purple Heart and Bronze Star from Afghanistan, and among the other company sergeants his tag is 'Fuckin' Liberal,' but what was extraordinary about Bravo, the miracle that only gradually became apparent to Billy, was the presence in the squad of not one but two demonstrably superb warriors, neither of whom had any use for the prevailing orthodoxies. When Vice President Cheney made his morale-boosting stop at FOB Viper, Dime and Shroom had cheered with such sick abandon that even Captain Tripp registered the savage mockery of it. Woooo-woooh, yeanh, Dick! Give 'em hell! Bring it *awn*! Woooo-woooh, let's kick some raghead ass! The entire platoon snickering and giggling, about to piss their pants, finally the captain passed a note to Dime saying to 'tone it the fuck down *now*,' though Cheney seemed well pleased with his reception. Standing there onstage in his L.L.Bean khakis, hands in his pockets, NASA windbreaker zipped to his neck, he complimented Viper on its fighting spirit and offered up encouraging news about the war. *There is no doubt,* he said. *The latest intelligence,* he said. *Our commanders in the field,* he said, all in that modulated dial-tone Cheney voice that made everything sound so fucking reasonable. So what was it he said? Oh, right. The insurgency was on its last legs, he said.

'Albert!' Dime calls out. 'Billy thinks Hilary Swank is weird.'

'Wait. No.' Billy turns, and there's Albert coming down the steps, smiling with a bemused sort of West Coast cool. 'I just said I thought it's weird she'd wanna play a guy.'

'Hilary's all right,' Albert says mildly. 'In fact she's one of the nicest ladies in Hollywood. But if you think about it, Billy' – the young soldier is always shocked when Albert calls him by name; Dude, he wants to say, not necessary, you don't have to remember my actual name – 'that's the supreme challenge for any actor, playing the opposite sex. I can see why she'd be interested.'

'He doesn't want a chick playing him,' Dime says. 'He's scared people are going to think he's a pussy.'

'Albert, don't listen to anything he says.'

Albert chuckles, and for a second Billy thinks of Santa Claus, another jolly man of girth. 'Stay loose, guys. We've got a long way to go before you have to worry about that.'

Albert's target is a hundred thousand down for each Bravo's life story, plus all manner of arcane fees, points, percentages, and other unintelligible stuff they will just have to trust him on. For the past two weeks he's been jumping in and out of the *Victory Tour,* meeting up with Bravo in DC, then jetting out, another meeting in Denver, then jetting out, Phoenix and out, and now here at the tour's end, Dallas. Two weeks ago he said they'd have a deal by Thanksgiving, and while it looks like everything's under control Billy senses an inchoate diminishing of heat, a barely perceptible laboring on Albert's part to keep it stoked. None of the other Bravos has said anything, so maybe Billy is wrong. Probably he's wrong. Dear God please let me be wrong. If he could come out of this just a little bit rich all monies would be devoted toward a most worthy cause. When Billy joined the platoon at Fort Hood, Dime and Shroom rode him 24/7 with taunts of punk, thug, delinquent, and not in a friendly way. For some reason they had it in for him, and with deployment looming, not to mention three and a half years left on his Army contract, he was screwed if he couldn't get them off his back. So one day they come upon him lifting weights in the gym and there it is again, the whole shitbag punk-ass gangbanger line. Billy follows them out to the lobby and addresses them in his most formal manner. Sergeant Dime, Sergeant Breem, I'm not a delinquent or a punk or a gangbanger, so please stop calling me that. I'm just a guy busting his ass as hard as he can to be a credit to his platoon and his company.

No, Shroom said, you are a fucking delinquent punk. Only a punk would trash another man's car.

The fuck, Billy thought, how'd they know about that? 'Depends on whose car,' he said.

So whose?

My sister's fiancé. Ex-fiancé.

This got their attention. What kind of car? Dime asked.

A Saab, Billy told them. Convertible five-speed with graphite-alloy rims, three months off the lot. By then they were ready to hear him out, so Billy told them about Kathryn, his middle sister and the star of the family, an extremely beautiful girl and gentle and smart who won a partial scholarship to TCU. So far so good. Majors in business, joins a sorority, makes dean's list every term. All good. Becomes engaged to a guy three years her senior who's getting his MBA, kind of a tight-ass pussy boy and far too impressed with himself, but it's still good, mostly, sort of, even though Billy secretly hates the guy. Then one rainy May morning at the end of her sophomore year Kathryn's driving to work, she has a job as receptionist and broker-trainee at the Blinn Insurance Agency, all good except she's T-boned on Camp Bowie Boulevard by a hydroplaning Mercedes in a flat spin, this enormous dark object windmilling her way and it's the sound she remembers more than anything, the *whoof whoof whoof* of its rotary vortex like the flapping wings of the angel of death. Next thing she knows she's lying flat on her back and three grizzled Mexicans are standing over her, trying to shield her from the rain with a sheet of cardboard. Kathryn always cries when she gets to this part. She simply cannot talk about it without breaking down, describing the three men hovering there wide-eyed and scared, their soaked clothes, their whispered Spanish, the delicate way they held the cardboard like an offering of some sort.

Never even thanked them, Kathryn will say. I just laid there looking up at them, I couldn't talk. In fact all the doctors said she should have died. Fractured pelvis, fractured leg, ruptured spleen, collapsed lung, and massive internal bleeding, then the complicated lacework on her face and back, 170 stitches below the neck, 63 above. You're gonna be fine, the plastic surgeon tells her the day after. It may take a couple of years but we'll get you there, I do this all the time. But pussy boy can't handle it. Three weeks after the wreck he drives to Stovall and breaks off the engagement, whereupon the gentle Kathryn *thumps* the engagement ring in his face, thumps it as you'd thump a spider or slug you found crawling on your hand. But Billy felt called to a more active response. His sister, family honor, basic goddamn human decency, all these and more seemed crucially at stake. He drives to Fort Worth, locates the pussy-boy Saab outside the pussy-boy condo, and proceeds to reduce said vehicle to scrap and spare parts with the True Value crowbar he bought along the way. A sanctifying calm came over him as he mounted the roof and prepared for that first mighty swing at the windshield. He had a job to do, that was his sense of the moment, and after a frazzled adolescence marked by much conflict with authority and numerous self-inflicted fuckups, he was determined to get this right. He swung calmly, picking his spots with real care and deliberation. The work was pleasing. Even the shriek of the car alarm couldn't shake his concentration. The feeling had been building for quite some time that something drastic needed to happen, and now it was.

He was two weeks away from graduating. After several meetings and much official jerking around, the school board decreed that Billy would receive his diploma, but only by mail. He would not get to 'walk,' i.e., do the traditional senior passage across the stage to receive his diploma. 'You will not walk,' the chairman of the school board announced in the darkest, direst tones of churchly reproach, and Billy thought his throat would burst from holding in the laughs. Like he gave a flying fuck! Ooooo, I don't get to walk? Ooooo, my life is over! The lawyer who cut the deal with the school board had to work rather harder to keep him out of jail. The demo job on the Saab wasn't so much the problem as chasing p. boy across the parking lot. With the crowbar. 'I wasn't gonna hurt him,' Billy confessed to the lawyer. 'I just wanted to see him run.' In fact Billy had been laughing so hard that he could barely stand up, much less manage anything like a credible chase.

The DA agreed to drop the felony charge down to criminal mischief if Billy joined the Army, which seemed as good a place as any to be sloughed off, better than jail and being raped every night by guys with names like Preacher and Hawg. Thus he came to be a soldier at the age of eighteen, a private in the infantry, the lowest of the low.

So how's your sister? Shroom asked when the story was done.

She's better, Billy said. They say she's gonna be okay.

You're still a fucking delinquent, Dime said, but after that they didn't ride him so hard.

25

IT IS MOSTLY IN YOUR HEAD
BUT WE HAVE CURES FOR THAT

Billy hopes Josh brings some Advil soon. The five Jack and Cokes made his hangover worse, but now that he's stopped drinking it hurts worse still. Dime and Albert are standing in the aisle and Dime is telling him about Shroom's funeral yesterday, how what should have been the most solemn service ever, a tribute to the spirituality of the man with readings from the Tao, Allen Ginsberg's 'Wichita Vortex Sutra,' and prayers from an elder of the local Crow tribe, had instead turned into a freak show of Christian wingnuts, a little group standing outside the church with signs like GOD HATES YOU 2 THESS. 1:8 and U.S. SOLDIERS ARE GOING TO HELL, screaming chants about abortion and dead babies and God's curse on America.

Crazy, Albert says. Disgusting. Outrageous.

'Hey, Albert,' Crack calls, 'make sure you get that in the movie.'

Albert shakes his head. 'Nobody would believe it.'

The Goodyear Blimp is making labored passes overhead, bucking like a clipper ship in a storm.

26

The Jumbotron is airing a video tribute to the late, great 'Bullet' Bob Hayes, and displayed along the rim of the upper loge are the names and numbers of the Cowboys 'Ring of Honor.' Staubach. Meredith. Dorsett. Lilly. This is the undeniable big-time, there is no greater sports event in the world today and Bravo is smack in the frothy middle of it. In two days they will redeploy for Iraq and the remaining eleven months of their extended tour, but for now they are deep within the sheltering womb of all things American – football, Thanksgiving, television, about eight different kinds of police and security personnel, plus three hundred million well-wishing fellow citizens. Or, as one trembly old guy in Cleveland put it, 'Yew ARE America.'

Billy always thanks people for these sentiments, though he has no idea what they mean. Right now he's thinking maybe if he pukes he'll feel better. He tells Mango he's going for a piss, and Mango glances around to see if Dime's watching, then murmurs, 'Wanna get some beers?'

Hell yeah.

They take the steps two at a time. A few people call out greetings from the stands, and Billy waves but won't look up. He's working hard. He's climbing for his life, in fact, fighting the pull of all that huge hollow empty stadium space, which is trying to suck him backward like an undertow. In the past two weeks he's found himself unnerved by immensities – water towers, skyscrapers, suspension bridges and the like. Just driving by the Washington Monument made him weak in the knees, the way that structure drew a high-pitched keening from all the soulless sky around it. So Billy keeps his head down and concentrates on moving forward, and once they reach the concourse he feels better. They find the head – he pees, forgoes the puke – then buy beers at Papa John's. Technically they aren't supposed to drink while in uniform, but what's the Army gonna do, *send us to Iraq*? The Bravos do, however, ask for their beers in Coca-Cola cups, but before taking a drink Billy hands his to Mango and rips off fifty push-ups right there on the concourse. He can't stand how soft he's gotten. For the past two weeks it's been all planes and cars and hotel rooms, no time for working out, no way to stay sharp. The pussification of Bravo, that's what the past two weeks have been, so now they'll return to the war all stale and crusty with a corresponding falloff of effectiveness.

His head is pounding when he stands, but the rest of him feels better. 'Push-ups, beer chaser,' Mango says.

'You got it.'

'Think they water the beer down?'

'Dude, just taste it.'

'They say they don't but you can tell they do. It's just not the same.'

Billy nods. 'But we're still drinking.'

'We're still drinking.'

28

They stand against the wall and drink their beers, content for the moment to watch the crowd moving past. With all the varieties on display it's like a migration scene from a nature documentary, all shapes, ages, sizes, colors, and income indicators, although well-fed Anglo is the dominant demographic. Having served on their behalf as a frontline soldier, Billy finds himself constantly wondering about them. What are they thinking? What do they want? Do they know they're alive? As if prolonged and intimate exposure to death is what's required to fully inhabit one's present life.

'What do you think they're thinking about?'

Mango hesitates, then smiles his long-lipped coyote smile. 'Heavy stuff. You know, like God. Philosophy. The meaning of life.' They laugh. 'Nah, dawg, just look at 'em. They're thinking about the game, whether their boys gonna cover the spread or not. Where they're sitting, is it gonna rain on their ass. What they're gonna eat, how long is it till next payday. Shit like that.'

Billy nods. That sounds about right. He doesn't blame them for such pedestrian thoughts, and yet, and yet . . . the war makes him wish for a little more than the loose jaw and dull stare of the well-fed ruminant. Oh my people, my fellow Americans! See the world with prophet's eyes! Virtually everyone is wearing Cowboys gear of one kind or another, parkas and caps stamped with the blue star logo, oversized jerseys, hoodies, scarves of silver and blue, dangly earrings or other forms of team bling, some have little Cowboys helmets painted on their cheeks. Billy finds this touching, how earnestly they show devotion to their team. The women display more aptitude for game-day style than the men, who lumber around with Cowboys jerseys hanging past their coattails and their pants bagged around the heels of their boots, a fatal foreshortening of vertical line that makes them look like a bunch of hulking twelve-year-olds.

Oh my people. The soldiers finish their beers with the air of a job well done, and going back to their seats Billy aims his gaze firmly on the aisle steps and away from all that nullity clawing at his face. It freaks him, the monstrous void of it dangling there, the vast empty center creates a vacuum of sorts and all the gravity seems to flow in a reverse-flush action toward that huge gaping blowhole at the top. Billy reaches his seat in an actual sweat. Some of the Bravos are texting, others staring at the field, still others chewing gum or spitting dip into cups. Then Mango gets careless and rips a seismic burp that might as well scream *Beer!*, and Dime swings about like a shark smelling blood.

'Where's Major Mac?' Billy alertly asks. A crude diversion, but it works. Dime frowns, looks left and right.

'Where's Major Mac?' he woofs at the squad. Bravo does a collective bobble-head waggle, then bursts out laughing. Braaaah! Major Mac has disappeared!

'Billy! Mango! Go find Major Mac.'

Up the stairs again, Billy hunching his shoulders against all that horrible space. The stadium is huge. It is deformed. It is a deformation of the human mind. They head straight to Papa John's and buy two more beers. This time a small crowd gathers as Billy does his push-ups; they count off and give him a cheer when he's done. 'Do it again!' someone cries, but Billy hoists his beer in salute, and drinks. He and Mango start walking.

'This should be easy.'

'Right. Only, what, like eighty thousand people here?'

'If you were Major Mac, where would you go, and when would you go there?'

'Dude, maybe he's back at the mother ship.'

They laugh. Major Mac rarely speaks, hardly ever eats or drinks, and has never been seen to relieve himself, prompting speculation among the Bravos that their PA escort might be a new kind of human being, one that consumes and voids through the pores of his skin. Thanks to mysterious back channels Sergeant Dime discovered that on the major's very first day at the war he was blown up not just once but twice, resulting in profound but as-yet-to-be-determined hearing loss. For now he's been parked in public affairs while the Army figures out what to do with him. The major is a chiseled, cleft-chinned, iron-spined specimen, he looks every inch the ideal Joe, which might explain why he's hung on this long, because in truth the man is deaf as a post, not to mention prone to spells of extreme dissociation. As in, checked out. Stroked. Spaced. Peed on the fire and called in the dogs, everybody gone. Dime calls it the major's thousand-yard Prozac stare.

The search for Major Mac is one of the million pointless tasks that make the Army what it is, but Billy is happier doing this than sitting on his ass, plus he feels all right with Mango at his side, not just for the street cred of having a Latino best buddy but for the calm, companionable vibe his friend exudes. Mango is rock-steady in both war and peace. Tough as hell, never complains, can carry major pounds on a stocky five-foot-eight-inch frame and has photographic recall of stats and timeline-oriented facts, such as, for instance, he can rattle off the names of not just the U.S. presidents but the *vice* presidents as well, which tends to put a quick stop to any illegal-alien talk. The one time Billy ever saw his buddy break down wasn't in a firefight, nor any of the times they were mortared, rocketed, sniped at, or roadside-bombed, not even the time he was blown out of the Humvee's turret and asked, 'Is anything sticking out of my head?' Rock-steady, except for the day a car bomb blew up Third Platoon's checkpoint, and Bravo was tasked to pull security in the after-math. A bad day by any standard, but it was only when they fanned out to search for the correct number of severed limbs that Mango sank to his knees in a blubbering heap.

But now they're walking, and how fine it would be if they could out-walk the war by sheer force of will. Billy checks his cell and there's a text from Kathryn, his sister with the divot in her cheek. *Where r u* she wants to know, and he texts *stadium*. Then it's *mom worried ur cold* and he answers *kid is smokin,* and she sends back the smile sign. He and Mango grunt whenever a good-looking female passes, though everyone's so bundled up there's only so much you can see.

'Can you believe those girls last night?'

'Ridiculous,' Billy agrees. 'Everybody says Dallas has the best strip clubs.'

'No shit. Like sensory overload, dawg, where do they all come from? That place we were, not the last place, the one before that, the one with the cage dancers—'

'Vegas Starz.'

'—Vegas Starz, I'm like, damn, girl, why you workin' here? Any one a those girls could be models, I mean like real models, not just stripper hos.'

Mango seems truly distressed, as if confronted by a tragedy in progress, one he could prevent.

'Dunno,' Billy says, 'maybe talent is cheap. Too many hot girls out there.'

'You know that ain't right.'

Billy laughs, but he's struck by a broader notion about young lively bodies and the human meat market and supposedly inexorable laws of supply and demand. Society may not need you, strictly speaking, but some sort of use can usually be found.

'Maybe they're there because they wanna be,' Billy says, but he's just talking now. 'So they can meet fine young men such as ourselves.'

Mango laughs. 'That must be it. It's not the money, dawg. They were really into us.'

Which is what Sykes said on returning from his private dance in back. *She was really into me. It wasn't about the money.* Still in shock from Shroom's funeral that afternoon, Bravo changed into civvies at the hotel and emerged forthwith to get extremely drunk, and at one point or another in the course of the evening they all got blown. *She was into me* became the big joke of the night, but today the memory just makes Billy depressed. It is its own hangover, a scum around his psyche like a bathtub ring, and he decides blow jobs suck, just by themselves. Well, sometimes they're all right. Okay, usually they're awesome as far as they go, but lately he feels the definite need for something more in his life. It's not so much that he's nineteen and still technically a virgin as it is this famished feeling deep in his chest, this liposucked void where his best part should be. He needs a woman. No, he needs a *girlfriend,* he needs someone to mash into body and soul and he's been waiting for it to happen these entire two weeks, the girlfriend, the mashing, *two weeks* he's been traveling this great nation of ours so you would think that after all the miles and cities and positive press coverage, all the love and goodwill,

34

all those smiling cheering crowds, he would have found someone by now.

So either America's fucked up, or he is. Billy walks the concourse with his aching heart and awareness that time is running out. They report to Fort Hood at 2200 tonight, tomorrow will be PACK YOUR SHIT day, and the day after will commence their twenty-seven hours of flying time and the resumption of their combat tour. It seems to Billy a flat-out miracle that any of them are still alive. So they've lost Shroom and Lake, *only two* a numbers man might say, but given that each Bravo has missed death by a margin of inches, the casualty rate could just as easily be 100 percent. The freaking *randomness* is what wears on you, the difference between life, death, and horrible injury sometimes as slight as stooping to tie your bootlace on the way to chow, choosing the third shitter in line instead of the fourth, turning your head to the left instead of the right. Random. How that shit does twist your mind. Billy sensed the true mindfucking potential of it on their first trip outside the wire, when Shroom advised him to place his feet one in front of the other instead of side by side, that way if an IED blew low through the Humvee Billy might lose only one foot instead of two. After a couple of weeks of aligning his feet just so, tucking his hands inside his body armor, always wearing eye pro and all the rest, he went to Shroom and asked how do you keep from going crazy? Shroom nodded like this was an eminently reasonable question to ask, then told him of an Inuit shaman he'd read about somewhere, how this man could supposedly look at you and know to the day when you were going to die. He wouldn't tell you, though; he considered that impolite, an intrusion into matters that were none of his business. But talk about freaky, huh? Shroom chuckled. Looking that old man in the eye and knowing he knows.

'I don't ever wanna meet that guy,' Billy said, but Shroom's point was made. If a bullet's going to get you, it's already been fired.

Billy realizes that Mango hasn't spoken for the past five minutes, so he knows his friend is also thinking about the war. He's tempted to raise the subject, but really, what can you say short of everything? As if once you opened your mouth would you even be able to stop, though in the end it all amounts to one and the same thing, how the hell are they going to get through eleven more months of it.

'You've been lucky so far, right?'

This was Kathryn, talking to Billy over backyard beers.

I guess I have, he answered.

'So keep on being lucky.'

Sometimes it feels as easy as that, just remembering to be lucky. Billy thinks about this as he eyes the fast food outlets that line the stadium concourse, your Taco Bells, your Subways, your Pizza Huts and Papa John's, clouds of hot meaty gases waft from these places and surely it speaks to the genius of American cooking that they all smell pretty much the same. It dawns on him that Texas Stadium is basically a shithole. It's cold, gritty, drafty, dirty, in general possessed of all the charm of an industrial warehouse where people pee in the corners. Urine, the faint reek of it, pervades the place.

'Fierce,' Mango says in hushed tones of wonder.

'What?'

'All these thousands of gringos, and not a single Major Mac.'

Billy snorts. 'You know we're never gonna find that mofo. He's a grown man anyway, like why are we even looking for him.'

'He knows where he is.'

'You would think.'

They look at each other and laugh.

'Let's go back,' Billy says.

'Let's go back,' Mango agrees.

First they stop at Sbarro and get a couple of slices of pizza, then stand there munching off paper plates, content for the moment not to be recognized. Being a Bravo means inhabiting a state of semi-celebrity that occasionally flattens you with praise and adulation. At staged rallies, for instance, or appearances at malls, or whenever TV or radio is present, you are apt at some point to be lovingly mobbed by everyday Americans eager to show their gratitude, then other times it's like you're invisible, people just see right through you, nothing registers. Billy and Mango stand there eating scalding hot pizza and know that their fame is not their own. Mainly it's another thing to laugh about, this huge floating hologram of context and cue that leads everyone around by the nose, Bravo included, but Bravo can laugh and feel somewhat superior because they know they're being used. Of course they do, manipulation is their air and element, for what is a soldier's job but to be the pawn of higher?

Wear this, say that, go there, shoot them, then of course there's the final and ultimate, *be killed.* Every Bravo is a PhD in the art and science of duress. Billy and Mango finish their pizza and start walking. With some food in their bellies they're feeling stoked, and on a whim they wander into Cowboys Select, the highest-end of all the on-site establishments offering Cowboys apparel and brand merchandise for sale. The dizzying scent of fine leathers meets them at the door, along with a brightly lit Texas Lottery machine. Flat-screen TVs mounted in the walls are playing a highlights reel from the Aikman years. Billy and Mango are a little bit punchy coming in, they're primed for an ironic retail experience, and in seconds the place has them laughing out loud. It's not just the racks and racks of upscale clothing, the fine jewelry, the framed and certified collector memorabilia, no, you had to admire the determination, the sheer marketing *balls* of stamping the Cowboys brand on chess sets, toaster ovens, high-capacity ice makers, personal oxygen bars, and laser-guided pool cues. Dude, check it out! An entire line of Cowboys kitchenware. The two Bravos grow so rowdy that other customers start to give them some space. As far as Billy and Mango are concerned, the store is a museum, these are all things to look at but nothing a Bravo could buy, and the humiliation of it makes them a little wild. His 'n' hers cotton terry-cloth robes, like, four hundred dollars. Authentic game jerseys, a hundred fifty-nine ninety-five. Cashmere pullovers, cut-crystal Christmas ornaments, Tony Lama limited-edition boots. As their shame and sense of insult mount the two Bravos become rough with each other. Dude, check it out, sick bomber jacket. Only six hundred seventy-nine bucks, dawg.

Is it leather?

The fuck you mean, hell yeah it's leather!

'Cause, dawg, I don't think so. I think that's pleather.

The fuck it's pleather!

Unh-unh, dumbshit. It's just you're so fucking ghetto you don't know from pleather—

Suddenly they're grappling, they've hooked arms in a fierce shoulder clench and lumber about like a couple of barroom drunks, grunting, cursing each other and butting heads, laughing so hard they can hardly stand up. Their berets go flying as they tear at their ears. It hurts and they laugh harder, they're gasping now, *bitch, shitbag, cum-slut, faggot,* Mango jabs at Billy with stinging uppercuts,

39

Billy crams a fist into Mango's armpit and off they go on a left-tilting axis, pottery wheel and pot rolling loose across the floor. *Can I help you!* someone is shouting, jumping in and out of the way. *Gentlemen! Fellas, guys, can I help you? Whoa there!*

Billy and Mango separate, come up flushed and laughing. The salesman – store manager? a middle-aged white guy with thinning hair – he, too, is laughing, but it's clearly a situation for him, what with two obvious lunatics on his hands. Everyone else, staff, customers – the few who haven't fled – is standing well back.

'Is this leather?' Billy asks, lifting a sleeve from the rack of bomber jackets. ''Cause moron here's trying to tell me it's pleather.'

'Oh no sir,' says the manager, 'that's genuine leather.' He's chuckling, he knows they're putting him on, but in the manner of straight men since the beginning of time whose job it is to bring order to a sick and comical world, he launches into a fruity description of this full-grain aniline lamb's-leather jacket, the special tanning and dyeing processes and so forth, not to mention the coat's superior construction qualities. Uh huh, uh huh, uh huh, the Bravos hear him out with the rapt expressions of cavemen watching popcorn pop.

'See, dumbfuck' – Billy cuffs Mango's shoulder – 'I told you it was leather.'

'Like you know so much about fashion. I bet you ain't even wearing underwear—'

They swat at each other, start to grapple, but the manager's gulpy Whoa! calls them off.

'So, hunh. You sell a lot of these?' Billy asks, fingering one of the jackets.

'Five or six a game. When we're winning we might do better than that.'

'Damn. Your peeps got some juicy cash flow, huh.'

The manager smiles. 'I guess that's one way to put it.'

The Bravos thank the manager and leave. 'Dawg,' Mango says once they're outside. 'Six hundred seventy-nine dollars,' he says. 'Billy,' he says, then, 'Shit.' And that's all they say about it.

THE HUMAN RESPONSE

'Fifteen million,' Albert is saying as Billy and Mango resume their seats. 'Fifteen cash against fifteen percent of gross, a star can do that when they're running hot. And Hilary's running very hot these days. Her agent won't let her read without a guarantee.'

'Read what?' Sykes asks. Albert's eyes slowly track that way, followed by his head.

'The script, Kenneth.'

'But I thought you said we don't have a script.'

'We don't, but we've got a treatment and we've got a writer. And now that Hilary's interested, we can slant it in a way that really speaks to her.'

'I love it when he talks like that,' says Dime.

'Look, the script's not the problem, just telling your story's gonna make a compelling script. The hard part's getting the damn thing in her hands.'

'You said you know her,' Crack points out.

'Hell yes I know her! We got bombed off our ass a couple of months ago at Jane Fonda's house! But this is business, guys, everything she reads has to go through her agent, and he won't let her so much as touch a script unless it comes with a firm offer from a studio. That way she knows if she says yes, the studio's on the hook. She can't get turned down.'

'Uh, so, do we have a studio?' Crack asks. He knows he should know this, but everything about the deal seems so abstract.

'Robert, we do not. There's tons of interest out there, but nobody wants to commit until a star commits.'

'But Swank won't commit until they do.'

Albert smiles. 'Precisely.' The Bravos emit an appreciative *ahhhh*. The paradox is so perfect, so completely circular in the modern way, that everyone can identify.

'That's kind of fucked,' says Crack.

'It is,' Albert agrees. 'It's totally fucked.'

'So how do you make it happen?' asks A-bort.

'By making it inevitable. By making it a goddamn force of nature. By scaring these guys so bad that somebody else is gonna buy it that they have to commit or their heads'll explode.'

'People,' Dime announces, 'I think I just figured out what Albert does.'

Billy and Mango are sitting at the end of the row, then it's Crack, Albert, Dime, Day, A-bort, Sykes, and Lodis, then an empty seat for Major Mac. Billy has noticed that Albert is never far from Dime. Not that Bravo needed proof of how special their sergeant is, but it arrived anyway in the form of Albert and his instant fascination with the Bravo leader. Billy has decided that Albert is gay for Dime, in a nonsexual sense. Dime interests him, Dime the person and Dime the soldier, the entire phenomenon of Dime-ness loosed upon a square and unsuspecting world. In the pantheon of Albert's attentions, Dime comes first and Holliday a distant second, and even that seems more of a proximate sort of interest, conditional, complementary, a function of Day's black yin yoked to Dime's honky yang. Day deigns not to notice his secondary status, like now, for instance, as Albert and Dime huddle in intense conversation while Day perches on his seat back surveying the field like an African king high on his throne, looking down on all his little subject bitches. And as for the rest of Bravo, they might as well be so many shares of corporate stock that happen to talk and walk and drink a lot of beer. 'Dime the *property*,' as Day muttered to Billy last night, in a rare drunken moment of resentful candor. 'The rest a you just the *produck*.'

Which made Shroom what? Shroom and Lake, were they *produck* too? Bravo's talk these days is so much about money, *moneymoneymoney* like a bug on the brain or a hamster spinning his squeaky wheel, a conversation going nowhere at tremendous speed. Billy would just as soon move on to other subjects, but he won't call his fellow Bravos on it. The way they obsess, it's as if a big payday involved more than mere buying power, as if x amount of dollars cooling in the bank could bring your ass safely through the war. He intuits the spiritual logic of it, but for him the equation works in reverse: The day the money comes through, the actual day his check clears, that will be the very day he gets smoked.

So he attunes to the movie talk with pronounced conflictedness. Bravo peppers Albert with questions. What about Clooney? What's going on with Oliver Stone? How about the guy who said he could get Robert Downey Jr? Then the distinguished-looking gentleman seated behind Albert leans over and asks if he's in the movie business.

Albert freezes, head cocked to the side as if he's heard the call of some rare and wonderful bird. 'Why, yes.' he answers sweetly. 'Yes I am in the film industry.'

'Director? Writer?'

'Producer,' Albert allows.

'L.A.?'

'L.A.,' Albert confirms.

'Listen,' says the man, 'I'm a lawyer. I do white-collar criminal defense and I've got a great idea for a legal thriller–type script. Care to hear it?'

Albert says he'd be delighted, as long as the lawyer can describe it in twenty seconds or less. Meanwhile a couple of dozen Cowboys players have taken the field and begin warming up. This isn't the real warm-up, explains Crack, who played a year of college ball at Southeast Alabama State, but the pre-warm-up warm-up for the guys who need some extra loosening up. Billy's attention is soon drawn to the Cowboys punter, a slope-shouldered, moon-faced, paunchy fellow with hardly any hair, the kind of guy you'd normally find behind your supermarket meat counter, except this guy can kick a football to oblivion and back. *Foom*, the soggy thump of each kick resounds in Billy's gut as the ball rockets off on a steep trajectory, up, up, onward and upward still, your eye falters at the spot where the ball should level off and yet it climbs higher still as if some unseen booster charge has fired and straight for the bottomless dome it goes. Billy tries to mark the absolute highest point, that instant of neutral buoyancy where the ball hangs or dangles, actually pauses for a moment as if measuring the fall that even now begins as the nose rolls over with a languid elegance, and there's an aspect of surrender, of grateful relinquishment as it yields to the gravitational fate. After seven or eight kicks Billy feels a kind of interior vaporization taking place, a dilution or relaxation of self-awareness. He feels calm. Watching the kicker is restful for his mind. The peak moments give him the most intense pleasure, a bristling in his brain like tiny lightning strikes as the ball sniffs eternity's lower reaches, strokes the soft underbelly of empty-headed bliss for as long as it lingers at the top of its arc. Billy can imagine that's where Shroom lives now, he is a citizen of the realms of neutral buoyancy. It's sort of a childish and sentimental thought, but why not, if Shroom has to be somewhere then why not there? Bravo has long since been reduced to bestselling *produck*, but even the long arm of marketing can't touch Shroom now.

It's a Zen thing, watching punts, as absorbing in its way as watching goldfish paddle around an ornamental pond. Billy would happily watch punts for the rest of the afternoon except the fans behind him start pounding his back, crying, Look! Look! Check out the Jumbotron! And there on the screen loom the eight operational Bravos literally bigger than life, plus Albert, who's smiling like a proud new papa. Small pockets of applause spark off here and there. The Bravos assume postures of masculine nonchalance. Mainly they're trying not to stare at themselves on the screen, but so pumped with the moment is Sykes that he starts mouthing off and flashing gangsta signs. To a man Bravo tells him to shut the fuck up, but after a moment the screen cuts to a flags-waving, bombs-bursting cartoon graphic against a background of starry outer space, and from within these inky depths enormous white letters suddenly zoom to the fore

**AMERICA'S TEAM PROUDLY HONORS
AMERICAN HEROES**

which disappears, clearing the way for a second wave

THE DALLAS COWBOYS

**WELCOME HEROS OF AL-ANSAKAR
CANAL!!!!!!!**

STAFF SGT. DAVID DIME

47

STAFF SGT. KELLUM HOLLIDAY

SPC. LODIS BECKWITH

SPC. BRIAN HEBERT

SPC. ROBERT EARL KOCH

SPC. WILLIAM LYNN

SPC. MARCELLINO MONTOYA

SPC. KENNETH SYKES

As if drawing down energy through the stadium's blowhole, the applause slowly gathers volume and heft. People moving in the aisle stop and turn their way. The fans behind Bravo come to their feet, the prompt for a slow-motion standing ovation that rolls through their section in a gravity-defying backward wave. Soon the Jumbotron cuts to a hyperactive ad for Chevy trucks, but too late, people are already heading Bravo's way and there is just no help for it and no escape. Billy rises and assumes the stance for such occasions, back straight, weight balanced center-mass, a reserved yet courteous expression on his youthful face. He came to the style more or less by instinct, this tense, stoic vein of male Americanism defined by multiple generations of movie and TV actors, which conveniently furnishes him a way of being without having to think about it too much. You say a few words, you smile occasionally. You let your eyes seem a little tired. You are unfailingly modest and gentle with women, firm of handshake and eye contact with men. Billy knows he looks good doing this. He must, because people totally eat it up, in fact they go a little out of their heads. They do! They mash in close, push and shove, grab at his arms and talk too loud, and sometimes they break wind, so propulsive is their stress. After two solid weeks of public events Billy continues to be amazed at the public response, the raw wavering voices and frenzied speech patterns, the gibberish spilled from the mouths of seemingly well-adjusted citizens. *We appreciate,* they say, their voices throbbing like a lover's. Sometimes they come right out and say it, *We love you.* We are so grateful. We cherish and bless. We pray, hope, honor-respect-love-and-revere and they *do,* in the act of speaking they experience the mighty words, these verbal arabesques that spark and snap in Billy's ears like bugs impacting an electric bug zapper

> terrRr
>> Eye-rack,
>>> Eaaaar-*rock,*
>> Sod'm
> freedoms

>> nina leven,
>>> nina leven,
>>>> nina leven

49

hero

      sacrifice,

   soooh-preeeeme sacrifice

  Bush

                     Osama

               values

                  dih-mock-cruh-see

No one spits, no one calls him baby-killer. On the contrary, people could not be more supportive or kindlier disposed, yet Billy finds these encounters weird and frightening all the same. There's something harsh in his fellow Americans, avid, ecstatic, a burning that comes of the deepest need. That's his sense of it, they all need something from him, this pack of half-rich lawyers, dentists, soccer moms, and corporate VPs, they're all gnashing for a piece of a barely grown grunt making $14,800 a year. For these adult, affluent people he is mere petty cash in their personal accounting, yet they lose it when they enter his personal space. They tremble. They breathe in fitful, stinky huffs. Their eyes skitz and quiver with the force of the moment, because here, finally, up close and personal, is the war made flesh, an actual point of contact after all the months and years of reading about the war, watching the war on TV, hearing the war flogged and flacked on talk radio. It's been hard times in America – how did we get this way? So scared all the time, and so shamed at being scared through the long dark nights of worry and dread, days of rumor and doubt, years of drift and slowly ossifying angst. You listened and read and watched and it was *just, so, obvious,* what had to be done, a mental tic of a mantra that became second nature as the war dragged on. *Why don't they just* . . . Send in more troops. Make the troops fight harder. Pile on the armor and go in blazing, full-frontal smackdown and no prisoners. And by the way, shouldn't the Iraqis be thanking us? Somebody needs to tell them that, would you tell them that, please? Or maybe they'd like their dictator back. Failing that, drop bombs. More and bigger bombs. Show these persons the wrath of God and pound them into compliance, and if that doesn't work then bring out the nukes and take it all the way down, wipe it clean, reload with fresh hearts and minds, a nuclear slum clearance of the country's soul.

Americans fight the war daily in their strenuous inner lives. Billy knows because here at the contact point he feels the passion every day. Often it's in their literal touch, a jolt arcing across as they shake hands, a zap of pent-up warrior heat. For so many of them, this is the Moment: His ordeal becomes theirs and vice versa, some sort of mystical transference takes place and it's just too much for most of them, judging from the way they choke in the clutch. They stammer, gulp, brainfart, and babble, gum up all the things they want to say or never had the words to say them in the first place, so they default to old habits. They want autographs. They want cell phone snaps. They say thank you over and over and with growing fervor, they know they're being good when they thank the troops and their eyes shimmer with love for themselves and this tangible proof of their goodness. One woman bursts into tears, so shattering is her gratitude. Another asks if we are winning, and Billy says we're working hard. 'You and your brother soldiers are preparing the way,' one man murmurs, and Billy knows better than to ask the way to what. The next man points to, almost touches, Billy's Silver Star. 'That's some serious hardware you got,' he says gruffly, projecting a flinty, man-of-the-world affection. 'Thanks,' Billy says, although that never seems quite the right response. 'I read the article in *Time*,' the man continues, and now he does touch the medal, which seems nearly as lewd as if he'd reached down and stroked Billy's balls. 'Be proud,' the man tells him, 'you earned this,' and Billy thinks without rancor, *How do you know?* Several days ago he was doing local TV and the blithering twit-savant of a TV newsperson just came out and asked: What was it like? Being shot at, shooting back. Killing people, almost getting killed yourself. Having friends and comrades die right before your eyes. Billy coughed up clots of nonsequential mumblings, but as he talked a second line dialed up in his head and a stranger started talking, whispering the truer words that Billy couldn't speak. *It was raw. It was some fucked-up shit. It was the blood and breath of the world's worst abortion, baby Jesus shat out in squishy little turds.*

Billy did not seek the heroic deed, no. The deed came for him, and what he dreads like a cancer in his brain is that the deed will seek him out again. Just about the time he thinks he can't be polite anymore the last of the well-wishers drift away, and Bravo takes their seats. Then Josh shows up and the first thing he says is, Where's Major McLaurin?

Dime is casual. 'Oh, he said something about needing to take his meds.'

'His meh—' Josh begins, but catches himself. 'You guuuuyyyyyzzzzzz.' The very picture of young corporate America on the move, is Josh. He is tall, toned, handsome as a J.Crew model, with a nose straight and fine as a compass needle and a brilliant shock of glossy black hair, the sight of which triggers subliminal itchings in the Bravos' peach-fuzz scalps. It has already been a matter of some debate as to whether Josh is gay, the consensus being no, he's just your basic corporate pussy boy. 'He's whatcha call one a those metrosexuals,' Sykes said, whereupon everyone agreed that Sykes was gay just for knowing such a word.

'Well,' Josh says, 'I guess he'll turn up. You guys feel like getting some lunch?'

'We wanna meet the cheerleaders,' says Crack.

'Yeah,' says A-bort, 'but we wanna eat too.'

'Okay, hang on.' Josh consults his walkie-talkie.

The men exchange WTF looks. The vaunted Cowboys organization seems to be winging it with Bravo, the planning somewhere between half-assed and shit-poor. During a lull in the walkie-talkie confab Billy motions Josh closer, and the ever-alert Josh flexibly squats by his seat. 'Advil,' Billy says, 'were you able to find me any—'

'Oh *shit*,' Josh exclaims in a hot whisper, then 'Sorry,' in his normal voice, 'sorry sorry sorry, I'll definitely get that for you.'

'Thanks.'

'Still hungover, dude?' Mango asks, and Billy just shakes his head. One night, eight men, and four strip clubs, all to no real purpose except that transactional blow job there at the end, thoughts of which make him want to shoot himself. Like a dental procedure it was, a blunt-force plumbing job, the memory of that girl's head bobbing in his lap. Bad karma, for sure. Billy has overdrawn his karma account, that running tally of good and evil that Shroom described to him as the expression, the mental crystallization, as it were, of the great cosmic tilt toward ultimate justice. Billy scans the field but the punter is gone. His gaze sweeps the stadium's upper reaches where the punts topped out, but it's just air, he needs the concrete marker of the punts' arc to get that vibe of Shroom hovering on the other side.

Shroom, Shroom, the Mighty Shroom of Doom who foretold his own death on the battlefield. When their deployment was done and he got his leave he

54

was going on an ayahuasca trek to Peru, 'going to see the Big Lizard,' as he put it, 'unless the hajjis send me first.' Unless. Guess what. And on that day Shroom knew. Wasn't that the meaning of their last handshake? Shroom turning in his seat just as they hit the shit, Mango already opening up on the .50 cal as Shroom reached back and took Billy's hand. 'I'm going down,' he yelled into the racket, which at the time Billy heard as *it's*, 'It's going down,' his ear rounding off the weirdness so the words made sense. Later he'd cycle back to that moment and know it for what it was, the words and Shroom's eyes with their hint of far remove, like he was looking up at Billy from the bottom of a well.

If Billy thinks about this for more than a couple of seconds a synthesized hum starts up in his head like a tremendous swell of organ music, not the sickly calf bleatings they played at Shroom's funeral but a thunderous massing of mighty chords, the subsurface rumble of a tidal wave as it rolls unseen through the ocean depths. Spooky as all shit, not that he fights it; the big sound might be God banging around his head or some elaborately coded form of essential truth, or maybe both, or maybe they're one and the same thing, so put *that* in your fucking movie, if you can. *Were you good friends?* asked the reporter from the *Ardmore Daily Star*. 'Yes,' Billy said, 'we were good friends.' *Do you think about him a lot?* 'Yes,' Billy said, 'I think about him a lot.' Like, every day. Every hour. No, every couple of minutes. About once every ten seconds, actually. No, it's more like an imprint on his retina that's always there, Shroom alive and alert, then dead, alive, dead, alive, dead, his face eternally flipping back and forth. He saw the beebs dragging Shroom into the high grass and thought Oh fuck or maybe just Fuck, that was the extent of Billy's inner reflections as he scrambled off his belly and made his run. Weirdest thing, though, he retains this sense as he got to his feet of knowing exactly how it was going to turn out, the visualization so intense that it shook loose a kind of double consciousness that lingers to this day. His memory of the battle is mostly a hot red blur, but the premonitory memory is sharp and clear. He wonders if all soldiers who do these radical things get a brief sightline into a very specific future, this telescopic piercing of time and space that instills the motivation to do what they do. The ones who live, maybe. Maybe they all think they see, but the ones who don't make it, they were wrong. Only the ones who survive are allowed to feel clairvoyant and canny, though it occurs to him now that Shroom, too, saw with equal clarity, just with the opposite result.

Hooah, Shroom. It feels like too many things to have to think about at once, movie deals and interviews and what it means to wear a medal plus that hard-core thing underneath it all, the primal and ultimately unfathomable facts of their engagement on the banks of the Al-Ansakar Canal. Your mind is not calm. You aren't sick but you aren't exactly well. There's an airy sense of dangling or dangerous incompletion, as if your life has gotten ahead of itself and you need some time to let it back and fill. This feels right, this grasping of the time problem, here is the possible square one on which to build except Josh gives the word, *Lunch!*, and they rise. Little rockslides of applause tumble across the stands, and Sykes, the butthead, waves to the crowd like it's all for him. Josh leads them bravely onto the stairs and it's a long slow slog to the top, trudging upward in column like those poor doomed fucks near the end of *Titanic* striving against the horrible voids of sea and sky. If you relax even for a second, it will take you, thus a strategy is revealed: Don't relax. Once they reach the concourse Billy feels better. Josh leads them up a spiral ramp where the wind shears into tight coiling eddies, tossing trash and dust around in little tantrums. A kind of coagulatory effect attends Bravo's route as people stop, shout out, gape, or grin according to their politics and personality type, and Bravo blows through it all, polite and relentless, an implacable flying wedge of forward motion until the crew of a Spanish-language radio station grabs Mango for an interview, and all that good clean energy goes to hell. People gather. The air turns moist with desire. They want words. They want contact. They want pictures and autographs. Americans are incredibly polite as long as they get what they want. With his back to the railing Billy finds himself engaged by a prosperous-looking couple from Abilene who have their grown son and daughter-in-law in tow. The young people seem embarrassed by their elders' enthusiasm, not that the old folks give a damn. 'I couldn't stop watching!' the woman exclaims to Billy. 'It was just like nina leven, I couldn't stop watching those planes crash into the towers, I just couldn't, Bob had to drag me away.' Husband Bob, a tall, stooped gent with mild blue eyes, nods with the calm of a man who's learned how much slack to give a live-wire wife. 'Same with yall, when Fox News started showing that video I just sat right down and didn't move for hours. I was just so proud, just so' – she flounders in the swamps of self-expression – '*proud*,' she repeats, 'it was like, thank *God*, justice is finally being done.'

'It was like a movie,' chimes her daughter-in-law, getting into the spirit.

'It *was*. I had to keep telling myself *this is real*, these are *real* American soldiers fighting for our freedom, this is *not* a movie. Oh *God* I was just so happy that day, I was *relieved* more than anything, like we were finally paying them back for nina leven. Now' – she pauses for a much-needed breath – 'which one are you?'

Billy politely introduces himself and leaves it at that, and the woman, as if sensing the delicacy of the question, doesn't press. Instead, she and her daughter-in-law embark on a spoken-word duet of patriotic sentiments, they are 100 percent supporting of Bush the war the troops because defending szszszsz among nations szszszsz owl-kay-duzz szszszsz szszszsz szszszsz, the lady keeps leaning into Billy and tapping his arm, which induces a low-grade somatic trance, thus he's feeling comfortably numb when the lid of his skull retracts and his brain floats free into the freezing air

terrRr,

wore on terrRr

double y'im dees
proud, so proud
and

praaaaaay
we
pray and
hope and
bless and

praise

from whom all things

blow

HOOAH BRAVO

PACK YOUR SHIT!

No matter their age or station in life, Billy can't help but regard his fellow Americans as children. They are bold and proud and certain in the way of clever children blessed with too much self-esteem, and no amount of lecturing will enlighten them as to the state of pure sin toward which war inclines. He pities them, scorns them, loves them, hates them, these children. These boys and girls. These toddlers, these infants. Americans are children who must go somewhere else to grow up, and sometimes die.

'Dude, that lady back there,' Crack says when they're moving again, 'the blonde with the little kids? When her husband was taking our picture she was totally grinding her ass up against my rod.'

'Bullshit.'

'No lie! Like instant wood, dude, she was shoving her ass right in there. Five more seconds and I woulda come, I shit you not.'

'He's lying,' Mango says.

'Swear to God! Then I'm like, hey, give me your e-mail, let's stay in touch while I'm back in Iraq, and it's like she doesn't know what I'm talking about. Bitch.'

Mango demurs, but Billy thinks it's probably true – women will do some crazy shit around a uniform. He drops back a couple of paces and checks his cell. Pastor Rick has sent him another Bible text—

Know that the Lord is God!
It is He that made us and we are His.

60

The guy is relentless, he is a used-car salesman in sheep's clothing. Billy deletes the text, wondering if it's bad luck to dis a preacher, even a worthless one. 'Aren't you *cold*?' a passing woman asks, and Billy smiles and shakes his head, No, ma'am. Truly he's not, though he doesn't begrudge the fans their sumptuous fur coats, their puffy parkas, their bear-paw mittens and ninja masks. A lot of men are wearing fur, now there's fashion for you. Major Mac suddenly falls into step at his side.

'Major McLaurin, sir!'

The major gives him a dopy look. Billy remembers to raise his voice.

'WE WERE WORRIED ABOUT YOU SIR! WE DIDN'T KNOW WHERE YOU'D GONE!'

The major transitions to frown. 'Look alive, soldier, I've been right here. Get those cobwebs out of your eyes.'

Affirmative and copy that, in the major's mind he's been right here and for a grunt that's all that matters, *roger SIR*! Billy becomes nervous and awkward, hyper as a setter pup, while the major strides along in brooding contemplation of his shoes. Try, fool, Billy tells himself. Like when're you gonna get a better shot than this? He needs knowledge that Major Mac might have, knowledge and guidance having to do with death, grief, the fate of the soul, if nothing else he seeks the means for verbalizing such matters without shitting all over their very real power. When people ask does he pray, is he religious or specifically *saved* or

61

Christian, Billy always says yes, partly because it makes them happy and partly because he feels that's pretty much the truth, though probably not in the way they're thinking. What he'd like to say is that he's lived it, if not the entire breadth and depth of the Christian faith then certainly the central thrust of it. The mystery, the awe, that huge sadness and grief. Oh my people. He felt Shroom's soul leave his body at the moment of his death, a blinding *whoom!* like a high-voltage line blowing out, leaving Billy with all circuits fried and a lingering haze like he'd been whacked by a heavyweight who knows how to hit. A kind of concussion, is what it was. Sometimes he thinks his ears are ringing still.

The soul is an actual, tangible thing, Billy knows this now. For two weeks he's been traveling this great nation of ours in the good-faith belief that sooner or later he'll meet someone who can explain his experience, or at least break it down and properly frame the issue. There was Pastor Rick, to whom he confided in a moment of weakness, but the pastor turned out to be an egotistical pain in the ass. Dime is too close to it, and anyway Billy needs more of the profile of the stable adult. For a while he thought Albert might be the one, a man of wide experience and impressive education who seems to know so much about so many things and can talk the sun down and up again, but lately Billy despairs. It's not that Albert lacks compassion – though there is that cool way he looks at you sometimes, like you're the next bite on his hamburger – but rather the irony with which he views all sides, including his own. Albert is wise to himself, as any man of the world must be, but it's this ingrown worldliness that limits him in precisely the way that Billy needs him most.

Which leaves Major Mac as the best available candidate, Major Mac the sphinx, the zombie, the rarely speaking and never-taking-a-piss wraith, the guy who seems about 60 percent there about 40 percent of the time. *That* Major Mac. Thus it's in a state of extreme frustration that Billy accompanies the senior officer along the concourse. He wants to know what happened that day in Ramallah. Did the major lose men that day? Friends? Did he watch them die? Billy feels a terrible need to connect, heart to heart, man to man, warrior to warrior, he craves that rough and necessary wisdom and yet can barely manage small talk with officers, much less crack the code of the major's vacancy to access something so personal and real. How is he supposed to break the ice? YO MAJOR, CHECK IT OUT, THEY GOT HEINEKENS ON TAP! He feels his chance slipping away as Josh diverts them down a side corridor to a restricted-access escalator. A pair of beefy, unconfident security men in coats and ties glance at the Bravos' game credentials and wave them on. 'Dude, stairway to heaven!' Sykes cries as the escalator rides them up, yukking like he's the soul of wit. Standing one deferential step below the major, Billy decides it's hopeless.

He lacks the nerve and he lacks the bullshit, plus there's the major's disability and the corresponding sense that certain subjects should not be discussed at roadhouse volume. Death, grief, the fate of the soul, these beg congress in tones of sober thoughtfulness, you can't scream back and forth about such matters and hope to get anywhere.

So he says nothing, not that the major notices. They step off the escalator onto something called the 'Blue Star Level,' and Josh leads them to an elevator marked RESTRICTED – STADIUM CLUB ONLY. He swipes a card through the little access gizmo and everyone boards. Two well-dressed couples join them for the ride up, they are old enough to be any Bravo's parents but money shaves off a good ten years. No one acknowledges anyone else. The doors close, concentrating the women's perfume, a shrill citral musk like lemon trees in heat. The elevator has just clunked into gear when necessity rumbles Billy's bowels, precursing a monstrous anal belch. He clenches with all his might and hangs on. An almost imperceptible tremor runs through the Bravos; several more are stiffening, shifting their feet, opening and closing their fists. Oh God, please God, not here, not now. They grit their teeth and stare straight ahead. What is it about close confines that so reliably excites the fighting man's lower GI tract?

Dime speaks with the steel of a man born to lead. 'Gentlemen.' He pauses. 'Do not even think about it.'

64

BY VIRTUE OF WHICH
THE MANY BECOME THE ONE

Saddling up to the sumptuous buffet, Sykes keeps calling it 'brunch' like this makes him some big-stick metrosexual stud until Dime finally tells him to *shut,* this is *lunch,* yo, or Thanksgiving *dinner* if you want to get technical about it, and indeed they are faced with a postcard-perfect orgiastic feed, no less than sixty linear feet of traditional and nouveau holiday fare glistening like an ad in a Sunday magazine supplement. Billy palms a clean plate off the stack and thinks he might be sick. It's just too much for his hangover, all the mounds, slabs, sheets, hummocks, and hillocks of edible matter resembling a complex system of defensive earthworks, and it's that thingness, the sheer molecular density on display, that gives him the lurch. He stands there swaying for a moment – will he lose it? – then his stomach asserts the primal need and growls.

'Load up, guys,' Dime tells them. 'Then we'll talk about how do the little people live.' With its establishment odors of gravy and furniture wax, this is clearly the game-day hangout for the

65

country-club crowd. You pay ten bucks just to pass the door, then $40 plus tax and service for the meal – gratis for heroes, Josh says, to which Bravo answers *troof* – though the 'club' isn't much to look at, a rambling, low-ceilinged space with a bar at one end and at the other full-length windows overlooking the field. The light is a nerve-jangling palette of hards and softs, the rancid-butter mizzle of the overhead fixtures cut by the harsh silver glare from all those giant windows, a constant wrenching of visual tone and depth such that the patrons' eyes never properly adjust. The carpet is coal-slurry gray, the furnishings a scuffed, faux-baronial mélange of burgundy vinyls and oxblood veneers reminiscent of a 1970s Holiday Inn. Clearly, all expense has been spared save for the bare minimum to keep a captive market from outright rebellion.

Billy gets how shitty the place makes him feel, the quick sink of depression in his gut, but he thinks it's just an allergic reaction to rich people. He clenched the moment he walked in and felt the money vibe. He wanted to back right out of there. He wanted to punch someone. Rich people make him nervous for no particular reason, they just do, and standing by the hostess station in his kudzu-green class A's Billy felt about as belonging here as a wino pissing his pants. But – surprise! As Bravo stood there waiting to be seated, the Stadium Club patrons rose as one and achieved a stately round of applause. Several of the nearby millionaires stepped over to shake hands, while farther back in the room a group of patriots, drunk from the sound of it, offered up a woozy ballpark cheer. The manager *himself*, a slender, oleaginous fellow with the unctuous patter of an undertaker murmuring pickup lines in a bar, showed them to their table, and in a way this was worse, having all these high-powered people looking at you. Billy felt his stride going wonky, his arms starting to flail, but a quick glance at Dime settled him down. Shoulders square, eyes forward, head tipped six degrees as if dignity was a shot glass you balanced on your chin – he assumed the Dime tilt, and immediately everything clicked into place.

Fake it till you make it, he reminds himself. This is how he's survived Army life so far.

Josh sees to it that they're served and seated, then announces he has to leave them for a short while.

'Dawg, you gotta eat,' A-bort says. 'You're getting skinnier just standing there.'

Josh laughs. 'I'll be okay.'

'When do we meet the cheerleaders?' Holliday wants to know.

'Soon,' Josh answers over Crack, who's saying the hell with that, bring on Destiny's Child, he wants some quality 'facial' time with Beyoncé.

'They gonna give us some lap dances?' Day persists. Josh hesitates. 'I'll ask,' he says in perfect deadpan, and everybody haws. Josh. Jaaaaassssshhhhh. Jash is all right for a pussy boy. They are seated at a big circular table near the

67

windows with an excellent view of the playing field, on which nothing much is happening at the moment. Dime allows them one Heineken with lunch, *one,* he says, glancing at Major Mac, who nods. Billy has made sure to sit next to Dime and Albert, because whatever they say he means to hear it. He knows he doesn't know enough. He doesn't know anything, basically, at least nothing worth knowing, the measure of worth at this point in his life being knowledge that quiets the mind and calms the soul. So he makes it his business to sit next to Dime, and where Dime sits, that's the head of the table. Albert is to Dime's right, then A-bort, Day, Lodis, Crack, Sykes, Major Mac, Mango, and finally, rounding off the circle, Billy. So how about a couple of place settings for Shroom and Lake? This is his private mental ritual at the start of group meals that he does in lieu of prayers. Another ritual: Never cross a threshold with your left foot leading. And others: Fasten body armor from the bottom up, do not start sentences with the letter W, don't masturbate within six hours of a mission. Yet he'd adhered to all such tics and talismans on the day of the canal so maybe it doesn't matter a damn that they stayed at the W Hotel in Dallas last night, or that said hotel featured an upscale club called, how fucking weird, the Ghost Bar. So many omens, so many signs and portents to read. It's the randomness that makes your head this way, living the Russian-roulette lifestyle every minute of the day. Mortars falling out of the sky, random. Rockets, lob bombs, IEDs, all random. Once on OP Billy was pulling night watch and felt a sick little pop just off the bridge of his nose, which was, he realized as he tumbled backward, the snap of a bullet breaking the sound barrier as it passed. Inches. Not even that. Fractions, atoms, and it was all this random, whether you stopped at the piss tube this minute or the next, or skipped seconds at chow, or were curled to the left in your bunk instead of the right, or where you lined up in column, that was a big one. At first they were hitting the lead Humvee, then they switched to number two, then it was a toss-up between two, three, and four, then they went back to one, and don't even talk about the never-ending mindfuck debate as to your odds in any particular seat inside the vehicle, on any given day it could be anything, anywhere. 'You can dodge an RPG,' he said to a reporter a couple of days ago. He hadn't meant to reveal such a fraught and intimate fact, and felt cheap, as if he'd divulged a shameful family secret, but there it was, *you can dodge an RPG*, that damn crazy thing lamely fluttering at you, spitting and smoking like a cheap Mexican firework, *tttttthhhhhhhhpppppppffffffttttt-FOOOM*! What he'd meant to say, been trying to say, is that it's not a lie, sometimes it really happens in slow-motion time, his ultimate point being just how strange and surreal your own life can be. Lately he thinks he could have tapped it as it flew by, sent it spinning off to nowhere like thumping a balloon instead of merely dodging as it sputtered past on its way to making such a christfuck mess back there. What's happening now isn't nearly as real as that, eating this meal, holding this fork, lifting this glass, the realest things in the world these days are the things in his head. Lake, for instance. 'Lake,' that's all it takes to get this bleak little movie going, a night shot of, say, the berm road in pale moonlight, crickets cheeping, dogs barking faintly in the distance, the slow suck and gurgle of the nearby canal. So there is the berm road on a quiet night, then a slow tracking shot that peels off the road and gradually keys on something in the high grass. A leg. Two legs. Lake's. Peaceful. Those crickets, the soft moonlight, the purring canal. As if waking from a long sleep, the legs begin to stir. Tentative at first, they move with a childlike air of sweetly baffled innocence, but eventually they rise, shake themselves off, and set off in search of the rest of Lake. It could be a Disney movie about a couple of household pets mistakenly left behind, for they are as brave as that, as trusting and loyal, how can they know they're screwed from the start for Lake is six thousand miles and an ocean away? Not that these are appropriate thoughts for mealtime, but once these little movies get going in your head—

'Billy!' woofs Dime. 'You're flaking on me.'

'No, Sergeant. I'm just thinking about dessert.'

'Thinking ahead, good man. God-*damn* I trained them well.'

'They certainly can eat,' Albert observes. 'Hey, guys, you can slow down. It's not going anywhere.'

'It's chill,' Dime answers. 'Just keep your hands and feet away from their mouths and you won't get hurt.'

Albert laughs. He is having only a mixed green salad and fizzy water, along with a barely touched 'Cowboyrita' on the side. 'I'm gonna miss you guys,' he tells them. 'It's been an experience getting to know you fine young men.'

'Come with us,' says Crack.

'Yeah, come to Iraq,' A-bort urges. 'We'll have some laughs.'

'No,' Holliday objects. 'Albert gotta stay here and make us rich, ain't that right, Albert.'

'That's the plan,' Albert responds in a studiously mild voice, and *there,* Billy thinks, *there* it is in that soft deflation at the end, the almost imperceptible slackening of ego and effort that denotes the triage mode of the consummate pro. 'I'd just get in the way,' Albert is saying, 'plus I'm pretty much your classic pacifist twerp. Listen, the only reason I went to law school was to stay out of Vietnam, and lemme tell you guys, if my deferment hadn't come through, I would've been on the bus for Canada that night.'

'It was the sixties,' Crack observes.

'It was the sixties, exactly, all we wanted was to smoke a lot of dope and ball a lot of chicks. Vietnam, excuse me? Why would I wanna go get my ass shot off in some stinking rice paddy just so Nixon can have his four more years? Screw that, and I wasn't the only one who felt that way. All the big warmongers these days who took a pass on Vietnam, look, I'd be the last person on earth to start casting blame. Bush, Cheney, Rove, all those guys, they just did what everybody else was doing and I was right there with 'em, chicken as anybody. My problem now is how tough and gung-ho they are, all that bring-it-on crap, I mean, Jesus, show a little humility, people. They ought to be just as careful of your young lives as they were with their own.'

'Albert,' says Mango, 'you should run for something. Run for president.'

Albert laughs. 'I'd rather die. But thanks for the sentiment.' The producer is clearly enjoying himself, a smiling, avuncular presence not so much slumped in his chair as taking full advantage of it, as comfortably shored against gravity's downdraft as Jabba the Hut on his custom throne. 'Why's he fucking calling us?' Crack asked when Albert first got in touch, after a quick Internet search confirmed that he was what he said he was, a veteran Hollywood producer with three Best Picture Oscars from the seventies and eighties, plus the distinction of having produced *Fodie's Press and Fold*, the biggest money-losing film in the history of Warner Bros. 'It was that year's *Ishtar*,' he likes to say, laughing, wearing the flop like a badge of honor, for only an A-list player could engineer that kind of legendary bust, and anyway the third Oscar came a couple of years later, so he was redeemed. The midcareer sabbatical was his choice. The paradigm was shifting, the studios moving away from long-term producer deals, plus he'd just gotten married for the third time and was starting a new family. He had all the money he'd ever need and decided to step back for a while, but now, three years on, he's itching to get back in the game. Thanks to old friends he's got a solo shop on the MGM lot, with a secretary and assistant provided by the studio. 'I like where I am right now,' he told Bravo in their first face-to-face. 'No overhead, no pressure. I feel like a kid again, I can do whatever I want.'

And if his hot young wife (Bravo googled her too) is miffed that he's not home on Thanksgiving Day, well, she's a good kid. She understands the demands of his work. Albert watches with interest as several Stadium Club patrons stop to pay their respects. The men have the hale good looks and silver hair of successful bank presidents or midsized-city mayors, tanned, fit sixty-year-olds who can still bring the heat on their tennis serves. Their wives are substantially but not offensively younger, all blondes, all displaying the taut architectonics of surgical self-improvement. *So proud,* the men say, going around shaking hands. *So grateful, so honored. Guardians. Freedoms. Fanatics. TerrRr.* The wives hang back and let their men do the honors, they look on with vaguely wistful smiles and not an ounce of evident lust.

Enjoy your meal, the men say in parting, with the stern yet coaxing manner of white-glove waiters. 'They sure do love you guys,' Albert observes after the group moves on. Crack snorts.

'If they love us so much, how about if their wives—'

'Shut,' Dime woofs, and Crack shuts.

'I mean *everybody* loves you guys, black, white, rich, poor, gay, straight, *everybody*. You guys are equal-opportunity heroes for the twenty-first century. Look, I'm just as cynical as the next fella, but your story has really touched a nerve in this country. What you did in Iraq, you went head-to-head with some very bad guys and you kicked their ass. Even a pacifist twerp like me can appreciate that.'

'I got seven,' Sykes says, which is what he always says. 'Seven for sure. But I think it was more.'

'Listen,' Albert says, 'what Bravo did that day, that's a different kind of reality you guys experienced. People like me who've never been in combat, thank God, no way we can know what you guys went through, and I think that's why we're getting push-back from the studios. Those people, the kind of bubble they live in? It's a major tragedy in their lives if their Asian manicurist takes the day off. For those people to be passing judgment on the validity of your experience is just wrong, it goes beyond wrong, it's ethics porn. They aren't capable of fathoming what you guys did.'

'So tell them,' says Crack.

'Yeah, tell them,' says A-bort, and Bravo strikes

up a spontaneous chant, *tell them, tell them, tell them* like a frog chorus or monks at prayer. The nearby Stadium Club patrons smile and chuckle like it's all a high-spirited college prank. As abruptly as it started, the chanting stops.

'Tell Hilary to tell them,' says Dime.

'I'm trying, hoss. Lotta moving parts to this deal.' Albert's cell hums and the first thing he says is, 'Hilary's officially interested.' Then: 'Sure she is. It's a very physical role and she's a very physical actress. Plus she's a patriot. She really wants to do this.' Pause. 'I'm hearing fifteen million.' Pause. 'Will there be politics?' Albert rolls his eyes for Bravo's benefit. 'Larry, you know what von Clausewitz said, war is simply politics by other means.' Pause. 'No, you illiterate, not *The Art of War*. The German guy, the Prussian.' Silence. 'My ass you read *The Art of War*. You might've read the CliffsNotes for it. I could believe you read the blurbs.' Albert's eyes glower down as he listens. Big listen. Mouth twitching, hairy fingers fribbling the tablecloth.

'Tell me this, Larry, how could you make a movie about this war and *not* be political? You want a video game, is that what we're talking about?'

The Bravos glance at one another. Could do worse, is the general thought.

'Okay look, how about this for politics. My guys are heroes, right? Americans, right? They're unequivocally on the right side and they also unequivocally kicked ass, now when was the last

75

time *that* happened for this country? There's your politics, Lar, it's all about feeling good about America again. Think *Rocky* meets *Platoon* and you're on the right track.' Pause. Eye roll. Uh huh, uh huh, uh huh. 'Listen, we're at the Cowboys game right now and I'm telling you, I've never seen anything like it. They can't take a step without getting mobbed, it's like the Beatles all over again. People respond to these guys in a very visceral way.'

The Bravos look at one another. What's amazing is a lot of what he says is true.

'Look, talk to Bob. He could use a hit right now, and I'm bringing him one on a goddamn silver platter.' Silence. 'Jesus.' Silence again. 'Well fuck me, it *is* Thanksgiving. Just trust me when I say Hilary's interested. You'll be glad you did.'

'Problems?' Dime asks when Albert clicks off.

'Nah. All normal.' Albert takes a drink of Cowboyrita and winces. 'It's all accountants running the studios these days. Midgets in Maseratis, tiny men in big suits. They have to google themselves every morning just to remember who they are.'

'Didn't you say Oliver Stone went to Nam?' Sykes asks.

'Yes I did, Kenneth. Did I fail to also mention he's a lunatic? And he can't bring the money anyway. Look, if I have to hit the street to make this film that's what I'll do, that's how much I believe in you guys.'

No one knows what this means exactly, but the

buffet beckons. When they go back for seconds – only Dime, Albert, and Major Mac stand pat – a long line precedes them, but as soon as people notice Bravo standing there they move aside and urge the soldiers forward. At first Bravo declines, which triggers a merry hue and cry. *Go on!* people insist in mock-scolding tones. *Get on up there, go!* They nod and chuckle as the Bravos pass, heartened by the sight of these fine, strapping American boys with their big broad shoulders and excellent manners and ability to eat everything in sight. Everyone is happy. It is a Moment. A point has been made, assumptions proved, and now they can all go forth and enjoy the day. Billy's hangover has been shocked into remission by the onslaught of calories, and on this second pass he marvels once more at the gorgeous food, the woody grain of the turkey beneath its golden crust, the lush, moist plaids of the vegetable casseroles, the luxuriant mounds of stuffing, and the six different kinds of mashed and whole potatoes, including an exotic purple variety with the strangely pleasing texture of leavened mildew. Here in the God-blessed realms of mainstream America you eat civilized meals and take civilized dumps, indoors, in peace, on toilets that flush, in the common decent privacy that God intended as opposed to the wide-open vistas of the barbarous desert, nature nipping at your ass like a pit bull puppy. So perhaps, it occurs to Billy, this is the whole point of civilization, the eating of beautiful meals and the taking of decorous dumps, in which case he is for it, having had a bellyful of the other way.

Walking back to the table they start giggling. No reason, they're just punchy, the food has given them a glucose high, but on arrival Dime tells them to sit the fuck down and shut up and he is not messing around. Something has happened. What happened? Soon they will learn that the powerful producer-director team of Grazer and Howard has relayed its desire to make the Bravo movie, Universal Studios has even verbally committed, but all on condition that the story relocates to World War II. But for now the only thing Bravo knows is that Dime is suddenly OTR, on the rag, while Albert carries on as if everything's cool, placidly keying in a message on his BlackBerry. 'A master of the psyche,' Shroom said of Dime, after the sergeant spent the better part of a morning smoking Billy's ass for leaving his night-vision goggles in the Humvee overnight. Push-ups, crunches, stress positions with sandbags, then six deadly laps in hundred-degree heat around the FOB's inner perimeter, roughly the equivalent of four miles. 'You'll never figure him out, so don't even try,' Shroom advised.

'He's an asshole,' said Billy.

'Yeah, he is. And that just makes you love him more.'

'Fuck that. I hate the son of a bitch.'

Shroom laughed, but then he could, he and Dime had served together in Afghanistan and he was the only Bravo who Dime never smoked. This exchange took place in the shade of the conceal-ment netting that Shroom rigged up outside his Conex, to which he would repair in his leisure hours to smoke and read and ponder the nature of things from the camo camp chair he bought in Kuwait. It calms Billy to think about him thus arranged, barefoot, shirtless, cigarette in hand, and with a book in his lap, *Slowly Down the Ganges*. He was heavy into the whole ethnobotanical mystic trip and even *looked* like a giant shroom, a fleshy, slope-shouldered, melanin-deficient white man with the basic body type of a manatee, yet he possessed a prodigious blue-collar strength. He could one-hand the SAW like a pistol and ready-up the .50 cal, and forty-pound sacks of HA rice were like beanbags in his grasp. Every other day he shaved his head, a surprisingly delicate orb that seemed a couple of sizes too small for the rest of him. In heat conditions his face lit up in swirling lava-lamp blobs, and he didn't so much perspire as *secrete*, producing an oily substance that covered his body like a slick of stale pickle juice.

'If people lived on the moon,' Dime liked to say, 'they would all look like Shroom.'

It was Shroom who told Billy that Dime's father was a high-powered judge back in North Carolina. 'Dime is money,' he said. 'But he doesn't want people to know. And you know what that means.'

No, Billy said. What does it mean?

'It means that money's *old*.'

They made the oddest of odd couples, handsome Dime palling around with mooncalf Shroom, and they seemed to know more about each other than would be considered healthy in a normal environment. From time to time Dime would allude to Shroom's horrific childhood, an apparently epic tale of hard knocks that included a stint in some sort of religious institution for waifs, or, as Dime called it with never a batted eye from Shroom, the Anal Redemptive Baptist Home for Misplaced Boys of Buttfuck, Oklahoma. Billy supposed that's where Shroom came by his impressive repertoire of Bible verses, in addition to such gnomic pronouncements as 'Jesus was not a U-Haul' and 'We're all God's Pop-Tarts whether we like it or not.' In Shroom World, bricks were 'earth biscuits,' trees were 'sky shrubs,' and all frontline infantry 'meat rabbits,' while media pronouncements on the *progress* of the war were like 'being lied to on your tombstone.' Early on, before they'd seen any real action, Billy asked him what being in a firefight was like. Shroom thought for a moment. 'It's not like anything, except maybe being raped by angels.' He'd say 'I love you' to every man in the squad before rolling out, say it straight, with no joking or smart-ass lilt and no warbly Christian smarm in it either, just that brisk declaration like he was tightening the seat belts around everyone's soul. Then other Bravos started saying it but they hedged at first, blatting 'I love you man' in the tearful desperate voice of the schmuck in the

Budweiser ad, but as the hits piled up and every trip outside the wire became an exercise in the full pucker, nobody was playing anymore.

I'm going down. Like a slide show, alive, dead, alive, dead, alive, dead. Billy was doing about ten different things at once, unpacking his medical kit, jamming a fresh magazine into his rifle, talking to Shroom, slapping his face, yelling at him to stay awake, trying to track the direction of the incoming rounds and crouching low with absolute fuck-all for cover. The Fox footage shows him firing with one hand and working on Shroom with the other, but he doesn't remember that. He thinks he must have been cutting Shroom's ammo rack loose, pulling the release on his IBA to get at his wounds. Is this what they mean by courage? Simply doing all the things you were trained to do, albeit everything at once and very fast. He remembers the whole front of his body being covered in blood and half-wondering if any of it was his, his bloody hands so slick he finally had to tear open the compression bandage with his teeth, and when he turned back to Shroom the big bastard was sitting up! Then going right back down, Billy sliding crabwise to catch him in his lap, and Shroom looked up at him then with his brow furrowed, eyes burning like he had something crucial to say.

'He's your sergeant,' Shroom said that day outside his Conex. 'It's his job to make your life as miserable as possible.' Then he went on to explain to Billy how Dime's mastery of the psyche involved intermittent

81

doses of positive reinforcement, intermittent being a more effective behavior-modification tool than a consistent program of same. Whatever. From all his reading Shroom knew lots of useless stuff, but what Billy is thinking here at the Stadium Club is, Thank you for making us feel like shit, *Sergeant*! Thank you for ruining this delicious *meal*! Probably the last non-Army-issued or contracted-for meal they will get for some time, but no matter, they are scum-sucking shitbag frontline grunts and their task at this moment is to shut up and eat.

Dime snaps, 'A-bort, what the fuck are you doing?'

'I'm texting Lake, Sergeant. Just saying what up.'

Dime can't very well object to that. He scans the table for other targets, but everyone's staying low to his plate, shoveling it in. Then Albert starts chuckling.

'Here, take a look at this.' He passes the BlackBerry to Dime.

'Dude's serious? Can't be serious.'

'I'm afraid he is.'

Dime turns to Billy. 'Dude's saying our movie's another *Walking Tall*, but in Iraq.'

'Ah.' Billy has never seen *Walking Tall*. 'Was Hilary Swank in that?'

'No, Billy, Hilary Swank was not – Jesus, never mind. Albert, who *are* these people?'

'Twerps,' Albert says. 'Nerds, wimps, liars, they're a bunch of skinny mutts with not much brains chasing a fake rabbit around a track. Content scares them, no, absolutely terrifies them. *"Is this any good? Ewwww, is it bad? Ewwww, I just can't tell!"* It's pathetic, all that money and no taste. You could hit them over the head with another *Chinatown* and they'd say let's stick a couple of cute little dogs in it.'

Dime is casual. 'So you're saying we're screwed.'

'Whoa, did I say that? Did I say that? Oh no indeed, I don't think I did. I've made a living in this business for thirty-five years, do *I* look screwable?' The Bravos laugh – well, no, screwable does not leap to mind when considering Albert. 'Hollywood's a sick, twisted place, I will most certainly grant you that. Corrupt, decadent, full of practicing sociopaths, roughly analogous to, say, the court of Louis the Sun King in seventeenth-century France. Don't laugh, guys, I'm serious, sometimes it helps to visualize these things in concrete terms. Gobs of wealth floating around, *obscene* wealth, complete over-the-top excess in every way, and every jerk in town's got their hustle going, trying to break off their little piece of it. But for that you've got to get to the king, because everything goes through the king, right? But that's a problem. Huge problem. Access is a problem. You can't just walk in off the street and pitch the king, but at any given moment there'll be twenty, thirty people hanging around the court who can get to the king. They've got access, influence, they're tapped in – the key is getting one of those guys attached to your deal. Same thing in Hollywood, there's maybe twenty, thirty people at any one time who can make a project go. The names might change from year to year, but the dynamic's the same, the number stays about the same. You get one of those people attached to your deal, you're gold.'

'Swank,' Crack offers.

'Swank is gold,' Albert confirms.

'Wahlberg?' Mango asks.

'Marky can make a project go.'

'How 'bout Wesley Snipes,' says Lodis. 'Like, you know, say we got him to play me.'

'Interesting.' Albert ponders a moment. 'Not this movie, but I tell you what, Lodis. I'll see if I can get you the bitch part in his next film, how about that.'

Aaaaaaaannnnnnnhhhhhhh, everybody slags on Lodis, who just grins with food mashed all over his teeth. They're interrupted by a Stadium Club patron who wants to say hello. It's never the young or middle-aged men who stop to speak but always the older guys, the silverbacks secure in the fact that they're past their fighting prime. They thank the soldiers for their service. They ask how is lunch. They offer praise for such assumed attributes as tenacity, aggressiveness, love of country. This particular patron, a fit, ruddy fellow with some black still in his hair, introduces himself with a lavish trawling of vowels that comes out sounding like 'How-Wayne.' Soon he's telling them about the bold new technology his family's oil company uses to juice more crude out of the Barnett Shale, something to do with salt water and chemical fracturing agents.

'Some of my friends' kids are serving over there with you,' How-Wayne tells them. 'So it's a personal thing with me, boosting domestic production, lessening our dependence on foreign oil. I figure the better I do my job, the sooner we can bring you young men home.'

'Thank *you*!' Dime responds. 'That's just excellent, sir. We certainly do appreciate that.'

'I'm just trying to do my part.' And that was cool, Billy will later reflect. If he'd just said *enjoy your meal* like everybody else and returned to his lucrative patriotic life, but no, he got greedy. He had to squeeze just a little bit more from Bravo. So, he says, just from your own perspective, how do you think we're doing over there?

'How're we doing?' Dime echoes brightly. 'Just from our own perspective?' The Bravos fold their hands and look down at their plates, though several can't help smiling. Albert cocks his head and pockets his BlackBerry, suddenly interested. 'Well, it's a war,' Dime continues in that same bright voice, 'which is by definition an extreme situation, people trying very hard to terminate each other. But I'm far from qualified to speak to the big picture, sir. All I can tell you with any confidence is that the exchange of force with intent to kill, that is truly a mind-altering experience, sir.'

'I'm sure, I'm sure.' How-Wayne is gravely nodding. 'I can imagine how hard it is on you young men. To be exposed to that level of violence—'

'No!' Dime interrupts. 'That's not it at all! We *like* violence, we *like* going lethal! I mean, isn't that what you're paying us for? To take the fight to America's enemies and send them straight to hell? If we didn't like killing people then what's the point? You might as well send in the Peace Corps to fight the war.'

'Ah ha,' How-Wayne chuckles, though his smile has lost some wattage. 'I guess you've got me there.'

'Listen, you see these men?' Dime gestures around the table. 'I love every one of these mutts like a brother, I bet I love them more than their mommas even, but I'll tell you frankly, and they know how I feel so I can say this right in front of them, but just for the record, this is the most murdering bunch of psychopaths you'll ever see. I don't know how they were before the Army got them, but you give them a weapons system and a couple of Ripped Fuels and they'll blast the hell out of anything that moves. Isn't that right, Bravo?'

They answer instantly, with gusto, **Yes, Sergeant!** Throughout the restaurant, dozens of well-coifed heads whip around.

'See what I mean?' Dime chortles. 'They're killers, they're having the time of their lives. So if your family's oil company wants to frack the living shit out of the Barnett Shale, that's fine, sir, that's absolutely your prerogative, but don't be doing it on our account. You've got your business and we've got ours, so you just keep on drilling, sir, and we'll keep on killing.'

How-Wayne opens his mouth and flaps his jaw once or twice, but nothing comes out. His eyes have receded deep into his head. Behold, Billy thinks, the world's most mindfucked millionaire.

'I've gotta go,' How-Wayne mumbles, glancing around as if checking his escape route. Don't talk about shit you don't know, Billy thinks, and therein lies the dynamic of all such encounters, the Bravos speak from the high ground of experience. They are authentic. They are the Real. They have dealt much death and received much death and smelled it and held it and slopped through it in their boots, had it spattered on their clothes and tasted it in their mouths. That is their advantage, and given the masculine standard America has set for itself it is interesting how few actually qualify. *Why we fight*, yo, who is this *we*? Here in the chicken-hawk nation of blowhards and bluffers, Bravo always has the ace of bloods up its sleeve.

By the time How-Wayne leaves, the Bravos are openly sniggering. 'You know, David,' Albert says, gazing thoughtfully at Dime, 'once you're out of the Army, you really ought to consider acting.'

The Bravos hoot, but Albert seems serious, and Dime does too because he asks quite solemnly, 'Was I too hard on him?' which cracks everybody up, yet he sits there completely straight-faced. Several Bravos start chanting *Holly-wooood* while

Day tells Albert, 'Dime ain't no act, he just like fucking with people,' to which Albert answers, 'What do you think acting is?' which inspires another round of hoots. As all this is going on Dime leans toward Billy and murmurs:

'Now dammit, Billy, why did I give that man such a hard time?'

'I don't know, Sergeant. I guess you had your reasons.'

'Dear Jesus. And what might those be?'

Billy's pulse takes off. It's like being called on in class. 'Hard to say, Sergeant. Because you hate bullshit?'

'Yeah, maybe. Plus I'm an asshole?'

Billy declines to answer. Dime laughs, sits back and waves for a waiter. When he turns back to Billy there it is again, The Look, his gaze so frank and open-ended that Billy can't help but wonder, Why me? At first he feared it was the start of some hideous gay thing, gay being virtually his sole reference point for prolonged eye contact from a fellow male, but lately he doubts it, a conclusion that required no small broadening of his view of human nature. Dime is after something else, some acknowledgment or as-yet-to-be-determined insight, though Billy knows if he described it to your average third party it would come out sounding gay, just based on a strict visual rendering of the trigger event. You had to be inside it to understand the pure human misery of that day, the desolation, for instance, one among many, of seeing Lake up on

88

the table fighting off the docs, howling and flailing and slinging blood like he wasn't being saved but skinned alive. Billy has come to see that as the breaking point, the bend in his personal arc that day. There was before and there was after, and whatever of his shit he still had together he lost it then, broke down sobbing right there on the aid station ramp. Surely his mind would have cracked from shock and grief had not Dime shoved him into a supply pantry, slammed him up against the wall and pinned him there as if bent on bodily harm. By then Dime was weeping too, both of them hacking, gagging on snot, covered in mud and blood and sweat as if they'd just that moment climbed gasping and retching from some elemental pit of primordial sludge. *I knew it would be you,* Dime was hissing over and over, his mouth a butane torch in Billy's ear, *I knew it would be you, I knew it I knew it I so fucking knew it I am so fucking goddamn proud of you,* then he grabbed Billy's face in both his hands and kissed him full on the lips like a stomp, a whack with a rubber mallet.

Billy's mouth was sore for days. He kept waiting for Dime to say something about it, and when that didn't happen he'd put his fingers to his mouth and feel the bruise on his lips. You couldn't put this in a movie and have people understand, not based on any movie Billy's ever seen. If you could then he'd say, Okay, put it in, he could give a flying fuck if people think it's gay, but it would have to be done with real shrewdness and skill, you

89

couldn't just throw it out there and expect people to understand, but now Swank has totally screwed up his thinking here. If she plays him and Dime both, where does it go? Like, good luck kissing yourself. Good luck saving yourself. Maybe in the movie they will all just have to lose their minds.

Fuck it, nobody knows about it anyway. Dime orders another round of Heinekens for the table, though he requires that the empties be cleared away first. After the waiter leaves another waiter arrives and asks would they like coffee. Coffee? *Hell yes, coffee!* Caffeine being one of the essential drugs. Crack asks if there's Red Bull and the waiter says he'll check, which prompts orders for Red Bull all around. Everyone rises to go for desserts but Billy needs to find the head. He's too shy to ask where it is so he wanders the outer sanctums of the club for a while, which is fine, he needs a break anyway, and viewing forty years' worth of pro football memorabilia is as good a way as any to numb the mind. There's a poster-sized photo of the Hail Mary catch, Staubach's cleats from Super Bowl VI, Mel Renfro's grass-stained jersey from the Cowboys' last game at the Cotton Bowl, every item curated with all the pomp and reverence of relics from the Holy Roman Empire. Billy finds the men's room and takes his time. Everything is so clean. Iraq is trash, dust, rubble, rot, and bubbling open sewers, plus these maddening microscopic grains of sand that razor their way into every orifice of the human body. Lately he's noticed the crud is even in his lungs. It whines when he takes a deep breath, a faint screeching down there like bagpipes playing deep in the valley, and he wonders if it's a permanent thing or just a temporary backup in the filtration system.

He takes a long time washing his hands, watching himself in the mirror. Growing up in Stovall he knew a boy named Danny Werbner, the older brother of his friend Clay. Danny had a distant manner and rarely spoke, but he'd narrowly survived a car accident in which his two best friends died, and for this reason everybody just shrugged off the strange things Danny did. Such as, he'd strip naked in the room he and Clay shared and stare at himself in the mirror for long periods of time, not caring if the door was open or how cold it was or whether posses of younger boys were tromping through. This was just one of the weird things Danny Werbner did, disturbed behavior with its own inarguable logic, Danny staring in the mirror to make sure he was there.

Billy thinks about this lately when he looks in mirrors. Out in the hall he meets Mango coming the other way with one of the waiters, a stocky young Latino with a gold hoop earring and the high-fade haircut of the ghetto cat. They're smirking. Something is up. Mango pulls Billy aside, and right there under a photo of Tom Landry shaking hands with Ronald Reagan, he whispers, 'Wanna get high?'

Hell yeah. The waiter leads them through the kitchen, down a cluttered service corridor, and into a junky storeroom with no heat, and from there they exit into a trapezoidal pocket of outdoor space, a kind of hutch hollowed out of the stadium's armature. It's a mistake, a design flaw neatly tucked out of sight, hardly big enough for the three of them. The waiter, whose name is Hector, has to bend to clear the I-beam cutting across his corner.

'What is this place?' Billy asks, because he has to ask something.

Hector laughs. 'It's not nothing.' He kicks a chunk of wood under the door. 'It's nowhere, man, it's one of them places don't exist. Me and some of the guys, we use it for smoke breaks.'

They laugh. The cold air feels good. A neutered sort of daylight filters down to them, strained and sifted through the steel fretwork. For several moments Billy imagines the stadium as an extension of himself, as if he's wearing it, strapped into the most awesome set of body armor ever known to man. It's a fine, secure feeling until his chest starts to labor under the weight of all that steel, but the joint coming around helps with that.

'Nice,' Mango says appreciatively.

Hector nods. 'Takes the edge off, *vato*. Gets you through the day.'

'That it does,' Billy sagely agrees. Certain lights are switching on in his head, others switching off. 'That's some dank-ass bud.'

'Hey, you know, gotta support the troops.' Hector laughs and takes his hit. 'You guys ain't worried about pissing hot?'

Mango explains that, no, they aren't worried about it. Bravo has deduced that the Army is loath to risk all this good PR by tagging Bravo with random drug tests, so for the duration of the *Victory Tour* they feel safe. 'And what'd they do if they nailed us, yo, send our ass back to Iraq?'

Hector shakes his head with stoned gravitas. 'No way, not for a blunt. Even the Army ain't that harsh.'

Billy and Mango hesitate. Command seems sensitive about this, Bravo's imminent return to Iraq. The Bravos are not to deny they're redeploying if the subject comes up, but higher would prefer to omit this detail from the *Victory Tour* conversation.

Mango grins, cuts Billy a look. 'Dude,' he tells Hector, 'we *already* goin' back.'

Hector squints. 'Shittin' me.'

'Shit you not. Leaving Saturday.'

'The fuck you gotta go back.'

'Gotta finish out our tour.'

'The fuck! The fuck you gotta go back, after all you fuckin' done, fuckin' heroes? Where's the fuckin' right in that? You guys done kicked your share a ass, like whyn't they let you just coast on out?'

Mango laughs. 'The Army don't work that way. They need bodies.'

'Shit.' Hector is scandalized. 'For how long you gotta go?'

'Eleven months.'

'Fuck!' Sheer outrage. 'You *wanna* go back?'

The Bravos snort.

'Man. Fuckin' harsh. That just ain't right.' Hector

93

casts about. 'Ain't they supposed to be making a movie about you?'

Uh huh.

'And you still gotta go back? Fuck, so what happens if you, uh, you, uh—'

'Get smoked?' Billy offers.

Hector turns away, stricken.

'No worries, homes,' Mango says, 'that's a totally different movie.' The Bravos laugh, and Hector smiles bashfully, grateful to be absolved for raising the spectre of their deaths. The joint makes another circuit. The light in their little space takes on a pearly, numinous glow. The war is out there somewhere but Billy can't feel it, like his sole experience with morphine when he could not feel pain. At one point he even tried as an experiment, stared at his cut-up arms and legs thinking *hurt,* but the notion simply gassed into thin air. That's how the war feels now, it is at most a presence or pressure on his mind, awareness without content, an experiential doughnut hole. When he tunes back into the conversation, Hector is asking if they're going to meet Destiny's Child, the headliner for today's halftime extravaganza and currently number one on the national wet-dream charts.

'They ain't said nothing about that.' Mango's English is getting looser, leaning toward the street. Not that he's slurring, just taking the corners wide. 'Ain't told us much of anything, like we're supposed to be in the halftime show? They said we're gonna meet the cheerleaders.'

'Shit, *vato*, everybody meets the cheerleaders, fucking Boy Scouts meet the cheerleaders. You guys are rock stars, they oughta get you with Beyoncé and her girls. Shit, heroes 'n' all, they oughta let you bone those bitches fah real.'

Bonemfahreal, Billy says to himself. Not possible. Not that he necessarily would if given the chance, though probably. Maybe. Okay, definitely. Or it depends. He decides he wants both more and less. He'd like to hang with Beyoncé in a nice way, get to know her by doing small pleasant things together like playing board games and going out for ice cream, or how about this, a three-week trial run in some tropical paradise where they can hang together in that nice way and possibly fall in love, and meanwhile fuck each other's brains out in their spare time. He wants both, he wants the entire body-soul connect because anything less is just demeaning. Has the war done this to him, he wonders, inspired these deeper sensitivities and yearnings of his? Or is it just because he's going on his twentieth year of life?

Time is growing short. They need to get back to the unit, but the engine's dropped out of their urgency. The joint has burned down to a glowing squib when Hector confides that he's thinking of joining the Army.

The Bravos groan. *Don't.*

'Yeah, I know it's fucked, but I got a kid and her moms don't work so it's all on me, which I accept, I mean I wanna take care of 'em and all, but the way it is now it just ain't happening. I got the job here, I work five days a week at Kwik Lube and don't get insurance neither place, and I gotta have insurance for my little girl. And I got debts. Like, you know, who don't have debts.' Billy notes that Hector is worried in the way a man worries, not freaking and thrashing around like a fuckwit kid but soberly taking the measure of his trouble, manning up to live it every day. He says the Army is offering enlistment bonuses of $6,000, and once he's in he wouldn't have to worry about insurance.

'So you gonna do it?' Billy asks, panged by the $6,000. The Army got his carcass for absolutely free.

'Dunno. You guys think I should?'

Billy and Mango lock eyes. After a couple of seconds they all bust up laughing.

'It pretty much sucks,' says Billy. 'I don't know why the hell we're laughing.'

'Hell yeah,' Mango says, 'all those days I'm thinking, Yo, I am so fuckin' done with this shit, and then I'm like, Okay, so I get out when my time's up, what the fuck's waiting for me gonna be any better? Like, fuck, workin' at Burger King? Then I remember why I signed up in the first place.'

Hector is nodding. 'That's sort of my whole point. What I got out here sucks, so I might as well join.'

'What else is there,' Mango says.

'What else is there,' Hector agrees.

'What else is there,' Billy echoes, but he's thinking of home.

BULLY OF THE HEART

They got two nights and a day. Sykes went to Fort Hood, to the tiny on-post house where his daughter and pregnant wife live, at the edge of the artillery drop zone. Lodis went to Florence, S.C., which is also the hometown, or so he claimed, of his fourth or maybe second cousin Snoop Dogg. A-bort went to Lafayette, La., Crack to Birmingham, Mango to Tucson, and Day to Indianapolis. Dime went to Carolina. Lake continued his long-term residency at the Brooke Army Medical Center in San Antonio, and Shroom was being held against his will at the Merriam-Gaylord Funeral Home in Ardmore, Oklahoma. And Billy, Billy went to Stovall, to the three-bedroom, two-bath brick ranch house on Cisco Street with sturdy access ramps front and back for his father's wheelchair, a dark purple motorized job with fat whitewalls and an American flag decal stuck to the back. 'The Beast,' Billy's sister Kathryn called it, a flanged and humpbacked ride with all the grace of a tar cooker or giant dung beetle. 'Damn thing gives me the willies,' she confessed to Billy, and Ray's aggressive style of driving did in fact seem to strive for maximum creep effect. *Whhhhhhhiiiiirrrrrrr*, he buzzed to the kitchen for his morning coffee, then *whhhhh-hiiiiirrrrrrr* into the den for the day's first hit of nicotine and Fox News, then *whhhhhhhiiiiiirrrrrr* back to the kitchen for his breakfast, *whhhh-hiiiiirrrrr* to the bathroom, *whhhhhhiiiiirrrrrr* to the den and the blathering TV, *whhhhhhiiiiirrrrrr, whhhhhhiiiiiiirrrrr, whhhhhhiiiiiiirrrrrrr*, he jammed the joystick so hard around its vulcanized socket that the motor keened like a tattoo drill, the piercing *eeeeeennnnnhhhhh* contrapuntaling off the baseline *whhhhiiiiirrrrrrr* to capture in sound, in stereophonic chorus no less, the very essence of the man's personality.

'He's an asshole,' Kathryn said.

To which Billy: 'You just now figured that out?'

'Shut up. What I mean is he *likes* being an asshole, he *enjoys* it. Some people you get the feeling they can't help it? But he *works* at it. He's what you'd call a *proactive* asshole.'

'What does he do?'

'Nothing! That's my whole point, doesn't do shit! Won't do his physical therapy, never goes out, just sits in that damn chair all day watching Fox and listening to fat-ass Rush Limbaugh, won't even talk unless he wants something, and then he just grunts. Expects us to wait on him hand and foot.'

'So don't do it.'

'I don't! But then it all falls on Mom and she wears herself out and I'm like, Okay, whatever,

I'm in. As long as I'm living here I might as well be part of the problem.'

Somewhere in the house there's a trunk full of glossy promotional photos of rock and metal bands from the seventies, eighties, and into the nineties, 'the mullet years' as Kathryn has tagged that primitive era, most of these bands long forgotten and mercifully so, though Ray's collection does contain a few bona fide stars. Meat Loaf. .38 Special. Kansas. The Allman Brothers. Proximity to talent as well as the empire of his own considerable ego propelled Ray to a minor local stardom all his own, and while the pop music juggernaut of love, lust, and endless adolescence powers on and on, it endures without the oral gifts of Rockin' Ray Lynn, who in the 9-11 climate of recessive economics found himself out on his downsized and too-old ass. We love ya, big guy, but you're gone. And all those years he'd kept apartments in Dallas and Fort Worth, that era came to a sputtering and ignominious end too, though he was plotting his comeback in between the odd jobs that came his way, emceeing local beauty pageants and Rotary Club banquets, 'monkey gigs' he called them in the bitter, waspish voice he used at home, the one best suited to his default settings of contempt, sarcasm, and general hatefulness. The way he could switch from that to his professional voice was something to see, a kind of ventriloquist's trick, no dummy necessary. He'd be berating you for, say, failing to lather the tires with sufficient

Armor All to achieve that lustrous showroom shine, and in the midst of his ruptured sewer line of fucks and damns and worthless-piece-of-shits his cell would ring and it was like a switch flipped, all at once he was the hip, happy voice of ten thousand drive-times and the perennial metro-area Arbitron champ.

Billy hated that. Not just the lie of it but the affront to nature, like someone's head changing shape right before your eyes. But the comeback. That was his mission. Through research Ray concluded that the market could support yet one more aggrieved white male defending faith and flag from America's heartland. He studied the masters, followed the news, logged serious hours on the Internet. He began making demo tapes and sending them out; the family became his test audience for ever more baroque elaborations of conservative creed. 'America's Prick,' Billy's elder sister, Patty, called him after an especially inspired riff on the welfare state. He'd leaped straight from rock 'n' roll to hard-core right wing with no stops in between. It was a remarkable feat of self-actualization, but at what cost, what stresses of body and soul, a bending of the psyche beyond human limits such as might be endured on a space voyage to Mars. The man existed in a 24/7 paranoid clench. He had TV and radio for intellectual affirmation, a two-packs-a-day habit for sensual sustenance, and none of the mundane distractions of fresh air or exercise. Thus he was operating at peak efficiency until the day he rose punch-drunk from the couch, staggering, sloshing his words, comically swatting his head like a man trying to ward off a swarm of bees.

Stroke. Then another before the EMTs arrived, the one that nearly killed him. Now he mumbles and mewls like the Tin Man pre–lube job, and Billy makes not the slightest effort to understand. Kathryn understands him, and their mother, Denise, and Patty, who drove from Amarillo with her toddler son, Brian, just to spend these two nights and one day with Billy, she mostly understands. Not that Ray tries to talk except where his personal needs are concerned, and therein lies the family secret which dare not speak its name. It wasn't that he screwed around during all those years of keeping an apartment, which he *had* to do, keep an apartment that is; as the morning DJ for a succession of Metroplex radio stations no way he could handle the daily commute from Stovall, and Stovall was where they chose to raise the kids, steeped in the neighborly virtues and core American values of small-town Texas. Plus Denise had a pretty good job there, so the arrangement was he'd stay in the city during the week working his fingers *to the bone,* and would return home in triumph on the weekends. Extramarital sex wasn't the terrible family secret, neither the screwing around nor the evidence thereof, the surfacing after his stroke of the alleged teenage daughter and the lawsuit for acknowledgment of paternity and child support. A sorry business to be sure, but no secret, no tiptoeing around the smirch to family honor. But that other shame they never spoke of, thrilling though it was. You felt bad about feeling good, was what the shame amounted to. Ray wouldn't – couldn't? – talk: ! The famous silver tongue was finally stilled, and what a relief and secret joy that was for everyone.

'Some days I think I'm living in a bad country song,' Kathryn said, and she told Billy about walking into the den one day to find Ray whimpering on the floor, stuck between the coffee table and the sofa. He'd clearly been there awhile, judging from the dark stain across the front of his pants, and not ten feet away Denise sat at her desk paying bills and shuffling insurance forms. Mom! Kathryn cried. Don't you see Dad lying there? Denise gave her husband a breezy glance. 'Oh,' she said, turning back to the desk, 'he's okay. He'll get up when he's good and ready.'

Kathryn laughed when she finished the story. 'I swear I think she'd let him die if I wasn't around.'

You couldn't please him, not if you happened to be his son, not even if you came home a national hero. There was a noisy happy scene when Billy walked in the door, his mother crying, his sisters laughing and crying, little Brian swinging among their knees and crying too, everyone lumped in a big sloppy blob of a hug. Ray was in the den watching TV. He glanced up when Billy entered, gave a noncommittal grunt, and turned back to the tube. Billy stood at parade rest and sized up the situation. Still dyeing your hair I see, he said, and indeed the old man's brick of a pompadour was the glossy jet-black of a fresh oil spill. Nice boots, Billy went on, nodding at the brown ostrich quills, never creased. New? Ray cut him a look, eyes glittering with dangerously high IQ. Billy chuckled. He couldn't help it. Still the dude with his Bible-black hair and prickly attention to grooming and dress, the pretty pink candies of his fingernails gleaming from a house-call manicure. He wasn't tall, he had a pinched dirt-dauber sort of build and his sharp-featured face was just this side of handsome, but a certain class of woman had always gone for him. Waitresses, hairstylists, receptionists, the moment he opened his mouth they were hormone mush. Secretaries were a specialty; his own, others'. Much had been learned in the course of the lawsuit.

'Your chair's looking all spiff. You get it waxed?'

Ray ignored him.

'Looks like a little Zamboni, anybody ever told you that?'

Still Ray didn't react.

'So does it make that beeping sound when you put it in reverse?'

For dinner Denise served up a spectacular chicken tetrazzini feed. She'd had her hair done. She'd put on makeup. She wanted everything perfect, which Ray deftly sandbagged by cranking up the volume for Bill O'Reilly and chain-smoking through dinner. 'It's every daughter's dream to die of secondhand smoke,' Kathryn wistfully crooned, then she turned to Billy and laughed. 'Listen, if he could stick the whole pack in his mouth and smoke it all at once he would, nothing would make him happier.' Ray just ignored her. He pretty much ignored them all, and that night it struck Billy as never before how completely they were all bound up in one another. You can deny him, he thought, watching his father across the table. You can hate him, love him, pity him, never speak to or look him in the eye again, never deign even to be in his crabbed and bitter presence, but you're still stuck with the son of a bitch. One way or another he'll always be your daddy, not even all-powerful death was going to change that.

Denise waited on her husband's every need, though she was never quick about it, Billy noticed, she seemed quite fine with him harrumphing a second and third time, and when she did get around to fetching, pouring, cutting, she performed with a multitasky air of distractedness, like she was watering plants while talking on the phone. She was sneaky. She had those passive-aggressive wiles. Her hair was an indeterminate washed-out chemical color, and most of the emotional muscle tone was gone from her face, though she was still capable of sad, skewed smiles from time to time, forcing the cheer like Christmas lights in the poor part of town. She strove mightily to keep the conversation upbeat, but family troubles kept leaking in around the edges. Money troubles, insurance troubles, medical-bureaucracy troubles, Ray-being-a-stubborn-pain-in-the-ass troubles. Halfway through the meal young Brian grew restless. 'Hey!' Kathryn cried. 'Hey, Briny, watch this!' She stuck two of Ray's Marlboros in her nose and bought them five more minutes of peace.

'She called today,' Denise said, helping herself to a third glass of wine.

'Who called?' Billy asked, not knowing any better. His sisters hooted. 'That *hussy*!' Kathryn answered with a berserk-debutante sort of shriek. She plucked the cigarettes from her nose and returned them to Ray's pack. 'Mother knows she's not supposed to talk to her. Everything's supposed to go through the lawyers.'

'Well,' Denise said, 'she called. I can't help it if the woman keeps calling my house.'

'Doesn't mean you have to talk to her,' Patty pointed out.

'Well, I can't just hang up. That would be rude.'

The girls yelped. 'That woman,' Kathryn began, and had to pause for a fit of dry-heave laughs, 'that woman had an *affair* with your husband, and you can't be *rude*? Ye gods, Mom, she did your old man for eighteen years, they had a *kid* together for Christ's sake. Be rude, please. Like that's the least you could do.'

Billy wanted to point out that Ray was sitting

105

right here – as if the situation called for a certain delicacy? But this was how they did, apparently, the women talked about and around him as if discussing the price of bleach, and Ray, for his part, might as well have been deaf for all the notice he took. He kept his eyes on O'Reilly and worked his fork with a fist grip, like little Brian.

'Mom,' said Patty, 'next time she calls, you need to tell her your lawyer said you can't talk to her.'

'I do, I tell her every time. But she keeps calling anyway.'

'So hang up on the bitch!' Kathryn cried, cackling, widening her eyes at Billy. *See? See what a bunch of lunatics we are?*

'I don't know what difference it makes,' Denise answered. 'We might as well talk, I mean, it can't do any harm, it's not like either of us has any money the other could take. "I've got bills," she says, "how'm I supposed to raise this child? What'm I gonna do about sending her to college?" Tell me about it, I say, I'm in the same boat as you. If you can find any money you're more than welcome to it, just take his medical bills too.'

Kathryn was laughing. 'Oh come on, Mom, say it. Say it! She can take *him* too!'

What was soothing and not something Billy had even anticipated was the pleasure of masturbating in his old room. He walked in and all the old associations mugged him, the twin beds with their plain blue bedspreads, the plastic sports trophies lined up across his dresser, the faint musk of adolescence lingering in the air like the loamy smell of last year's mulch. He tossed his duffel on the bed, shut the door to change clothes, and *boom*, the Pavlovian response reared its angry head below. He was done in ninety seconds so it wasn't like he kept anybody waiting, then next was the pleasing discovery that his old shirts were tight from all the muscle he'd packed on, his size 30 blue jeans slack through the waist. That night he had another j.o. session after turning in, then again first thing in the morning, and each time with this relaxed mood of easy reconnection, as if a fond former girlfriend had welcomed him back with open arms. What a luxury not to have to meet your masculine needs in some stinking horror of a port-a-potty, or even worse in a hardpan Ranger grave out in the field with mortal enemies all about and always, *always,* **always** some torment of nature with which to contend, bugs, rain, wind, dust, extremes of temperature, no misery too small for such a small thing as a man. So give it up for America, yes! And God shed His grace on thee, where a boy can grow up having a room of his own with a door that locks and a bottomless stash of Internet porn.

'Nice to be home,' he said at breakfast, which was Cheerios, bacon and eggs, raisin-cinnamon toast, orange juice, coffee, and Krispy Kreme doughnuts. For lunch there would be homemade split-pea soup, Waldorf salad, fried bologna sandwiches, and warm brownies. For dinner, a slow-cooked pot roast with carrots, potatoes, and scallions, braised brussels sprouts, a citrus congealed salad, and double-fudge chocolate cake with Blue Bell ice cream. Denise had taken the day off from work, 'this special day' she kept saying at breakfast, which Kathryn echoed in swoony Hallmark tones, then Ray tumped the coffeepot and placidly motored into the den, leaving the mess for everyone else to clean up. As they hurtled around the kitchen with rags and paper towels, the Fox News theme came thundering from the den.

'Does he watch that all day?' Billy asked. His mother and sisters turned to him with long-suffering eyes. *Welcome to our world.*

After breakfast Billy took his little nephew out to play. It was a mellow fall morning, the blue sky-dome stretched high and tight with that sweet winesap smell in the air, the honeyed, vaguely melancholy scent of vegetable ferment and illegal leaf burns. Billy figured they were good for ten, maybe fifteen minutes before he, Billy, was bored out of his mind, but half an hour later they were still at it. Based on his highly limited experience with small children, Billy had always regarded the pre-K set as creatures on the level of not-very-interesting pets, thus he was unprepared for the phenomenal variety of his little nephew's play. Whatever came to hand, the kid devised some form of interaction with it. Flowers, pet and sniff. Dirt, dig. Cyclone fence, rattle and climb, grit links between teeth. Squirrels, harass with feebly launched sticks. 'Why?' he kept asking in his sweetly belling voice, its tone as pure as marbles swirled around a crystal pail. Why him wun up the twee? Why him nest up theah? Why him gadder nuts? Why? Why? Why? And Billy answering every question to the best of his ability, as if anything less would disrespect the deep and maybe even divine force that drove his little nephew toward universal knowledge.

What to call it – the spark of God? Survival instinct? The souped-up computer of an apex brain evolved from eons in the R&D of natural selection? You could practically see the neurons firing in the kid's skull. His body was all spring and torque, a bundle of fast-twitch muscles that exuded faint floral whiffs of ripe pear. So much perfection in such a compact little person – Billy had to tackle him from time to time, wrestle him squealing to the ground just to get that little rascal in his hands, just your basic adorable thirty-month-old with big blue eyes clear as chlorine pools and Huggies poking out of his stretchy-waist jeans. So is this what they meant by *the sanctity of life*? A soft groan escaped Billy when he thought about that, the war revealed in this fresh and gruesome light. Oh. Ugh. Divine spark, image of God, suffer the little children and all that – there's real power when words attach to actual things. Made him want to sit right down and weep, as powerful as that. He got it, yes he did, and when he came home for good he'd have to meditate on this, but for now it was best to *compartmentalize,* as they said, or even better not to mentalize at all.

Patty emerged from the house, shading her eyes against the sun. She took a seat on a lawn chair at the edge of the patio.

'You guys having fun?'

'You bet.' Billy was rolling Brian around as if breading a fish filet, coating his sweater with crunchy brown leaves. 'He's an amazing little guy.'

Patty snuffled a laugh around the cigarette she was lighting. Former hell-raiser, high school dropout, teenage bride; in her midtwenties she seemed to have slowed down enough to start thinking about it all.

'He sure doesn't lack for energy,' Billy called.

'Briny's got two speeds, fast and shut off.' Her lips produced a tight funnel of smoke.

'How's Pete?'

'Fine,' she said, a bit wearily it seemed. Her husband, Pete, worked the oil rigs around Amarillo. 'Still crazy.'

'Is that good?'

She just smiled and looked away. In Billy's memory she was always so lithe and bold; now she was packing saddlebags on her hips and thighs, spare tubes on her upper arms. With the extra weight had come an almost palpable air of apology.

'When do you go back?'

'Saturday.'

'You ready?'

'Well.' Billy gave Brian a last roll, and stood. 'I guess I'd just as soon stay here.'

Patty laughed. 'That sounds like an honest answer.' Billy walked over and sat on the low patio wall near her chair. Brian remained where Billy left him, lying flat on his back, staring up at the sky. Patty cut her brother a shy look. 'How does it feel to be famous?'

Billy shrugged. 'I wouldn't know.'

'All right then, sort of famous. A lot more famous than the rest of us'll ever be.' She had a taste of her cigarette, tapped off the ash. 'You know, you sort of surprised a lot of people around here. I don't think this was what they were expecting when they put you up in front of that judge.'

'I know I didn't have the best reputation around here. But I wasn't the worst fuckup in my grade.'

She laughed.

'Or maybe it's just . . .'

'What.'

'I just hated school so much, hated everything about it. I'm starting to think that was what was fucked up, a lot more than me? Keeping us locked up all day, treating us like children, making us learn a lot of shit about nothing. I think it made me sort of crazy.'

Patty chuckled, a low gunning of the sinuses. 'Well, I guess you showed them. What you did over there—'

Billy hooked his thumbs in his belt loops and looked away.

111

'—that was something. And we're all really proud of you, your family. But I guess you already know that.'

Billy tipped his head toward the house. Out here the roar of the TV was an underwater growl. 'Not him.'

'No, him too. He just doesn't know how to show it.'

'He's an asshole,' Billy said, lowering his voice for Brian's sake.

'That too,' Patty acknowledged pleasantly. 'You notice I was never much interested in hanging around the house? Mainly I just feel sorry for him now. But then I don't have to live with him, do I.' She shrugged, examined her cigarette. 'You heard the latest? About the house?'

'I don't think so.'

'It's kind of fucked.' She did that gunning chuckle again, a nervous habit. Billy wished she'd stop. Out in the yard Brian was sweeping his arms and legs back and forth, making leaf angels.

'Mom wants to take a loan out on the house. She says there's a hundred, hundred ten equity in it, she wants to use that to pay down the medical bills. Kathryn looked into it and she's like, no way, you can file for bankruptcy and wipe out most of the medical bills, plus you get to keep the house. But if she does the equity loan and then can't make the payments, she and dad lose the house. And even with the money from the equity loan, they're still gonna owe a ton of medical bills.'

A ton. Define ton. Billy was afraid to ask. Random neighborhood sounds came their way – a dog barking, a car door slamming somewhere, a stack of two-by-fours clattering to the ground.

'What do you think she should do?'

'No-brainer, dude. File for bankruptcy and keep the house.'

'So why won't she?'

'Because she's worried what everybody else might think. And Kat and me are like, who gives a flyer what people think, you can't gamble the house.' Patty crushed her cigarette against the patio wall. 'You know what Idis McArthur told her after church one day?'

'No.'

'She said the reason our family's had so many problems is because we didn't pray hard enough.'

'Well, isn't that special.'

'It's a sick little town,' Patty agreed.

'Hey' – Kathryn poked her head out the door – 'anybody want a beer?'

They did, though until that moment they hadn't realized. For the rest of the morning his mother and sisters kept asking him what he wanted to do. See a movie? Drive around? Go out to eat? But this was enough, just chilling on a warm Indian-summer day, a sweet abeyance in the golden tone of the light and nothing to do but sit in lawn chairs or sprawl on blankets and let the morning lazily take its course. Two years ago Billy couldn't have done this, the very notion of family time would have sent him running down the street tearing off his clothes. I am a changed man, Billy solemnly told himself. The person you see before you is not the person you were. Maybe it's age, he thought, leaning back on his blanket, watching the sun do its stately pinwheel through the trees. Or maybe not so much a function of calendar days as the way Iraq aged you in dog years, and how with that kind of time under your belt you could bide here in the company of your mother and sisters and somewhat hyper little nephew and be, if not exactly calm, then still. Taking it slow and letting it be what it would be. Perhaps this was what came of being a soldier in Iraq, and the farther perspective war brought to things.

He had a beer now and then, nothing major. Ray stayed inside with the TV and that was fine with everybody, though whenever he wanted something, which was often, he'd wheel to the storm door and thump the glass until Denise or Patty or Kathryn rose to serve his needs. Worse than an infant, Kathryn observed, and when Patty pointed out no diapers were involved, Kathryn said, Don't give him any ideas. A few of the neighbors got word of Billy's visit and dropped by with cakes and casseroles, as if there'd been a death in the family. Mr and Mrs Wiggins from church. Opal George from across the street. The Kruegers. We are so proud. We always knew. So brave, so blessed, so honored. *Edwin!* I yelled, *come quick! Billy Lynn's on TV and he's taking out a whole mess of al-Qaedas!*

Nice people but they did go on, and so *fierce* about the war! They were transformed at such moments, talking about war – their eyes bugged out, their necks bulged, their voices grew husky with blood-lust. Billy wondered about them then, the piratical appetites in these good Christian folk, or maybe this was just their way of being polite, of showing how much they appreciated him. So he smiled his modest hero's smile and waited for them to leave so he and his sisters could go back to drinking beer. After her third of the morning – she was keeping pace with Billy – Kathryn pranced out of the house with his Purple Heart pinned over her left breast and the Silver Star pinned over her right, the medals flopping around like stripper's tassels. Billy and Patty howled, but their mother was not amused. 'What? Oh, these?' Kathryn answered in a ditzy coo when Denise asked just *what* she thought she was doing. 'Why, Mother, I'm merely displaying the *family jewels.*' Denise pronounced the whole thing indecent and ordered Kathryn to return the medals to Billy's room, but she was still sporting the hardware when Mr Whaley stopped by, and it was worth virtually any amount of money to see this eminence's eyes bug out at the sight of Kathryn, not just the medals riding high on her proud perky breasts but the whole tanned, taut, leggy length of her.

Eh-hem. Ah ha. Ha ha. He was Denise's boss so there was some awkwardness about imbibing in the A.M., but Whalers was a sport and pretended not to notice. Balding, liver-spotted, about forty pounds overweight, with a wardrobe that ran to checked blazers and stay-pressed slacks, he was what passed for money in Stovall, the founder of the moderately prosperous oilfield-services company where Denise had worked as office manager for fifteen years. 'Miz Lynn's the real boss around here,' he liked to tell visitors, laughing affectionately in her direction. 'I just try to stay out of the way and let her run the place.' They served him a Diet Coke and moved the chairs into the shade just off the patio. Denise and Patty sat on either side of their guest, while Billy took a perch on the patio wall. Kathryn lolled like a lioness on a nearby beach towel. Brian was somewhere in the house, ostensibly in the care of his chain-smoking grandfather.

'Your mother tells me you're home just for today,' said Mr Whaley.

'That's correct, sir.' It was a challenge, maintaining eye contact while spuming your beer-breath off to the side.

'No rest for the weary, eh.' Mr Whaley chuckled. 'Where've they sent you so far?'

Billy rattled off the cities. Washington, Richmond, Philadelphia, Cleveland, Minneapolis–St Paul, Columbus, Denver, Kansas City, Raleigh-Durham, Phoenix, Pittsburgh, Tampa Bay, Miami, and practically every one, as Sergeant Dime pointed out, happened to lie in an electoral swing state. Though Billy didn't say this.

Mr Whaley took a dainty sip of Coke. 'What's your reception been like?'

'People've been really nice everywhere we go.'

'I'm not surprised. Listen, the vast majority of Americans strongly support this war.' Whenever Whaley's gaze happened to land on Kathryn, he practically fainted with the effort of tearing his eyes away. 'Nobody wants to go to war, goodness sakes, but people know sometimes it's necessary. This terror thing, I think the only way to deal with that type of agenda is to go straight to the source and rip it out by the roots. Because that crowd's not going away by themselves, am I right?'

'They're extremely committed, a lot of them,' Billy replied. 'They don't back down.'

'There you go. Either we fight them over there or we fight them over here, that's the way most Americans see it.'

Denise and Patty nodded with bovine agreeableness. Kathryn, meanwhile, had sat up straight and pulled her knees to her chest; she was following the conversation with real attention, looking from Billy to Mr Whaley as if their talk contained a code she was trying to break. *Heroes,* Whaley said. *Iraq. Freedoms. Gaining freedoms to make our own freedoms more secure.* Then he asked about the movie deal, sagely nodding as Billy explained their progress to date.

'You'll want a lawyer to take a look before you sign anything.'

'Yes sir.'

'I can fix you up with my firm in Fort Worth, if you like.'

'That would be great. I'd sure appreciate that, sir.'

'Son, it's the least I can do. You've made us all proud, not just your family and friends but all of us here, the entire community. You've given this whole town a tremendous boost.'

Billy summoned his most modest chuckle. 'I don't know about that, sir.'

'Listen, everybody's so damn proud of you, pardon my French, if word got out you were home today there'd be cars lined up from here to the airstrip. Oh yes!' he cried in a playfully ferocious voice. 'Now, we didn't know soon enough to get it together this time, but next time you're home we want to have a parade in your honor. I already spoke with Mayor Bond and he's on board, he talked with the city council and they're on board. We want Stovall to honor you in the way you deserve.'

'Thank you, sir. I do appreciate that.'

'No, son, thank *you*. What you've done just says so much about who we are—'

'He has to go back,' Kathryn broke in.

Everyone turned to her.

'To Iraq,' she added, as if this wasn't entirely clear.

'Yes,' said Mr Whaley in mournful tones, 'your mother told me that.'

'So they're gonna get another shot at him.'

'Kathryn!' Denise scolded.

'Well it's true! If it's supposed to be this great *Victory Tour* then why can't he just stay home?'

Mr Whaley's voice was gentle. 'It's fine young men like your brother who are going to lead us to victory.'

'Not if they're dead.'

'*Kathryn!*' Denise cried again. Billy felt like an innocent bystander in all this. It wasn't his place to say one way or the other.

'We will pray every day for Billy's safe return,' said Mr Whaley, soothing as the doctor with the best bedside manner. 'Just as we pray for all our troops, we want them all to come home safely.'

'Oh God, he's going to *pray*,' Kathryn snarled to herself, then she screamed, a guttural *urrrrrrgggggghhhhh* like an in-sink disposal backing up. 'I'm losing my *mind* out here,' she cried, and like a sword being drawn from its sheath she rose in one swift motion and stalked toward the house. The rest of the group sat quietly for several moments, waiting for the area turbulence to subside.

'That young lady's been through a lot,' Mr Whaley ventured. Denise started to apologize, but he waved her off. 'No, no, she's had to deal with so much in her young life. When's her next surgery?'

'February,' said Denise, 'then one more after that. The doctors say that ought to be the last.'

'She's made a remarkable recovery, that's for

119

sure. The past year hasn't been easy on the Lynns, has it, and with Billy doing all he's doing overseas, I know that makes it a special sacrifice. And Billy, if it'll ease your mind any, I want you to know you've got a standing offer to come work for me when you're done with your military service. All you've got to do is say the word.'

Now there was a depressing thought, although Billy could see how it might come to that, assuming best-case scenario he made it home with all his limbs and faculties intact. He'd go to work for Whalers hauling oil-field pipe and blowout protectors all over the wind-scrappled barrens of Central Texas, busting his ass for slightly more than minimum wage and shitty benefits.

'Thank you, sir. I may be taking you up on that.'

'Well, I just want you to know you've got options here. I'd be honored to have you on our team.'

Billy had been trying to avoid a certain thought, a realization born of his recent immersion in the swirl of limos, luxury hotels, fawning VIPs; he knew intuitively the thought would bring him down and so it did, mushrooming into awareness despite all best efforts. Mr Whaley was small-time. He wasn't rich, he wasn't particularly successful or smart, he even exuded a sad sort of desperate shabbiness. Mr Whaley will return to the forefront of Billy's mind on Thanksgiving Day as he hobs and nobs at the Cowboys game with some of Texas's wealthiest citizens. The Mr Whaleys of the world are peons to them, just as Billy is a peon in the world of Mr Whaley, which in the grand scheme of things means that he, Billy, is somewhere on the level of a one-celled protozoan in a vast river flowing into the untold depths of the sea. He's been having many such existential spasms lately, random seizures of futility and pointlessness that make him wonder why it matters how he lives his life. Why not wild out, go off on a rape-and-pillage binge as opposed to abiding by the moral code? So far he's sticking to the code, but he wonders if he does just because it's easier, requires less in the way of energy and balls. As if the bravest thing he ever did – bravest plus truest to himself – was the ecstatic destruction of pussy boy's Saab? As if his deed on the banks of the Al-Ansakar Canal was a digression from the main business of his life.

Mr Whaley left. Kathryn did not appear for lunch. After the meal, Ray and Brian went down for naps, Denise and Patty went to the store, and Billy had a relaxing jack-off session in the friendly confines of his room. Then he repaired to the backyard and laid himself down on a blanket in the sun. He dozed. Dreams came and went like fish drifting through the wheelhouse of an old shipwreck. He stirred, took off his shirt so that the sun would toast his chest acne, and dozed again. He dreamed in paisleys now, big atom-bomb swirls of biomorphic colors that presently resolved into a parade. His parade. He was in it yet watching from slightly above, and he was happy, safe, he'd made it back home. No worries! It was a sunny winter day and everyone was bundled up except for the strippers riding by on floats, blazingly naked but for G-strings and long evening gloves. A high school band stomped by, trombones and trumpets flashing in the sun, then there was Shroom far back in the crowd, his pale onion of a head sticking out of the general mass. His eyes met Billy's and he laughed, raised a big Bud Light cup in salute. Yo, Shroom! Shroom! Get your ass up here! He kept yelling at Shroom to join him on the float, but Shroom seemed happy where he was, content to be just another face in the crowd. Shroom. Fuck. Get up here, man. The dream contained awareness that Shroom was dead so there was the huge anxiety of an opportunity missed, the parade moving on and Billy's float being carried with it, this ridiculous paper barge coasting down the river of life and the banks lined with all these thousands of cheering folks who – dear Jesus! terrifying thought! – were they all as dead as Shroom?

His sleep broke with that throb of panic, a desperate lunge into waking. Someone was leaning over him, breathing in his face. He tipped open one eye to find Kathryn staring down at him through big Angelina Jolie–style sunglasses.

'You better be careful over there,' she murmured darkly. 'If anything happens to you, I'm going to kill myself.'

Hunfh. He opened both eyes, lifted his head.

His sister was stretched out beside him on a beach towel, propped on an elbow with her frontage facing him. She was also, he couldn't help noticing, wearing a bikini, the sight of which cracked his lungs even if she was his sister. Despite the divot in her cheek she was undeniably hot: long, tan legs, an amply palmable rack, tummy flat and golden-brown as the most perfect pancake.

'Why would you do that?'

'Because I'm the reason you're over there.'

'Oh, right.' He closed his eyes and let his head drop back. 'Your bad, getting whacked by that Mercedes. Getting dumped by whatsisface, yeah, thanks. Thanks for getting me in the shit, Kat.'

She snickered, a breathy whiffling like wind through a microphone. 'Yeah, but anyway. Sorry, dawg.'

'Not a problem,' he mumbled, sounding sleepier than he was. Though if he kept his eyes shut sleep would come. Kathryn rustled about, doing female preening sorts of things.

'Mom's pissed at me,' she said.

'Imagine that.'

'Whalers, gimme a break, a fucking *parade*. Those guys are talking about a *parade,* and you might *die.*'

Billy had to laugh. It was refreshing, having someone put it right out there. Living at home as she had for the past sixteen months, enduring all she'd endured by way of health and family troubles and getting dumped by p. boy, Kathryn had undergone drastic and interesting changes. For one thing, her trials had burned off all her baby fat, her tendency to pudge toward the rounder, gentler line of wholesome Christian voluptuousness. Now she sported the lean, rangy frame of a girl bartender in some kick-ass honky-tonk, if such places even existed anymore. A glossy track of keloid tissue looped over her shoulder and down her back like the dangling tail of a coil of rope. Her face was 'eighty-seven percent' recovered, she told him, utterly deadpan as she emphasized that 'eighty-*seven* percent' like a dimwit sportscaster flogging statistics. She loved that her orthopedic surgeon's name was Dr Stiffenbach, whom she endowed with a jaw-breaking German accent. 'High ham Dock-terr Shhhtiffen-bock, jah! You vill do dese exercises for your healdth, jah!' She called Billy's commander in chief 'idiot-head,' as in 'What was it like meeting idiot-head?' which had provoked scolding shushes from their mother. 'Well he is!' Kathryn protested. 'He's got the brains of a cicada!' Billy's sweet, beautiful, studious, supremely square sister who'd always been so reverent toward authority, who thought only good clean all-American thoughts and never cursed or denigrated anyone, she'd become a punchy hell on wheels.

She reached into the cooler by her side and brought out two Tecate beers. 'You miss drinking over there?' she asked, handing one to Billy.

'At first. But after a while, not so much.' He

popped the top and savored that happiest of fizzy sounds. 'There's days, though, you'd give about anything for one.'

'No shit. Listen, I think drinking's way under-rated in our society, like for its therapeutic values? Lets you bust out from time to time, take a little vacation from yourself. It's hard living in your own head twenty-four/seven.'

'You sort of go insane.'

'Explains a lot, eh, all those preachers getting caught doing hookers. I just hope I never have a drinking problem, then I'd have to quit.'

They drank. A healthful sense of well-being enveloped them.

'So tell me about the *Victory Tour*.'

'The tour. Huh. Well, it's kind of a blur.'

'Then just tell me about the groupies.'

He laughed but could feel himself flushing from the shoulders up. A puritanical mood came over him. 'Haven't been any groupies,' he muttered.

'Lie.'

'No lie.'

'You are a lying sackful of it. Listen, boy, you better be out there hitting it! Like, get out there and get some for me.'

'Kathryn, stop.'

'The truth, dude, I'm going a little crazy in this burg.'

'You'll be gone soon enough.'

'Soon, maybe, yeah, but not soon enough. Not one decent guy in this freakin' town, believe me,

I checked. Some nights I'm like, whatever, maybe I'll drive over to Sonic and hit on the high school boys, like, hey bubba, come take a ride with me! Once you've had a chick with a scar on her face you never go back.'

'Kathryn,' Billy pleaded.

'I should be graduated by now. I could be making sixty thousand a year someplace.'

'You'll get there.'

'Yes, I will,' she said firmly.

'You're getting there,' Billy amended.

'If I don't go crazy first.'

Her last two surgeries were scheduled for spring. In January she'd start a couple of classes at community college, which she had to do, otherwise the compassionate bankers at College Fund Inc. would start charging penalty interest on her student loans. 'You know what's funny,' she said, 'everybody around here's such a major conservative till they get sick, get screwed over by their insurance company, their job goes over to China or whatever, then they're like, "Oooooh, what happened? I thought America was just the greatest country ever and I'm such a good person, why is all this terrible shit happening to me?" And I was one of 'em, man. Just as stupid as the rest. I never thought anything bad would happen to me, or if it did there was a system that would make it all right.'

'Maybe you didn't pray hard enough.'

She coughed up a laugh. 'Yeah, that must be it. The power of prayer, dawg.'

They drank. Kathryn touched the cold beer can to her cheeks, her neck, her navel, each touch triggering starbursts in Billy's brain. He asked what their mother planned to do about the home equity loan.

Kathryn frowned. 'Who knows what that woman's going to do. She's not rational, Billy. She's not dealing with the facts. Look, don't you worry about the damn loan. Not your life, not your problem, or mine either, really. She and dad are gonna do what they're gonna do, and we can't stop them.'

'How much do we owe on the medical?'

'*We?* You mean *they*. Or I suppose me too, if you want to get technical.' She consulted her beer. 'Four hundred thousand, give or take. Bills keep coming in from stuff they did a year ago.'

Four. Hundred. Thousand. It was like God appearing in all his nuclear glory, omnipotent, all-consuming, incomprehensible.

'No way.'

Kathryn shrugged. The numbers bored her.

'Not your prob, Bill. Let it go. And anything you get from your movie deal, keep it. Don't be blowing it trying to bail those two out.' When Billy said nothing, she laughed and rolled onto her stomach, her bottom smartly rising from the small of her back like an island appearing on a tropical sea.

'You know what Dad bought that girl when she turned sixteen?'

'What girl?'

'Come on, Billy, our *sister*. *Half* sister.'

'No, I don't know what he bought her when she turned sixteen.'

'A damn car.'

Billy swallowed, turned away. He could be cool about this.

'Mustang GTO, dawg, right off the lot. This was before he got fired. But still.'

Billy could feel the air hardening in his chest. 'New?' He hated that his voice cracked.

'Total cherry.' She laughed. 'So don't be a sap. Anything you do for him or Mom, they'll just dump on it. Look after yourself and let them do whatever they're going to do.'

Billy managed to refrain from asking the color of the car. 'Well.' He reached beyond the blanket and pulled up a twist of dry grass. 'It's not like I've got anything to give them anyway.'

Kathryn brought out two more beers. Billy's philosophy was, any buzz you caught during daylight hours was a bonus; that time didn't count against your total allotment here on earth, therefore the daytime buzz was that much sweeter. And today, what could be more perfect than lying in the sun, drinking beer with an extremely hot blonde in a bikini? The only problem, of course, being that the girl was his sister, but what was the harm in pretending for a few short hours? The afternoon took on a spangling beer-buzz glow. He didn't mind that Kathryn probed him about life 'at the front,' as she called it. How's the food?

How's your quarters? The Iraqis, what are they like, and do they all hate us yet? She kept touching him, tapping his shoulder and squeezing his arm, pushing her bare feet up against his blue-jean legs. All the contact simultaneously sharpened his senses and made him passive, relaxed, as if an especially fine drug was kicking in.

'What's gonna happen when you get back?'

He shrugged. 'The same, I guess. Patrol, eat, sleep. Then get up and do it again.'

'Do you dread it?'

He pretended to consider. 'It doesn't matter what I feel about it. I've gotta go, so I'm going.'

She was lying on her side with her head propped on an elbow. A small gold cross lay on the swell of one of her breasts, a tiny mountaineer going for the top.

'How do the other guys feel?'

'The same. I mean, look, nobody *wants* to go back. But it's what you signed up for, so you go.'

'Then let me ask you this, do you guys believe in the war? Like is it good, legit, are we doing the right thing? Or is it all really just about the oil?'

'Kathryn, Jesus. You know I don't know that.'

'I'm just asking what you believe, what you personally think. It's not a quiz, dude, I'm not looking for the big objective answer here. I just want to know what's going on in your head.'

All right. Well. Since she asked. He found he was strangely grateful that someone had.

'I don't think anybody knows what we're doing

over there. I mean, it's weird. It's like the Iraqis really hate us, you know? Just right there in our own AO, we're building a couple of schools, we're trying to get their sewer system up and running, we bring in tankers of drinking water every day and do a meal program for the kids, and all they wanna do is kill us. Our mission is to help and enhance, right? And these people are living in shit, literal shit, their government did nothing for them all these years, but we're the enemy, right? So what it ends up coming down to is survival, I guess. You just pull in, you aren't thinking about accomplishing anything, you just wanna get through the day with all your guys alive. So then you start to wonder why we're even over there.'

Kathryn heard him out. She set her jaw.

'All right, how about this. What if you didn't go back.'

He flinched. Then he laughed. No. No way.

'I'm serious, Billy. What if you said nope, no thanks, been there, done that, you think they'd have the guts to come after you? The big hero and all? Think of the headlines, "Hero Staying Home, Says War Sucks." You've got major cred, it's not like anybody's going to say it's because you're scared.'

'But I am scared. Everybody's scared.'

'You know what I mean, like scared scared. Like coward scared, like if you never went to begin with. But with everything you've done nobody's going to doubt you.' Then she made a somewhat frantic speech about a website she'd found that

130

listed how certain people had avoided Vietnam. Cheney, four educational deferments, then a hardship 3-A. Limbaugh, 4-F thanks to a cyst on his ass. Pat Buchanan, 4-F. Newt Gingrich, grad school deferment. Karl Rove, did not serve. Bill O'Reilly, did not serve. John Ashcroft, did not serve. Bush, AWOL from the Air National Guard, with a check mark in the 'do not volunteer' box as to service overseas.

'You see where I'm going with this?'

'Well, yeah.'

'I'm just saying, those people want a war so bad, they can fight it themselves. Billy Lynn's done his part.'

'Kat, it just doesn't matter. They did what they did. I'm doing what I'm doing. There's no point in us trying . . .' Two fat tears seeped out from under her sunglasses, and he had to turn away.

'What about *us*, Billy, think about that. With everything this family's been through, what do you think it'll do to us if something happens to you?'

'Nothing's going to happen to me.'

She paused long enough for him to want that one back.

'Billy, there's a way to do this. There's a group down in Austin, they help soldiers. They've got lawyers, resources, they know how to handle these things. I did some research, and it looks like they're really good people. So if you decided . . . look, I'm just saying, you'd have some help with this.'

'Kathryn.'

'What?'

'I'm going.'

'Dammit!'

'I'll be okay.'

'*You don't know that!*'

She was so fierce. He was touched. Then he felt scared.

'I guess I don't. But we get a lot more of them than they get of us. And they can't get all of us.'

She began to weep. He put his arm around her shoulders and held her close in a brotherly, determinedly nonsexual way. She cried harder and rested her head on his shoulder. Her hair had a clean woody smell, with hints of spice like fennel or freshly rained-on ferns. There was something peaceful about her crying, some sort of music or psychic nourishment in the sound. Her tears dribbled across his chest like hatchling turtles. The last thing he remembered before falling asleep was that she'd gone inside to get some Kleenex, saying she'd be right back. He wasn't even aware of falling asleep until being waked in the most unpleasant way by the *whoom* of the back door bursting open as if fireballed, blown out by a breaching charge, then the *whhhhhhiiiiiiiirrrrrrrr* of the latest in assisted mobility systems. Son of a bitch! Heart going like a speed bag, eyes sparking tiny gigabytes of shock, Billy spun onto his belly, wrenching various small muscles in his back, and there was Ray buzzing across the patio. What the FOCK!!! Is that any way to wake a combat soldier? The startle reflex triggering a highly refined set of quick-response skills, i.e., had Billy happened to have his M4 handy, Ray would be a steaming pile of hamburger right about now.

Bastard, he probably meant to do it. He didn't acknowledge his son or even glance Billy's way, but Billy detected a faint smirk in the set of his mouth, a crimping of flesh at the corners of his lips. Ray motored down the ramp and into the yard. Billy felt sick from all the adrenaline jamming his system, but he scruffed up on one elbow and had a look around. Kathryn was gone. His mouth was skunky from all the pre-nap beers. The afternoon had turned overcast, the sun bleared by the clouds like a soap ball floating in a tub of dirty bathwater. Out in the yard Ray paused to light a cigarette. A real piece of work, that one, Billy mused. Highly intelligent and glib as hell, you couldn't beat him in any argument. Never went to college but made a shit ton of money, back in the day. Ray snapped his lighter shut and trundled farther into the yard, his chair waddling over all the little bumps and rills. It had a sad lack of dignity when viewed from behind, as graceless in motion as a hippo's backside, and the American flag decal stuck there dead center seemed like a cruel and tasteless joke, someone's lame attempt at satire.

Billy leaned back on his elbows and watched his father. You'd think family would be the one sure thing in life, the gimme? Points you got just for

133

being born? So much thick, meaty stuff bound you to these people, so many interlocking spirals of history, genetics, common cause, and struggle that it should be the most basic of all drives, that you would strive to protect and love one another, yet this bond that should be the big no-brainer was in fact the hardest thing. For proof all you had to do was take a quick poll of Bravo. On Holliday's last visit home before shipping out, his brother told him, I hope you fuckin' die in Iraq. When Mango was fifteen his father cracked his skull with a monkey wrench, and Mrs Mango's comment was, So maybe now you'll stop pissing your father off. Dime's grandfather and one of his uncles were suicides. Lake's mother was an OxyContin addict who'd done time, his father a dealer who ditto. When Crack was eleven years old his mother ran off with the assistant pastor of their church. Shroom, he barely *had* a family. A-bort's father had been the deadbeat poster dad for the state of Louisiana, and Sykes's father and brothers blew up their house cooking meth.

Yes, family was key, Billy decided. If you could figure out how to live with family then you'd gone a long way toward finding your peace, but for that, the finding, the figuring out, you needed a strategy. So where did you go for that? Age by itself didn't do it for you, obviously. Maybe books, but they took so long, and in the meantime the thing was always coming at you. When violent animal forces were in play, who had the fucking

134

time for books? The morning after 9-11 Ray was on the air advocating 'nuclear cleansing' of certain Middle East capitals, playing 'Bomb Bomb Iran' by Vince Vance and the Valiants and 'The Ballad of the Green Berets.' Billy remembers thinking, Is this how it works? Terrible things had happened, which meant more and greater terrors were on the way, as if the process was not merely automatic, but absolute. Those days and weeks have since acquired an aura of prophecy in his life. Billy thinks he sensed the fatedness of it even then – war was coming and he was bound for the war, and some occult, irresistible father-son dynamic was at work to ensure that this was so. If the father loved the war, how could the son stay away? Not that love for the war would necessarily translate into love for the son.

Whhhhiiiirrrr, stop. *Whhhhiiiirrrr,* stop. What was he doing? Ray paused at the flowers growing along the fence, a stand of powder-blue puffballs on tall, skinny stems. Something blue mist, they were called – Billy had asked his mother that morning, after he and Brian counted seventeen monarch butterflies feeding on the blooms. All day the monarchs had been wobbling through the yard on their way south, pausing to snack on the something-blue-mist before continuing on their way to Mexico. Ray lit another cigarette and sat there smoking, watching the monarchs flutter around. Billy had never seen his father do such a thing, spend any amount of time in contemplation of nature. This was a man whose chief relation to the natural world was that of a carnivore toward his steak, but with him sitting there quietly observing the butterflies, Billy sensed, if not an opening, then some potential or possibility that threw him back on himself. It made him a little desperate, this feeling. If the opportunity came along, would he know what to do? If there could be some minor good between them and they lacked the skills to make it happen, well that would be a damn shame and maybe even tragic, given that this might be their final day together. Then the door banged open, *boom*, not so loud this time, and here came Brian trotting across the patio.

'Hey, Billy,' he chirped, so sweetly matter-of-fact that Billy had to smile. Brian jogged across the yard to Ray and climbed onto the back of the old man's wheelchair. Ray smiled and wheeled the chair about, and they went rattling across the yard. 'Make it jump!' Brian cried. Ray pulled back the joystick, then rammed it forward; the chair bucked, its front rising an inch off the ground. The thing did maybe three miles per hour, max, and Ray somehow juiced a wheelie out of it. Brian squealed and called for more, and off they went on a wide loop, popping and bucking, Ray gaming the chair for all it had while Brian hung on the back and laughed himself silly. Their loop gradually brought them around to Billy, and thinking about it later he will recall that he was smiling not just out of a general sense of pleasure, but in a specifically feeling way toward his father. In these later reflections, Billy will realize he'd been thinking he and Ray might have a Moment, and what he got instead was one of the great silent fuck-offs of all time. How exactly Ray did this Billy will never figure out, though it seemed to happen mostly in the eyes, in the cool, dismissive edge to their sidelong cut, that briefest of glances as the wheelchair tractored by. Some vast rejection was rendered in that moment, but Billy couldn't describe it any better than as his father's way of saying, This isn't for you. You aren't part of it, you don't belong. Ray was keeping the Moment all to himself; he could make Brian love him whenever he wanted and none of the rest of them even deserved his effort.

All of which went to prove the point, that without a strategy you were a big fat target dangling out there, chum in the shark tank of family dynamics. At dinner that night Bill O'Reilly raged on the TV, Denise and the girls bickered about the home equity loan, Brian was tired and started acting like a little shit, the roast was overdone, Ray wouldn't stop smoking, and Denise broke down crying because she wanted everything perfect and of course it couldn't be. Mom, Billy said, laughing, putting his arms around her, plumbing reserves of serenity he didn't know he had, Mom, don't worry about it. I'm happy. I'm home. Everything's cool. What was amazing was this actually seemed to help. His mother calmed down. Brian fell asleep in the high chair. Patty and Kathryn got the giggles and opened another bottle of wine, and Billy felt so much older than nineteen, as if blessed with wisdom beyond his years. Had the war done this? All that ever got talked about was how war was supposed to fuck you up, true enough but maybe not the whole truth. He tumbled into bed that night buzzed on chocolate cake and wine, closing his eyes with the satisfaction that disaster had been averted, something crucial salvaged. There was no such thing as perfection in this world, only moments of such extreme transparency that you forgot yourself, a holy mercy if there ever was one.

A limo would come for him at 0700, courtesy of some well-to-do patriot who either wished to remain anonymous or whose name Billy forgot. A limo. For him. Whatever. He slept poorly and woke hungover, his mouth fouled with a reechy copper scum out of all proportion to the wine he'd consumed. He knew this taste, knew what it meant – fear, loathing, and bad karma beyond the wire – but he still had enough sass for one last jack-off in the friendly confines, a comical momentousness attending the act as if this farewell shot was the historical equal of Troy Aikman's final game at Texas Stadium. *Folks, he's at the forty! The thirty! He may go all the way! The twenty! The ten! The five! And . . . touchdown!* Thus refreshed, he showered and shaved, got his kit together, made his bed, and placed his duffel by the front door. Then there was nothing left to do but face the family.

'Ya gonna miss me?' he crowed cheerfully as he entered the kitchen, but the women just stared at him, stricken. They were miserable. So was he, but if he showed it they would be more miserable yet. The kitchen windows seemed to have been laminated during the night, nothing in them but smooth unadulterated gray. Gusts of wind thumped the house like a bellows; hard little pellets of rain popped and rattled across the roof. The season's first winter storm was pushing across the plains, the same front that would deliver snow and freezing rain by Thanksgiving Day.

'Where do you go next?' Patty asked. Billy's sisters drank coffee and watched him eat. Denise was upright and mobile, a one-woman strike force for small kitchen tasks.

'Fort Riley, they've got a rally scheduled there. Then Ardmore. For, you know.' He glanced at their mother. 'Then Dallas. I think.'

'The big game!' Kathryn mooed. 'You gonna meet Beyoncé?'

'You know as much as me.'

'You will, dude, for sure. So don't blow it. This'll probably be your only chance to sweep her off her feet.'

'No doubt.'

'So, listen, start by telling her how nice she looks.'

'Kathryn, it's Beyoncé. She doesn't need me to tell her she's hot.'

'Dude, women can never get enough of that stuff! What you wanna do is come at her like, "Bey, yo, you crushin' it, girl, lookin' all funky-fresh and fly, your hair so jump and everything, what say we hang after the game?" Patty, wouldn't it be so cool to have Beyoncé for a sister-in-law?'

'Very cool.'

'Guys, come on. I'm a grunt. She's not going to have the time of day for me.'

'Bull hockey! A handsome young stud like yourself, a *hero*? She's gonna be all over your junk!'

'Isn't she dating that Jay-Z guy?' Patty asked.

Denise began to cry. She was wiping down counters and started weeping, the same way she might hum any old tune that happened into her head. Kathryn clicked her tongue as if angry, vexed. Patty's eyes pinked up but she held it together. Just get through it, Billy told himself. Once he was in the car he'd be okay, but there was a lump in his throat the size of a charcoal briquette. This was worse than when he shipped out the first time, which surprised him; it should be easier the second time around. But it seemed like he had more to lose now, though what that was he couldn't say. So there was that, whatever it was, plus this time he knew the nature of the gig he was going back to.

'Now, where is Ray,' Denise said vaguely, as if talking to herself might help. 'Maybe one of us should . . .'

Kathryn and Patty glanced at each other, then looked to Billy. He shrugged. Ray's presence did not seem essential to their happiness this morning. As if in answer to the logical follow-up, Brian padded into the kitchen in his footie pajamas, his cheeks plump and rosy with the fullness of sleep.

He climbed into his mother's lap and snuggled close, clinging like a baby koala bear in the bush.

You want some juice?

No.

Cereal?

No.

You just want to sit with Mommy for a while.

Yes.

His presence had the effect of settling everyone down. He stared and stared at Billy, not so much out of curiosity, it seemed, as in witness, as if channeling some ancient gravity. Billy's beret in particular seemed to hold his attention. As long as he didn't start with the whys they would be okay, Billy thought. Denise poured more coffee for him. Kathryn cleared away his plate. The clock on the microwave was two minutes faster than the stove clock, which was in turn a minute faster than the wall clock, and every time you looked at one you had to look at the others in a never-ending quest for congruity. It was awful, watching those clocks. One by one they sequenced to 7:00 and beyond, then Kathryn was hissing *'shit'* under her breath. From the kitchen they could look through the dining room and out the front window, where a black Lincoln Town Car was pulling into the driveway.

A small melee erupted. Kathryn took off down the hall for the front door. Denise turned to the sink and just bawled. Somehow Brian ended up in Billy's arms, so he was right there in the middle when Billy hugged his weeping mother, Billy purposely blurring his senses as he leaned in because it was just too much, the crying, the bleakness, the whole tragic vibe, but at least Brian was there to muffle some of the shock. 'Bye, Mom,' Billy whispered, then he was moving down the hall with Brian in his arms, Patty following so close she kept clipping his heels. Out in the driveway Kathryn was helping the driver load Billy's gear in the trunk.

'Take care of yourself,' Patty said on the porch. She was a teary, phlegmy spongeball of hiccups and sobs. 'Don't do anything crazy. Just get your butt home.'

Billy took a last sniff of his nephew's head, rich with notes of spring grass and warm homemade bread, and handed him back to Patty. A scumbled three-way hug ensued.

'You tell him,' Billy murmured to his sister in the clutch, 'if I'm not around you tell him, I said don't ever join the Army.'

Kathryn was waiting at the car. She was crying, and laughing at herself for crying, outdone by the sheer unmitigated suck of it all. Later he would recall the scrabbling action in her hug, as if she were sliding down a cliff face and clawing for purchase. She shut the door behind him and stepped back, then tossed off a windmilling cartoon salute. Billy could not have been more spent if he'd just run a marathon. It felt like organ failure, like his face was melting, but the car was backing down the driveway and the worst was over. Kathryn waved from the yard as the Town Car pulled away. Patty was waving from the porch with Brian slung to her hip, and behind them, thinned out by the glare of the storm door, Ray was watching from his chair. Billy cursed to himself and leaned back in his seat. The Town Car gathered speed. So his father made an appearance, what was he supposed to do with that?

'You want some music?' the driver asked. He was a heavyset black man, pushing sixty. A thick lip of flesh spilled over his suit collar.

Billy said no thanks. They went several blocks before the driver spoke again. 'Hard on the families,' he said in a lilting preacher's voice. 'But something wrong if it weren't, I guess.' He glanced at Billy in the rearview. 'Sure you don't want some music?'

Billy said he was sure.

WE ARE ALL AMERICANS HERE

Billy is thinking if you took every person he's ever known in his life and added up the sum total of their wealth, this presumably grand number would still pale in comparison to the stupendous net worth of Norman Oglesby, or 'Norm' as he's known to the media, friends, colleagues, legions of Cowboys fans, and the even mightier legions of Cowboys haters who for whatever reason – his smug, kiss-my-ass arrogance, say, or his flaunting of the whole America's Team shtick, or his willingness to whore out the Cowboys brand to everything from toasters to tulip bulbs – despise the man's guts even as they're forced to admit his genius for turning serious bucks. Norm. The Normster. *Nahm.* He figures prominently in the fantasy lives of fans everywhere, the antagonist in endless imagined arguments and the medium for all manner of secret wish fulfillment. For days Sykes has been rehearsing his big moment with fuck Norm this and fuck Norm that, gon' give my boy Norm boocoo shit for dealing Tresbnoski, like, hey, what the fuck, Norm! You trade your all-world linebacker for steroids on a stick? But when it's

Sykes's turn to meet the Cowboys owner, he rolls over and does a shameless bitch flop.

'It's an honor to meet you, sir,' he says in hushed, reverent tones. 'I just want you to know, I've been a huge Cowboys fan my entire life.'

'Well it's *my* honor to meet *you*, Specialist Sykes,' Norm rips right back. 'I've been a huge fan of the United States Army for *my* entire life!'

The crowd gives up a big round of applause. Hooah, Norm! They are in a large bare room deep inside the stadium's bowels, a chilly space with concrete walls and cheap all-weather carpet that wicks the cold up through the floor in a palpable draft. Bravo has been brought here for an intimate meet-and-greet with the Cowboys brass and selected guests, perhaps two hundred people have gathered with many family units on display, as is surely right and fitting on this Thanksgiving Day. It's a class crowd, the men dressed in coats and ties, the women spiff in tailored suits with matching shoes and purses, though some of the hipper, edgier set make a winter fashion statement with skintight leathers and long fur coats. They could be the congregation of the richest church in town, Our Anorexic Lady of the Upscale Honky Bling; the only people of color here are the waitstaff and several gregarious former players, fan favorites from yesteryear who invested wisely and kept their noses clean. Billy and Mango appreciate that best behavior is called for at this top-shelf event, and thanks to Hector's primo herb they are close to losing it. It is next to impossible not to bust up laughing and if they do no telling where it will end. An elderly priest with a lisp almost sets them off, then a lady whose hair resembles an exploded poodle. They are in that perilous state of stoned paranoia where surely everyone sees they've been toking up, which is terrifying and just the funniest thing ever.

'*Be cool,*' they hiss at each other, giggling like deranged asthmatics. Think of something horrible – rectal bleeding, sucking chest wounds, tapeworms dangling from your nose.

'Okay, how do I look?'

'Fucked up.'

They're whispering out the sides of their mouths.

'How about now?'

'Still fucked up.'

Billy boots Mango with a behind-the-back crossover kick, Mango sends a quick jab to Billy's ribs, and they furtively cuff each other until Dime gives them a look. It has the feel of a high-speed spinout, the *whhheeee-hai!* of serious G's plus awareness that it's probably going to turn out badly, but when Norm & Co. approach for the big introduction it is time to square up and get straight for real.

Norm. It is Himself in the flesh. So much of life consists of inertia and drift, the brief savory or sour of any particular day tends to blur into the next so that it all becomes one big flavorless wad. There are so few moments you can point to and say, Yes, that was historic, greatness happened that day, and evidently this is supposed to be one of those moments because photographers and video cams follow Norm's every move. He glows, which isn't to say he's a handsome man but rather shimmers with high-wattage celebrity, and therein lies the problem, the brain struggles to match the media version to the actual man who looks taller than the preformed mental image, or maybe broader, older, pinker, younger, the two versions miscongrue in some crucial sense which makes it all a little unreal, and anyway Billy is freaking. He has met the president himself, but if nerves are any measure this is a bigger deal, a greater challenge to his fluid definition of self. Meeting famous people is a touchy business. Will he be enhanced by the coming encounter? Affirmed? Diminished? Yesterday he asked Dime, What do I say to him? Dime snorted. You don't have to say shit, Billy, Norm'll do all the talking. Just say yes sir and no sir and laugh when he makes a funny, that's all you have to do.

Norm works his way down the receiving line. By the time he reaches Billy, the young soldier is feeling faint. 'Specialist Lynn,' he says, pausing to give Billy an appraising up and down, 'I've been looking forward to meeting you,' and Billy can feel himself levitating, borne upward on a froth of white-hot video lights and stinging camera flashes, a kind of fulminating photo-op meringue, and being stoned gives it all a swoopy, slow-motion feel. Norm grips his hand, *yow,* a real alpha-dog crunch – dude, just hike up your leg and spray the room! *Pride,* he says, but like a tape played too slow the word warps and fattens in Billy's ear, ppp*rrrRRIIiii*ddde. Then courage, coo*o-OUURR*raaage. Service, ssss*errrRRRrvvvi*ccce. Ssss*acccrRRRIiiif*fffice. Hoo*ooONNn*norrrr. Deeet*errRRRminaaaAAA*tion.

'You're a Texas boy,' Norm says, and there's a chewiness to his words, a faint thickening of the palate like he's got those braces that go behind your teeth. 'From Stovall, correct? Out there in the oil patch?' He takes note of the medals on Billy's chest and asserts that he's especially proud of Billy 'as a fellow Texan,' but not surprised, not at all surprised, it's only natural that a native-born Texan would distinguish himself in military service.

'Everybody knows Texans make the best fighters,' Norm continues, and he's smiling, it's not exactly a joke but more a teasing form of Texas boosterism. 'Audie Murphy, the heroes of the Alamo, you're part of a famous tradition now, did you know that?'

'I never thought of it that way, sir.' Billy must have said the right thing because a warm swell of laughter rises from the crowd, yes, people are watching, their faces rim the bubble of media lights with a fish-eye arcuation and ovoid bulge. Adrenaline sings in his head like a power saw. Norm is talking. Norm is making an entire little speech. He stands an inch or so taller than Billy, a fit, stout-necked sixty-five-year-old with peach-tinted hair and a trapezoidal head, wide at the bottom, then narrowing through the temples to the ironed-down plateau of hair on top. His eyes are a ghostly cold-fission blue, but it's the proving ground of his face that awes and fascinates, the famously nipped, tucked, tweaked, jacked, exfoliated mug that for years has been a staple of state and local news, Norm's very public saga of cosmetic self-improvement. The result thus far is compelling and garish, like a sales lot for reconditioned carnival rides. His mouth seems winched a couple of screws too tight. The vaguely Asiatic folds at the corners of his eyes speak of seductive and even feminine sensitivities, as if modeled on a sexy illustration of the Pocahontas myth. His complexion is the ruddled, well-scrubbed pink of an old ketchup stain. For all that work the sum effect is neither good nor bad, just expensive, and Billy will later reflect that you could get pretty much the same result by plastering your face with thousand-dollar bills.

'You have given America back its pride,' Norm is saying, information that takes the form of tiny bubbles effervescing in Billy's brain. America? Really? The whole damn place? But people are clapping and Billy lacks the nerve to argue, then he's being introduced to Mrs Norm, a well-maintained lady of a certain age with a poufed-out cloud of dark hair. She's pretty. Her dark violet eyes don't quite focus. She smiles but it's purely social, gives nothing of herself, and Billy decides she's either medicated or ruthlessly conserving energy. If it's a snob thing he's just fine with that, for what woman is more entitled to the rights and privileges of flaming bitchdom than the First Lady of the Dallas Cowboys? In fact her bitchiness makes him a little bit hard – *Dude*, he's thinking, *DOWN, she's old enough to be your mom* – but now the rest of the clan is coming at him, Norm's children, the husbands and wives of the children, then the teeming gaggle of grandkids, every one of them blessed with the Oglesby quadrilateral head, and once they've had their turn the receiving line collapses into a genteel rave. People are pumped; proximity to Bravo jazzes them full of fizzing good spirits, even these, the high-profile and the well-to-do, they go a little out of their heads around Bravo. Is it because they smell blood? Strangers make free with Billy's young body, kneading his arms and shoulders, clutching his wrists, clapping a manly hand to his back. They gush. They swear allegiance and undying gratitude. A regal older lady asks how old he is, 'You look so young!' she cries, and at his answer she tosses her head and turns away in disbelief. Little boys in coats and ties ask for his autograph. Someone hands him a Coke in a plastic cup. Before the *Victory Tour* he hated big parties with all their nervous chitchat and stressful shifting around, but it's not so bad when people actually want to talk to you.

'You were at the White House,' one man queries him.

'That's right.'

'You met George and Laura?' the man's wife says hopefully.

'Well, we met the president and Cheney.'

'That must have been such a thrill!'

'It was,' Billy says agreeably.

'What did yall talk about?'

Billy laughs. 'I don't remember!' And it's true, he doesn't. There was a certain amount of joking around, good-natured guy stuff. Lots of smiles, lots of stage-managed posing for pictures. At some point Billy realized he was expecting the president to act, well, embarrassed? Ashamed? For how fucked up everything obviously was. But the commander in chief seemed well pleased with the state of things.

'You know,' the woman says, leaning close like she's divulging privileged information, 'we sort of claim George and Laura as our own. They're moving back to Dallas when their time in Washington is up.'

'Ah.'

'We were at the White House a couple of weeks ago,' the man says, 'they had a state dinner for Prince Charles and Camilla. Listen, those royals are just the finest people, no pretensions whatsoever. You can talk to Prince Charles about anything.'

Billy nods. There's a silence. Just in time he asks, 'What did you talk about?'

'Hunting,' the man answers. 'He's a bird man like me. Grouse and pheasant, mostly.'

Several tanned, glamorous couples have engaged Major Mac in intense conversation. The major nods, frowns, purses his lips – he does an expert mime of undivided attention. Dime and Albert have been absorbed into Norm's entourage, and Billy finds it reassuring, this proof that Dime's stuff is so strong that it flies even at these lofty altitudes. *Americans,* he says to himself, gazing around the room. *We are all Americans here* – it's like suddenly becoming aware of your tongue inside your mouth, an issue where there was none before. But they are different, these Americans. They are the ballers. They dress well, they practice the most advanced hygienes, they are conversant in the world of complex investments and fairly hum with the pleasures of good living – gourmet meals, fine wines, skill at games and sports, a working knowledge of the capitals of Europe. If they aren't quite as flawlessly handsome as models or movie actors, they certainly possess the vitality and style of, say, the people in a Viagra advertisement. Special time with Bravo is just one of the multitude of pleasures available to them, and thinking about it makes Billy somewhat bitter. It's not that he's jealous so much as profoundly terrified. Dread of returning to Iraq equals the direst poverty, and that's how he feels right now, *poor,* like a shabby homeless kid suddenly thrust into the company of millionaires. Mortal fear is the ghetto of the human soul, to be free of it something like the psychic equivalent of inheriting a hundred million dollars. This is what he truly envies of these people, the luxury of terror as a talking point, and at this moment he feels so sorry for himself that he could break right down and cry.

I'm a good soldier, he tells himself, aren't I a good soldier? So what does it mean when a good soldier feels this bad?

Don't be scared, Shroom said. Because you're going to be scared. So when you start to get scared, don't be scared. Billy has thought about this a lot, not just the Zen teaser of it but what exactly does it mean to be scared out of your mind. Shroom, again: Fear is the mother of all emotion. Before love, hate, spite, grief, rage, and all the rest, there was fear, and fear gave birth to them all, and as every combat soldier knows there are as many incarnations and species of fear as the Eskimo language has words for snow. Spend any amount of time in the realms of deadly force and you will witness certain of its fraught and terrible forms. Billy has seen men shrieking with the burden of it, others can't stop cursing, still others lose their powers of speech altogether. Loss of sphincter or bladder control, classic. Giggling, weeping, trembling, numbing out, classic. One day he saw an officer roll under his Humvee during a rocket attack, then flatly refuse to come out when it was over. Or Captain Tripp, a pretty good man in the clutch, but when they're really getting whacked his brow flaps up and down like a loose tarp in a high wind. His soldiers might feel embarrassed for him, but no one actually thinks the worse of him for it, for this is pure motor reflex, the body rebels. Certain

153

combat-stress reactions are coded in the genes just as surely as cowlicks or flat feet, while for a golden few fear seems not to register at all. Sergeant Dime, for example, an awesome soldier who Billy has seen walking around calmly eating Skittles while mortars rained down mere meters away. Or a man will be fearless one day and freak the next, as fickle and spooky as that, as pointless, as dumb. Works on your mind, all that. The randomness. He gets so tired of living with the daily beat-down of it, not just the normal animal fear of pain and death but the uniquely human fear of fear itself like a CD stuck on skip-repeat, an ever-narrowing self-referential loop that may well be a form of madness. Thus all our other emotions evolved as coping mechanisms for the purpose of possibly keeping us sane? And so you start to sense the humanity even in feelings of hate. Sometimes your body feels dead with weariness of it, other times it's like a migraine you think you can reason with, you bend your mind to the pain, analyze it, break it down into ions and atoms, go deeper and deeper into the theory of it until the pain dissolves in a flatus of logic, and yet after all that your head still hurts.

So these are Billy's thoughts while he makes small talk about the war. He tries to keep it low-key, but people steer the conversation toward drama and passion. They just assume if you're a Bravo you're here to talk about the war, because, well, if Barry Bonds were here they'd talk about baseball. Don't you think . . . Wouldn't you agree . . . You have to admit . . . Here at home the war is a problem to be solved with correct thinking and proper resource allocation, while the drama and passion arise from the terrorists' goal of taking over the world. *Ire way of life. Ire values. Ire* **Christian** *values.* Billy can feel his head emptying out.

'Excuse me,' a Cowboys executive interrupts, 'our soldier's looking a little dry there. How about a refill?'

Billy rattles the ice in his cup. 'Thank you, sir. Another Coke would be nice.'

'Come on. Excuse us, folks.' The executive rudders him by the elbow toward the bar, a take-charge guy. It is apparently the Cowboys' corporate culture that all executives must resemble sales managers at a Ford dealership, and this one – he introduces himself, Bill Jones – fits the mold. Plain, balding, full in the face, with a second-trimester heft to his middle, yet he radiates a vibe that Billy feels at once, a good working tool of controlled aggression. A rubbery impatience seems to flow through all his movements.

'Enjoying yourself?'

'Yes sir.'

Mr Jones laughs. 'You looked like you could use a change of scenery back there.'

Billy smiles, shrugs. 'They're nice people.'

Mr Jones laughs again, rather more harshly this time. 'Yes indeed, they certainly are. And they're thrilled to meet you fellas. You're an impressive group.'

'Thank you.' Billy notices a bulge in the vicinity of Mr Jones's armpit. He's packing. Billy resists a brief but powerful urge to smash Mr Jones's esophagus into the back of his neck and disarm him, just for safety's sake.

'You won't find many dissenters in this group. They're strong for the war, strong for America. And not at all shy about speaking their minds.'

'Yes sir.'

'Listen, I'm as political as anybody, but I'd rather talk about football any day than politics. How about you?'

'Sir, I'd rather talk about just about anything than politics.'

Mr Jones gives a quick hard laugh. Billy seems to be saying all the right things, but he won't let himself relax.

'You're the one from Texas?'

'Yes sir.'

'You a Cowboys fan?'

'All my life.' Billy puts some oomph in it, just for flattery's sake.

'That's what I like to hear. We'll try to give you a win today. Harold,' he says to the black bartender, 'how about an ice-cold Coke for our young friend. Anything in it?' He turns a raffish eye to Billy.

'A little splash of Jack Daniel's would be nice. Though technically I'm not supposed to.'

'No worries, we'll keep it on the down-low. Anything else I can get for you?'

Billy wonders why he's going to so much trouble

for him. 'Well, to be honest, sir, I've got kind of a headache. Some Advil or something would be nice.'

'Hang on.' Mr Jones pulls out his cell and taps faster than one would believe from such blunt fingers, which boast not one but two Super Bowl rings. Billy tries not to gawk at these bulbous crustaceans of the jeweler's art. He accepts his drink and turns to face the room. From deep within the crowd Mango shoots him a look of stunned hilarity, then the sightline quickly shuts and that seems like part of the gag. The crowd is thickest around Norm, a bee swarm of hovering bodies, and Billy decides this is a learning opportunity, a chance to see a master schmoozer up close. Norm's skill at working a room is legendary. Charisma, charm, command presence, he brings all these to bear in the smile and personal word he has for each and every guest, he is the indisputable pivot point and center of the room and Billy can see the skill with which he manages things, and yet, and yet . . . He is so *on*, is Norm. He is working so hard. He has all the right moves but betrays a salesman's stress in the doing, or that of a mediocre actor who hits his points but seems cramped by a too-tight collar, a twist in his underwear. Norm is confident, absolutely, he is the king of self-esteem, but this is the confidence of self-help tapes and motivational mantras, confidence learned as one learns a foreign language, and so the accent lingers in his body language, a faint arthritic creak in every smile and gesture.

Painful to watch, and lacking in essential dignity

– is this why he's always getting dissed? Tales abound of weird encounters – Norm mooned en masse on South Beach in Miami, mooned again from the infield at Churchill Downs, roughed up by a gang of frisky young hedge-fund managers in the men's room of '21' in New York City. And yet he *is* the owner, so it must be working for him on some level. Billy runs his gaze over the rest of the Oglesby clan and they are working every bit as hard as Norm, they are keys jangling on the same live wire, all spark and flash and brassy salesmanship, and Billy tries to imagine living at such a pitch, always on, always playing to the wider stage, channeling all your best energies into the public realm.

Jesus Christ, it looks like a hell of a lot of work. More than sympathy Billy feels respect for them, for the discipline it must take to get up every day and carry the entire Cowboys nation on their backs.

Mr Jones clicks off and turns to Billy. 'Some Aleve's coming down for you right now.'

'Thank you, sir.' Billy tries not to look at the holster bulge. 'And thank you for all this.' He waves his cup at the crowd. 'This is really nice.'

'Well, we appreciate you fine young men being with us today. It's an honor to be your host.'

'You know what I'd like to know,' Billy blurts, suddenly bold or careless with that fresh hit of bourbon in his gut, 'is how you do it? I mean, business. All this. How do you make it happen?' He falters, racks his brain for intelligent-sounding business vocabulary. 'I mean, okay, like where do you start, where does the money come from for, well, the stadium? The land and construction and everything, then paying the players, the coaches, I mean we're talking about some serious cash outlay here, am I right?'

Mr Jones laughs, not unkindly. 'Pro football's a capital-intensive business, that's true,' he says in a patient, teaching-a-retard voice. 'The key is leverage relative to cash flow, whether you can generate enough of a revenue stream to service your debt and still cover your current obligations. So it's a fair question. In a way it's *the* question. You've definitely put your finger on it.'

Billy nods as if he knew all along. 'Uh huh, but just from a tactical standpoint' – whoa, *nice* – 'say when Mr Oglesby decided he wanted to buy the Cowboys, what did he do? I mean, I know he didn't just whip out his credit card and say, Hm, I think I'll buy the Cowboys today.'

'No' – Mr Jones smiles – 'it wasn't quite like that. But let me tell you, leverage is a beautiful thing. In the right hands it can literally move mountains, and Norman Oglesby, well, let's just say my boss is a genius when it comes to structuring deals. I've never known anybody with his feel for numbers, and he's the best negotiator I've ever seen. I've watched him take on a roomful of New York investment bankers and come away with the deal he wanted, and let me tell you, those are some big boys. They're used to getting what they want, but not on that day.'

Holy shit, Billy thinks, we're talking business. He is having an actual adult business conversation with a high-ranking Cowboys executive, an extraordinary Moment in his life even though he knows he's barely or not even hanging on and Mr Jones is totally humoring him. But still. He's here. They're talking. 'Debt ratio,' Mr Jones is saying,

equity / return on equity
income stream //revolving credit

fixed Assets > borrowing *against*

marketing

branding

goodwill

Balance sheet

depreciation

%s over time

lenders group

or

equity in lieu

*there*of

PLAYERS' UNION!!!!!

𝕾𝖆𝖑𝖆𝖗𝖞 𝕮𝖆𝖕

sinking

fund

debentures

Mr Jones's cell phone chirps. He checks the screen, flashes a smile at Billy, and steps away. Billy gets a refresher shot for his Coke and stands off to the side of the bar, thinking. Life in the Army has been a crash course in the scale of the world, which is such that he finds himself in a constant state of wonder as to how things come to be. Stadiums, for example. Airports. The interstate highway system. Wars. He wants to know how is it paid for, where do the billions come from? He imagines a shadowy, math-based parallel world that exists not just beside but amid the physical world, a transparent interlay of *Matrix*-style numbers through which flesh-and-blood humans move like fish through kelp. This is where the money lives, an integer-based realm of code and logic, geometric modules of cause and effect. The realm of markets, contracts, transactions, elegant vectors of fiber-optic agency whereby mind-boggling sums of mysterious wealth shoot around the world on beams of light. It seems the airiest thing there is and yet the realest, but how you enter that world he has no idea except by passage through that other foreign country called college, and that ain't happening. He will not return to the classroom, ever, the mere thought

161

inflames a whole host of piss-offs and associated grudges that go all the way back to kindergarten, not to mention the sheer soul-sucking boredom of those years. If there is real knowledge to be had in the Texas public schools he never found it, and only lately has he started to feel the loss, the huge criminal act of his state-sanctioned ignorance as he struggles to understand the wider world. How it works, who gains, who loses, who decides. It is not a casual thing, this knowledge. In a way it might be everything. A young man needs to know where he stands in the world, not just as a matter of basic human dignity but as determinants in the ways and means of survival, and what you might hope to gain by application of honest effort—

Owwwwww!!!

'Gotcha, dawg. You're flaking on me.'

'Damn, Sergeant!'

'If this was Iraq, you'd be dead.'

'If this was Iraq there wouldn't be chicks in leather pants. Jesus, Sergeant.' Billy straightens his clothes, gingerly touches his chest. While he was absorbed in thought, Sergeant Dime snuck up behind him, clotheslined his throat, and gave his left nipple a ferocious twist.

'I think you ripped my titty off, Sergeant.'

Dime laughs. He asks for a Sprite at the bar. He is a Sprite man, always Sprite, diet if you got it.

'Sergeant Dime, what is leverage?'

Dime blows a little of his Sprite. 'What, Lynn,

you been reading *Forbes* behind my back? Where did you hear about leverage?'

'That guy over there' – Billy tips his chin at Mr Jones – 'he said leverage is the key to Norm's success.'

'He said that, huh.' Dime studies Mr Jones. 'Leverage, Billy, that's a fancy way of saying other people's money. As in, borrowing. Debt. Credit. Hock. Using other people's money to make money for yourself.'

'I don't like debt,' Billy says. 'Owing money makes me nervous.'

'Historically that is the sane position.' Dime bites down on a chunk of ice, *scrunch*. 'But I'm not sure sanity counts for much anymore.'

'What about Norm?'

'What about him?'

'Are you saying he's not sane?'

'I'm not sure he even exists.'

Billy laughs, but Dime does not crack a smile. 'I do know one thing, though.'

'What, Sergeant?'

'He's got a big old boner for Albert.'

Billy opts for silence.

'I guess once you've conquered the NFL there's nothing left to do but take on Hollywood. He's all over Albert about the movie biz.'

'What's Albert doing?'

'He's cool, dawg. He's working it.'

'For our movie?'

'Better be. We're the ones who got him here.'

They fall silent. Mr Jones has joined a group of well-dressed guests. Even when he laughs, Mr Jones's eyes stay sharp, his body alert. Young and strong as he is, even with his military training, Billy thinks he would have a hard time taking Mr Jones in a fight.

'See that guy over there, the one I was talking about? He's packing.'

Dime is not impressed. 'I thought everybody packed in Texas.'

'Yeah, but here? It's bullshit.' Billy is surprised by the intensity of his disgust. 'Only a dick would pack at a game, like, what, there's only about a million cops here? Maybe he thinks he's gonna take out all the terrorists by himself.'

Dime turns to Billy and laughs. Then he stiffens, wheels to Billy's front and stands so close that their noses almost touch. Billy holds his breath but it is too late.

'You motherfucker, you're still drinking.'

'A little, Sergeant.'

'Did I give permission for further consumption of alcohol?'

'No, Sergeant.'

Dime glances at the cup in Billy's hand. 'Do you have a problem?'

'No, Sergeant.'

'We're back in the shit in two days, have you forgotten that?'

'No, Sergeant.'

'You better get your shit wired to a T, and I mean fast.'

'I am, Sergeant Dime. I will.'

'You think the beebs are going to give us a pass just because we've been the big shit over here?'

'No, Sergeant Dime.'

'Hell no, they're gonna be gunning for us. And if I can't count on you . . .' Dime steps back. He seems suddenly aggrieved. 'Billy, I'm gonna need you. You gotta help me keep the rest of these clowns alive. So don't be flaking on me.'

And fast as that, Dime breaks his heart. He is the kind of man for whom you'd rather die than disappoint.

'I'm fine, Sergeant. I'm good. Really.'

'Really?'

'I am, Sergeant. Don't worry about me.'

'All right. Drink some water. Don't get wasted on me.'

So Billy is drinking water when A-bort and Crack approach, grinning like cheetahs with bits of flesh and bone stuck between their teeth.

'What?'

'Norm's old lady.'

'Yeah?'

'We wanna do her. Two on one.'

'Shut up. Dude, she's like, fifty-five.'

'I don't care how old she is,' says A-bort, 'check her out. That bitch is tight.'

'I always wanted to bone a rich bitch right up the ass,' Crack offers.

'That's just rude,' Billy says, with feeling; his puritanical recoil puzzles even him. 'You guys are disgusting. We're her guests and you're showing disrespect.'

Mango has joined them. 'Ain't disrespect if it ain't never gonna happen. It's just *werds*. They ain't gonna tap that lady.'

'Watch,' Crack promises. 'Five to one I do her, hundred bucks.'

'Bullshit,' Billy says, still on his choirboy streak.

'I'll take that,' says Mango.

'Me too,' says A-bort.

'What,' Crack says, 'like you mean if I nail her, or you too?'

But before they can clear this up a Cowboys executive joins them, and it's like a video splice, one second the Bravos are the sludgiest sort of street-corner pervs, and the next they are the nation's very spine and marrow, yes, near to holy they are, angelic warriors of America's crusader dreams. The executive sets a stack of *Time* magazines on the bar and asks for their autographs, there, on the cover, and again on p. 30 where the story starts, 'Showdown at Al-Ansakar Canal': 'The tiny hamlet of Ad-Wariz on the Al-Ansakar Canal is a backwater even by Iraqi standards, a loose collection of mud-wattle huts and subsistence farms. But for two brutal hours on the morning of October 23, this remote village became the epicenter of America's war on terror.'

166

There follow six pages of copy and photos, plus a 3-D schematic with arrows and labels that bears no relation to any battle that Billy can recall. It is not even a Bravo on the cover but Sergeant Daiker from Third Platoon, a dramatically blurred close-up of his clenched and fearsome face. 'It seems this particular group of insurgents wished to die,' Colonel Travers told *Time*, 'and our men were more than willing to oblige them.' True on both counts, but not until the very end did they offer themselves up, a little kamikaze band of eight or ten bursting from the reeds at a dead sprint, screaming, firing on full automatic, one last rocks-off martyrs' gallop straight to the gates of the Muslim paradise. All your soldier life you dream of such a moment and every Joe with a weapon got a piece of it, a perfect storm of massing fire and how those beebs blew apart, hair, teeth, eyes, hands, tender melon heads, exploding soup-stews of shattered chests, sights not to be believed and never forgotten and your mind simply will not leave it alone. Oh my people. Mercy was not a selection, period. Only later did the concept of mercy even occur to Billy, and then only in the context of its absence in that place, a foreclosing of options that reached so far back in history that quite possibly mercy had not been an option there since before all those on the battlefield were born.

The Bravos sign. They've signed dozens of *Time*s over the past two weeks, and some have turned up on eBay, but whatever. The executive gathers up the magazines with the gingerly air of a lawyer who's just pulled a fast one.

'Destiny's Child here yet?' Crack asks him.

'Not in the loop on that one, fella.'

'We were hoping we could hang with them a little.'

The executive laughs. 'You friends of theirs?'

This seems a bit fresh. He might be laughing at them.

'We're fans,' Mango says steadily.

'Son, I'd be worried if you weren't. Tell you what, I'll go find out.'

Sure. The Bravos bar up for a quick round of Jack and Cokes, and Harold's a sport, he keeps the bottle belowdecks as he pours. They slam down the drinks just in time to be rounded up and led into the chilly hall, where Josh gives them the drill for the press conference. He has a clipboard now. His hair is a perfect delta wedge. His entire person looks freshly dry-cleaned.

Will the cheerleaders be there?

'Yes, there will be cheerleaders.'

Yaaaaaaahhhhhh-woof! What about those lap dances?

'No lap dances in front of the press, guys.'

What are we supposed to do at halftime?

'I don't have those specifics yet. I do know Trisha has some kind of role for you.'

Who the fuck's Trisha?

'Guys, come on, Mr Oglesby's daughter. You just met her. She's been planning the halftime show for the past six months.'

Tell her we can sing!

'I'm sure you guys are great singers, but we've got Destiny's Child for that.'

Yeah, we wanna meet—

'I know I know I know, but guys, it's Destiny's Child. Getting you in there might be a little above my pay grade.'

You dah man, Jash.

'I'll ask. But I can't guarantee anything.'

More laughs, a smattering of wolf cheers. Bravo is pumped. They stand around long enough to realize they are waiting for something, for Norm it turns out, at last he arrives with his cloud of an entourage that includes a photographer, a video guy, several family members, and a big chunk of the Cowboys' upper management.

'Ready?' Norm asks, beaming at the Bravos. 'I expect you guys are pros at this by now.' He scoops one of his grandsons into his arms and off they go through the stadium labyrinth, as intricate as the guts of a battleship. Billy's head is pounding, but Josh, so alert and duteous in other matters, has forgotten his Advil again. The ache forms a kind of aura or envelope around his head, with localized boreholes of quite specific pain, as if a nail gun is firing spikes into his skull.

Outside the media room Norm hands off his grandson and waits by the door while the Bravos form up. 'Great,' he is murmuring, 'super,' 'fantastic,' 'outstanding,' a gaseous blather of free-form superlatives aimed at no one in particular.

It is a little embarrassing to see him this way, like watching the fattest kid at a birthday party circling the cake, clearly wishing he could have it all to himself. In any case Norm is first through the door and his entry cues a cataclysmic shriek, from the cheerleaders Billy sees when he crosses the threshold, a pom-pom waving, boot-stamping, thunderclap howl that jumps abruptly to a 4/4 dogtrot chant, a cheer!, and well why not, it's their job:

> *American soldiers strong and true,*
> *The best in the world at what they do,*
> *Thanks for keeping us safe and strong*
> *Against all those who'd do us harm!*

Billy takes a seat onstage with the feeling that the war has attained new heights of lunacy. Norm is urging the medias to stand up! up!, a mostly male crowd of forty or fifty reporters who don't seem terribly thrilled to be stage-managed, yet they stand, they clap, they break into grudging smiles, they are lifted by the moment in spite of themselves, and Norm gestures toward Bravo and raises his arms as if to say, Look at what I brought for you!

He is said to be a marketing genius, is Norm, and sitting there amid the flaming hairball of media lights Billy has the weirdest feeling that none of them exists except in Norman Oglesby's mind. Norm is beaming, clapping, gesturing toward the Bravos. His blue eyes glitter with a special, no, a *holy* light, he is so completely certain of the Cowboys brand that God is surely on his side. What higher calling could there be? What greater good in life? Any profit to the team is truly God's work, and all creation must bend to His will.

The room is a hothouse of plastic and epoxy smells, the burnt-dust fug of large electronics. 'U-S-A!' a cheerleader yells, and the rest take up the chant, 'U-S-A! U-S-A! U-S-A!' and Norm is chanting and clapping, rocking with the beat. So many cheerleaders, enough to line three walls of the room – the sheer volume of exposed female flesh sends Bravo into a mild state of shock. Photographers crab-walk close and flash off in Bravo's face, singeing eyes and probably cauterizing pieces of brain. Camera crews are bunched at both sides of the stage, a two-foot-high riser with the fudgy give of plywood underfoot. The stage is backed by an incurving bulkhead of sorts, a fabric screen stamped with the Cowboys star and Nike swoosh logo. It's actually kind of a crummy room, more like a union hall or under-funded rec center: fluorescent lights, that horrible all-weather carpet everywhere, steel-tube chairs with hard plastic shells. Norm takes the last seat at the table and bellies up to the microphone.

'*I*,' he begins, but has to pause for the handful of cheerleaders who simply can't shut up. He smiles, looks down at his hands, and chuckles at their zeal, which draws a responsive chuckle from the medias.

'I,' he resumes, and waits out the last shrieks as the cheerleaders finally get a grip on themselves, 'I' – another pause, this time for effect – 'and the entire Cowboys organization' – *kai-boiz,* Billy mouths to himself, scratching an itch on his inner ear – 'are pleased, privileged, and extremely honored to have with us today the outstanding young men of Bravo squad, these true American heroes here to my left. If you want to talk about a group that knows how to suit up and show up, here they are. They are the best our nation has to offer, and our best is absolutely the best in the world, as they proved on the battlefields of Iraq.'

The cheerleaders cry out, their orgasmic shriek quickly morphing into the lockstep U-S-A! chant. Have they been told to interrupt, Billy wonders, or do they just know to do it on their own? The role of cheerleader being secondary by definition, yet cheerleaders themselves exhibitionists by nature, he starts to sense the conflict at the core of every boy and girl who ever fanned the fires of team spirit, the private anguish of always cheering for others when you're the one busting it body and soul. Nobody cheers for the cheerleaders! And how that must hurt, the goad for many a deafening scream of crazed enthusiasm. Norm is chuckling, shaking his head as if to say, Those girls. Off to the side, the Cowboys brass are chuckling too.

'I'm sure,' Norm resumes, 'everyone is familiar

by now with the Bravos' exploits, how they were the first to come to the aid of the ambushed supply convoy, they went straight into the battle with no backup, no air support, outnumbered against an enemy who'd been preparing this attack for days. They didn't think twice about the odds stacked against them, they even suspected it was a trap, and yet they went right in without hesitating—'

Several of the cheerleaders cry out, but Norm holds up his hand. He will not be interrupted now.

'Fortunately for us, a Fox News crew was embedded with the group that arrived shortly thereafter, so it's possible for us to see for ourselves what these fine young men did that day. And I have to say, I have *never*' – Norm's voice grows husky, he hunches close to the microphone – 'I have *never*, been prouder, to be an American, than when I saw, that, footage. And if you haven't seen it, I urge you to do so at your earliest opportunity . . .'

Billy's mind wanders. Now that he's settled down somewhat he can give the cheerleaders his first considered look, and he had no idea there are *so many* of them, they are a life-sized sampler of rapturous female flesh with all colors on display, all flavors of sculpted tummy and supple thigh, scooped waist, contoured flare and furl of hip, and such breasts, oh Lord, such volumes of majestically fulsome boob overflowing the famous tail-knotted half shirt, yes, at any moment an avalanche could burst forth and bury them all, only a few

173

scant inches of besieged cloth save Bravo from utter annihilation.

'It's my personal feeling,' Norm is saying, 'that the war on terror may be as pure a fight between good and evil as we're likely to see in our lifetime. Some even say it is a challenge put forth by God as a test of our national mettle. Are we worthy of our freedoms? Do we have the resolve to defend our values, our way of life?'

Billy makes a few of the cheerleaders for strippers – they have the tough slizzard look of the club pro – but most of them could be college girls with their fresh good looks, their pert noses and smooth necks, their scrubbed, unsullied air of wholesome voluptuousness. Don't stare, Billy tells himself; don't be a creep. Albert and Major Mac are sitting together in the back row, and he tries to imagine what they might talk about. This seems funny. From time to time Albert looks up from his BlackBerry to check on Bravo, his eyes keen, not without affection, much like a rich man watching his prize Thoroughbred taking a jog around the track.

'To all those who argue this war is a mistake, I'd like to point out that we've removed from power one of history's most ruthless and belligerent tyrants. A man who cold-bloodedly murdered thousands of his own people. Who built palaces for his personal pleasure while schools decayed and his country's health care system collapsed. Who maintained one of the world's most expensive armies while he allowed his nation's infrastructure to crumble. Who channeled resources to his cronies and political allies, allowing them to siphon off much of the country's wealth for their own personal gain. So I would ask all those who oppose the war, would the world be a better place today with Saddam Hussein in power? Because what is America *for*, if not to fight this kind of tyranny, to promote freedom and democracy and give the peoples of the world a chance to determine their own fate? This has always been America's mission, and it's what makes us the greatest nation on earth.'

Billy wonders if Norm will run for office someday. He's as polished a public speaker as any of the politicians Bravo has encountered over the past two weeks. He has the presence, the *werds,* plus he's mastered the wounded, vaguely petulant tone that is the style of political speech these days. If there's a grating artificiality in the performance – Norm's awareness of himself as performer, sneaking peeks at a mental mirror off to the side – it's no worse than any other fixture of the public realm. Billy has noticed that audiences don't seem to mind anyway. All the fakeness just rolls right off them, maybe because the nonstop sales job of American life has instilled in them exceptionally high thresholds for sham, puff, spin, bullshit, and outright lies, in other words for advertising in all its forms. Billy himself never noticed how fake it all is until he'd done time in a combat zone.

'I had the pleasure of visiting with our president recently, and he assured me we are winning this war. We are winning, make no mistake. We have the best troops in the world, the best equipment, the best technology, the best home-front support, and as long as we maintain our resolve, it's only a matter of time before we prevail.'

The medias look, if not downright sullen, then definitely peckish and bored. Norm is talking longer than anyone expected, and even the Bravos, who are tired of answering questions from the press, grow impatient. Billy's attention swings back to the cheerleaders and he does an experiment, walking his gaze down the row of women to his right. As he catches each cheerleader's eye she breaks into pyrotechnic smiles – it's like flipping on a row of klieg lights, bam bam bam bam. But somewhere down the line his gaze stops, backtracks of its own accord to a petite, fair-skinned girl with a teased-out corona of strawberry-blond hair, soft bolts of which drape the rising tide of her chest. She smiles again, then silently laughs and crinkles her eyes at him. He knows it's her job, but still; his stomach does a drop-kick sort of bounce. A nice girl doing her part to support the troops.

The press is definitely sulking. All the little recording gadgets they were holding up at first, all of these have disappeared. Billy forces himself not to look at the cheerleader for the next thirty seconds, but he's careful not to look at the TV cameras either. Nothing makes you feel more like a geek than seeing yourself on the tube staring straight back at yourself, there's some peculiar

176

quality of guilt or cluelessness that the camera seems to catch in the direct gaze.

'Ladies and gentlemen, nine-eleven was our national wake-up call. It took a tragedy of that magnitude for us realize there's a battle going on for the souls of men. This is not an enemy that can be appeased or reasoned with. They don't negotiate; terrorists do not unilaterally disarm. In a war like this, mixed signals only encourage our enemies . . .'

When Billy at last looks back, she's waiting! She gives him a stupendous smile, then another eye crinkle, then winks. Of course it is all professional courtesy but Billy allows himself to pretend that, yes, she really digs him, that they'll meet, exchange digits, go out on a date, go out on more dates, have sex/fall in love, marry, procreate, raise excellent children, and have incredible sex for the rest of their lives and why the hell not, dammit, humans have been doing it since the dawn of time so why can't Billy have his turn? He has looked away, and when he looks back they both smile and silently chuckle over this little thing they have, whatever it is.

'. . . these fine young men, these true American heroes,' Norm says, and at last he serves up Bravo for direct consumption. *Welcome to Dallas,* says their first interlocutor, which prompts cheers and pom-pom-flapping from the cheerleaders.

What have you been doing since you got here?

The Bravos look at one another. No one speaks. After a moment everyone laughs.

177

'Here, Dallas, or here at the stadium?' Dime asks.

Both.

'Well, in Dallas, we got in late yesterday afternoon, checked into the hotel, and went out for something to eat. Then we did some sightseeing.'

At night?

'You can see lots of interesting things at night,' Dime says straight-faced. This gets a nice laugh.

Where are you staying?

'The W Hotel downtown, which is probably the nicest place we've stayed the whole time. We feel like rock stars there.'

'W Hotel,' Lodis pipes up, 'that have anything to do wif—'

Nooooooo, half the room bellows at him.

'Hunh. 'Cause I just thought maybe the president—'

No no no no no.

What's been your favorite city so far?

'You mean besides Dallas?' Sykes says, which gets a shout-out from the cheerleaders.

Have you had any trouble sleeping, readjusting to life back home?

The Bravos look at one another. Nah.

What was your most unusual mission?

The raid on the chicken farm.

Hardest mission?

When we lost our guys.

Hottest?

Any trip to the port-a-pot.

Are we making a difference over there?

'I think we are,' Dime says carefully. 'We are making a difference.'

For the better?

'In some places, yes, definitely better.'

And other places?

'We're trying. We're working hard to make it better.'

We've been hearing a lot lately about the Sadr insurgency. What can you tell us about that?

'The Sadr insurgency. Well.' Dime reflects for a moment. 'I wouldn't bet on any group whose leader looks like Turtle on *Entourage*.'

Big laugh.

Do you play any sports over there, like intramural stuff?

'It's too hot for sports.'

What do you do during your downtime, for fun?

MASTURBATE!!! they all shriek, or would, except Dime would slowly kill them one by one. 'The Army's real good at task saturation,' he says, 'so we don't have a whole lot of downtime. Most days we're putting in twelve, fourteen hours, lots of days more than that. But when we do get some kick-back, I don't know. Guys, what is it we do for fun?'

Play video games.

Lift weights.

Buy stuff at the PX.

'I like to kill my enemies and listen to the lamentations of their women,' Crack says in a lumbering

German accent. The room freezes, then exhales a laugh when he adds, 'That's from *Conan*. I just always wanted to say that.'

Billy and his cheerleader continue their face work – glances, smiles, brow-scrunching mugs, then this amazing soulful stare that lasts for several seconds. He feels strangely porous, as if his vital organs have turned into Nerf balls.

What was it like meeting the president?

'Oh the president,' Dime enthuses, 'what a totally charming guy!' The rest of the Bravos strain for studiously blank expressions, as Dime's loathing for the Yale brat – his words – is well-known within the platoon. When their deployment began, Dime soaped 'Bush's Bitch' on the front passenger door of his Humvee with an arrow shooting up to the window, where he, Dime, usually sat, but the Lt. finally noticed and made him wash it off. 'He made us feel incredibly welcome and relaxed, like, say, if you went down to your local Chase branch to get a car loan, he's the nicest banker you'd ever hope to meet. He's friendly, easy to talk to, you could sit down and have a beer with this guy. Except, hunh, I guess he doesn't drink anymore, does he.'

This evokes a few sniggers from the medias, a few hostile stares, but mostly it's business as usual.

What's the food like over there? Do you have Internet? Cell service? Can you get any sports channels? The Bravos have this much in common with POWs, they are asked the same questions over and over. Someone asks about the day-to-day challenges of life in Iraq. Crack tells them about the camel spiders, A-bort talks about the horrible biting fleas, then Lodis gets off a free-associative riff about his skin problems, 'how my skin dry out and get all crack and ashy, my boy Day always on me about moisturizer an' I'm like *snap,* den gimme somma dat Jergens, dawg!' This goes on for a while.

Would any of you say you're religious?

'Each of us in our own way.' Dime.

Have you become more so in your time over there?

'Well, you can't see some of the things we've seen and not think about the big questions. Life, death, what it all might mean.'

We keep hearing they're going to make a movie about you. What's up with that?

'Yeah, right, the movie. Let me just say, we call Iraq the abnormal normal, 'cause over there the weirdest stuff is just everyday life. But based on what we know of Hollywood so far, that might be the one place that out-abnormals Iraq.'

Laughs. Big laugh. Albert shoots them the high sign without looking up from the BlackBerry. *Please, God,* Billy prays, *do not let it be Swank.* Then a reporter asks what 'inspired' Bravo to do what it did that fateful day at the Al-Ansakar Canal. Everyone looks to Dime, and Dime looks to Billy, and all eyes follow Dime's.

'Specialist Lynn was the first to recognize what was happening out there, and he was the first to react. So I think he's the appropriate one to answer your question.'

Oh for the fuck of shit. Billy's not ready for this, plus he's having a hard time with *inspired*. Inspired? This seems like a prissy way to put it, but he tries, he's anxious to answer properly, to correctly or even approximately describe the experience of the battle, which was, in short, everything. The world happened that day, and he's beginning to understand he will spend the rest of his life trying to figure it out.

Everyone's staring, waiting. He starts talking just before the silence gets weird. 'Well, ah' – he clears his throat – 'to tell you the honest truth, I don't remember all that much about it. It's like I saw Shroo – Sergeant Breem, and, ah, just seeing him there, basically at the mercy of the insurgents, I don't know, it was pretty clear we had to do something. We all know what they do to their prisoners, you can go into any street market over there and buy these videos of what they do. So I guess that was on my mind, in the back of my mind, not like I clearly had a conscious thought about it. There wasn't much time to think about anything, really. I guess my training just kicked in.'

He feels like he talked too long, but at least it's done. People are nodding, their faces seem sympathetic, so maybe he didn't sound too much like an idiot. But they are coming at him again.

You were the first person to reach Sergeant Breem?

'Yes. Yes sir.' Billy feels his pulse starting to shred.

What did you do when you got to him?

'Returned fire and rendered aid.'

He was still alive when you got to him?

'He was still alive.'

The insurgents who were dragging him away, where were they?

'Well.' He glances to the side, coughs. 'On the ground.'

They were dead?

'That was my impression.'

The medias laugh. Billy hadn't meant to be funny, but he sort of sees the humor in it.

You shot them?

'Well, I had engaged those targets in route. There were several exchanges of fire. They basically dropped Sergeant Breem so they could engage, and we exchanged fire.'

So you shot them.

A rank nausea is spreading out from his armpits. 'I can't say that for sure. There was a lot of fire coming from a lot of different directions. It was a pretty crazy time.' Billy pauses, gathers himself; the words take so much effort. 'I mean, look, it's fine with me if I did shoot them—'

He means to say more, but the room erupts in thunderous applause. Billy is stunned, then worried that they have missed the point, then he's sure they've missed the point but is too unconfident of his communication skills to try to force a clarification down their throats. They're happy, so he will leave it at that. The flash cameras are really going now, and like so much of his nineteen years' experience of life it has become mainly something to get

183

through, then the applause dies down and he's asked if he'll be thinking of his friend Sergeant Breem during the playing of the national anthem today, and he says *yes* just to keep it upbeat and on track, *Yes, I sure will,* which sounds obscene to his ears, and he wonders by what process virtually any discussion about the war seems to profane these ultimate matters of life and death. As if to talk of such things properly we need a mode of speech near the equal of prayer, otherwise just *shut,* shut your yap and sit on it, silence being truer to the experience than the star-spangled spasm, the bittersweet sob, the redeeming hug, or whatever this fucking *closure* is that everybody's always talking about. They want it to be easy and it's just not going to be.

'I'm sure we'll all be thinking of him,' he adds, a final dollop on this big steaming turd of sentiment. Bitch of it is, he *will* be thinking of Shroom. And he loves the national anthem as much as anybody.

Who's going to win today?

'Cowboys!' yells Sykes, and the cheerleaders shout their approval, and with his maestro's feel for the ripeness of things, Norm stands and brings the press conference to a close.

DRY-HUMPING FOR THE LORD

The front page of tomorrow's *Dallas Morning News* will feature an enormous close-in photo of A-bort amid the post-press-conference scrum, a trio of cheerleaders cowled about him as he addresses a quiver of microphones. 'Cowboys Host American Heroes' the caption header will read, then: 'Specialist Brandon Hebert of Bravo Squad being interviewed yesterday at Texas Stadium. Spc. Hebert and Bravo visited Dallas on the final leg of their national victory tour. Cowboys lost, 31–7.'

Billy will notice several things about this news item, first and foremost being the screwup of A-bort's name, which will result in his being known forever afterward as 'Brandon' to his fellow Bravos. Or rather, *Bran*-dunn, always pronounced with a teacher's-aide's sort of pissy severity, as in *Bran*-dunn will be on the .50 cal this time out. *Bran*-dunn will go in first after Crack breaches the door. *Bran*-dunn grazed some wiring in the new shower stalls and got the living shit shocked out of him. Next, Billy will notice that while A-bort is turned quarter-profile to the camera, facing the

185

unseen people with the microphones, the three cheerleaders are smiling directly at the camera, which has the effect of reducing A-bort to a prop. And, third, how happy he looks. He's twenty-two, which makes him ancient in Billy's eyes; not until he sees A-bort's ecstatic smile in the photo, his headlong, boyish pleasure in the moment, will Billy appreciate that his squad mate is basically just a kid, a guy who reads the Harry Potter books over and over and once sent a 'letter' home to his dog, which was a rag he'd kept stuffed under his arm for several days.

It will make Billy anxious, this photo. He'll see too much trust in A-bort's face, too much heedless good faith in the presumed blessings of being born American at a certain point in time, but at the moment of its taking Billy has his own hands full. It must be that every cheerleader has been given a specific charge, for as soon as the Bravos step off the stage each soldier is received by exactly three girls, a moment that packs the force, if not the content, of divine intercession. Billy is shy about actually touching them but they spoon right in with sisterly nonchalance. Their pancake makeup disappoints him a little, but he decides he doesn't mind because they're *just so pretty* and genuinely nice, and *toned,* good God, their bodies firm as steel-belted radials. *Such an honor to meet you! Welcome to Texas Stadium! We're so proud and thrilled to have you with us today!* Oh mother of all fuck even a man with a pounding migraine feels restored among these girls, no, these women, these *creatures* with their thickets of fragrant hair and palmable little butts and Alpine crevasses of dizzying cleavage into which a man could fall, never to be seen or heard from again.

And that would be all right, just to disappear down there, vanished by a kind of reverse-rapture action into chasms of sheltering female flesh. Such tender feelings their bodies evoke in him, an almost irresistible instinct to root and nuzzle, to say *I love you. I need you. Marry me.* Candace's boobs, incidentally, are fake, not that it matters a damn, those are regular warheads punching out from her chest, whereas Alicia and Lexis sport the more pliable slope of the real. By any measure they are all three stunning women with their sharp little noses and blinding white teeth and such tiny tiny isthmuses of biscuit-brown waists that it's all he can do not to grab them, just to try those sylphy flexures out for size.

'You havin' a good day so far?' Candace asks.

'Outstanding,' Billy says. 'I hope I didn't talk too much up there.'

'What?'

'Are you kidding?'

'No way!'

'You were super,' Lexis assures him. 'Everybody was incredibly moved by your words.'

'Well, it just felt weird. Usually I don't talk that much.'

'You were excellent,' she says firmly. 'Believe me. You were very concise and to the point.'

'And it's not like you were putting yourself forward,' Alicia observes. 'They kept asking you questions, what're you gonna do?'

'Personally I thought it was kind of rude, some of the stuff they were asking,' says Lexis.

'You have to be so careful around the media,' Candace says.

Photographers and TV cameramen eddy through the crowd, along with reporters, team executives, and persons of no discernible purpose. Billy spots Mr Jones sharking around the fringes, armed and presumably dangerous, or at least a pain in the ass to have to think about. It turns out that the cheerleaders have their own photographer, a balding, raw-faced little jockey of a man who dashes about barking 'Hold!' before each shot, showing no more sensibility for the splendors of his subjects than a peeler at a meat-packing plant. Hold! – *snnnizzzck*. Hold! – *snnnizzzck*, the shutter spasming like an old man's sphincter giving way. In between photo ops the girls tell Billy about the USO tour they did last spring, with stops in Baghdad, Mosul, Kirkuk, and points beyond, plus a volunteers-only foray into Ramadi, where their Black Hawk helicopter could have taken fire.

'I don't see how yall do it,' says Alicia. 'That's some hard living over there, boy, just how dry it is, all that wind and sand. And those people, the Iraqis, their houses? All those dirt huts, they're like something Jesus might've lived in.'

'Your service is just so much more meaningful

to us now,' Lexis tells him. 'We have a lot more appreciation for the job you're doing.'

'The food was pretty good,' says Candace, 'the *chow*. We only had to eat MREs a couple of times.'

'A *lot* of carbs,' adds Lexis.

'I swear, ever since we got back? I cry whenever I hear the national anthem,' Alicia admits.

Billy was hoping to meet his strawberry-blond cheerleader but knows he should be grateful for what he has right here, three beautiful and voluptuous Dallas Cowboys cheerleaders. They are so sweet, so utterly gorgeous. They smell so good. They cry out and give him high-fives on discovering he's a Texan just like them. Their wonderful breasts keep noodging up against his arms, setting off sensory bells and whistles like a run of bonus points in a video game. Whenever any of the medias approach, the girls hook their thumbs into their hot pants and stand there cock-hipped and saucy as if daring the press to give their Billy a hard time. And the medias, the men, they cannot deal straightforwardly but throw out smirks, sidelong looks, ironical tones of voice. *Yeah, yeah, we see you, hoss,* they as much as say to Billy. *Rock star and everything, ain't you the shit.* Viewing himself through the medias' eyes, Billy understands how close the cheerleaders come to rendering him absurd, the pimp excess of not just one or two but *three* beautiful girls. He's fully aware it's all fake, and surely they know he knows, so is this put-on scorn their way of manning up to him?

189

He begins to resent the situation. The reporters waft a few pro forma questions his way. Did he play sports in high school? Is he a Cowboys fan? What does it mean to be home for Thanksgiving this year?

'Well, technically,' Billy points out, 'I'm not at home. I'm here.'

They don't even have to take notes, just hoover up his words with sleek little recording gadgets that look like protein bars. Merely by standing there they manage to be incredibly annoying, a middle-aged bunch of mostly big-assed white guys dressed in boring-as-hell business casual, such a sad-fuck sampling of civilian bio-matter that for a moment Billy is actually glad for the war, hell yes, so much better to be out there shooting guns and blowing shit up than shuffling around like scenery on a bad sitcom. God knows the war sucks, but he sees no great appeal in these tepid peace-time lives.

Through the crowd he spots his cheerleader, who's been assigned – gah! – to Sykes. The proceedings are definitely getting on his nerves. She catches him looking and sends back a seemingly warm and genuine smile, then tips her head in concern or puzzlement. His abs contract as if from a body blow.

When the medias finally leave he turns to Lexis and asks, 'Do you have to be single to be a cheerleader?'

She gives a curt laugh; a look passes among the

cheerleaders. Oh Christ, they think he's hitting on them.

'Well, no,' she says, very crisp and businesslike, 'you don't, and we've always got some married girls on the squad. Me and Candace and Al, we aren't married, but we've all got steady boyfriends.'

Billy's head is bobbing in manic agreeableness, uh huh, uh huh, *of course* you do! 'I was just, you know, um, curious.'

The girls exchange another look. *Sure you were.* He is trying to figure out how to nicely say it's not you particular three I'm interested in, but before this formulation is revealed to him he's summoned by Josh. Showtime. The medias want a photo op, Norm and the Bravos together. A space is cleared in front of the stage, chairs pushed back, bodies herded. One of Norm's small grandsons darts past playing tag with the cheerleaders, the sturdy little stub of his erect penis straining against his pants. As everyone takes their places a reporter asks Norm about his plans for a possible new stadium. An *oh-ho* sort of razzing rises from the medias.

'Well, obviously we're playing in an aging facility,' Norm answers. 'But Texas Stadium has been a wonderful home for the Cowboys. I don't see that changing any time soon.'

'But,' the reporter prompts, drawing laughs. Norm smiles. He's happy to play the straight man in this routine.

'But for the long-term health of the organization, I think it's something we'll have to look at.'

'Some of the Irving city council think you already are. They're saying that's why you cut the stadium maintenance budget by seventeen percent.'

'No, not at all. We just did our review in the normal course of business and found a few places where some fat could be trimmed. We have every intention of maintaining Texas Stadium as a first-class facility.'

'Any chance you'll move the team back to Dallas?'

Norm merely smiles for the cameras, which click away like parakeets cracking seeds. A few of the medias keep on about the stadium, but Norm ignores them. Billy begins to get a sense of the dynamic here, a power equation along the lines of the CEO of a giant corporation vis-à-vis the urinal puck he so thoughtfully studies as it's drenched with his mighty personal stream. It is Norm's job to maximize the value of the Cowboys brand, and it is the job of the medias to soak up every drop, dab, and dribble of PR he sends their way. As sentient human beings endowed with reason and free will, they naturally resent such treatment; perhaps this explains their sourpuss attitude, the karmic dampness that breathes off them like the towel hamper at a gym. Tomorrow he'll read the newspaper and wonder why this, too, isn't part of the story: that the press, however grudgingly, gathered as instructed to record in its stenographic capacity Norm's presentation of Bravo Squad, a blatantly formulaic marketing event that enlightened no one, revealed nothing, and served no tangible purpose other than to big-up awareness of the Cowboys brand.

The bullshit part of it, isn't that part of the story too? But not a word, not a murmur, not a peep from the press about how thoroughly they've been used, and no hint of their personal feelings toward Norm, which, as Billy infers from the body language, consist in roughly equal measure of resentment and fear. If he so wished, Norm could probably get any one of them fired. Could probably get them killed, if he wished. Not that he would. Probably. Billy spots Mr Jones nearby, discussing the line with several other suits. Cowboys by four? 'Boys by three? They chuckle like men comparing the talents of a carnally shared woman, and Billy would like to go over there and beat their faces in. He doesn't know why he's so offended, but he is, maybe it's Mr Jones's gun that sets him off, something about the presumption of it, the ignorance, the sheer fucking *ego* of carrying around an instrument of deadly force. Like you *know*? You wanna see what deadly force can do? Bravo can show you, Bravo does deadly like you wouldn't believe, the kind that will break your mind and make you wish you'd never spilled out of your mother's crack.

When the photo op is done Billy decides he needs a moment. He takes up position with his back to the wall, just to the left of the stage where the arc of the backdrop as it curves inward shields him from much of the room. He stands at parade rest and works on smoothing out his breathing. A couple of medias see him and here they come. Well fuck. What the hell. Billy sucks it up.

'Hey.'

'Hello.'

'What up.'

They introduce themselves. Billy gave up trying to remember names long ago. They talk a little while for the recording gadgets, then one of them asks has Billy considered writing a book about his experiences in Iraq. Billy laughs and gives him a *Dude!* sort of look.

'A lot of soldiers are doing it,' the man tells him, 'there's a market for that right now. It'd be a way to get your story out there and make some money. Paul and me could help you with that, we've ghostwritten a couple of books. We'd be interested in working with you on something like that.'

Billy shuffles his feet. 'I never saw myself ever trying to write a book. I hardly even ever read, till I joined the Army and a buddy started giving me books.'

What, the medias want to know.

'Well, okay. You really wanna know? *The Hobbit.* Kerouac, *On the Road.* This book *Flashman at the Charge,* which was hilarious. Why don't they tell you about these books in school? Like maybe then they'd get people to actually read. Let's see, the *Hell's Angels* by Hunter S. Thompson. *Fear and Loathing in Las Vegas. Slaughterhouse Five, Cat's Cradle. Gorky Park* and another one with that same guy, the Russian dude.' All books given to him by Shroom.

'What did you think of the Thompson books?'

'They made me wanna get high,' Billy says, and laughs so they'll know it's a joke. 'No, seriously, I think you'd have to say the man's a total lunatic, but in a way it makes sense, like it's a normal response to the situations he puts himself in. Though why a person would do a lot of the shi – stuff he does . . . I bet he'd have some interesting things to say about Iraq, like if he went, if he could see it the way the soldiers see it. I'm not saying I endorse his lifestyle or anything. I just like the way he writes.'

'Would you say there's much drug use among the soldiers over there?'

'I wouldn't know about that. I'm only nineteen. I can't even drink beer!'

'You can vote and die for your country, but you can't walk into a bar and buy a beer.'

'I guess that's one way to put it.'

'How do you feel about that?'

Billy takes a moment to reflect. 'It's probably for the best.'

Again the medias raise the idea of writing a book. Billy becomes aware of a radiant heat source on his right, and glancing over he sees it's her standing patiently at his side. His pulse takes off at gazelle speed, oh God oh God oh God oh fuck fuck fuck fuck, meanwhile the medias natter on about markets, contracts, agents, publishers, and God knows what. He gives them his e-mail address just so they'll leave him alone, and when at last they do he turns to her. She regards him steadily, with an air of frank expectation. Somehow he has the poise to look her up and down, not a leering perv look but more like that of a childhood friend encountering the splendid grown-up version of the knock-kneed, noodle-armed, grass-flecked little girl he used to chase around the playground in first grade.

'So you're gonna write a book?'

'*No,*' he gruffs, and they both laugh. Suddenly he's barely nervous at all. 'Don't you get cold out there, cheering in that rig?'

'We move around so much it's almost never a problem, though I'm tellin' you, last week in Green Bay I thought I was gonna freeze my you-know-what off. We do have coats for really cold weather, but we hardly ever wear them out on the field. I'm' – sounds like *pheasant?* She shifts her pom-poms and holds out her hand.

'Say again?'

She laughs. 'Faison. F-a-i-s-o-n. I know who you are, Billy Lynn from Stovall. My grandmother was Miss Stovall 1937, how about that?' She laughs easily, a husky trilling from deep in her chest. 'Everybody said she had a shot at winning Miss Texas that year. A bunch of local business guys got together and financed her wardrobe, voice lessons, all her travel expenses, they really wanted it for the town. Back then Stovall was sort of a big deal, with all the oil they were pulling out of the ground.'

'So how'd she do?'

Faison shakes her head. 'Second runner-up. Everybody said she should've won, but the fix was in. You know how those pageant deals work.'

And with his vast experience in beauty pageants, Billy eagerly nods. For the moment people are leaving them alone.

'Not much you could call a big deal about Stovall these days.'

'That's what I hear. Haven't been since I was a kid, but when I saw one of the Bravos was from Stovall, I was like, Hey, Stovall! I felt like I kind of knew you in a way, I mean, *Stovall*, come on, out of all the places a person could be from? It just seemed funny.'

She grew up in Flower Mound, she tells him, and works part-time as a law firm receptionist while paying her own way through UNT, a mere six credits to go before she earns her degree in broadcast journalism. He guesses she's twenty-two, twenty-three, a compact, curvy package with a pert, inquiring nose, green eyes strewn with flecks of amber and gold, and the kind of cleavage that makes men weep. At the moment she's telling him how much his comments at the press conference meant to her, but he barely hears, so absorbed is he in the beautiful shapes her mouth makes as it forms the words witness

　　　　　　　　bearing

　　　　　　　　　witness

　　　yr

　　　words

　　　deeds

acks

　　　　　　　acks of *sack*-rih-*fice*

　　　　free-dom

　　freest in the world

　　　　　　　　ire values

and

　ire way of life

　　　　ire

　　　way

　　　　　　　of . . .

　　　　ire

　　　　　　　　　life

198

'You were so incredibly eloquent up there.'

'I don't know about that.'

'No, yeah, you were! You put it right out there and that's strong, a lot of people can't talk about those kinds of things. I mean, like, death, your friend's death? And you were right there with him? It can't be easy talking to a room full of strangers about that.'

Billy inclines his head. 'It is sort of weird. Being honored for the worst day of your life.'

'I can't imagine! A lot of people would just shut down.'

'So what's it like being a cheerleader?'

'Oh, great! A *lot* of work but I love it, it's a lot more work than people realize. They see us on TV and think that's all there is to it, just dressing out for the games and dancing and having fun, but that's really just a very small fraction of what we do.'

'Really,' he says encouragingly. He feels light inside, refreshed, a physical state of hopefulness. Talking to this beautiful girl makes him realize just how precious his unremarkable life is to him.

'Yeah, community service is really the main part of our job. We do lots of hospitals, lots of stuff with underprivileged kids, appearances at fund-raisers and stuff like that. Like right now that it's the holidays? We're doing four or five service events per week, then practice and games on top of that. But I'm not complaining. I'm grateful for every minute of it.'

'Did you do the USO tour last spring?'

'Oh my God NO and I SO would've gone but I only made the squad this summer. Listen, I'm DYING to do a trip like that, no way they're gonna keep me off that plane next time it happens. The girls who did it? They came back so enriched and that's the thing about service, people say, "Oh, you're so good to be giving so much of yourselves," but really it's the other way around, we get so much back. To me that's been the most satisfying thing about being a cheerleader, serving others. The spiritual aspect of it. Like it's another stage in the journey, the quest.' She pauses; her eyes hold Billy's for a long, searching moment, and just before she speaks he knows what's coming.

'Billy, are you a Christian?'

He coughs into his fist, looks away. The confusion is genuine, but he rarely goes to the trouble of showing it.

'I'm searching,' he says finally, dipping into his repertoire of Christian buzz words, which, thanks to growing up in small-town Texas, is extensive.

'Do you pray?' She's become softer in her manner, more solicitous.

'Sometimes. Not as much as I should, I guess. But some of the stuff we saw in Iraq, the little kids especially . . . Praying doesn't come so easy after that.'

So if he's laying it on a little thick, so what. His sensors haven't picked up a false word yet.

'You've been tested in so many ways, I know. But a lot of the time that's how it works, life gets so dark until we think all the light's gone out of us. But it's there, it's always there. If we just open the door a crack the light comes pouring in.' She smiles and ducks her head, emits a shy chuckle. 'You know how we kept looking at each other during the press conference? And I was thinking to myself, Now, why out of all the people here does he keep looking at me and I keep looking at him? I mean you're cute and everything, you've got gorgeous eyes . . .' She giggles, regroups her seriousness. 'But now I think I know why, I really do. I think God wanted us to meet today.'

Billy sighs, his eyelids flutter and his head tips back, meets the wall with an understated *thunk*. For all he knows every word she says is true.

'We're all called upon to be His lights out in the world,' she continues, brushing a pom-pom against his arm, and thirty seconds into the story of how she came to a personal relationship with Jesus Christ, Billy quietly, slowly, firmly, reaches underneath her pom-pom and takes her hand. Because, why not. Because he's moved. Because in two days he's back in the shit and what's the worst that can happen compared to that? Faison doesn't falter, in fact her rate of speech gathers speed. Her sternum lifts and swells; hothouse blooms of plum purple and fireball red dapple the regions of her face and neck. Her pupils dilate to twice their former size, and faint, shallow pantings swirl and ripple through her words as if she's just trotted up five flights of stairs.

God

God-ly

Him
    and

      the light within

Jews,

   the Jews

         Jerusalem

           from the Jordan

      to the sea

            healing and annealing

          goodness and light

died for us

      his *disobedient* and *gainsaying*

        people

   died

       died for us

          died

  Oh

my

Lord

Billy is stepping backward, pulling her with him. One, two, three short steps and they are cached in the small dim space behind the backdrop's flared edge, so that someone would have to stand flush with the wall in order to spy them out. Billy pivots, Faison's back snugs up against the wall, and now she isn't talking anymore. Her face is puffy, slack, a new thickness has filled out her cheeks and lips, the suddenly heavy swag of her free-swinging jaw. She could be falling asleep, she's that yielding, and leaning toward her Billy knows that six weeks ago he wouldn't have conceived of such a move, much less followed through. Three weeks ago, same, three days, check, so evidently something has happened to him. He keeps his eyes open the whole way in, and Faison's eyes gradually merge into a single brilliant ball like a picture of Earth as seen from outer space. The first kiss feels like a pressure release, like bursting a bubble with a touch of the lips. He pulls back and discovers pleasure in the restraint. They stare at each other from a couple of inches' distance. She seems stoned, out of it, then lifts her face and they kiss again. He wants to tell her how amazing her lips are, softer than anything he's ever touched. *Did you know* he wants to say, but the tool is otherwise engaged as they linger, mouths drunk on soft-tissue probings, then it's like a starting gun has fired because they're going at each other like a couple of sophomores under the bleachers, a high-energy bout of gymnastical making out that seems to have as its goal the cramming, the actual forcing of their entire bodies down each other's throat.

'This is *crazy*,' she whispers when they come up for air. 'I could get kicked off the *squad* for this.' With that they fall on each other again, and for as long as it lasts Billy wants nothing more.

'What is it *about* you?' she murmurs at the next surfacing. 'What's happening to me?' When they lock lips again his pelvis drops and scoops into hers like a spoon driving into soft ice cream, pure motor reflex from the lower brain stem. He pulls back at once.

'Sorry.'

'It's okay.' She watches him for a moment, then her eyes lose focus and some settling or shift in her lumbar regions signals he can press in again. *Home* he thinks, leading with his crotch, and her core seems to part and flow around him. They're trembling. It's so hard not making any noise. On the other side of the backdrop people are talking and carrying on with their idiot lives. Faison seems near tears as she grabs his lapels and wraps her legs around his waist, cowgirl boots and all. He clutches her from below, her compact little bottom fits neatly in his hands and he conjures up a mental picture of that, his hands full of fabled hot-pants ass and it strikes him in a blaze of exploding pheromones, *Holy shit, I'm making out with a Dallas Cowboys cheerleader!* Faison, meanwhile, has forged ahead, she's rolling her hips and breathing mansions of glory in his face and on this day Billy will let himself believe he's special because she comes in fewer than a dozen strokes, with a mighty clench and up-curving heave, a dolphin squeal stuck deep in her chest. That last torque of her hips nearly breaks his back, at least that's the way it feels as he hangs on with every bit of life's breath squeezed out of him, his vertebrae popping like bubble wrap. Then it's done, except for a few lingering after-shocks. Like a shipwreck survivor dragging herself onto a beach, Faison releases first one leg, then the other. Her boots find the floor. She slumps against him.

'You okay?'

She mumbles something, then glances to the side to make sure no one's watching. 'My God,' she murmurs, and like a child whose attention is wholly elsewhere, she reaches up and gives his Silver Star an idle pull. When she draws back and looks up at him there are tears in her eyes.

'I've never moved this quick with anybody,' she whispers. 'But it's not wrong. I know it's not.'

He shakes his head, which of its own accord tips toward her. 'It's not,' he mumbles into her hair.

'It's just you, something about you. Maybe it's the war.' She grabs him by the short scruff of his neck and gets him where she can see his eyes. 'How old are you?'

'Twenty-one.'

He forces himself to meet her stare. In a second or two his retinas ache.

'You have an old soul.'

He thinks that might be from a movie but doesn't mind. There may even be a kind of truth in it, the way Iraq ages you in dog years. He gives her a tug and she promptly collapses against his chest.

'We better go,' she murmurs.

'You're incredible.'

She sighs. Neither of them moves. The voices are moving away, toward the back of the room. His erection is active and painful but apparently there's just nothing to be done about it.

'I'm gonna be honest with you,' she whispers, 'I'm not a virgin. I've had three boyfriends, but they were all long-term relationships. I'm not casual with my body, I just want you to know that.'

He nods and dips down for a whiff of her neck. Beneath the floral scents of perfume and soap he discovers a dense, rooty smell like sweet potato paste. Her smell. He can't remember ever being so happy.

'It's a really serious thing for me,' she whispers. 'Being intimate with somebody.'

'Me too,' virginal Billy mouths into her neck.

'But it's like if you really care about someone and trust them and know they feel the same way about you, I think it's okay to be physically intimate. But it takes time, you know? To build that kind of trust. It doesn't happen after one or two dates or a couple of weeks, it takes *time*, a real commitment to honoring each other. Like for me, just where I am in my life right now, I need to be with somebody for at least three months before I get to the trust point.'

All of which seems like a lot of information, but Billy doesn't mind. He knows what his fellow Bravos would say: Let's fuck now and I'll owe you three months.

'That's all right,' he whispers. 'But I'd sure like to see you when I get back.'

She lifts her head. 'Back from where?'

'Well, Iraq. We've gotta finish out our tour.'

'You – *what*?' She's still whispering, but barely. 'You're going *back*? But nobody said, wait, everybody just *assumes*, oh my God, yall were done. Oh my God. When are you leaving?'

'Saturday.'

'*Saturday?*' she cries, her voice breaking. She lifts her hair with one hand as if to rip it out, an ancient gesture that makes Billy weak in the knees. *Only women*, he thinks – only his mother, his sisters, and now Faison, only they have ever shown real grief for his sake, and his eyes burn with gratitude for all womankind. Faison rises on her toes for a furious kiss, and Billy's erection, which had been napping at half-mast, instantly springs to attention.

207

'Oh my God,' she whispers, 'if we could just—'

'Cheerleaders!' barks a female with a drill sergeant's voice, 'form up in the hall!'

'Oh shoot, I've gotta go.' Faison gives him a last kiss, then cups his cheek with her hand. 'Listen . . .'

'Give me your digits.'

'I just got a new phone!' Meaning – ???? 'Come find me, I'll be at the twenty-yard line.'

She pokes her head past the backdrop's edge, then turns. '*Billy,*' she murmurs, and tries to smile, but falters when her eyes meet his. Then she's gone.

JAMIE LEE CURTIS
MADE A SHITTY MOVIE

Billy has no idea how they got here. That part is blank, like a concussion knocked him clean out of time's flow into the next half hour, for he finds himself deposited on the playing field. The Bravos, Norm & Co., they are milling around the flats near the end zone, deep in the stadium's horseshoe curve where the wind tears around in stinging freshets and flukes, a regular toilet bowl of rotary action down here. The transect of sky through the open dome is the color and texture of rumbled pewter, an ominous boil of bruised sepias and ditchwater grays that foretells all kinds of weather-related misery. 'Gonna snow,' says Mango, their winter-conditions expert, 'I can smell it,' but nobody pays any attention to him. Their little huddle is a-swirl with movie talk. Something has happened, Billy infers, new developments have been breaking while he was otherwise engaged. Howard and Grazer are out, apparently. Hanks is definitely out, Stone was never in, and Clooney's people keep assiduously not returning Albert's calls, but suddenly looming in the breach is Norman Oglesby with the promise, or let's say the *potential*, or at least the not-so-far-fetched *possibility*, of robust millions in production financing—

'He's intrigued,' is how Albert puts it, *intrigued* implying a level of interest higher than running your yap but short of laying the actual lucre on the table. 'He likes the idea, and he likes you guys. But it's early days yet.'

Early days, but Bravo has only two left, a woefully short fuse in the labyrinthine world of the movie deal. First *this* has to happen and then *that* has to happen and then about thirty more things simultaneously or in sequence without any previous item crapping out on you, the process fed, as far as Billy can tell, by outrageous verbal plyings of fear and greed. You make it happen by convincing everyone it's happening, belief in the first instance being a vaporous construct of duplicity, puff, evasion, cant, and bald-faced lies. A con, in other words. Not that Billy thinks less of Albert because of this. It seems the process has huge margins for treachery built in; everyone just assumes everyone else is lying until a critical mass erupts from the sheer tonnage of bullshit put forth, and then they aren't. Lying, that is. A sort of truth has been made to happen. Whether this business model has anything to do with the quality of the product that Hollywood turns out, Billy hasn't had time to consider.

Someone, somebody's *people* – Hanks's? Grazer's? Swank's? – said it didn't matter shit, or actually what they said was *nickels out of a monkey's butt*, that the Bravo story is true, that *truth* is a *nonfactor* in the pricing of the deal. Which offended the soldiers, but Albert told them to shake it off. 'They're assholes,' he said. 'Don't worry about it.'

Except the assholes always seem to be the ones with the money. At the moment Albert is standing off to the side, briary hair clawing the wind as he takes a call. Equidistant on Bravo's other side, Norm is having his own cell session.

'Maybe they're talking to each other,' says A-bort.

Dime just shakes his head and hunkers down against the cold. He's slumping. He's bored. His energy is low. Major Mac has wandered over to the sideline, where he stands gazing up at the goalpost as if signs and wonders are being revealed.

'Tole my moms I'ma buy her a car,' Lodis says. 'Hunred thousand, Momma, go on up to the lot and pick it out! She pick it out and now she sittin' at home, wonderin' where the money at.'

'Look,' Crack says to the squad, 'Norm's loaded, right? Pretty much a billionaire, right? So all he's gotta do to get the movie going is basically write a check.'

'Write *us* a check,' says Day. 'Our story, yo.'

'True that. And like as soon as fucking possible.'

'Don' forget Wesley Snipes gonna play me!'

'Your momma gonna play you.'

'Fuck that, she's not ugly enough. Urkel plays him.'

'Richard Simmons. Dark him up.'

'No, that black midget dude, the wrestler. Master Blaster.'

'So why won't he write the check?' Crack whines, appealing to Dime. 'Like, just write it, bitch, don't you wanna support the troops? How do you get a guy like that to put it out there?'

Well, Billy thinks but doesn't say, we could walk over there, pick him up, turn him upside down, and just shake him until all the money falls out. Dime is unresponsive through all of this. It's a classic Dime funk, not unheard-of when he's bored or his blood sugar dips, but he's funking right at the moment Billy needs his counsel most, namely, what to do with the miracle that's just blown up his life. Thoughts of Faison crank his brain the way he's heard crack does, a power-ball straight to the neural pleasure zones, and while it's not the full-system freak-out of the hard-core fiend he is definitely feeling things he cannot control. *Dude, she was into you.* Fuck that, *she GOT OFF on you.* It occurs to him to wonder was it even real. It's too perfect, just exactly the sort of delusion a desperate soldier would dream up, your normal, frustrated ADD grunt whose inner life is mostly overcooked sex fantasies anyway. But then self-doubt has always been there for Billy, self-doubt and its cousin the berating voice, these faithful companions have always been on call to help him through the critical junctures of his life, and yet, and yet . . . his lower back hurts like hell. Her scent lingers on his hands and chest. Strands of reddish-gold hair glint on his sleeves like signals from a distant mountain range. So if he's not delusional and not on crack, what is he supposed to do? To make it real, that is. To make it stick. He needs to consult with his sergeant as soon as possible, because time is of the essence.

'Boys, things are looking up,' says Sykes. Half a dozen cheerleaders, none of them Faison, are heading this way, plus Josh with a duffel bag slung over his shoulder. He walks up to Bravo, unslings the duffel, and dumps a bunch of footballs at their feet.

'What's this?'

'These are your balls,' says Josh.

Our balls.

'Yeah, they want you guys holding footballs when we do the shoot.'

A couple of Bravos grunt, but nobody says anything. They eye the footballs, nudge them with their toes, gaze off into the distance as if none of this has anything to do with them. Billy waits for an opening to speak with Dime alone. The cheerleaders sheep together nearby, shoulders hunched, legs pressed together for warmth, pom-poms clutched to their chests like giant muffs. Bravo shoots longing looks that way, but no one quite musters the courage to walk over there.

'Yo, Josh, any word on halftime?'

'Not yet. I'll let you know as soon as I hear something.'

'You're gonna look out for us, right, Josh? Don't make us do anything lame.'

'Or hard.'

'Or hard, right. We don't wanna look like a bunch of morons on TV.'

'No worries, guys,' Josh assures them. 'I think it's going to be just fine.'

An especially chill gust shuts everyone up for a moment. 'Why we gotta wait out here in the *cole*?' Lodis wails.

'The network said their guys would be here,' says Josh.

'Well they ain't!'

'Hang loose. I'm sure they'll be here in a minute.'

'Put Norm on they ass.'

Everyone turns and looks at Norm.

'Who he talking to?' Day asks. Josh furrows his brow, as if the answer will come with sufficient concentration, or the pretense thereof.

'I'm not sure, actually.'

'Whyn't you go find out, yo.'

Josh staggers a little. 'I can't do that!'

Day gives him a sour, pitying look. 'Whatchoo sayin', you can't walk?'

'Well of course I can walk.'

'Then cruise on by, thas all I'm sayin'. He talkin' about makin' our movie or what, all we wanna know. Think you can handle that?'

'I'm not sure that's exactly ethical.'

214

Day snorts. He's not above using his cool as a bullying tool when it comes to finicky white-boy sensibilities.

'Look, you see the man standin' right there. He in public, right? This confidential, he go inside, slip off someplace private.'

'Uh, maybe. But I'm not sure what it would accomplish anyway.'

'Come on, man, intel! Knowledge power, every motherfucker know that! Just walk on by like you got business over there, ain't no thing. Your job be looking out for us, right? It's cool, just walking by. He ain't markin' you nohow.'

The other Bravos join in, mainly for something to do; they cajole and browbeat so relentlessly that at last Josh consents. With actorly nonchalance he saunters past Norm, loops around the entourage, greets the cheerleaders, then swings back toward Norm, in whose vicinity he casually kneels to tie his shoe. The Bravos follow every move. *A hundred thousand bucks.* By the time he returns they're climbing out of their skins.

'He's getting the injury report.'

Awww fuck. They're dying out here. Billy scoops up a football and flips it at Dime. 'Hit me!' he barks, and without waiting to see if Dime actually catches the ball Billy sprints off with an agonal *aaagggghhhh*, legs churning through all the arterial muck of the day's heavy intake of food and alcohol. Three, four steps and his legs start to get it, his arms gear into the rhythm of the stride. He jukes through random people standing along the sideline, breaks left across the end zone and looks back. The ball – shit! – is right on him, tightly spinning like a drill bit's business end and in that split second he sees everything, speed-loft-trim computes to ETA while his eye travels the ball's trajectory back to the source, the big bang of Dime's arm and the suddenly animate genius of his snarling face, like a Viking leaping ashore with ax in hand.

He's unloaded a real bullet, too. The ball sings like silk tearing along a seam and Billy knows there will be no mercy in it, but he does just like the pros, eyes it all the way in and folds his stomach around the blow, a smothering *oooooph*—

Touchdown. He throws the ball back to Dime and angles deeper into the end zone, legs stroking, lungs feeding on fresh cold air. It feels so good to run, to just: run. Dime leads him too far with the next pass and he has to stretch, full extension in midstride and – *hands*! A cheer rises from the end-zone stands as he pulls the ball in, and Billy breaks off a little touchdown dance, uh *huh*, uh *huh*, taking it to the *house*. On the next pass Dime waves him long, then launches a bomb that floats over Billy's head and into his arms, like rocking a baby the way that ball cuddles up to him, and the end-zone crowd sends up another cheer.

Billy is on. He's feeling it. There's a tingling sentience in every inch of his body, his receptors keyed to near-orgasmic pitch with a corresponding sureness of motor control. Is this how professional athletes feel all the time? Such pleasure in the sheer physicality of every moment, the meaty spring of your feet off good firm turf, the razor-strop of cold air in and out your lungs. Even food must have a heightened savoriness for them, and sex, dawg, don't even talk about it. Naturally he hopes Faison is watching, and there's the half-conscious thought that she did this, their encounter somehow altered his brain chemistry with one result being this quantum boost to his athletic skills.

He pivots, plants his feet for the throw back to Dime, and finds one, two, three footballs sailing at him, air support for an all-out incursion onto the field. Mango launches a line-drive kick that screams past Billy's head. Lodis rams into Sykes from behind, knocking him to the ground. Crack and A-bort go long for a pass from Day, elbowing and trash-talking stride for stride, stumbling, nearly falling they are laughing so hard. 'Jerry Rice,' Dime says as he jogs past Billy, then he kicks into gear and goes streaking off, looking back for Billy's pass. The end-zone crowd is really cheering now and why not, what fan hasn't dreamed of doing this very thing, a hell-all dash around the Valhalla of pro football fields? Bravo falls into a loose game of razzle-dazzle, modified tackle-the-man-with-the-ball with fluid or basically nonexistent teams and no apparent goal, just a bunch of guys tearing around the end zone, slamming into each other and laughing their asses off. And if it was just this, Billy thinks, just the rude mindless headbanging game of it, then football would be an excellent sport and not the bloated, sanctified, self-important beast it became once the culture got its clammy hands on it. Rules. There are hundreds, and every year they make more, an insidious and particularly gross distortion of the concept of 'play,' and then there are the meat-brain coaches with their sadistic drills and team prayers and dyslexia-inducing diagrams, the control-freak refs running around like little Hitlers, the time-outs, the deadening pauses for incompletes, the pontifical ceremony of instant-replay reviews, plus huddles, playbooks, pads, audibles, and all other manner of stupefactive device when the truth of the matter is that boys just want to run around and knock the shit out of each other. This was a mystery Billy's mother was never able to fathom. After having two daughters she couldn't accept why from the earliest age her son would purposely slam into walls, doors, shrubbery, wrestle the ottoman around the den, or spontaneously tumble to the ground for no apparent reason other than it is there. Football seemed a constructive outlet for this impulse, and at various times during his youth Billy played organized ball, 'organized' being the code word for elaborate systems of command and control where every ounce of power resides at the top. It seemed that football must be made to be productive and useful, a net-plus benefit for all mankind, hence the endless motivational yawping about teamwork, sacrifice, discipline, and other modern virtues, the basic thrust of which boiled down to shut up and do as you're told. So despite the terrific violence inherent in the game a weird passivity seeped into your mind. All those rules, all the maxims, all the three-hour practices where you mostly stood around waiting your turn to be screamed at by an assistant coach, they produced an almost pleasurable numbness, a general dulling of perception and responsiveness. In a way it was nice, constantly being told what to do, except after a while it got boring as hell, and at a certain age you started to realize that most of the coaches were actually dumb as rocks.

So fuck that, he was done with football after his sophomore year, except the Army is pretty much the same thing, though the violence is, well, what it is, obviously. By factors of thousands. But for the moment Bravo has found some measure of peace as they bounce off each other like lottery balls, great gouts of tension release with every hit and they are laughing like absolute maniacs. The end-zone crowd – the cheap seats, the rednecks, the blue-collar rowdies – they're standing and cheering them on. Bravo is running wild over hallowed ground and – *weird!* – nobody is stopping them. Then three obese men in Cowboys parkas and caps roll up in a stretch golf cart, and the fattest of the three, a guy with steel-framed glasses and swollen ass cheeks for jowls, yells at Bravo to *Get the hell off my field, NOW.*

'Get the HELL off his field!' Crack screams, and

Mango screams it back and in an instant all the Bravos are bellowing at each other, *Get the HELL off his field! His field, dude, get the HELL off his field! He wants his field back NOW! Get the HELL OFF!* They gather up the footballs with a geriatric shuffle-trot, pausing every couple of steps to scream *HELL!* and *FIELD!*, and the three fat guys just sit there and scowl. A couple of cops saunter over but don't say anything, and the Bravos keep yelling at the tops of their lungs because the bastard couldn't even be *nice* about it, couldn't append a civil *please* or gracious *thank-you* for these brave American soldiers, these *youngsters*, as General Colin Powell (ret.) calls them, these loyal, honorable youths who bared their breasts to the foe for the sake of your freedoms, you fat fuck, you disgrace to the notion of man-in-God's-image, you whale-ass keeper of other people's grasses. *Dude, maybe they don't hate our freedoms, maybe they hate our fat!*

The end-zone rowdies send up a boo when they see what's happening, a blowsy, cynical sort of *Screwed again!* howl. Norm & Co. greet the Bravos as they trot off the field. Norm is laughing. 'Sorry, fellas,' he says with that mouthful-of-salad chewiness, 'I should've warned you. Bruce is pretty touchy about his field.'

But isn't Norm the boss? So it seems like he could . . . Whatever.

'It's a really nice field,' A-bort says.

'Dude, best field you'll ever see,' says Crack. 'I

bet Mango'd love to have a run at that turf. Crank up the John Deere and go at it, I mean, you know, just being a Mex and all.'

'It's Astroturf, moron,' Mango points out.

'I'm just saying—'

'Ethnic clichés demean us all,' Mango says.

'All I'm saying is any beaner would love—'

'—to do your mother like I did?'

Norm is laughing. What cards these Bravos are, what a grab-ass band of brothers. Okay, so maybe they aren't the greatest generation by anyone's standard, but they are surely the best of the bottom third percentile of their own somewhat muddled and suspect generation. Over in the flats a network camera crew is setting up while two media-type women discuss 'the shoot.' The six cheerleaders are there, waiting. Josh is there, hovering, and Albert, texting. With a certain habituated weariness Billy notes that Major Mac is nowhere to be seen.

'Right here, guys,' calls the younger of the two women, who turns out to be the network producer for their *shoot*. 'Line up right along here.'

'Well, facing more this way,' says her middle-aged colleague, a high-ranking Cowboys PR executive who has the swat to call Norm 'Norm.' Intense women, these two, competitive, willful, dressed all in black, their faces set with the pinched look of angry vegans. Billy is angling to speak with Dime about the Faison situation, but Norm has glommed onto the sergeant and keeps him all to himself.

'I've got serious problems with Hollywood anyway,' says the Cowboys owner as everyone footsies around their marks. 'I think they're way out of step with the rest of the country, the concerns and value systems of mainstream Americans. Someone needs to get out there and start making films that reflect what America's really all about.'

'I think we need that,' Dime replies. 'I think the time is now.'

'Just the way they've been giving you the runaround, you start to wonder where their loyalties lie. Whether they really want America to win this war.'

'You start to think they might be a little gutless,' Dime observes.

'Listen, Ron Howard's made some great films, *Splash* is one of my all-time favorites. But for him and Glazer—'

'Grazer,' Dime corrects.

'—Grazer to say you have to set your story in World War Two, that's just outrageous.'

'They're playing hardball, sir, that's a fact.'

'World War Two gets its due, there've been plenty of great movies about World War Two. *The Longest Day, The Big Red One,* those are great, great movies. But Bravo's story is all about the here and now, and I think that context should be honored.'

'I think all of us would agree with you there, sir.'

'Listen, I sure don't see any signs of *Iraq fatigue* out there. The vast majority of Americans support this war, and they sure as heck support the troops fighting the war. If anybody has any doubts about that, they should just look at the reception you've gotten here today.'

The women herd Bravo into a quarter-circle line with garlands of cheerleaders on each flank. Norm and Dime stand front and center in the starring roles. There is a script, which everyone has memorized. 'Hold your footballs up, like this,' the PR woman instructs, clutching an imaginary football to her breast. Though it's dorkish and lame, the Bravos do it.

'No, lower,' says the producer.

'For Christ's sake,' moans the PR lady, rolling her eyes.

'Well it just looks unnatural up there. It doesn't look right.'

'We're at a football game, hel-*lo*? It looks completely natural.'

Presently everything is ready for the first take. Norm's personal videographer stands off to the side, filming Norm being filmed. 'Bravo squad would like to wish you and your family a Very HAPPY **THANKSGIVING,**' Dime booms, then veers off-script: 'And to our brother and sister soldiers out in the field, we say **PEACE THROUGH SUPERIOR FIREPOWER!**' Thus everyone is laughing when Norm, the cheerleaders, and all the Bravos shout, 'Go Cowboys!' but the media people are pissed. Excuse me, is that in the script? That is not in the script so don't say that, you can't say that, don't you know you can't say that? Dime apologizes. He mumbles something about getting carried away. Everyone settles in for take two.

'Bravo Squad would like to wish you and your family a Very HAPPY **THANKSGIVING!**' Dime starts, and then, oh God, he's doing it again, 'and to our brother and sister soldiers out in the field, we say, shoot first! SHOOT STRAIGHT! **PUNISH THE DESERVING!**'

'Yaaah, go Cowboys!'

Now the medias are really pissed. 'People, we've got four minutes to get this done,' the producer lectures them. 'I suggest you get serious real quick or we can forget it.' Norm is laughing as hard as the Bravos, but he urges them to settle down and play it straight. 'A lot of people out there want to hear from you,' he assures them. On take three Dime obligingly follows the script, but so primed are they for mischief that Lodis and Sykes bust up laughing. Take four goes smoothly until the end, when a fan leans over the front-row railing and screams, 'Chicago Bears suck horse cock!'

At this point a short break seems in order. Extra cops are summoned to secure the taping area. Billy keeps trying to speak with Dime, but Norm and the sergeant are talking again. Billy almost butts in – he's that desperate – but instead forces himself to fall back three paces as an exercise in impulse control. And runs straight into a huddle of cheerleaders.

'Whoa. Sorry!'

The cheerleaders smile and nod. There are three of them, two white and one black.

'Are you guys sisters?'

They hoot.

'Ooooh, how can you tell?'

'We thought it was our little secret!'

'Hey, it's obvious. You could even be triplets.'

More hoots. As with all the cheerleaders they are stunning specimens of buff femininity, soft where they are soft and firm where firm all in accordance with the Photoshopped ideal of fashion magazines, except these women are real. Jesus. Bullshit spews from his mouth, he has no idea what he's saying but they're laughing, so he must be doing all right. The cheerleaders stamp their feet and shirr wintry breaths through their teeth to dramatize how cold they are. 'Seniority,' they tell him when he asks why Faison wasn't included in the Thanksgiving shoot.

'She's brand-new, and everything goes by seniority. We get first dibs on TV spots based on years of service.'

'So the TV spots are a big deal?'

The girls shrug, make blasé.

'It doesn't hurt.'

'Hurt what?'

'Well, you know. Your career.'

'Ah. I didn't know cheerleaders have careers.'

'What's that?' one of the cheerleaders asks, pointing to, almost touching, Billy's shiniest medal.

'That's a Silver Star.'

'What's it for?'

Billy flails. He has no bullshit for this, nor anything else that will serve for polite conversation. 'For gallantry, I guess,' he says, then resorts to the language of the actual citation. 'For conspicuous gallantry and intrepidity in action against an enemy of the United States.'

The cheerleader gives him a blank look. 'Cool,' she says, and all three women abruptly turn away. Somehow Billy has killed the conversation. Did they think he was bragging? The medias order everyone back for take five. They find their marks and wait. And wait. And wait some more. Then groan when told there's a technical problem. They're instructed to stay put while the glitch is fixed.

'There's your man,' Norm murmurs, nodding at Albert pacing the sideline with the cell to his face. 'Looks like he's working it.'

'He's a machine,' Dime says. Standing just to the side and slightly behind them, Billy has no choice but to eavesdrop.

'How long have you been associated with him?'

'Well, officially about two weeks, I guess. That's when we met him face-to-face. Though we were doing e-mails and phone calls before that, while we were still in Iraq.'

'You've got a contract, I'm assuming.'

'We signed some papers, yes, sir.'

'And I assume it's been a positive experience so far?'

'Yes sir, we like Albert a lot. He really believes in our story. And he's doing everything he can to get us the best deal possible.'

Norm clears his throat and says nothing for several moments. Billy leans forward a couple of millimeters, anxious for someone to speak.

'Hilary *Swank*,' Norm says at last.

'Sir?' Dime inquires.

'Hilary *Swank*,' Norm repeats. 'Albert says she's one of the stars interested in your project.'

'Yes, sir.'

'He said she wants to play you.'

'Apparently so.'

'That strikes me as sort of nutty. What do you think?'

'I'll be honest, sir, I'm having a hard time getting my head around it.'

'They should stay true to the story, not go twisting it around just to suit some star's whim. I'll tell you frankly, the narcissism of Hollywood people never ceases to amaze me.'

'I only know what I read in the tabloids.'

'I don't think a whole lot of her as an actress anyway.'

'Ah.'

'I saw her in that movie with Schwarzenegger, the one where she plays his wife and he's in the CIA, but supposedly she doesn't know it? Kind of a silly movie. I didn't think much of that movie at all.'

'I think that was Jamie Lee Curtis, sir,' Dime says.

'Pardon?'

'I think that was Jamie Lee Curtis who played the wife, not Swank.'

'Really? Well. It was still a shitty movie.'

Billy happens to look at Albert just as he pockets the phone, his shoulders rising and falling in a tectonic heave. Such a gesture would seem to suggest defeat, but Billy thinks he looks more thoughtful than worried, like a consummate old pro plotting his next move. So *do* something, Billy silently urges, and he finds himself wishing the producer had more skin in the game. The deal craters, Albert goes back to L.A., back to his Brentwood home and his hot young wife and his office with the three Oscars sitting on the shelf. Meanwhile it's back to the war for Bravo, deal or no deal. Iraq has never been less than a life-or-death proposition for them, but the deal hanging in the balance seems to make it more so.

They nail the next take and everyone cheers, even the camera crew adds its own jaded bray. Norm doles out old-school high-fives. 'Hang on to those footballs,' he tells Bravo, 'they're yours to keep. But they'll look better with some ink on them, don't you think?' He grins. 'Follow me, men.'

XXL

They are huge. They could be a new species, or throwbacks to some lost prehistoric age when humans the size of Clydesdales roamed the earth. TV's toy-soldier scale doesn't do them justice, these blown-up versions of the human frame with their beer-keg heads and redwood necks and arms packing softball-sized bulges, plus something not quite right about their faces, their eyes too close or too far apart, a thumb-mashed puttiness to cheekbone and nose. All the parts are there but the whole is out of joint, a hitch of proportion, of cranial size relative to facial scheme, as if by achieving superhero scale the players have outstripped the blueprint of the human face.

'Arncha glad you aren't that guy's toilet seat?' A-bort whispers to Billy, nodding toward that pile of human spam known as Nicky Ostrana, the Cowboys' All-Pro offensive guard. Where else but America could football flourish, America with its millions of fertile acres of corn, soy, and wheat, its lakes of dairy, its year-round gushers of fruits and vegetables, and such meats, that extraordinary pipeline of beef, poultry, seafood, and pork, feedlot gorged, vitamin enriched, and hypodermically immunized, humming factories of high-velocity protein production, all of which culminate after several generations of epic nutrition in this strain of industrial-sized humans? Only America could produce such giants. Billy watches as tight end Tony Blakely pours an entire box of cereal into a mixing bowl, follows that with a half gallon of milk, and serenely falls to with a serving spoon. One. Entire. Box. Any other country would go broke trying to feed these mammoths, who blandly listen as Norm speaks from the center of the room. *Real American heroes . . . freedoms . . . that we might enjoy . . .* 'So let's give them our warmest Cowboys welcome,' Norm exhorts, and the team responds with a round of applause. For all their exalted status, the players are, technically speaking, Norm's employees, so Billy supposes they have to do what he says.

Norm turns to Coach Tuttle. 'George, would you mind if our guests got a few autographs while they're here?'

Coach answers with a marked lack of enthusiasm, 'That would be fine,' all but adding, *Then get the fuck out of my locker room.* He is a large, dour, slope-shouldered man, in size and shape not unlike an old bull walrus. His skin is the same oatmeal shade as his salon-tinted hair, a bushy quiff that he combs straight back for a retro Deep South prison warden look. On their way down to

230

the locker room Josh handed out Sharpies to the Bravos – *still* no Advil, he lashed himself for forgetting – and now the soldiers fan out to gather autographs.

'I wonder if Pat Tillman played with any of these guys,' Dime muses in a bright voice. Several players give him a look, but no one answers. So there's Dime, staking out his psychic territory, and there's Sykes and Lodis scurrying off to collect as many signatures as possible, and here is Billy, hanging back. He's never really seen the point of autographs anyway, and the players' size is such that he doesn't even want to look at them directly, much less approach in supplicant mode. He's not comfortable here. He feels exposed, diminished. If the painful truth be known, he feels less of a man right now than he did five minutes ago. The players seem so much more martial than any Bravo. They are bigger, stronger, thicker, badder, their truck-sized chins could bulldoze small buildings and their thighs bulge like load-bearing beams. Testosterone, these guys are cranking it, and their warrior aura ramps up exponentially as they assemble themselves for the game. As if these human mountains needed more bulk? Elaborate systems of shock and awe are constructed about their bodies, arrays of hip pads, thigh pads, knee pads, then the transformative lift of the shoulder pads, these high-tech concoctions of foams, fabrics, Velcros, and interlocking shells, with girdling skirt extensions to cradle mere mortal ribs. Tape for the

231

hands, tape for the wrists. Roll pads. Elbow pads. Pads for the forearm. The top shelf of each locker displays no fewer than four pairs of brand-new shoes.

All the gear, all this *stuff*, depresses Billy further. Such tedium it involves; the players probably spend more time getting dressed than the most pampered models and actresses, and they show it, they are surly and closed off, thoroughly into their suiting-up ritual. They don't want to be messed with, which Billy gets; it's a mental thing, the mental feeding off the physical, getting their heads set to deal some serious hurt because aggression against one's fellow man is not a casual thing. Dude, been there! Totally feeling it! He recognizes the process, even the hurt-music pounding from the lockers is the same, but starting a conversation along these lines would just seem like sucking up.

Billy gets Kervan McClellan's autograph because, well, he's standing right there and it would seem rude not to. He knows it's Kervan McClellan because his name and number are stenciled in jaunty script across the top of his locker. Billy moves on to the next player, Spellman Taylor, # 94. Tucker Rubel, # 55. DeMarcus Carey, # 61. The players are all business. They take the Sharpie and scrawl their names and most of them don't even look up. A few manage to nod when Billy thanks them. Indurian Kashkari, # 81. Tommy Budznick, # 78. Then Billy comes to Ed Crisco, # 99, an enormous white guy standing perfectly still while a trainer winches his shoulder pads tight. Crisco holds out his arms and doesn't speak, doesn't blink, just stares straight ahead like a beast of burden submitting to the harness for yet another day.

Billy opts not to bother Ed Crisco. Two pale, thin, completely hairless children are moving about the room collecting autographs, accompanied by their bravely smiling parents and a team representative for each family group. The kids' skin gives off a bleached silver glow, the radiance of cirrus at high altitudes. Whatever they have, it must be bad; Billy can't tell if they are boys or girls, so extreme is their condition.

He continues down the line. Durrell Sisson, # 33. D'Antawn Jeffries, # 42. Octavian Spurgeon, # 8. Octavian speaks as he takes the ball.

'What it do.'

'Solid. Yourself?'

Octavian nods. He is sitting in a chair in front of his locker, and save for his helmet he's completely suited up for the game. He's coiled, cool, broad through the shoulders and slim through the hips, with a long, tapering nose and high, almost delicate cheekbones. Elaborate tats crawl up his neck and twine around his arms, and a black do-rag is knotted at the nape of his neck. He scratches the pen across Billy's ball and hands it back.

'Thanks.'

'No probl'h. Yo, hang ona second.'

Billy turns back. For a second the Cowboy seems at a loss for words.

'Like, you been in Iraq an' all?'

'Um, yes.'

Again he seems to struggle for words. Billy is tempted to think the Cowboy is punch-drunk from years of taking blows to the head, but his eyes are quick and alert.

'So whas it like?'

'What's it like? Well, it's hot. Dry. Dirty. Boring as hell, a lot of the time.'

Octavian speaks in a slushy murmur. 'Butchoo, like, ona front line an' all? You been in some battle?'

'I've been in some battles, yes.'

D'Antawn and Durrell step over. They are the same physical type as Octavian, lithe, dark, supremely controlled. A look passes among the players, but Billy can't read it.

'Huh, fah real doe. But like you ever cap some-body you know of? Like, fire yo' piece and dey go down, you done that?'

That. It doesn't occur to Billy that he doesn't have to answer.

Yes, he says. The players glance at each other. Billy sees it is an intense moment for them.

'So whas it like? You know, like what it feel like?'

Billy swallows. The hard question. That's where he bleeds, exactly. Someday he'll have to build a church there, if he survives the war.

'It doesn't feel like anything. Not while it's happening.'

'Hunh. Yeah.' A few more players have drifted over. Billy realizes that the entire Cowboys starting secondary has gathered around. 'So whatchoo carry?'

'What do I carry? It depends. It depends on the mission and what my assignment is. Most of the time my weapon's the M4, standard semiautomatic assault rifle. A few times I've had the M240, that's a fully automatic, heavy-volume weapon, lays down nine hundred fifty rounds per minute. Then if you're riding top on the Humvee you're gonna be on the .50-cal.'

'M4, what kind a round it take?'

'Five-five-six mil.'

'You carry a side?'

'Beretta nine-millimeter.'

'You ever use dat?'

'Sure.'

'Like, up close?'

Billy nods.

'They issue you knives?' asks Barry Joe Sauls, a white guy old enough to have lost most of his hair.

'Ka-Bars,' Billy says. 'But you can carry pretty much any blade you want. A lot of guys get their own knives online.'

'What about AKs,' someone asks, 'you carry those?'

'AK's an insurgent weapon, we aren't issued those. Though plenty of guys've picked them up along the way.'

'They bad?'

'Bad enough. The AK fires a bigger round, so

there's more of a crush factor. You definitely don't wanna take an AK round.'

'Huh. Aiight.' Octavian glances at his teammates, chews his lip a moment. 'So what it do, you know, yo' M4. When you pop somebody.'

Billy laughs, not that it's funny. It's not anything, in fact. He wonders if nothing's an actual feeling, or just nothing.

'Well, it fucks them up.'

'Like, one pop? Stoppin' power what I'm gettin' at.'

'Body shot, no. It's a high-velocity round and usually passes right through. But they go down, yeah.'

'But they ain't dead.'

'Maybe not with a body shot. That's why we aim for the face.'

The players suck in their breath. 'Unh,' someone murmurs, as if biting into something juicy and sweet.

'The 240,' says Sauls, 'you said that's fully automatic. What does it do?'

'What does it *do*? Fuck, what can I say. The 240's pure evil.'

'Yeah?'

'You hit somebody with the 240, it fucking takes them apart.'

Before they can ask him anything else Billy says thanks good luck nice talking to you, and leaves. He is definitely done getting autographs, which more than ever seems like a dumb and pointless exercise. After some furtive casting about he spots Dime at the far end of the room, studying the giant greaseboard on which the team's depth chart is displayed. 'So if it's not a democracy,' Dime is murmuring as Billy approaches from behind, 'and it's not communist, then what is it?'

'What is what?'

'Nothing. Enjoying yourself, Billy?'

'I guess.' He sidles closer to Dime and lowers his voice. 'Some of these guys are crazy, Sergeant. Not right in the head.'

Dime laughs. 'And we are?'

Whatever. He notices Dime's football is bare of autographs.

'Sergeant, can we talk?'

'Yes.' Dime is back to studying the depth chart.

'It's kind of a personal matter.'

'I'm the best friend you're ever going to have.'

'Well, what happened is, well, I met a girl. Like, today. A little while ago. One of the cheerleaders, actually.'

A flummery *blat* sprays off Dime's lips. 'Congratulations.'

'Yeah, I mean, no, I mean we all did, I know. But this girl and I, Sergeant, we sort of connected.'

'Billy, don't be a moron.'

'No, Sergeant, we did. Something happened.'

Dime perks up. 'She blow you?'

'Well, no. But we made out.'

'Bullshit.'

'Swear to God.'

'Bullshit! When did this happen?'

Billy briefly describes the encounter, though for the sake of honor and decency he says nothing about Faison's orgasm.

'You bastard,' Dime says softly. 'You aren't lying, are you.'

'No, Sergeant, I'm not.'

'I can see that.' Dime starts laughing. 'You are a motherfucker, Lynn. Though how the hell you talked her into—'

'Actually I let her do most of the talking.'

'Brilliant. Smart man. I think you're gonna get laid a lot in your life, Billy.'

'Thanks. But what I wanted to ask you . . . well, the reason I wanted to talk . . .'

Dime eyes him patiently.

'Well, I don't wanna lose her, Sergeant. How do I keep from losing her?'

'*What?* Jesus Christ, lose *what*, Billy, how long were you with her, ten minutes? You guys mugged down, great, excellent, I'm really happy for you, but I don't think you've got anything to lose. She was being *nice*, all right? You're a hero, she was doing something *nice* for the troops. And we're on post as of twenty-two hundred tonight, so I don't know when you think you're gonna see her again. Tell you what, see if you can get her e-mail, maybe that way yall can e-fuck once we're back in Iraq.'

Billy feels sick. Of course Dime is right, it is absurd to hope for any kind of future with Faison, but then he thinks about how tenderly she cupped his cheek, how knowingly her hips absorbed his thrusts. Her wide-mouthed kisses. Her tearful eyes. Her bone-crushing climax. Not to be a shallow bastard, but how much realer does it get?

One of the equipment managers notices them standing there and asks would they like a tour of the equipment room. We'd love it, Dime says. Ennis, the man says, holding out his hand. He is a wiry sixty-year-old with a starter paunch and the tumbleweed twang of the native Texan. 'We sure are proud to have you boys with us today,' he says, leading them past the dispensary counter to a side door. 'Everybody treating you right?'

'Everyone's been excellent.'

'Glad to hear it. We sure try to take care of our special guests.' Inside the door they're hit with a stiff blast of plastic and leather smells.

'Whoa. How do you not get high in here?'

'Listen, open up on a Tuesday morning when it's been locked up for a day, man, you *will* get high.'

The equipment room is the size and dimensions of a small air-plane hangar, with row upon farther receding row of cabinets, shelves, scaffoldings for bins and crates, steam tables, work benches, step-ladders on wheels, and every fixture from carpet to doorknobs coordinated in team colors of blue and silver-gray, a very narrow palette. 'Now, you can't field a world-class football team without a world-class equipment operation,' Ennis declaims, and Billy suspects they're at the top of a well-honed tourist spiel. 'Football is an equipment-centric sport, and when you're talking about the four or five tons of materials we deal with here, inventory and organization are a must. You gotta have it to find it, right? And you gotta find it to use it, the best gear in the world won't do you any good if it's pulling down dust in a closet somewhere. And we're talking over six hundred categories of items here.'

'That sounds like a lot,' says Billy.

'It is, young man, you should see our travel list. It takes a team of detail-oriented individuals to work an operation like this. Zero tolerance for error, that's our standard.' They pause at the neatly racked jerseys in home and away colors. Ennis points out the spandex panels to ensure tight fit, the extra-long tails with spandex hems, the moisture-wicking qualities of the space-age fabric. Billy pulls out number 78 and holds it up by the hanger; they share a chuckle over its impossible size, enough fabric to clothe an average family of four. Then it's on to the shoes, an entire section of wall shelved floor to ceiling with shoes, shoes, shoes, shoes, and nothing but more shoes.

'Wow,' says Dime. 'Look at all the shoes.'

'Impressive, hunh. And we'll use 'em. We burn through close to three thousand pair a season, and that number goes up every year. Listen, at training camp? I've seen it so hot out there the shoes just fall apart, and these are top-quality product, not your Wal-Mart knockoffs.' Each player, Ennis continues, requires three kinds of Astroturf treads, one for dry, one for damp, and one for wet conditions, plus a molded-form shoe with fixed cleats for grass, plus another grass shoe with interchangeable cleats, four kinds of cleat styles for all different weathers. Then to the shoulder pads stacked on steam tables, stack upon stack and row upon row like bones in an Old World catacomb. Twelve styles, which is to say a style for each position, four sizes per style plus flak-jacket extensions plus infinite customizations possible. Now, your helmet. Most important piece of gear we have. The helmet is a world unto itself, a high-tech engineering marvel born of the latest in orthopedic and impact science. Outer shell made up of cutting-edge polymers, resins, and epoxies that can take a hit like *this*, **WHAM,** both soldiers jump back as Ennis slams the helmet to the floor with astounding violence. See, look here. Nothing. Impressive, hunh. Not quite your Kevlars, but then again my guys aren't dodging bullets. Inside, just as important, you can build an individual-type matrix of jaw pads, foam inserts, and air bladders to ensure perfect fit and maximum protection. Here, air pumps to inflate the bladders, there's your nipples right there along the edge of the shell. Even then we get concussions, lots of 'em. Those guys can hit. Here you've got your face masks, fifteen different styles, chin straps in six distinct configurations, mouth guards in a multiplicity of styles and colors. Quarterback helmets come equipped with wireless radio for instant coach-to-QB communication. Every week we strip off the helmet decals and put on new ones, clean the shells with SOS pads, polish them up with Future floor wax.

Lotta work, you bet. Chewing gum, we provide five flavors for the guys, you're looking at twenty twenty-five-hundred-count boxes right there. Velcro strips and tags here, to keep your gear snug and tight, you don't wanna be giving the enemy any handles to grab. Hip, thigh, and knee pads sorted by style, size, and thickness. Tact gloves for receivers, padded gloves for linemen. Orthopedic insoles, all sizes. Baseball caps. Knit caps. Electric drills for changing out cleats. Talcum powder. Sunscreen. Smelling salts. Twenty-two different kinds of medical tapes. Gels, creams, ointments, antibacterials, and antifungals. Coolers. Cartons of powdered Gatorade. Whoa ho, fellas, there's more. For cold-weather conditions such as we face today, skullcaps, thermal underwear, mittens, muffs, chemical hand warmers, cold-weather cream, thermal socks, heating units for the benches. Water-repellent thermal overcoats, specially designed to fit over shoulder pads. Rain ponchos, same design. We go through seven hundred towels per game, double that for wet or extra-warm conditions.

'Where do you keep the steroids?' Dime asks.

'Unh-unh, that's a dirty word around here. Now, game balls. As the home team we're responsible for providing thirty-six brand-new balls for the game, plus an additional twelve balls that get delivered directly from the manufacturer to the refs, which they'll mark "K" for exclusive use in the kicking game.' Farther along, practice jerseys and shorts here, sweatshirts and pants there. A quick look into the industrially scaled laundry room, then on to the coaches' gear. Notebooks, clipboards, small and large greaseboards, Magic Markers, grease pens, headphones, bullhorns. A shoebox-sized bin filled with shiny silver whistles, another full of Casio stopwatches. Wireless communication and video in there, always locked down, for obvious reasons. When we're on the road it takes two semis to haul all our gear, we're talking nine, ten thousand pounds of equipment.

By the end even Dime seems a little dazed. It is simply too much, these mind-numbing quantities of niche-specific goods and everything labeled, sorted, sized, collated, stowed, and stacked, a testament to the human genius for logistics and inventory control. Billy's headache is worse, from breathing all the fumes, he guesses, and as they backtrack the length of the equipment room he feels a tightness in his chest, a stunting of breath as if his lungs have been short-sheeted somehow. Allergies, maybe; or maybe a heart attack? The thought arrives on the wings of a mental shrug; he's too caught up in the mysteries of the equipment room to waste much time fretting over his health. How does it all come to be, that's what he wants to know, not just the how but the why of all this *stuff*. Only in America, apparently. Only America could take such a product-intensive sport and grow it into the civic necessity it is today.

He's not sure what he's just seen in here, but it seems to have made him sick.

'You know,' Ennis shyly confides, 'I did a couple years in the Army, back in the day. But pretty much ever-body did. We had a draft, you know.'

'Vietnam?' Dime asks.

'Just missed it. Got out in '63 and damn glad I did. I knew guys who didn't come back from there.'

'Lotta those,' says Dime.

'You ain't kidding. I just want you fellas to know how much we appreciate the job you're doing over there. If it watten for yall God knows what'd be going down here, I guess we'd all be praying to Allah and wearing towels on our heads.'

'You got anything for a headache?' Billy asks. 'Advil? Aleve?'

'Tons of the stuff,' Ennis replies. 'You hurtin'? Listen, son, I'd love to help you out, but I can't, legal liability and all that. Every single item that goes through those windows' – he points to the dispensary counter – 'gets recorded and tallied. You wouldn't think it, but even just a couple of little pills could lose me my job.'

'That's okay,' Billy says. 'I don't want you to lose your job.'

Ennis apologizes again. At the door to the locker room Dime asks him to autograph his ball. Ennis rears back. He's chuckling but his eyes are wary.

'Why you want that? I'm just an old equipment hand, nobody cares about my autograph.'

'As far as I'm concerned you run the team,' Dime answers, so Ennis laughs and takes the Sharpie and signs his name to Dime's ball, and this will be the only autograph that Dime collects today. Back in the locker room the players have almost finished suiting up. The air is a pungent casserole of plastics, b.o., farts, melon-woody colognes, and the rancid-licorice reek of petroleum liniments. Norm stands on a chair in the center of the room and calls Bravo to him, then instructs the team to circle around. Bravo has heard its quota of speeches today but here comes another, what can you do. The players dutifully approach, and as they assemble here in the middle of the room Billy tries to imagine the vast systems that support these athletes. They are among the best-cared-for creatures in the history of the planet, beneficiaries of the best nutrition, the latest tech-nologies, the finest medical care, they live at the very pinnacle of American innovation and abun-dance, which inspires an extraordinary thought – send them to fight the war! Send them just as they are this moment, well rested, suited up, psyched for brutal combat, send the entire NFL! Attack with all our bears and raiders, our ferocious redskins, our jets, eagles, falcons, chiefs, patriots, cowboys – how could a bunch of skinny hajjis in man-skirts and sandals stand a chance against these all-Americans? Resistance is futile, oh Arab foes. Surrender now and save yourself a world of hurt, for our mighty football players cannot be stopped, they are so huge, so strong, so fearsomely ripped that mere bombs and bullets bounce off their bones of steel. Submit, lest our awesome NFL show you straight to the flaming gates of hell!

'Now, I just want to say,' Norm begins, but there's some chatter at the back, and someone's boom box is burbling Ludacris. 'SHADDUP!!!!!' Coach Tuttle bellows, and for a moment they could all be back in eighth-grade gym.

'Well,' Norm resumes, 'I hope everyone's had a chance to visit with the very special guests we have with us today, the soldiers of Bravo squad. I'm sure by now everybody is familiar with their story – under fire, pinned down, large numbers of their colleagues killed or wounded, but these young men, the young soldiers of Bravo, they would, not, quit. There on the banks of the Al-Ansakar Canal they were faced with the biggest challenge of their lives, and thanks to God's help they rose to the challenge, and they've made our entire country proud. I had the privilege of speaking with President Bush not long ago, and he . . .'

The players have tuned out. Billy can see it in their eyes, that flatness, the rheostatic dialing down of brains in sleep mode. Having stood in formation for countless hours, he knows the look when he sees it.

'. . . so maybe our challenges are different. Maybe

the challenges we face aren't as dramatic as theirs, but they're the tests God has put in our path to mold us into the people He wants us to be. Now, I know we've hit a rough patch in our season. We're struggling. Things haven't gone exactly to plan, but it's what we do when we're down, after we've taken the hit, that determines who we are. So do we say forget it, just pack it in . . .'

A cloud of chemical wrath seems to rise off the players. A Norm lecture is just an everyday pain in the ass, but to be shown up by Bravo? Contrasted? *Compared?* This stirs the bloody reservoirs of sibling rivalry. *Why can't you be more like him?* Not that Bravo wants anything to do with this, but it's too late to opt out of Norm's Sunday school lesson.

'. . . and so I challenge you, *all* of you, every individual on this team, from Vinny and Drew right down to Bobby' – a gurgling cry rises from somewhere behind the players, Bobby himself; Bravo met him earlier, the Cowboys' famous, mildly retarded ball boy – 'to rise to the challenge, to overcome. To be as brave and determined in facing the challenge as these young soldiers were facing theirs. It starts today, gentlemen. No time like the present. So let's go out there and kick some Bear butt!'

'Yeah!' someone cries, and the players erupt, more oomph in the cheer than Billy would expect. Then again, they are professionals. To lead them in prayer Norm calls on Pastor Dan, a pleasantly weathered man dressed in the same shiny track suit as the coaches. *Dear God,* prays the reverend in a melodic southern voice, all crushed-velvet vowels and chunky consonants, *please help us play to the best of our abilities. To conduct ourselves on the field in a way that fulfills your word and honors our faith. Guide us, lead us, protect us . . .* With his eyes shut tight Billy is thinking of Shroom's comment that the Christian Bible is mostly a compilation of old Sumerian legends, not something he particularly needed to know at the time but which has afforded some solace during these past two weeks of practically nonstop public prayer. America loves to pray, God knows. America prays and prays and prays, it is the land of unchained prayer, and all this ceremonial praying is hard on Billy. He tries, but nothing comes. You close your eyes and bow your head and at the first *thee* or *thine* it's like the signal cuts out, not so much as a stray spritz of static comes through. The thought that others might be having the same problem doesn't much help, but awareness that something came before – Sumerians, Hittites, Turkmen, an entire UN of ancient civilizations – that the thee-thine formula might not be the last word? – for some reason he finds comfort in this.

So who were the Sumerians?

'I'll tell you about it sometime,' Shroom said, strapping on his IBA. 'But not right now.'

Not now and not ever, as it turned out. Shroom swore off video games and rarely watched TV. Instead he read. All the time. 'I am constructing my personality,' he said of his reading. Even for whacking off he had an authoritative text, the ancient Egyptians this time, who believed – *no lie! I swear!* – that the first, the original, the nameless primeval god who created the universe did so through an act of masturbation, in effect bringing the cosmos into being by virtue of sheer ejaculatory force.

A-men, says Pastor Dan. **Tooooooh min-UUUUUUTTTTTES,** hollers an assistant coach, and in these final moments of preparation Billy finds himself invited, no, *summoned,* he'll think later, by a nod and lowdown flick of the wrist to Octavian Spurgeon's locker. Octavian, Barry Joe, a few others, they stand there with a stillness that suggests momentous events. Billy wishes he wasn't holding his dorky souvenir ball.

'Lissen, we wanna know . . .' Octavian's voice is barely a murmur. 'We, like, we wanna do somethin' like you. Extreme, you know, cap some Muslim freaks, you think they let us do that? Like we ride wit yall for a week, couple weeks, help out. Help yalls bust some raghead ass, we up for that.'

Billy sees that they are, up. They're up for it. He tries to imagine the world inside their heads, and can't.

'I don't think it works that way.'

'*Wha?* Whatchoo mean, we offerin' to *help,* fah *free.* Nobody gotta pay us, we ain't askin' fah that.'

Billy knows better than to laugh. 'I just don't think the Army's gonna be too interested in that.'

'Hunh. Sheee-uh. Or why anybodys even got to know. Like we ride wit yall a couple weeks, nobody even gonna know we there. We offerin' to help, yalls sayin' you doan need the help?'

'Billy!' Mango calls. 'We're going.'

Billy nods and turns back to Octavian. 'Sure we could use the help. But – look, you wanna do extreme things, join the Army. They'll be more than happy to send you to Iraq.'

The players snort, mutter, cast pitying glances his way. *Fuck that. Shee-uh. Hell to the naw naw naw* . . . 'We got *jobs*,' Octavian impresses on him, 'this here our *job*, how you think we gonna quit our *job* go join some nigga's army? Fah like, wha, three *years*? Break our contract an' all?' Hilarious. They're laughing. Little squeals and snuffling yips escape their mouths. 'Go on,' Octavian says, waving Billy away. 'Go on now. Yo' boy over there callin' you.'

THIS IS EVERYTHING
THERE IS

So Billy decides first chance he gets he'll give his ball away. It's mere minutes before kickoff and the teams are on the field doing stretching and calisthenics, and Norm himself is leading Bravo along the main concourse, showing the skin, sprinkling some star power on the instantly smitten masses. All grudges, gripes, and man-on-the-street critiques melt like suet under the heat-lamp glow of his celebrity. Yo, Norm! Norm! We gonna do it today, Norm? Boyz by three, make it happen for me, Norm! It is the parting of the waters as the fans make way in a rippling furl of cell phone flashes, Norm striding through it all with his head held high and that same pleasant smile for everyone. Texas Stadium is his turf, his castle; no, his actual kingdom. A real king is rare these days but here Norm reigns supreme, and Billy sees how little it takes to make the peons happy, just a glimpse, a wave, a few seconds in his presence and they're stoked on that good strong celebrity dope.

Meanwhile Billy is looking for a certain kind of kid to give his football to. Not one of the money kids, nobody who could be on TV, tanned, smooth skinned, dazzlingly orthodontured, with the long clean limbs and good face that denote the genetic home run. No, he's looking for a little redneck kid, an undergrown runt with ratty hair and nails chewed down to bloody nubs, about as aware at ten years old as a half-bright dog and basically miserable, but doesn't know it yet. Billy is looking for himself. Outside the Whataburger booth he spots him, a smallish, twitchy kid with a head too big for his neck, ill dressed for the cold in a thin cotton hoodie and fake falling-apart Reeboks, and why the *fock* would parents spend hundreds of dollars on Cowboys tickets when their son lacks a proper winter coat? It is infuriating, the psyche of the American consumer.

'Excuse me,' he says, approaching, and the kid quietly freaks – *what'd I do?* His parents wheel about and what a pair they are, thick, soft, dull, clearly useless as humans and parents. Billy ignores them.

'Young man, what's your name?'

The boy's jaw falls off. His tongue is a liverish white.

'Son, tell me your name.'

'Cougar,' the boy manages.

'Cougar. You mean like the animal?'

The boy nods. He can't quite look Billy in the eye.

'Cougar! Radical name!' A lie; Cougar is a ridiculous name. 'Look, Cougar, I've got an autographed ball here, bunch of the Cowboys signed it for me down in the locker room. But I'm going back to

Iraq and I'll just lose it there, so I want you to have it. Are you all right with that?'

Cougar risks a quick look at the ball and nods. Clearly he thinks this is the setup for some low humiliation, a wedgie, a firecracker down the back.

'All right, young man. Here you go.'

Billy hands him the ball and walks away with no lingering, no looking back. He is sick of the squishy sentiments of the day and will not let this be yet another Moment. Mango has held up and is waiting for him.

'What'd you do that for?'

'Dunno. Just felt like it.' And on reflection he does feel better, though a strange melancholy fills his new mood. For several moments the two Bravos walk along saying nothing, then Mango gives his ball to a passing kid.

'Like, fuck their autographs,' Billy says. Mango laughs.

'If they win the Super Bowl we just gave away about a thousand bucks.'

'Yeah, well, a thousand bucks says they ain't winnin' no Super Bowl.'

Still no word about halftime, other than Norm's promise to 'showcase Bravo to the fullest extent,' which could be as harmless as standing there while your name is called, or as terrifying and onerous as . . . the mind boggles. Rumor has it that there are multiple bars in the owner's suite. The lower-ranking Bravos agree among themselves to get stinking drunk, then Billy thinks of Faison and privately amends his side of the bargain to sort of drunk. It was an impulse invitation – come watch the kickoff from my box! Norm has clearly caught a bad case of the Bravo disease, that burrowing spirochete of home-front zeal that inspires strippers to give free lap dances and upper-class matrons to bloodlust. A round of applause greets Bravo as they file into the suite, the polite, pro forma wittering of soft hands taking on real sizzle and pop. Yaaay for Bravo! Hooo-ray for the troops! Mrs Norm is there to greet them at the door, and if she's perturbed by the sight of ten largish, panting, booze-breath guests piling into her already crowded suite, she has the good grace not to show it.

So glad you could join us. So many friends eager to meet you. Billy takes it all in at a glance, the blue carpet, the blue furnishings with silver accents, giant flat-screen TVs implanted in every wall, two bars, hot and cold buffets, white-jacketed waiters, then a couple of steps down there's a second level that replicates the first, and farther on a steep-pitched bank of stadium seats, rows of upholstered chairs stair-stepping down to the glassed-in front and its postcard view of the playing field. The money vibe can be felt at once, a faint hum, a kind of menthol tingling of the lips. Billy wonders if wealth can be caught like a germ, just by virtue of sheer proximity.

Make yourselves at home, Mrs Norm is murmuring. *Help yourselves to refreshments.* Say no more, ma'am. Bravo breaks en masse for the free liqs as Dime mouths 'just one' with a stern look, but before the soldiers can bar up, Norm climbs onto a chair – he's got a thing for chairs? – and delivers a little speech about

    troops
       heroes
          guests
and just how

           pleased
             proud
               happy

is the entire Oglesby family for the opportunity on this Thanksgiving Day to

                  thank
                   honor
                    acknowledge

the Bravos for their service. Billy notes how closely his fellow guests listen to Norm's speech, how keen their facial expressions of faith and resolve. The men look wise, relaxed, in great shape for middle age, possessed of the sure and liquid style that comes of long success. They have good hair. They've wrinkled well. The women are slim and toned and internationally tan, their makeup sealed with a Teflon coat of cool. Billy tries to imagine the formula of birth, money, schools, and social savvy that lifts people to such a rarefied station in life. Whatever it is, they make it look easy just standing there, just by being who they are in this special place, being warm and safe and clean, being guests of Norm. Most have a drink or a plate of food in their hands. *Evil*, Norm is saying. *Terror. Mortal threat. A nation at war.* His speech describes the direst of circumstances, but at this moment, in this place, the war seems very far away.

'They have to leave us shortly,' Norm is saying, 'they're going to take part in our halftime show, but while they're here let's give them a big Texas welcome.' Everyone claps, hoots, cheers, let's get this party started; the ballers are feeling that good Bravo vibe. Billy is hailed by someone's craggy-faced granddad.

'Soldier, I'm damn glad to meet you!'

'Thank you, sir. It's a pleasure to meet you too, sir.'

'March Hawey,' the man says, sticking out his hand. The name and face are vaguely familiar to Billy, the kindly rumpled sag of his narrow features, the elfin tweak of his eyes and ears. Billy would hazard March Hawey is one of those celebrity Texans who's famous mainly for being rich and famous.

'Listen, when the news broke that night – when they started running that video of yall taking care of business? – that was one of the biggest thrills of my life, no lie. It's hard to put into words just what I was feeling, but it was, I don't know, just a beautiful moment. Margaret, tell him how I was.'

He turns to his wife, who looks a good twenty years younger, a statuesque six-footer with stiff blond hair and skin taut as a soufflé.

'I thought,' she says, *I thot* in the tart British accent of Joan Collins trashing a rival on a *Dynasty* rerun, 'he'd lost his *mind*. I hear him *screeeeeming* in the media room and I *ruuuussshhh* downstairs to find him *standing* on my good George Fourth library table, in, my *Gohd*, his *cowboy* boots, doing this *Rocky* thing' – she raises her arms and gives a couple of spastic fist-pumps – '"Mahch," I'm shouting, "Mahch, love, dear, what-*EVER*,"' – wot-*EVAH* – '"on *earth* has gotten *into* you?"'

Several couples have joined them. Everyone is smiling, nodding, evidently they are used to such antics from their good friend March.

'It was cathartic,' Hawey says, and Billy carefully repeats the word to himself, *cathartic*. 'Seeing yall John Wayne that deal, it's like we finally had something to cheer about. I guess the war'd been depressing me all this time and I didn't even know it, till yall came along. Just a huge morale boost for everybody.'

The other couples vigorously agree. 'You're among friends,' a woman assures Billy. 'You won't find any cut-and-runners here.'

Others chime in with variations on the theme. Margaret Hawey stares at Billy with enormous blue eyes that never blink. He senses that whatever judgment she's passing on him will be strict, swift, and without appeal.

'Let me ask you something,' Hawey says, leaning into Billy's space. 'Is it gettin' better?'

'I think so, sir. In certain areas, yeah, definitely. We're working hard to make it better.'

'I know! I know! Whatever problems we're having aren't yalls fault, we've got the finest troops in the world! Listen, I supported this war from the beginning, and I'll tell you what, I like our president, personally I think he's a good and decent man. I've known him since he was a kid – I watched him grow up! He's a good boy, he wants to do the right thing. I know he went into this with all the best intentions, but that crowd he's got around him, listen. Some of those folks are good friends of mine, but you've gotta admit, they've made one royal effing mess outta this war.'

This prompts much head-shaking, many sad mumbles of assent. 'It's been a fight,' Billy says, wondering how he might get a drink.

'I guess you'd know that better than anyone.' Hawey leans in again, closer now, but Billy stands his ground. 'Lemme ask you something else.'

'Yes, sir.'

'About the battle. But I don't wanna get too personal.'

'It's okay.'

'But it's just natural for people to wonder when somebody does something as fine and brave as you, I mean, we all saw the video. We know how rough it was out there. And for a fella to just go running through the middle of all that' – Hawey chuckles, shakes his head – 'we can't help wonderin', weren't you *scared*?'

The group shivers with a titillatory chill. Only Margaret is unmoved. She stands there watching Billy with those huge blue eyes that won't cut him any slack.

'I'm sure I was,' he answers. 'I know I was. But it happened so fast I didn't have time to think. I just did what my training told me to do, like anybody else in the squad would do. I just happened to be the guy in position.' He assumes he's done, but they're quiet, still primed for the payoff, so he has to think of something else. 'I guess it's like my sergeant says, as long as you've got plenty of ammo, you'll probably be okay.'

This does it; they throw back their heads and roar. In a way it's so easy, all he has to do is say what they want to hear and they're happy, they love him, everybody gets along. Sometimes he has to remind himself there's no dishonor in it. He hasn't told any lies, he doesn't exaggerate, yet so often he comes away from these encounters with the sleazy, gamey aftertaste of having lied.

New people join their group, others leave in a vigorous round robin of socializing. Billy is constantly shaking hands and forgetting people's names. Major Mac and Mr Jones are talking near the cold buffet; Mr Jones seems not to realize that the major couldn't hear a tank go by. Beyond them is the high-powered group of Albert, Dime, Mr and Mrs Norm, and several of what seem to be the gathering's heaviest hitters. Albert is laughing, quite at his ease, and that's as it should be, Billy reflects. Albert swims with the Hollywood sharks, he can handle this Dallas crowd standing on his head, but it's Dime who Billy focuses on now, the way he listens, holds himself, slips in a word here and there. 'Watch him,' Shroom used to tell Billy. 'Watch him and learn. Davey's spooky. He knows how to see in the dark.' According to Shroom this was Dime's particular gift, this intuiting ray he brought to the war, but the only way he could develop it was by testing himself, always putting it out there. The insurgents couldn't kill large numbers of Americans as long as the troops stayed on their bases; the flip side was, the only way the Americans could track down and kill insurgents was by leaving their bases, which made the whole business of patrols and checkpoints and house-to-house searches an exercise in the using up of nerve. But it was a form of war Dime forced them to accept. Bravo dismounted more than any squad in the platoon, in the entire battalion, probably. They could be anywhere, and Dime would order them clear to walk a couple of klicks with the Humvees lagging, following at a crawl. 'You won't know shit sitting inside that damn box,' he'd say. They were gambles, these little forays, they could easily get you killed, but they were Dime's way of banking knowledge, instinct, experience against the day when everything and everybody would be on the line.

Not that the Bravos liked it. Plenty of days they hated Dime for putting them out on the street. It seemed so pointless, the risk far out of proportion to the possible benefit, but if any Bravo bitched Shroom told him to shut up and do his job. So out they'd go, tromping through markets, humping down side streets, randomly walking into houses to find what they might find. One such day they're on the street and a small gang of boys approaches, they're fourteen, maybe fifteen years old, aspiring hustlers with fuzzy mustaches and not much better than rags for clothes. 'Mister,' they cry, swaggering up to Bravo, 'give me my pocket! Give me my pocket!'

'What the fuck,' Dime says, staring at them.

'I think they want money,' Shroom says, turning to Scottie for confirmation. Scottie was Bravo's interpreter at the time, so named for his resemblance to the former Chicago Bulls star Scottie Pippen. Scottie speaks to the boys.

'Yes, they want money. They say they are hungry, they are asking you to give them money.'

'"Give me my *pocket*"?' Dime laughs.

'Yes! Yes! Mister! Give me my pocket!'

'No, no, no, that's fucked, that's not the way you say it. Tell them I'll teach them how to say it, but we aren't giving them any money.'

Scottie explains. Yes! the boys cry. Yes! Okay yes! So there in the street Dime conducts a little

English lesson. 'Give me money.' Repeat. *Give me money.* 'Give me five dollars.' *Give me five dollars.* 'Give me five dollars, bitch!' *Give me five dollars beech!* 'Thank you!!' *Thank you!!* 'Have a nice day!!!' *Haf a naice day!!!* The boys are laughing. Dime is laughing. The rest of the Bravos are laughing too, laughing as they scan rooflines and doorways with their weapons raised.

'Thank you!' the boys cry when the lesson is done, and each boy ceremoniously shakes Dime's hand. 'Thank you! Mister! Thank you! Give me money!' And so they're bellowing as they walk down the street, Give me money! Give me five dollars! Give me five dollars beech!

'Wow,' Shroom says in hushed, trembling tones of New Age feelingness. 'Dave, that was just beautiful, man. That was a beautiful thing you did.'

Dime snorts, then lards up his voice with smarm. 'Well, you know what they say. Give a man a fish, he eats for today. But *teach* a man to fish—'

'—*and he eats for a lifetime,*' Shroom concludes.

Over time Billy came to see this kind of humor as another facet of his education in the realms of global bullshit. Abruptly he feels Shroom's loss like an awl in the gut, meanwhile noting on a parallel mental track how grief comes and goes, fattens and thins like the moon freestyling across foreign skies.

'I don't like it,' March Hawey is telling the group. 'I think it's bad psychologically and bad strategically. It's fine to keep the American public aware and all, but you keep harping on the terror thing twenty-four/seven, after a while you get a negative feedback loop going.'

'But March,' a woman objects, 'they want to kill us!'

'Sure they do!' March cuts Billy an amused look. 'The world's a dangerous place, nothing new in that. But you keep putting it in the public's face, *terrR, terrR, terrR,* that's bad for morale, bad for the markets, bad for anybody.'

'Except Cheney,' someone quips, and the group titters.

'Right,' March allows with a slow smile. 'Ol' Dick's got his own way of doing things. He and I've been friends a long time, but I have to say, we haven't talked in a while.'

A Jack and Coke arrives for Billy. How did they know? Somehow they knew. He nods and sips his drink and makes agreeable-sounding noises as people express their thoughts and feelings about the war. Here at home everyone is so sure about the war. They talk in certainties, imperatives, absolutes, views that seem quite reasonable in the context. A kind of abyss separates the war over here from the war over there, and the trick, as Billy perceives it, is not to stumble when jumping from one to the other.

'I'll say this for nina leven,' a man confides to him, 'it shut the feminists up.'

'Ah.' Billy consults his drink. The feminists?

'You bet,' the man says. 'They aren't so interested in being "liberated" now that we're under attack.

There's certain things a man can do that a woman just can't. Combat, for one. A lot of life boils down to physical strength.'

'Maybe we need a war now and then to get our priorities straight,' a second man says.

Clusters of subconversations orbit the main conversation, which is always about the war. Billy meets the man who owns – Coolcrete? Pavestone? One of those backyard leisure surfaces. The man tells Billy that the recent uptick in insurgent attacks is a sign that the tide is turning our way. 'It shows they're desperate,' he says. 'We're hitting them where it hurts.' 'Could be,' Billy concedes as an oak log of an arm falls across his shoulders, and their host, Norm himself, is snugging up to him. The group falls silent. Anticipation beams from every smiling face.

'Specialist Lynn.'

'Sir.'

'Is everything satisfactory?'

'Yes, sir. It's all good.'

People laugh as if he's said something terribly witty. Norm squeezes the back of his neck, gives his head a couple of shakes. 'What an honor,' he tells the group, 'what a privilege, having these young heroes with us today.' Billy catches a yeasty whiff of bourbon on Norm's breath. 'They are the pride and joy of our nation, and *this* one' – he gives Billy another couple of brain-rattling shakes – 'this young man, well, let me put it this way. Is anybody surprised that a *Texan* led the charge at the Al-Ansakar Canal?'

The group answers with a sharp burst of applause. Everyone in the vicinity turns and joins in. Billy is helpless, Norm has him pinned like a specimen to a board and there is nothing to do but stand there and smile like a shit-eater caught in the act. 'Look, he's blushing!' a woman cries, and it must be true, Billy can feel the heat pulsing off his face. Thus misery is taken for wholesome modesty.

'I think we've got another Audie Murphy on our hands,' March says, grinning at Billy. 'Now there was a great American hero. And a Texan.'

'He's a hero,' Norm agrees, hugging Billy close. 'That's why he wears the Silver Star. And I have it on good authority he was recommended for the Medal of Honor, but some desk jockey at the Pentagon shot it down.'

A zithering hum of disapproval roils the crowd. Billy hopes none of the Bravos is watching, but there is Dime placidly taking it all in, and Albert is smiling, no, smirking when he catches Billy's eye, and in this way Billy is given to understand the source of the leak. As soon as he can Billy excuses himself and heads for the nearest bar. Coke, he says. Just a plain regular Coke. After a minute Dime is squeezing in next to him.

'Billy, don't be flaking.'

Billy lifts his chin. 'That was bullshit.'

'What was bullshit?' They speak in barely audible murmurs.

'That. The Medal of Honor shit.'

'Oh, that. Billy, chill. You're a certified star.'

'Albert—'

'Albert knows what he's doing.'

'How the fuck did he even know?'

''Cause I told him, dipshit. Any booze in that drink?'

'No.'

'Good, I want you halfway sober for halftime. And no they haven't told me what we're supposed to do.'

Billy hunches over his drink. 'It's all bullshit.'

'You're being awfully touchy, Billy Sue.'

'Why the fuck did you tell him?'

Dime doesn't even bother answering that. They stay turtled up to the bar. The moment they turn away people will start talking to them.

'You know that old man you were talking to?'

'Well, yeah.'

'March Hawey.'

'I know who he is.'

'Mr Swift Boat himself. Dude's famous.'

Billy stares straight ahead. He won't give Dime the satisfaction of knowing he didn't know.

'Richer than God, and talk about tied in. So watch yourself around him.'

'Why should I watch myself?'

'Because in case you haven't noticed this is a highly partisan country we live in, Billy. Those guys are smart, they know who the enemy is. They aren't fooled by a couple of bullshit war medals.'

Billy glances at his chest, considering his medals in this possibly sinister light.

'I'm not the enemy.'

'Oh hooooo, you don't think? They decide, not you. They're the deciders when it comes to who's a real American, dude.'

Billy takes a sip of his Coke. 'I'm not planning on running for president, Sergeant.'

Dime nods, studies the skyline of liquor bottles behind the bar. 'You wanna know what my old granddaddy told me once, Billy?'

'What.'

'He said, Son, you want to live a good life, do these three things. Number one, make a lot of money. Number two, pay your taxes. And number three, stay out of politics.'

With that Dime picks up his drink and leaves. Billy tries to enjoy a quiet moment by himself, but his headache comes thundering into the void. He wonders if it's a migraine – how would he know? A migraine or something worse, something tragic and fatal, a brain tumor, cancer, a massive stroke. *Poor fella. So young. Died a virgin.* Tragic. In any case the headache is practically bad family history by now, a terrible pain and burden but who would you be without it? Cheers and applause suddenly roll through the suite, and too late he remembers not to turn from the bar.

'They just showed you on the Jumbotron!' a woman exclaims, and for a second Billy despairs – they showed him huckled up to the bar? – then realizes it was a repeat of the American Heroes graphic.

'I think it's wonderful yall are being honored today,' the woman enthuses.

'Thank you,' says Billy.

'It must be so exciting, traveling around the country!'

'And all at taxpayer expense,' a man – her husband? – adds. He chuckles, which means it's a joke. Ha ha.

'It's nice,' Billy says. 'It's been an experience. We've met a lot of nice people.'

'What stands out in your mind the most?' the woman asks. She is a bright-eyed, professionally peppy blonde of indeterminate age, blessed with dramatic cheekbones and a smile like silver lamé. Billy would guess she's a sales whiz of some sort, a high-powered realtress or Mary Kay honcho.

'Well, all the airports for sure,' he says. This gets a laugh from the group, seven or eight people have gathered now. And all the malls, he could add, and the civic centers and hotel rooms and auditoriums and banquet halls that are so much alike across the breadth of the land, a soul-squashing homogeneity designed more for economy and ease of maintenance than anything so various as human sensibilities.

'I really liked Denver,' he goes on, 'with all the mountains and everything? That was a beautiful place. I wouldn't mind going back there and spending some time someday.'

'Weren't you in Washington?' the realtress prods.

'Oh, yeah. Washington was awesome, definitely.'

'Isn't the White House so majestic?'

'It is, with all the history and everything. And I guess I never thought about people living there? I know, like why do they call it the White *House*, duh. But it was amazing, more like you'd expect a really elegant mansion to be.'

The realtress agrees; she and 'Stan' have been guests of the Bushes several times and it is truly an awe-inspiring place. Was there a dinner? There wasn't? That's a shame because formal state dinners are really quite the production, what with all the pomp, the protocol, the mingling with royalty and heads of state. Maybe next time, Billy says. Then someone asks are we winning and that opens the floor for discussion about the war, and Billy gets passed around like everybody's favorite bong. Why are they killing their own people? Why do they hate us? Why is it always seventy-two virgins? His brain switches to autopilot and his eye wanders. He spots Lodis over there, babbling about God knows what while his audience listens in polite horror. Then there is Crack hitting on someone's teenage daughter and doing pretty well from the looks of it, and Sykes staring clench-jawed into empty space, and Albert yukking it up with Mr and Mrs Norm. It dawns on Billy that his headache might be purely psychological, the naked ape of his mind asserting itself like the gorilla in that Samsonite commercial.

'. . . it's a code of honor that goes back to the Anglo-Saxon tradition, we don't attack unless we're attacked first. We aren't barbarians. *We* didn't attack on nina leven. Or at Pearl Harbor, for that matter.'

'No, sir.' Billy reenters the world of conversation.

'But when we *are* attacked, there's hell to pay, am I right?'

'I guess you could say that, yes sir.'

'I mean, if someone shoots at you guys, say you're on patrol and a sniper gets off a couple of rounds, what do you do?'

'We hit him with everything we've got, sir.'

The man smiles. 'There you go.'

Hey! Hey! Hey! People are shouting for silence, it is the summons for all persons to shut up and attend the singing of 'The Star-Spangled Banner.' Everyone turns to face the field. The sky has darkened to primer gray, a kind of dull celestial blister capping the stadium's paper-lantern glow. The light pools and thickens at field level in a lime-tinted aspic sheen. The singer and color guard step out from the home sideline with its legions of players, coaches, refs, medias, and VIPs, along with a circus train's worth of equipage. They could be an ancient army laying siege somewhere. The color guard presents the flag. The Bravos scattered about the suite snap to attention.

Ohhh-

oh

Ohhh-oh, ohhh-oh, ohhh-oh, an echo banging around the bruised hollows of your brain, *ohhh-oh*

270

as if you're standing at the mouth of a cave calling tentatively, hopefully into the dark. *Ohhh-oh, anybody there?* Ohhh-oh, ohhh-oh, ohhh-oh. That gulpy reggae drop-beat, *ohhh-oh,* Pavlovian cue for bursting of dopamine bombs and xylophone trills up and down your spine. Then the trapdoor springs beneath your feet

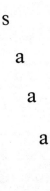

followed by the save, the safety net bottoming out and that *wheee* of a launch into the higher realms

seeeee???

youuuu

caaannn

Thence to the ritual torturing of a difficult song. The singer is a young white woman, raven haired, slight of frame, a C&W warbler with a classic high-plains heartbreak twang. Billy heard some-where that she is the latest American Idol, and

271

like all the American Idols pint-sized or not she is blessed with a huge barrel vault of a mouth.

WHHHHHHAAAAAAAAAATTTTTTTT
so
PRRRRRROOOOUUUUUDDDDLLLLL
YYYYY

Billy holds his salute. He makes it a point to think about Shroom and Lake and the hot red blur of that terrible day, but he's also, because he's young and still hopeful for his life, scanning the sideline far below for Faison. He systematically ticks his gaze from one cheerleader to the next, no, no, no, no, a dozen no's then *yes* and his head spins like a car on ice, an airy *whoosh* into sideways acceleration with all the nausea, the panic, the full butthole pucker, it is a roller-coaster ride to oblivion. Then his eyes snap back to their sockets and aim straight for Faison, sturdy little Koosh ball of female plenitude with that slash of amber hair like a lava spill, her right-hand pom-pom held to her heart. She is singing, even from here he can see her mouth moving, and so powerful is the bond between them that he leans several inches in her direction. *Dude, she was into you.* The singing triggers a soft detonation at his core, molten parts of him are flying everywhere and his ears ring to the tune of blast harmonics that only he can hear, but what is 'The Star-Spangled Banner' if not a love song?

                 at

            th'

         twi-

                  i-

                  i-

                  i-

                       i-

              light's

                    last

                         gleam-

                    ng

He has to remember to breathe. He feels calm
and agitated all at once, self-awareness teased to
such a screaming pitch that his skull might split
at any moment, and he moans, it is just too much
to hold in. The realtress glances his way and
answers with a sympathy moan. The next moment
she steps over and puts her arm around his waist,
and they stand so joined, Billy saluting, sweating,
standing ramrod straight, the realtress singing with
her right hand held to her heart and her left
clamped to Billy's hip.

Ore

            the RAAAMMMM-

prts

        we

          watched

This lady can really belt it out. Tears the size of lug nuts are tumbling down her cheeks but that's the kind of thing war does to you. Sensations are heightened, time compressed, passions aroused, and while a single dry-hump might seem a slender reed on which to build a lifetime relationship, Billy would like to think this is where the logic leads. He made Faison tremble, he made her *come*, surely there's meaning in that. Given all the shifting variables of existence, it's insane to plan or hope for any one particular thing, yet somehow the world comes to be every day. So if not this, then what? So why not this?

      GAAAAVE PROOOOOF

               through   the

NIIIIIGHT

The realtress pulls him closer. He doesn't sense that it's a sexual thing at all; it feels too brittle, more like a codependent clinginess or mothering clutch, which he can handle. Part of being a soldier

274

is accepting that your body does not belong to you.

Bah-ha-neeerrrrrrrr

   yeh-het
                      waaaaa-eh-eh-

      aaaaaavvve

Ore th' Laaa-ha-annnndddd of the Freeeeeeeeee
– HEEEEEEEEE

Then the pause, the teetering catch at cliff's edge, followed by the vocal swan dive—

      And th' ho-ommme
                              of
                                    thu-

      huuuh

Never do Americans sound so much like a bunch of drunks as when celebrating the end of their national anthem. In the midst of all the boozy clapping and cheering perhaps a dozen middle-aged women converge on Billy. For a second it seems they'll tear him limb from limb, their eyes are cranking those crazy lights and there is nothing they wouldn't do for America, torture, nukes, worldwide collateral damage, for the sake of God and country they are down for it all. 'Isn't it wonderful?' the realtress cries as she holds him tight. 'Don't you love it? Doesn't it make you just so proud?'

Well, right this second he wants to weep, that's how desperately proud he feels. Does that count? Are we talking the same language here? Proud, sure, he thinks of Shroom and Lake and all the blood-truths of that day and starts brainstorming quantum-theory proofs of *proud*. Yes ma'am, proud, Bravo has achieved levels of proud that can move mountains and knock the moon out of phase, but why, please, do they play the national anthem before games anyway? The Dallas Cowboys and the Chicago Bears, these are two privately owned, for-profit corporations, these their contractual employees taking the field. As well play the national anthem at the top of every commercial, before every board meeting, with every deposit and withdrawal you make at the bank!

But Billy tries. 'I feel full,' he says, and the women cry out and a pillowy sort of scrummage ensues with much hugging and pawing, many cell phone snaps, three or four conversations going at once and more than one woman shedding actual tears. It is a heavy Group Moment and about as much as he can handle, and when it finally tapers off he puts his head down and makes for the lower level because, like Custer's line of retreat at Little Bighorn, there's really no place else to go. People smile and greet him as he moves through the crowd. Someone holds out a drink, which he takes; later he'll realize they were merely waving at him. He comes to the bank of stadium seats and starts down the stairs. Three of his fellow Bravos are hunkered down on the bottom row, a refuge, a small redoubt amid this crowd of dangerously overstimulated civilians.

'Jesus Christ,' Billy says, dropping into a seat.

The other Bravos grunt. Being a hero is exhausting.

'Bears won the toss,' A-bort announces. 'Up fifty already, homes.'

Holliday snorts. 'You dah man, A. Showin' some real fine savvy with that call.' He turns to Billy. 'Where's Lodis?'

'Up there.'

'Actin' a fool?'

'He's doing all right. Any word about halftime?'

The other Bravos grimly shake their heads. They're all feeling it, not just the usual perfor- mance anxiety but the soldier's innate dread of cosmic payback. They've accomplished two weeks of remarkably glitch-free events, so perhaps the natural or even necessary climax of the *Victory Tour* – like they've been saving up! – will be the mother of all fuckups on national TV.

The Cowboys kick off to the Bears. Touchback. From the twenty-yard line the Bears run off tackle for three, up the middle for two, then a weakside sweep for four, but there's a flag. Between plays there is nothing much to do except watch bad commercials on the Jumbotron and worry about halftime.

'Do you think we're being rude?' Mango asks. Everyone looks at him.

'Sitting down here by ourselves. Not mingling or anything.'

'Rude as fuck,' Day says.

'Let's put up a sign,' A-bort suggests. '"Dysfunctional Vets, Leave Us Alone."'

They watch a few plays. Mango keeps sighing and squirming around. 'Football is *boring*,' he finally announces. 'You guys never noticed? It's like, start, stop, start, stop, you get about five seconds of plays for every minute of standing around. Shit is *dull*.'

'You can leave,' Holliday tells him. 'Nobody say you got to be here.'

'No, Day, I do got to be here. I gotta be wherever the Army says I gotta be, and right now it's here.'

The Bears punt. The Cowboys return to the twenty-six. There is a long wait while the chains are moved and the football replaced. The offense and defense trundle onto the field. The offense huddles while the defense mills around, huffing and puffing with their hands on their hips. Goddamn, Billy thinks, Mango's right. Between plays is sort of like sitting in church, if not for the infernal blaring of the Jumbotron everybody would keel over and fall asleep. One of the Filipino waiters comes by and asks would they care for anything. The Bravos check to make sure Dime isn't lurking, and since he isn't they order a round of Jack and Cokes. Billy chugs his accidental cranberry vodka and

278

keeps a fond eye on Faison. The drinks arrive. They help it be not so much like church. The Cowboys advance to the Bears' forty-two, then lose sixteen yards when Henson takes a sack, and Billy begins to intuit the basic futility of seizing ground you can't control.

'*Please* tell me there's no booze in those drinks,' Dime wharls. The Bravos jump. Dime drops into the seat next to Billy, a pair of binoculars swinging from a strap around his neck.

'Not hardly,' says A-bort. 'We were about to complain.'

'C'mon guys, I told you—'

'Yo Dime,' Day breaks in, 'Mango says football is boring.'

'*What?*' Dime instantly rounds on Mango. 'What the *fuck* do you *mean* football is *boring,* football is *great,* football kicks every other sport's *ass,* football's the fucking *pinnacle* of the sports world. What're you trying to say, you like *soccer?* A bunch of fruits running around in little shorts and knee socks? They play for ninety minutes and *nobody ever scores,* yeah, sounds like a lot of fun, the game of choice for the vegetally comatose? But *fine,* if you'd rather watch *fut-BOLL,* Mango, you can just go the fuck back to Meh-*hee*-co.'

'I'm from Tucson,' Mango answers mildly. 'I was actually born there, Sergeant. You know that.'

'You could be from Squirrel Dick, Idaho, for all I care. Football's *strategic,* it's got *tactics,* it's a thinking man's game in addition to being goddamn

279

poetry in motion. But you're obviously too much of a dumbfuck to appreciate that.'

'That must be it,' Mango says. 'I guess you've gotta be a genius—'

'Shut UP! You're hopeless, Montoya, you are a disgrace to the cause. I bet it was sad fucks like you who lost the Alamo.'

Mango giggles. 'Sergeant, I think you're a little confused. It was the—'

'Shut! I don't wanna hear any more of your gay revisionist crap, so just *shut*.'

Mango bides a couple of beats. 'You know, they say if the Alamo'd had a back door, Texas never woulda—'

'SHUT!'

The Bravos titter like a bunch of Cub Scouts. The Cowboys punt, but there's a penalty so they do it again, then everybody stands down for a TV time-out. Dime has the binoculars to his face.

'Which one is she?' he murmurs, understanding this is a private, no, a sacred matter.

'To the left,' Billy says in a low voice, 'down around the twenty. Kind of blondish reddish hair.'

Dime swivels left. The cheerleaders are doing a hip-rock fanny-bop routine, a fetching little number to pass the time. Dime watches for a while, then with the binoculars still to his face he extends his hand to Billy.

'Congratulations.'

They shake hands.

'Lady is bangin'.'

'Thanks, Sergeant.'

Dime continues to watch.

'You really mugged down with that?'

'I did. I swear, Sergeant.'

'You don't have to swear. What's her name?'

'Faison.'

'Last or first?'

'Uh, first.' Billy realizes he doesn't know her last.

'Umph. Damn.' Dime chuckles to himself. 'Depths and depths in young Billy. Who'da thought.'

When Dime leaves Billy asks if he can borrow the binoculars, and with grand, silent solemnity Dime drapes the lanyard around Billy's neck as if anointing an Olympic champion. Billy has a fine time with the binoculars. Mostly he keeps them trained on Faison, tracking her dance routines, her strenuous pom-pom shaking, her arm-waving exhortations to the crowd. The binos conjure a strange, delicate clarity from the material world, a kind of dollhouse fineness of texture and detail. So framed, everything Faison does is sort of miraculous. Here, she gives her hair a coltish toss; there, idly cocks her knee, thumps her toe on the turf while conferring with her sister cheerleaders. Billy conceives an almost delirious tenderness for her, along with sweet-sour roilings of nostalgia and loss, a sense of watching her not only from far away but across some long passage of time as well. Which means what, this melancholy, this mournful soul-leakage – that he's in love? The bitch of it is there's no time to figure it out. He and Faison need to talk – he needs her number! Along with her e-mail. And her last name would be nice.

'Hey.' Mango is nudging him. 'We're gonna hit the buffet. You comin'?'

Billy says no. He just wants to sit here with the binoculars and watch everything. The game doesn't interest him at all but the people do, the way the steam, for instance, rises off the players like a cartoon rendering of body odor. Coach Tuttle stalks the sidelines with the addled look of a man who can't remember where he parked his car. A sense of relaxing omniscience comes over Billy as he studies the fans, a kind of clinical, gorillas-in-the-mist absorption in how they eat, drink, yawn, pick their noses, preen and primp, indulge or rebuff their young. He lingers on all the hot women, of course, and spots no fewer than six people dressed up in turkey costumes. Often he catches people staring into space, their faces slack, unguarded, verging on fretfulness, fogged in by the general bewilderment of life. Oh Americans. Oh my people. Then he swings back to Faison and his vitals turn to mush. She's not just hot, she's *Maxim* and Victoria's Secret hot, she is world-class and he needs to get a plan together. A woman like her requires means—

'There's my Texan!'

He looks up. March Hawey is coming at him, sidling down the row. He starts to rise but Hawey palms his shoulder and guides him back down. He sits next to Billy and props his feet on the railing, and Billy immediately conceives a lust for his cowboy boots, a pair of lustrous sea-green ostrich quills with toecaps of silver filigree.

'How you doin'?'

'Really well, sir. And you?'

'All right, except I wish our boys would get their butts in gear.'

Billy laughs. He's only a little bit nervous, much less than he'd expect sitting next to a man who changed the course of history. Mr Swift Boat. He wonders if it's impolite to talk about that, not that he knows much about it one way or the other. Then there's the question of why he's even sitting here with Billy.

'Somebody said you're from Stovall.'

'Yes, sir.'

'Yall got some excellent dove hunting out that way. Some kinda weed yall got out there – guss-weed? gullweed? Big old tall yellow thing with these long seed pods, all *kind* a birds on that, doves love that stuff. You know what I'm talking about?'

'Not really, sir.'

'You're not a hunter?'

'No, sir.'

'Well, we had some great days out there. I'm telling you, man, we slayed 'em.'

Hawey asks if he can 'borry' the binoculars. In short order he reveals a whole repertoire of endearing senior tics – nose-snuffling, cuff-shooting, soft glottal pops. He smells of talcum powder and clean starched cotton, and wears a diamond horseshoe ring on his right hand. His wispy gray hair flops across his forehead in boyish Huck Finn bangs.

'You got any money on the game?' He's twiddling the focus back and forth.

'No, sir. Some of the guys do.'

'You don't bet?'

'No, sir.'

Hawey cuts him a glance. 'Smart man. We work too hard for our money just to throw it away.' He smiles when Billy asks what business he's in. 'Oh, buncha things,' he says, handing the binoculars back. 'Energy's our core business, production and pipeline, we've been doing that close to forty years. Do some real estate, a little on the hedge fund side, some arbitrage and whatnot.' He chuckles. 'And every once in a while we go raiding, if we see something we like. You interested in business?'

'I don't know. Maybe. After the Army. But not if it's going to bore me to death.'

Hawey sits up with a yelp and whacks Billy's knee. 'Man, I sure hear that. Why do it if you aren't having fun? In my experience the most successful people truly love what they do, and that's what I tell young people when they ask my advice. If you wanna make money, go find something you enjoy and work like hell at it.'

'That sounds like a good philosophy,' Billy ventures.

'Well, it fits my personality. Luckily I found a line of work I like, and I've been fortunate to have some success at it. You know, in a way it's like a game.' He pauses as the Cowboys go deep. The receiver stretches, snags the ball with his fingertips, then bobbles it out of bounds. 'What it boils down to is predicting the future, that's what business basically is. Seeing what's coming and getting the jump on everybody else, timing your move just right. It's like a puzzle with a thousand moving parts.'

Billy nods. This actually sounds interesting. 'So how do you do it?' he asks bluntly, thinking, What the hell. 'How do you get the jump on all those other guys out there trying to do the same thing?'

Hawey is chuckling again. 'Well, fair question.' He sits back and ponders for a moment. 'I guess I'd say, independent thinking. And inner peace.'

Billy smiles. He thinks Hawey might be putting him on.

'Inner peace – you need to know who you are, what you want out of life. You have to do your own thinking, and for that you better know who you are, and not just know but be secure in it, comfortable with yourself. Plus you gotta have discipline. Stamina. And luck sure helps. A little luck counts for a lot, including our great good luck of being born into the greatest economic system ever devised. It's not a perfect system by any means, but overall it's responsible for tremendous human progress. In just the past century alone, we've seen something like a seven-to-one improvement in the standard of living. I'm not saying we don't have problems, we've got a helluva lot of problems, but that's where the genius of the free market comes in, all the drive and talent and energy that goes into solving those problems. Now, look at this stadium, all this, the crowd, the game.' Hawey's arm sweeps left to right, then he points at the sky and the Goodyear blimp dangling in the early winter gloom. 'This is everything there is, you know what I'm sayin'? I'm not like that guy who goes around saying greed is good, but it can sure as heck be a force for good. Self-interest is a powerful motivator in human affairs, and to me that's the beauty of the capitalist system, it makes a virtue out of an innate human flaw. It's why you're gonna live better than your parents, and your kids are gonna live better than you, and their kids better than them and so on, because thanks to our system we're going to keep on finding more ways, easier and better ways, to solve the problems of living and accomplish so many things we never even dreamed of.'

Billy nods. America has never made so much sense to him as at this moment. It *is* an exceptional country, no doubt. As with the successful launch of a NASA space probe, he can take pleasure in the achievement, even feel some measure of partic-ipatory pride, all the while understanding that the mission has absolutely nothing to do with him.

'Now,' Hawey continues, 'right now we're going through a pretty rough patch. Two wars, the econ-omy's basically in the tank, the whole mood of the country's down. But we'll get through it. We shall overcome. Our system's been proving its resiliency for over two hundred years, and you youngsters, yall have a lot to look forward to. I think it's going to be an exciting time for you. If I could be your age – how old are you?'

'Nineteen, sir.'

Hawey has opened his mouth to speak, but he pulls up short. He looks at Billy as if puzzled, not profoundly so, just stumped for the moment.

'Nineteen. You sure act older.'

'Thank you, sir.'

'Shoot, I feel like I'm talking to a twenty-six-year-old lawyer, just the way you handle yourself.'

'Thank you, sir. I appreciate it.'

Hawey turns to the game. It seems he's lost his train of thought, but a moment later he's coming back at Billy.

'Is it true they put you up for the Medal of Honor?'

'My CO did, yes sir.'

'What happened with that?'

'I don't know. Higher tubed it, that's all they told me.' Billy shrugs. Whatever bitterness he feels is mostly secondhand.

'You know, I was never tested that way. Was too young for World War Two, though I remember it well. Now, Korea . . .' Hawey clears his throat, lets the thought die a natural death. 'You know things most of the rest of us will never know. The experiences you've had, you and your buddies . . .' Again he fails to finish the thought. Billy knows what they mean, these false starts, these snags of the psyche that stop a certain kind of *Victory Tour* conversation dead in its tracks. The old men struggle, and he can't help them. There's nothing he can say. He's learned it's best just to act like nothing's going on.

'Well,' Hawey says with the forced good cheer of a man shaking off bad news, 'I'm just proud to be able to spend this time with you. Nineteen years old, hell, I didn't know my ace from my elbow when I was nineteen.' He wishes his grandsons were here so they could meet Billy and see what a fine role model etc., etc., the laudatory verbiage is all fine and good but Billy would rather be learning something useful and new, or how about a job offer, that would be nice. *Come work for me! Let's get rich! I'll show you how it's done!* Hawey is still gassing about his grandsons when Faison flashes onto the Jumbotron, a Mount Rushmore–sized Faison leaning into the camera, smiling, tossing her head, shimmying those glorious pom-poms right in Billy's face and he can't help it, he sags in his seat and groans. In an instant Hawey sees what's going on.

'Um-umph, now there's a healthy girl.' He chuckles and taps Billy's knee, acknowledging the things a young man needs to stay alive. 'Goodness gracious, look out now. Norm's got some show dogs, don't he.'

BILLY AND MANGO
ARE OUT FOR A WALK

At the end of the first quarter they are asked to leave the suite. The Mexican ambassador is coming with his sizable entourage and the place is already packed to code, so somebody has to go. Norm apologizes. He seems truly distressed. 'You should see the security this guy rolls with,' he tells Bravo, shaking his head. 'I guess it's a drug war thing, but still. We're not too shabby on security ourselves.'

'Plus you've got us,' Sykes points out, 'sir.'

'That's right! We do! We've got the finest fighting men in the world right here! Oh man, if there was any way you guys could stay . . .'

Bravo is cool with it. Bravo could give a shit, basically. After big good-byes and a final round of applause Josh takes them back to their seats. Out come the cell phones, the iPods, the spit cups and dip. It's raining, sort of, the air pilled with a dangling, brokedick mizzle into which umbrellas are constantly being raised and lowered, up, down, up, down, like a leisurely game of whack-a-mole.

'Whoa, they scored.' Mango nods at the Jumbotron. Cowboys 7, Bears 0. 'When did that happen?'

Billy shrugs. He's not cold, which isn't to say he would mind being someplace warm. He finds two new texts on his cell. Kathryn: *Where u sitting?* Pastor Rick: *U r in our prayers 2day this special day of thanx. Lets talk b4 u leav overseas.* Pastor Rick, the tanned, portly founder of one of the largest megachurches in America, did the invocation for Bravo's rally at the Anaheim Convention Center. In a moment of – weakness? delirium? – Billy sought him out after the rally for an emergency counseling session. Something in the invocation had struck Billy as real, and while the rest of the Bravos signed autographs and posed for pictures, Pastor Rick and Billy sat down backstage and talked through Shroom's death. Shroom lying there wounded. Shroom sitting up. Shroom collapsing in Billy's lap, then his eyes zeroing in on Billy with such urgency, with so much pressing news, then the fade and his soul releasing, *whoom,* as if the life force is a highly volatile substance, contents stored under pressure.

'When he died, it's like I wanted to die too.' But this wasn't quite right. 'When he died, I felt like I'd died too.' But that wasn't it either. 'In a way it was like the whole world died.' Even harder was describing his sense that Shroom's death might have ruined him for anything else, because when he died? when I felt his soul pass through me? I loved him so much right then, I don't think I can ever have that kind of love for anybody again. So what was the point of getting married, having kids, raising a family if you knew you couldn't give them your very best love?

Billy cried. They prayed. Billy cried some more. He felt better for a couple of hours, but as day turned into evening and the hurt seeped in he found there was nothing for his mind to hold on to. What exactly had the pastor *said*? Billy remembered only the sound of it, a gauzy pambling and tinkling like easy-listening jazz. A couple of follow-up phone calls yielded similar uselessness, but now Pastor Rick won't let him go. He keeps calling, texting, sending e-mails and links. Billy gets what's in it for Pastor Rick; it's cool for the reverend to have a 'pastoral relationship' with a soldier in the field, it gives him cred, shows a stylish commitment to the issues of the day. Billy can hear the good pastor of a Sunday morning kick-starting his homily with a piece of Billy's soul. 'I was communicating the other day with one of our fine young soldiers who's serving in Iraq, and we were discussing blah blah blah . . .'

Billy answers Kathryn, deletes Pastor Rick. Here on his right, Mango can't get comfortable. He hunches over, flops back, peers left and right, twists around for a buggy look behind.

'Goddamn it,' Billy says, 'be still. You're making me nervous.'

291

'So stop being nervous.'

'You looking for something?'

'Yeah, your momma.'

'Fuck that, *your momma*. My momma's a nun.'

Mango laughs and sits back. He checks out the game clock and groans. Being honored feels a lot like work and it's worse out here on the aisle, sitting point for the Bravo-citizen interface. Yes sir, thank you sir. Yes ma'am, having a great time, absolutely. Billy passes programs down the row for everybody to autograph and has to make conversation while they come back. *It's getting better, don't you think? It was worth it, don't you think? We had to do it, don't you think?* He wishes that just once somebody would call him baby-killer, but this doesn't seem to occur to them, that babies have been killed. Instead they talk about *democracy, development, dubya em dees.* They want so badly to believe, he'll give them that much, they are as fervent as children insisting Santa Claus is real because once you stop believing, well, what then, maybe he doesn't come anymore?

So what do *you* believe in? Billy doesn't so much wonder as feel the question thrust upon him. Ha ha, well, okay. Jesus? Sorta. Buddha? Hm. The flag? Sure. How about . . . *reality.* Billy decides the war has made of him a rock-solid convert to the Church of What It Is, so let us pray, my fellow Americans, please join me in prayer. Let us pray for the many thousands gone, and those to follow. Let us pray for Lake and his stumps. Pray for

A-bort's SAW, that it may never jam in battle. Pray for Cheney, Bush, and Rumsfeld, father, son, and holy ghost, and all the angels of CENTCOM and the Joint Chiefs of Staff. Pray that it's really about the oil. Pray for armor for the Humvees. Pray for Shroom, who may or may not have eternal life in heaven but who is most definitely fucking dead here on planet Earth.

Billy sits up. He supposes he's been flaking. He cranes for a look down the sideline where Faison should be, but he's too close to the field and doesn't have the angle. For several minutes he tries to concentrate on the game, but it's too slow, like riding an elevator that stops on every floor. It's not like you're supposed to watch the actual game anyway, no, you watch the Jumbotron, which displays not just the game in real and replay time but a nonstop filler of commercials, a barrage of sensory overload that accounts for far more content than the game itself. Could it be that advertising is the main thing? And maybe the game is just an ad for the ads. It's too much anyway, what they want from it. Such a humongous burden the game has to bear, so many advertising dollars, such huge salaries, such enormous outlays for physical plant and infrastructure that you can practically hear the sport groaning under the massive load, and the idea of it stresses Billy out, the gross imbalance triggers a tweezing in his gut like the first queasy tugs of a general unraveling. He thinks back to his Moment in the equipment room, when all those cumulative tons of gear tried to smother him and there was Ennis doing the play-by-play for his demise, babbling about size-style-color-model-quantity and every-thing crammed into that ten-minute spiel, in one *breath* it seemed like, and even now Billy can feel his chest constrict.

He figures Ennis for batshit, but who wouldn't go crazy holding all that inventory in his head. Billy has these visions sometimes, these brief sightlines into America as a nightmare of super-abundance, but Army life in general and the war in particular have rendered him acutely sensitive to quantity. Not that it's rocket science. None of the higher mathematics is involved, for war is the pure and ultimate realm of dumb quantity. Who can manufacture the most death? It's not calculus, yo, what we're dealing with here is plain old idiot arithmetic, remedial metrics of rounds-per-minute, assets degraded, Excel spreadsheets of dead and wounded. By such measures, the United States military is the most beautiful fighting force in the history of the world. The first time he saw this demonstrated up close and personal sent him into a kind of shock, or maybe what they mean by awe. They were taking small-arms fire from somewhere above, sloppy, sporadic, deadly nonetheless. Finally it's sourced to a four-story apartment building down the street. There are flower pots in the windows, laundry strung from the sills. 'Call it in,' Captain Tripp radioed to Lt., so Lt. calls in the strike, two 155 mm HE rounds engage and the whole building, no, half the block goes down, *boom*, problem solved in a cloud of flame and smoke. So screw all the high-tech, precision-guided, media-whore stuff, the only way to really successfully invade a country is by blasting it to hell.

'Let's bounce,' Billy murmurs to Mango, and they're off, burning up the stairs two at a time.

'Where we going?'

'To see my girlfriend.'

Mango snorts. On the concourse they hit Papa John's for beers, then start walking.

'So where's this girlfriend?'

'You'll see. Shut up and drink your beer.'

'You never told me about no girlfriend, dawg.'

'Well I'm telling you now, *dawg*.'

'What's her name?'

'You'll see.'

'She hot?'

'You'll see.'

'She's here?'

'No, Arizona. Of course she's here, dumbfuck, how else we going to see her?'

The concourse is teeming with fans. The natives are restless. It has been a frustrating game thus far and they blow off steam by spending money. Happily there is retail at every turn so the crowd doesn't lack for buying opportunities, and it's the same everywhere Bravo has been, the airports, the hotels, the arenas and convention centers, in the down-towns and the suburbs alike, retail dominates the land. Somewhere along the way America became a giant mall with a country attached.

They take the section 30 tunnel off the main concourse and bomb down the aisle, shooting the gap of this human sea of fannies in the seats.

'Billy, where we going?'

'She's down here.' Billy is sucking in deep drafts of air, oxygenating his blood to counteract the booze. God forbid his new girlfriend should think him a drunk.

'Billy, what the fuck.'

'I told you she's down here.'

'Billy, dawg, come on. Dude, you've lost it.'

'Unh-unh, she's down here. She's a cheerleader.'

Mango actually screams, which makes it all the sweeter when Faison gives a little jump and yells Billy's name. The front-row walkway sits a good ten feet above field level; Billy leans over the railing and calls down to her.

'*Now* are you cold?'

She grins and shakes her head, hair tumbling everywhere. 'No, it feels great! They say it's supposed to snow!'

'This is my buddy Marc Montoya.'

'Hi, Marc!'

'*Say hello, numb nuts.*'

'Hello!'

'I'm so glad yall came to see me!' she calls up to them. 'You havin' a good time?'

'We're having a great time! Hey, you were on TV! They showed you on the Jumbotron!'

Seeing how happy this makes her crushes him a little. This is where the vital part of her energy goes, into the semi-mystical, all-consuming, positive-thinking hustle for exposure and notice, the miracle moment of prime time that will lead to the big break. She wants to be on TV. She wants to be a star. So how a common grunt like him is supposed to compete with that—

'You looked great,' he tells her, and she beams. 'That trippy little step,' he says, and breaks out a male approximation of her pom-pom routine, and this is funny, a U.S. soldier in dress uniform doing a shimmy-shimmy hip-slip sideways glide. She laughs; Mango is laughing too, half-draped on the railing he's laughing so hard. Billy has never known such happiness, and if thousands of fans at his back are watching, no matter. Let the entire world be witness to his love, except now a couple of security guys are walking up, telling the Bravos they have to leave.

'What, you don't like my dancing?' Billy says, but they just stare, all badass and bacdafucup, two doughy, middle-aged white guys with CORVINGTON SECURITY printed on their nylon bomber jackets, service-issue .38s bulging at the hip. Billy laughs. This makes it worse. He would guess they are moonlighting cops from some hick suburb, for they emanate the worst of both worlds, rural sloth plus urban malevolence.

'We're not terrorists,' Billy deadpans, pushing it.

'Move,' says one of the cops. 'Now.'

'We're just talking to my friend down there.'

'I don't care if you're talking to the president, you can't stand here.'

'You're blocking their view,' says the other cop, indicating the front row. 'These people paid good money for their seats.'

'What if they paid bad money?' says Mango, getting into the spirit, and the careful way the cops turn to him hums with all kinds of possibilities. For nothing Billy would gladly bust their heads, it's that fast, adrenal valves shoved full on and his brain hot-wired every which way, and wouldn't that do it, he thinks, busting their faces in, putting the truth of himself out there for all the world to see. If they make a move – but they don't, and Billy's homicide moment passes. He calls over the railing to Faison:

'These guys are saying we have to go.'

She's walked over and is right below them now. 'I think you better.' She's worried, Billy realizes. She's fearful of a scene.

'So I'll see you!' he calls down.

'At halftime!' She sends up a killer smile. 'I'll look for you on the field!'

He doesn't understand but nods anyway. Sure, on the field, in the stands, Brazil, wherever. He feels like he's known her all his life and loved her even longer. The Bravos mad-dog the cops with one last stare and head for the main concourse, where Mango staggers around like he's been maced. 'Billy,' he moans, 'Billy, Billy, a *cheerleader*?

Oh God she's fuckin' beautiful, Billy, how'd you get with that?'

Mango's slavering makes Billy cherish her even more. 'I don't know. We met at the press conference and just started talking.'

Mango turns wistful. 'She really likes you, man. You can tell just by the way she looked at you, all warm and chewy and everything.'

Billy wants to go straight back and see her again. Their hump session could have been a freak of nature, but this second encounter proved some things. Maybe there's hope for his love life after all. Maybe it didn't end with Shroom.

'Dude, you gotta get with her before we go,' Mango says.

'Don't see how. We're on post as of twenty-two hundred. Plus she's a Christian girl.'

'Fuck, you kiddin' me? Christian girls fuck like rabbits, *vato*. If you're gonna give up sin, you gotta sin, you know? You better go for it now, 'cause by the time we get back she ain't gonna know you, dawg. She'll be fucking some linebacker and you'll be like, Billy who?'

'Thanks, asshole.'

'I'm just sayin'! You better hit it while she's into you. That's just good advice.'

Billy's cell rings. He checks the screen. A-bort. 'Yo.'

'Where the fuck are you guys? Dime is *pissed*.'

'We went for a walk. We're on our way back.'

'They went for a walk,' A-bort says off-phone.

'They're on their way back.' Billy can hear Dime's growling response.

'He says get the fuck back asap.' A-bort pulls away again. 'Hang on, they're briefing us on half-time.' Another pause. 'What the fuck. They're saying – uh.' Pause. 'Oh Jesus.' There follows a longer pause, then A-bort resumes in a hushed voice. 'Dude, you don't even wanna know what they're gonna make us do.'

RAPED BY ANGELS

Billy knows they are truly in the shit when Lodis gives him a cockeyed grin and leans close, like he's about to impart some awesome piece of wisdom. 'Billy,' he mumbles. *Bih-yee*.

'What.'

'*Biy-yee*.' Lodis is so far gone he's in Buckwheat mode. 'Man, where we at?'

Dear Lord. 'Lodis,' Billy murmurs, 'we're down on the field. We're gonna do some drill, got it?'

Lodis grins and bobs his head. He's practically drooling.

'How many drinks you have up there?'

'Wonh' tha' many!'

Day peers around Crack. 'What's his problem?'

'He's hammered,' says Billy.

Crack sniggers. 'This oughta be good. He can't drill worth shit even when he's sober.'

'Don' be wishin' bad on me!'

'No worries, Load. You don't need my help to suck.'

Jesus Christ. Billy tells Lodis to key on him. Stay on my shoulder, just do everything I do. He wants

301

to tell Dime they have to call it off but Dime is clear on the other side of the formation, yes, thank you, in addition to everything else they have split Bravo in half to please some fascist bandmaster's jones for symmetry. Holliday, Crack, Billy, and Lodis stand four abreast on the home sideline. To the rear and sides the Prairie View A&M marching band is moving into position. It could be the setup for a night attack, there's that same edgy rustling of gear and clothes, the covert thump of boots on turf. Somewhere a lone drummer is marking time with his sticks, left, right, left, right, tick, tick, tick.

'Load, take some breaths. Clear your head.'

Scgggggck. Scgggggck.

'He dying over there?' Crack asks.

'*Coal!*'

'Hell yeah it's cold. Suck it up, bitch.' Thirty-four degrees, so they were informed by an unseen voice in the tunnel, and stepping onto the field they were met by a stinging crystalline mist, swarms of frozen micro-droplets like polar gnats. Ranks of young flag girls stood bravely in the cold, pinch-faced, pale, their bare legs pebbled and chapped, heads shiny with condensed mist. Lambs to the slaughter, Billy thought, as if they were truly forming up for battle, and farther on stood the high school bands in silent ranks, all those rows and rows of pink-cheeked baby faces so still and focused beneath their feathered caps, so seriously fixed on what they were about. Billy envied these kids the sincerity of their youth, their orderly student lives of classes, pep rallies, sleeping late on Saturdays. They looked so sharp! He felt tremendously tender toward them. They made him nostalgic. They made him feel so damn old.

The Prairie View drum line sets up at midfield, led by a towering black warlock of a drum major in high-church drum-major rig, cape, spats, golden braids and epaulets, a funnel cloud of a shako strapped to his head. The other four Bravos are somewhere to the left, and between their two contingents stands the United States Army Drill Team out of Fort Myer, Maryland, twenty drill grunts in flawless dress blues who can make their fixed-bayonet Springfields flip, twirl, spin, do cartwheels about the waist, loop the loop around the shoulder, sail through the air in a daring four-man diamond toss, and probably moonwalk if so ordered. A corps of ROTCs is positioned behind this front rank of Bravos and Drill grunts, the Rots stomping and huffing like water buffalo.

'Heeuunh, hoooo, hreeee, horrrr,' the warlock barks, and the drums erupt in a driving rataplan, *tatta-tottta tatta-totta drrrrp drrrrp boodly-boo,* a stirring take on the ructions of the smitten human heart. Then trumpets. Brass is jailbreak and bust out, the horns swinging in martial counterpoint as three slender women slip in from the side and take position front and center of the Drill grunts. It is Them. Billy floats a little outside of himself. The women's backs are to the soldiers, but even or maybe especially from behind there is no

303

question that Destiny's Child has arrived, the current undisputed world champs of mass-market pop, Colored Girl Division. Beyoncé takes the starring middle spot, while Michelle and Kelly – which is which? – decant themselves on the flanks. They wear tight low-rise pants, stiletto heels, flirty midriff tops with long lacy sleeves, and there's an awesome physical discipline in their stance, hips cocked, coaxialed to trunk and legs, backs sturdy and supple as flexed bows. Thus posed, they freeze. The music snaps to a halt. Cameramen are crab-walking around the singers, this is live TV happening as the girls raise the microphones to their lips, and soft as bedcovers being turned down for the night they croon in lush a cappella

        Ooooooo

                Ooooooo

                        Ooooooo

bending toward a reprise of the national anthem, it could tip that way with the slightest nudge, but their voices flower into something softer, sweeter, a rain of sugared rose petals batting the ears

Can
   you
      take
        me
          there

tooooooooh-
niiiiiiiiiiight

On the far sideline a stage has been concocted, a spangly three-tiered affair with a jigsaw backdrop of multicolored panels that seems to strive for a modernist stained-glass look. A dance troupe is freeze-framed on the various tiers, guys in shimmery white sweat suits and jumbo bling, women in tight slacks or cutoffs and artfully mangled Cowboys jerseys, ripped, cropped, sleeveless, no two alike. To Billy's right Lodis seems to be gagging on his snot. Destiny's Child reprises the *take me there* refrain, then the drums sound off and that's their cue, the entire formation steps out. The cameramen start backpedaling, going on faith. Up ahead the drum line peels left and right, clearing a route to the stage. Later, watching the performance on YouTube, Billy will start to piece together the enormous scale of it, at least five marching bands cycling on and off the field, the frantic sex-show choreography happening onstage, flag girls and drill squads from one end zone to the other, Rotcees, Bravos, Drill grunts, Destiny's Child. The proverbial cast of thousands. Someone will describe it as a production worthy of a Broadway musical, and though Billy has never set foot in New York, much less seen a musical of any kind, that will sound about right, but while it's happening he's just trying to hang on. A baton twirler skips by in a blur of skin and spinning chrome. High school drill teams in one-piece leotards are doing a shoop-shoop sort of booty-bump routine, they are training to be strippers apparently. Drum lines wheel alongside the soldier column, flying squads of flag girls zigzag across the route and Destiny's Child powers through it all with a back-leaning hip-heavy sashay strut that doesn't look quite possible from where Billy is, as if some mystical combination of diva mojo and StairMastered thighs keeps them upright when mere mortals would fall flat on their ass. Up ahead troupes of dancers flank the stage, guys in floppy shirts and pants, caps to the back, girls in silver sports bras and royal-blue tights. Already there's so much for the mind to absorb and then the disco lights get going, rows of blue and white strobes between the stage tiers, more strobes trimming the steel-pipe frame and everything flashing all at once, electro-visual spaz-pulse and epileptic overload, retinal scarring, frontal lobes blown to caterpillar fuzz—

This is yr brain on meth! Lodis is flinching, his poor head keeps swagging to the side, then the explosions start and they all flinch, *boom boom boom boom*, lum rounds are shooting off from somewhere backstage, smokers that explode with the arid crackle of cluster bombs scattering over a wheat field. A howl commences deep in Lodis's throat. 'It's cool,' Billy murmurs, 'it's cool, it's cool, *it's just fireworks*.' Lodis starts laughing, gasping for breath. On Billy's other side Crack is looking clammy and grim. If there was ever a prime-time trigger for PTSD you couldn't do much better than this, but lucky for Norm, the crowd, America, the forty-million-plus TV viewing audience, Bravos can deal, oh yes! Pupils dilated, pulse and blood pressure through the roof, limbs trembling with stress-reflex cortisol rush, but it's cool, it's good, their shit's down tight, no Vietnam-vet crackups for Bravo squad! You can march these boys straight into sound-and-light-show hell and Bravos can deal, but, damn, isn't it rude to put them through it.

The formation moves on eight-to-five step with the beat, *boody-Boom boody-Boom boody-bood-bood-BOOM*, snare drums make a fella damn proud to be a soldier. It's not a joke, Billy realizes. They spent too much money and went to too much effort for halftime to be intentionally ridiculous, which isn't to say that big expensive things can't be dumb. The *Titanic* was dumb. Enron was dumb. Hitler invading Russia, dumb. *Boom-diddy boom-diddy boom-buddah-dit-BOOM*, so go the Prairie View drums, thunder's wind chimes. Lodis knocks into Billy, steadies. 'Sorry, Biyee.' At the north hash mark all soldiers will about-face and march south while Destiny's Child proceeds to the stage. Billy is watching for his mark and trying not to hyperventilate. *Boom-diddy boom-diddy diddy-diddy BOOM*. Disco strobes, hump dancing, lum rounds and flares, marching bands marking time in regal high step, and here is Billy soldiering through the vast mindfuck of it, coiled into himself and determined to deal.

'Lay-dees A N D gennelmunnn,' booms the PA announcer in the fawning, basso profundo lilt of the pitchman who doesn't know he's a fool,

Puh-leeeeeze wel-cum

Kelly

Michelle

A N D

BEEE-YON-SAY

the hit singing sen-say-shuns

DESTINY'S CHILD

Such an unholy barrage of noise pours forth that Billy thinks he might be lifted off his feet. It is a dam bursting, bridges collapsing at rush hour, tsunamis of killer froth and boulder-sized debris revising the contours of the known world. *Just assume you're going to die,* so they were instructed the week before deploying to Iraq. Affirmative! Roger that! Sir yes sir! Carnage awaits us, we are the ones who will not be saved, the poor sad doomed honorably fucked front line who will fight them over there so as not to fight them here! A harsh thing for any young man to hear, but this is part of every youth's education in the world, learning the risks are never fully revealed until you commit. Destiny's Child is really laying into the strut, they could be wading through a storm surge up to their waists, *goddamn,* Billy thinks, watching them sling it, *goddamn,* so how is he supposed to redeploy with such sights in his head? Within days, no, *hours,* Bravo is back in the shit and he's waiting for them to say it again, he dreads it but the harsh words need to be said, *you're going to die,* just get that part of it over with please, but no, no one will do it, they get Beyoncé and her mouthwatering ass instead!

Maybe it's not supposed to make sense. Or maybe not for you, Billy reasons, because you are a duh-umb shit. Then they turn, he's missed the hash mark by half a beat, the Drill grunts razor-sharp on the mark while Bravo flops around like loose shoelaces. 'Change step *march,*' Day woofs sotto voce; as team leader he's responsible for getting them through halftime with some semblance of their dignity intact, and now he counts time with the Drill grunts, trying to shoehorn the Bravos into lockstep. 'Left, left,' the mantra settles Billy's mind and his feet start to follow, though it would help if he had a weapon in his hands. Just ahead are the Rots, a herd of shambling, big-assed kids, many of them no doubt older than Billy and yet they look so young from the back, their soft, fleshy, baby-fat necks practically screaming for the sacrificial ax to come down.

'Left *face,*' Day softly woofs. They've reached the

sideline. Bravo steps off seven strides, left face again, *halt*. For the moment their job is to stand next to the Drill grunts and look pretty. High school girls in fringed leotards go skipping past, waving long twirly streamers from six-foot poles. The Prairie View drum line has reconvened at midfield, glide-stepping to the beat of crunchy snare rolls, and everybody except Bravo is moving it seems, the field has become a huge jam-up of hip-hop choreographics and rigid blocks of synchronized marching-band mass. The stage apparatus belches gouts of flame and fireworks as Destiny's Child ascends with their prancing diva strut. The stage dancers go right on humping like the nastiest video on MTV as Beyoncé and her girls bring the microphones to their lips.

You say you gonna take me there

they sing in kittenish, pouty trills,

Say you know what I need
Show devotion to the notion of our mutual creed

The Drill grunts are doing their thing, snapping their Springfields around in the rock-star version of close order drill. *Chack, chack, chack,* the strike of palm to rifle stock a high-fiber sound, perhaps a skilled listener could follow the stunts just by cadence alone. Out here on the end Billy has only a peripheral view, the rifles flitting in the corner of his eye like cards shuffled and stacked.

> *You think it all in the moves*
> *Like some robot lover do?*
> *That ain't the way you get*
> *A grown woman into her groove*

Beyoncé slinks one hand down the inside of her thigh, then drags it toward her snatch, not quite cupping herself at the critical point; this is the PG-rated crotch grab, suitable for family viewing. The streamer girls go skipping by, their pale skinny legs like pogo sticks. Those strobes are doing a number on Billy's head. He narrows his eyes to slits and everything blurs, it is a rat-bite fever dream of soldiers, marching bands, blizzards of bodies bumping and grinding, whoofs of fireworks, multiple drum lines cranking go-team-go. Destiny's Child! Drill grunts! Toy soldiers and sexytime all mashed together into one big inspirational stew. How many dozens of times has Bravo watched Crack's Conan DVDs, many dozens, they know every line by heart, and out of all the streamings and veerings of his over-amped brain Billy flashes on the palace orgy scene, James Earl Jones as the snake king sitting on his throne while his stoned minions sprawl about the floor, slurping and licking and humping in glassy-eyed bliss. It creeps him, the overlay of that sludgy sex scene on what he sees before him now, the complete and utter weirdness of the halftime show and the fact that everybody seems okay with it. The stands are packed, the fans are on their feet and everyone is cheering, everything makes them happy today. Fine, be happy, is Billy's attitude. They can cheer and scream and holler all they want, but it's nothing, their show, just fluff, filler, it's got nothing to do with Billy or going back to the war.

I ain't scared, I'm comin' through,
I ain't scared, I ain't scared,

Big man can't you handle this good thing I'm offerin' you?

In the stands behind the stage a huge American flag appears, a card stunt, each one of a mass of twenty thousand fans comprising a pixel in this antique special effect. The cards spin, and now the flag is presented as if rippling in the wind, though on second look it's more like the thing's been badly pressed, the pattern gashed through with wrinkles and kinks. For several moments Billy's eyes play tricks with it, tweaking the perspective back and forth, then his inner ear jolts and the ground seems to tilt, a lurch that sets him down in a different place. It occurs to him that maybe he's wrong. Maybe the halftime show is as real as anything; what if some power or potent agency lives in it? Not a show but a means to something, something conferred or invoked. A ceremony. Something religious, so long as 'religious' extends to such cold-blooded concepts as mayhem, chance, nature out of control. He feels the pull of a superseding reality that trumps even the experiential truths of a grunt on the ground – the blood on your hands, the burn in your lungs, the stink of your unwashed feet. Merely thinking about it sets off a pounding in his skull, not his headache but a heavier sonar throb deep in the lower brain stem. And very clearly the thought comes to him, *that's where it lives*. The god in your head, all the gods – is that what's happening here? He's too self-conscious and church-averse to accept a completely straight notion of god, so how about this – chemicals, hormones, needs and drives, whatever is in us that's so supreme and terrifying that we have to call it divine.

> *Lemme break it down for you again,*
> *Stop actin' like a boy, stand up and be a man,*
> *What's sad is all your talkin' 'bout love and*
>   *affection,*
> *You get yours and leave me hangin' like a*
>   *prepubescent*

Billy is cold where the warmest part of him should be, as if meaning naturally registers first in the most delicate instrument he has, his balls. He's scared. He knows this is a bad place to be. They love to talk up God and country but it's the devil they propose, all those busy little biochemical

313

devils of sex and death and war that simmer at the base of the skull, punch up the heat a few degrees and they rise to a boil, spill over the sides. Do they even know? he wonders. Maybe they don't know what they know, given that what he sees before him is so random, so perfect, porn-lite out of its mind on martial dope. Short of blood sacrifice or actual sex on the field, you couldn't devise a better spectacle for turning up the heat.

Left face, Day softly woofs, and they step off, *right face* and they're crossing the field toward the belly of the beast, Lodis following Billy, Billy following Crack, Crack following Day, who tails the Prairie View drum corps through a blur of fancy uniforms and bared flesh. Individual sounds spire out of the din like guitar drones, the squeanings of whales. Time gears down to a lower speed. The strobes pulse in stretchy Day-Glo smears. Billy knows where they're supposed to end up though he's vague on the mechanics of getting there. As each Bravo crosses the sideline they face left, then they're hustled along a gauntlet of stressed-out handlers to a chaotic holding pen behind the stage. A tall slender woman in a knee-length parka pulls the Bravos out of line. She's pretty, at least the part of her that shows between the flaps of her Russian officer's cap. 'All right,' she says, gathering the Bravos into a huddle, yelling like a sailor in a gale, 'we're gonna get you guys in position backstage, then when we give you the go you step out and take the stairs down to the middle level. You'll be marching, right? Like this?' She mimes a military strut. 'You turn left on the middle tier and march out along there. Look for the purple X's, one for each of you, that's your mark. Then just turn and face the field and stand at attention.'

The Bravos nod. No one speaks. They're all quietly freaking.

'There's gonna be a lot going on out there but you guys don't move. That's your job, just stand there. No-brainer, right?' She smiles, gives Day a light cuff on the shoulder. 'You guys okay?'

The Bravos nod. Even Day seems rattled, his neck bulging like he's swallowed too much air. Crack is looking at the ground and mumbling to himself.

'Guys, come on, chill, you've got the easy part.' The woman laughs, exasperated by how tight they are. 'Once you're on your mark just stay there till the show's over, I'll come up and give you the all-clear.'

'This about to be *stoopih*,' Lodis grumbles, but the handler lady pretends not to hear. Bravos can deal, you bet, though none of them is looking particularly good at the moment. There's too many people running around, too much bug-eyed panic, all the freak-out flavors of an ambush situation without any of the compensating murderous release. Fireworks crews to their left and right keep shooting off nasty little rockets that hiss and sizzle like RPGs. Portable sets of metal stairs lead up to the highest stage level, and the Bravos are placed at the tops of these stairways, one Bravo per. A narrow catwalk is all that separates them from the stage backdrop, and Billy is standing there, a step below catwalk level, when a magnificent female creature bombs through the backdrop, it is a louvered sort of opening she steps around as several handlers swarm in. One takes her microphone, another offers Evian, a third presents some sort of small, furry garment that the woman proceeds to pull over her head. Beyoncé. If Billy chooses he could reach out and touch her thigh. Her hair springs free of the pullover like a solar flare, and from Billy's vantage point a foot below the catwalk she towers with a Rocky Mountain majesty. Up close her skin is the honeyed brown of apple butter, limned with a film of perspiration that holds the light. Michelle and Kelly have their own handlers farther down the catwalk. No one speaks. They are all business, these show people, as quiet and lethal as sniper teams. Beyoncé shoots her arms through the sleeves of the jacket, a cropped, off-shoulder sateen number with a fur-trimmed collar, and as she arranges herself inside the garment her eyes meet Billy's. Excuse me, he wants to say, go on, go on, she's so focused and fierce in the moment that he's sorry to impinge even to this small extent. Carrying the show in front of forty million people makes her one of the top human beings on the planet, and what strength of nerve that must take, what freakish concentrations of soul and energy. She's not even winded!

A yogic mastery of the mind-body balance. She inhabits some far distant astral plane, yet her eyes do something when they meet his, for an instant he seems to register there. In that split second Billy searches for something in her look – not mercy, exactly, nothing so grand as compassion, maybe just a bare acknowledgment of their shared humanity, but she's already turning, she takes the mike and one of the handlers is saying *kick butt* as she steps through the slot and disappears.

Someone pushes Billy onto the catwalk, then pulls him up short of the opening. The noise out there is just tremendous. He looks to his right and sees more Bravos similarly positioned, and at this instant he wishes he was back at the war. At least there he basically knew what he was doing, he had his training for guidance and the entire goddamn country wasn't watching to see if he'd fuck up, but this, this is all wing-and-a-prayer shit. *Middle level* a voice is yelling in his ear, *turn left and look for the purple X*. Abruptly the music gears down to a meat-grinding crawl, *kah-thunka, kah-thunka*, it is a trash compactor mulling over more than it can chew. On the lowest tier of the stage Destiny's Child is standing in front of three Prairie View drummers, the girls have taken the sticks and are pounding out the beat with the flailing elbows and lunging stance of fashionable women trying to jack up a car. By the time Billy gets stiff-armed onto the stage he's barely breathing. It's like stepping into a sun-filled cumulus cloud, a dazzling, cottony glow all about your person and nothing but air beneath your feet. He moves right-oblique toward the center stairs and arrives, small miracle, in sequence with the other three Bravos and everyone is marching more or less in step. He hears a rushing in his head and not much else. Directly in front of the stage the Drill grunts are doing the overhead rifle toss *with fixed bayonets,* the fuck, they could kill themselves and wouldn't that be the shit, stabbed through the eye on live TV with your own bayonet!

> *Need me a soldjah, soldjah boy*
> *Where dey at, where dey at*

Billy is last in file, thus he ends up on the purple X closest to center stage. Right face, halt. The rest of the Bravos have somehow appeared on the bottom tier, Dime-Sykes-Mango-A-bort all in a row. *Soldjah gonna be real fah me,* Beyoncé sings against Michelle's and Kelly's bass-line chant,

> *Soldjah gonna be real fah me*
> *Yeah dey will, yeah dey will*
> *Soldjah gonna get chill fah me*
> *Yeah dey will, yeah dey will*

They are serenading the bottom-tier Bravos, slinking and spooning about on dainty cat feet, mewling minor-key trills of do-me angst. The entire stage has become a blowup of foreplay

318

aerobics, rocket thrusting, shadow humping, knurling hips and ass, here on the second tier the dancers are twurking Bravo and not a damn thing you can do except stand at attention and get pole-danced in front of forty million people. It's not right. Nobody said anything about this. What might be merely embarrassing in real life is made obscene and hostile by TV. Billy hates to think of his mother and sisters watching this, then one of the guys starts dancing a little too close, punking Billy with glide-by swivels and squats. Like I really wanna see your junk, fool! Billy gives him a look; the guy smirks and spins away. Then he comes back around, and Billy speaks with all the feeling he can jam through his teeth:

Fuck off.

The guy laughs and he's gone again. The beat quickens as a line of Prairie View drummers comes marching down the stairs, *boom-Lacka-Lacka-Lacka boom-Lacka-Lacka-Lacka.* The Drill grunts are doing the Queen Anne Salute while troupes of smiling dancers decorate the flanks with jazzy kung fu moves. Down on the bottom tier Sykes is weeping. For some reason Billy is not surprised, he only hopes it will be over before all the Bravos lose their minds. Destiny's Child regroups at center stage as a gathering storm of lights and fireworks signals crescendo time. Sykes's back is a heaving pantomime of sobs, yet he maintains strict attention, chin up, chest out, and he has never seemed so brave or dear to Billy as at this moment.

I ain't scared, I'm comin' through,
I ain't scared, I ain't scared,
Big man can't you handle this good love I'm
offerin' you?

Far across the field the Cowboys cheerleaders have formed a kick line, and even at this distance, through the haze of sleet and fireworks smoke, Billy's eyes go straight to Faison, his groan a mere drop in the ocean of sound. Destiny's Child is mounting the stairs, pausing every few steps to throw sassy looks over their shoulders, T&A bait for the TV cameras. Billy doesn't so much as twitch when they pause on his tier, a fulmination of animal heat roaring at his side. For as long as they pose he doesn't move, but once they're gone he raises his eyes to the sky, then lifts his face a few degrees to get the weather's full effect.

The sleet stings, but he doesn't blink. He lets it come, the spray of ice like a billion needles showering down on him, then it's like the sleet is dangling and Billy's flying through it, zooming toward some unnamed but promising place. Everything else falls away and he's happy, free, the sting in his eyes is all speed and upward motion. It feels like escape velocity. It feels like the future. He's still standing there, rocketing toward the world to come, when Day taps him on the shoulder and says halftime is over.

IF IN THE FUTURE
YOU TELL ME THIS IS LOVE,
I WILL NOT DISAPPOINT YOU

No one comes for them. They gather around Sykes and wait as instructed for the woman in the Russian officer's cap, but Bravo has fallen through a crack in the collective mind and so they stand there marooned while a roadie crew swarms over the stage and ash from the fireworks settles on their heads. They have been through the wringer of a world-class spectacle and need some time for their nerves to recover. Like, about six years might do it? Bravo is roasted, toasted, and ready to pop, or maybe already popping in the case of Sykes, who sits himself down on the bottom step and weeps sparklers of racy little hopeless tears. 'I don't know why I'm fuckin' cryin'!' he squawks when Lodis asks. 'I just am, dammit! I just am!'

'You guys have to leave,' the roadie foreman barks at Bravo.

'Well fuck you too,' Mango mumbles as the guy stalks off, and the Bravos stay put. Day and A-bort sit down on either side of Sykes while the rest of them mill around feeling torn and frayed, fluttery hands shoved deep in their pockets.

'Dudes, we finally saw Beyoncé,' Crack points out.

'Woo, ain't we special.'

'Yeah, but we saw her up close.'

'Uh-huh, she's hot and everything. But I've had better.'

They manage a few yuks at that. Billy finds himself standing next to Dime, and confides:

'Sergeant, I feel sick.'

Dime gives him a once-over. 'You look okay to me.'

'Not like sick sick. More like bent. Baked.' He taps his head. 'Halftime sort of skitzed me out.'

Dime laughs, *at-at-at,* a machine-gun rattle high in his throat. 'Son, try to look at it this way. It's just another normal day in America.'

Billy's heart melts a little at that *son.* The stage is disappearing around them like a mortally wounded ship beneath the waves.

'I don't think I even know what normal is anymore.'

'You're fine, Billy, you're fine. I'm fine, you're fine, everybody's fine. He's fine.' Dime nods at Sykes. 'Everything is fine.'

Billy looks at Sykes and starts to ask, Yeah, what are we going to do about him? but the foreman is coming at them again, snapping at Bravo to get the hell off his stage.

'So where we supposed to go?' Crack snaps back. 'Nobody told us where to go.'

The foreman stops, spares them a harried moment's regard. He's well over six feet, bearded, broad shouldered, with a face slack and frowzy as a blown-out air bag, but there's a shot of chemical voltage in his eyes, the crazed-lumberjack look of the veteran roadie. His gaze lingers for a second on the hot mess that is Sykes.

'Look, I have no fucking idea where you're supposed to go, but you can't stay here.'

'All right, Rufus, tell you what,' Crack answers. 'We'll go right after you're done sucking my dick, how about that?'

Later, thinking back on it, Billy will be struck by the fact that he never saw an actual punch being thrown. It doesn't last long – ten, fifteen seconds at most? Though in the way of such things it seems to go on for hours. At first the foreman tries to *lift* Crack like he thinks he's going to bodily throw him off the stage, so he's bigger than Crack but not *that* much bigger, and what a bummer it must be for the guy when he finds himself locked in a young-buck clench. For an instant the two men hardly move. Only their bulging eyes and necks betray the tons of thrust at work, then they're twisting, spinning, they are the hub of a free-radical swirl of bodies that slides off the stage onto the field. People are pushing, chesting up, there's much half-assed shoving and garbled smack talk about who dissed who and who crossed whose line and of course everybody's gotta have their boy's back. A melee, you'd call it. A fracas. Not quite a throw-down brawl right here on the sacred turf of Texas Stadium. Billy is skying on a full-bore adrenaline rip as arms, hands, faces go crashing by, then there's Dime stroking past like a man swimming rapids, pushing through bodies to pry Crack clear. A roadie swipes at Dime's back and Billy grabs his collar and there's the guy's wild look as he twists around, and Billy thinks: Whoa shit, don't let go now. The guy reels as Billy rides him from behind, riding, riding, he wishes it didn't look so much like he's humping the guy but he hangs on until the cops wade in, and all it takes is a word from Dime for Bravo to disengage, 'like a bunch of excellent hunting dogs' as he likes to say of his squad.

Casualties, minor. Crack has taken an elbow in the eye; Lodis's lip is split and bloody; Mango's ear tenderized by a roadie headlock. The cops herd Bravo down the sideline and hear out their story, then send them packing across the field toward the home sideline. 'Somebody over there can tell you where to go,' the cops say, so like the remnants of some long-lost jungle patrol Bravo makes its straggling way across the field. They've passed the first hash mark when Billy looks up and sees, oh mother of mercy, Faison coming out to meet them, her head cocked at a questioning skew, face full of concern. She's pumped, Billy can tell. This is a girl who likes her drama.

'What happened?' She peers up at him, touches

his arm as they meet. The rest of the Bravos lapse into reverential silence.

'It was stupid, just this stupid little thing. We kind of got into it with the roadies over there.'

'Were yall fighting? We couldn't tell if yall were fighting or goofing around.'

'I guess we were fighting. Though you couldn't call it much of a fight.'

'All we did was ask if we could help!' A-bort says, and everybody yuks except Sykes, who breaks down all over again.

'Are you hurt?' Faison asks Billy, then she's speaking to all the Bravos. 'Is anybody hurt? Oh my God, look at your *lip*!' she cries at Lodis. 'Who's supposed to be taking care of you guys?'

She's incensed to learn that Bravo has been left on its own. 'All right,' she says, turning, motioning Bravo to follow, 'yall come with me, we'll get this figured out. I can't believe they just left yall stranded out here, that is *so* NOT the way we treat our guests.'

The Bravos clump about her in a loose bundle, murmuring their thanks. 'Listen,' she tells them, 'that stage crew? We've had problems with those guys before, it's like they think they own the place. They almost beat up Lyle Lovett a couple of weeks ago, they were like, *Get off the stage! Get off the stage right NOW!* And Lyle and his guys had all their equipment up there, it's not like they were gonna just walk off and leave it. Lucky security was right there or we mighta had a situation.'

'I think they're tweekin',' says Mango.

'They sure act like it, don't they, they act like they're on something. Somebody ought to speak to management about those guys.'

More cheerleaders are coming out to meet them, and it dawns on Bravo that this might turn out all right. A kind of mixer develops there along the home sideline, Bravos and cheerleaders chatting it up while calls are made upstairs on the soldiers' behalf. The fracas gives them something to talk about; the cheerleaders are shocked at first, then indignant as the story gets around, the flip side of which is a bonus serving of sympathy for Bravo. Ice is fetched for Crack's eye and Lodis's lip. A couple of cheerleaders tenderly probe Mango's rug-burned ear.

'What's wrong with him?' Faison asks, nodding at Sykes. She and Billy are standing somewhat apart from the others.

'Oh, that's Sykes.'

'Is he hurt?'

Billy considers Sykes, who's squatting in the lee of a portable equipment locker, quietly weeping.

'He misses his wife.'

'Wow.' Faison seems impressed. 'Really?'

'He's kind of an emotional guy.'

She keeps glancing over at Sykes. She's fascinated, or perhaps just troubled that nothing's being done about him.

'Does he have kids?'

'One on the ground, one on the way.'

'Oh my God, I can't imagine. Do you think I should go over and talk to him?'

'I think he just wants to be alone right now.'

'You're probably right. Sheesh, the *sacrifices* you guys make! How long did you say you're gonna be over there?'

'Through next October, unless we get stop-lossed again.'

'Oh Lord.' It comes out as a kind of rattling moan, *oh Lord,* like she's rollerblading on a gravel road. 'And you've been there how long already?'

'We infilled August twelfth.'

'Oh me. Oh my God. You must dread going back.'

'I guess. In a way.' Somehow their faces have ended up mere inches apart, and this seems like the most natural thing in the world, as basic as wind, tides, the magnetic north. 'It is what it is, I guess. But we'll all be together, that's something. That counts for a lot, actually.'

'I think I know what you mean. There's that whole bonding thing when you're challenged as a group.' While she talks Billy is trying to memorize her face, the supreme excellence, for example, of the delicate butterfly clasp of the bridge of her nose, or the smattering of freckles high on her forehead, the way their gingery carotene tint matches her hair exactly. The desire comes over him to stretch his mouth wide open, as wide as a lion's, say, and tenderly hold her perfect face between his lips for a while.

'Sometimes I wonder if the whole thing might be a mistake. I mean, I think we ought to be fighting terrorism and everything, but it's like, okay, we got rid of Saddam, maybe we should just bring our guys home and let the Iraqis work it out for themselves.'

'Sometimes we think that too,' Billy says, remembering something Shroom once said: *Maybe the light's at the other end of the tunnel.*

'Ha ha, no doubt.' She peers past his shoulder. 'The second half's gonna start in a minute,' she says, then pulls back and looks Billy in the eye. 'Listen, can I ask you something personal?'

'Sure.'

'Are you seeing anybody?'

'Not me,' he allows bravely, with breezy resignation. He doesn't care if she knows he's not a player.

'Me either. So how about if we stay in touch.'

'Ye-uh,' he says, half choking on it, then '*yes*. Yes, I think we should.'

'Good.' She's suddenly very brisk and business-like. 'You've got your phone? Get out your phone and I'll give you my information, then call me and leave a message so I'll have yours. Because, frankly, I don't wanna lose you.'

She says it just like that, a casually earthshaking statement of stupendous fact. Him, Billy, a person not to be wanted lost! His life has become miraculous to him. Maybe he should just go ahead and ask her to marry him.

'What's your last name?' He's got his phone out.

'Zorn.'

Billy clears his throat.

'I know, everybody thinks it's funny.'

Billy says nothing.

'It means "anger" in German.'

'Roger that,' he deadpans.

'Stop it! You're so funny.'

She's at his side, their heads practically touching as she watches him key in her information. The phone gives them socially acceptable cover for standing so close, good thing because it's happening in front of thousands of people. Billy breathes deep, pulling in her clean outdoors smell, the sharp vanilla tang of snow and winter wind. It's as if she's absorbed the sweetest essence that the season has to offer.

'Who's Kathryn?'

Billy is scrolling through his contact list. 'My sister.'

'You've got a call from her.'

'I know.' He highlights the next name. 'That's my other sister.'

'They older, younger?'

'I'm the youngest. There's ol' Mom.'

'Denise? Not "Mom"?'

'Well, that's her name.'

Faison laughs. 'Where's your Dad?'

'My Dad's disabled. He doesn't have his own phone.'

'Oh!'

'He had a double stroke a couple of years ago, impaired his speech.'

'I'm so sorry.'

'It's all right. It's life.'

She's holding his arm just above the elbow, her grip concealed by the bush of her pom-poms. 'Are you going to see them before you leave?'

Billy gets a sudden clutch in his throat. 'Ah, no.' He swallows. It's fine. 'We all said our good-byes yesterday.'

'That sucks.' She snugs a few millimeters closer.

'There's you.' He's scrolled all the way to the end.

'Zorn. I'm always last on everybody's list.'

'I'll change you to Anger, that way you'll be first.'

She laughs, looks over her shoulder. The cheerleaders are moving toward the tunnel to welcome the players onto the field. 'Sweetie, I gotta go,' she says, and gives his arm a squeeze. Her hand recoils as if electrically shocked, then she's squeezing again, then palpating his entire upper arm.

'*My God,* what a great body you've got. Do you have even an *ounce* of fat on you?'

'Not so much, I guess.'

'*Not so much I guess,*' she echoes in a gruff voice, and laughs. She's still feeling up his arm. 'You don't even know how good you are, do you? That makes it even better!' she declares with lip-smacking enthusiasm, then gives him a fierce fast hug, as if grasping a buoy before the storm tears her away. Billy practically keels over in a delirium of bliss. How wonderful, how absolutely holy to be appreciated for yourself, to be handled, petted,

330

groped, pawed, and generally hungered over. 'Okay, I gotta scoot,' she says, releasing him. 'Come see me at the twenty, same place.'

Billy says he will, and she goes trotting down the sideline after the rest of the cheerleaders. Bravo turns as she jogs past, their eyes helplessly drawn to the bounce of her bottom inside those teeny tiny cup holders that pass for shorts. Billy punches up her number and waits through six rings while watching her take position at the mouth of the tunnel. The first players come jogging onto the field like rhinos on the plod. The Jumbotron cranks up a Guns N' Roses riff, the cheerleaders rise on their toes and wave their pom-poms high, and a swell of applause rolls through the stands like thunder rumbling down the mountainside.

'Hi, you've reached Faison! I'm not able to take your call right now . . .'

It makes for an odd sensation, watching her real-time person in the middle distance while holding her disembodied voice to his ear. It puts a frame around the situation, gives it focus, perspective. It makes him aware of himself being aware of himself, and here is a mystery that seems worth thinking about, why this stacking of awareness should even matter. At the moment all he knows is that there's structure in it, a pleasing sense of poise or mental ordering. A kind of knowledge, or maybe a bridge thereto – as if existence didn't necessarily have to be a moron's progress of lurching from one damn thing to another? As if you might aspire to some sort of context in your life, a condition he associates with adultness. Then comes the *beep,* and he has to talk. The funny little message he leaves for her – two seconds after clicking off, he can't remember what he said.

TEMPORARY SANITY

The last few players are straggling out of the tunnel and here comes Josh trotting with them, looking like he just stepped out of a Polo ad. How does he do it? Every hair, every thread, every crease and pleat in place, as if he's sheathed in a varnish of pussy-boy perfection. *'My bad, my bad, my bad,'* he chants in a furious monotone, 'I am so so sorry guys, we blew it, *blew it,* no way you should've dropped off the radar like that,' and he launches into a detailed explication of post-halftime logistics, the gist of which is he's been waiting at prearranged point X for the past twenty minutes.

'So you're saying one of the clipboard chicks was supposed to bring us up,' Dime clarifies.

'Essentially, yes.'

'So how does that make it your bad?'

Josh opens his mouth, he's going to try to try, but Bravo saves him the trouble with a group razz. Jaaaaaassssshhhhhh! Dah Joshster. *Jash.* He is too damn nice for his own good, which is why Bravo loves the big lunk.

'Yo Josh, you hear about our fight?'

333

'Wait, what. What fight?'

'The one we just had.' Crack grins and holds up his ice pack.

'Yeah, Josh, that your bad too,' Day says.

'Wait, wait a second. You're kidding me. Oh shit, guys, what—'

'Jash, chill. It's cool.'

'Yeah, Josh, we like to fight. It's like our main thing to do.'

'You gotta remember, man, we're basically just a bunch of apes.'

Day asks about the after-party, which he defines as wherever Beyoncé and her girls are, which is where he'd like to be. Bravo offers this a unanimous second but Josh thinks Destiny's Child has already left the stadium. Billy is tired of asking about the Advil, so doesn't even. They take a freight elevator up to the first-level concourse. Crack, Mango, and Lodis head for the men's room to primp their injuries. The rest of the Bravos hang out on the concourse and phone home. *Didja see me? How'd I look?* Billy decides this is the grunt version of the after-party, calling up the fam. He pulls out his cell and dials Kathryn, but his sister Patty answers.

'Helloooo little brother,' she trills from deep in her cups, her voice all woozy and sickly sweet. 'You looked so handsome on TV! We're all really proud of you, baby bro.'

'Thanks.'

'Soooo' – she pauses for a sip of her drink – 'what's she like?'

'What's who like?'

'Beyoncé, fool!' Billy hears his mother wail in the background, *Please don't call your brother a fool.*

'Oh, her.' Billy affects a yawn. 'Yeah, she's okay. She's a little thick through the hips.'

Patty knocks that down with a braying *Hah!* 'Did you meet her?'

'Never got the chance.'

'But you were right up there onstage!'

'Yeah, but that's as close as I got. And it didn't seem like the best time . . .'

She wants to know if he's met any other celebrities. Billy doesn't mind, but it sort of brings him down, talking about those people. There was the actress from *Walker, Texas Ranger,* the blonde who played the spunky district attorney role. Senator Cornish, who has the largest head of any human Billy has ever seen. Jimmer Lee Flatley, medium-heavy country music star, and Lex, the Fort Worth hunk who made it all the way to the final round of *Survivor.* He throws out a few more names like change from a dollar bill.

'Listen, that thing you were doing at the end, what was that? We were all wondering.'

What thing?

'Well, right there at the end, when you were looking up at the sky. Like you were praying or something.'

'They showed that?'

'Well, yeah.' She laughs at the rise in his voice.

'Like a close-up?'

'Not *real* close, but they showed it. For a second it was pretty much just you on the screen.'

This freaks him, though he doesn't know why. 'Well, I sure wasn't praying.' He frets in silence a moment. 'Did it look weird?'

'No,' she laughs, 'it looked *sweet*. You were *cute*. We're really proud of you.'

'I don't remember that at all,' Billy says, though he remembers perfectly well. 'It was hot up there with all the lights and everything. Maybe I was just trying to get some air.'

She starts to tell him again how handsome and brave he looked, but Kathryn takes the phone from her.

'Hey.'

'Hey.'

'So no Beyoncé, huh.'

''Fraid not.'

'Just as well, she's probably a total bitch. Hang on a sec . . .' Doors open and close; the house noises fall away, replaced by an airy, bottomless quiet. Kathryn has stepped outside.

'Jesus Christ!'

'What?'

'Cold as dammit out here. I would *not* want to be wildlife today. You staying warm over there?'

'Warm enough.'

She tells him she and Brian spent several hours playing in the snow this afternoon, scraping enough together to make a runt snowman. 'He's crashed in your room right now, I think I wore his little

336

hiney out. We recorded halftime so he can watch you later. But, um, listen.' She lowers her voice. 'Patty told me what you said, about Brian. About telling him never to join the Army.'

Billy closes his eyes, silently curses.

'And I don't think you should go back.'

'Kathryn.'

'Just listen, just please hear me out, okay? I got in touch with some people, those people I told you about. The group in Austin.'

'I'm really not interested in talking about this.'

'Just listen, please, Billy, just listen for a minute. I talked to them twice, they're good people, they know what they're doing. They've got lawyers, resources, they aren't a bunch of flakes. And they really want to help you. They've been hoping somebody like you would reach out.'

'Somebody like me.'

'A war hero. Somebody the movement could really rally around.'

'Oh Jesus.'

'Just listen! One of these guys, one of their group, he's got like a ten-thousand-acre ranch where you can stay. I'm telling you, man, these people have some serious stroke. They can have some people meet you at the stadium and drive you to the airport, they'll fly you out to the ranch on a private plane tonight. You'd just disappear for a couple of weeks while the lawyers get everything set up.'

'That's AWOL, Kathryn. They shoot people for that.'

'Not you, not after everything you've been through. These lawyers know what they're doing, Billy, they have all kinds of strategies for cases like yours. And they'll have a PR firm on it too, these guys are pros. Can you imagine how shitty they could make the government look, prosecuting you? After the whole freakin' country saw what you did on TV?'

'I'm not psyche, if that's what the lawyers are thinking. So they can forget about that.'

'Of *course* you're not psyche, only a nut would want to go back to the war. We'll have the lawyers plead temporary sanity for you, how about that? You're too *sane* to go back to the war, Billy Lynn has come to his senses. It's the rest of the country that's nuts for wanting to send him back.'

'But, Kathryn.'

'But, Billy.'

'I sort of do want to go back.'

She screams. He thinks he can hear it echoing off the trees in the backyard.

'No, no way, I don't accept that. You *cannot* want to go back to that place.'

'But I do. I can't stay here if the rest of the squad's going back. If they're over there getting shot at, I want to be there too.'

'Then maybe all the Bravos should stay, how about that. Bush pinned medals on all you guys, nobody's going to think you're cowards for not going back.'

'That's not the point.'

'Okay, enlighten me here. What's the point?'

'Well, I signed up.'

'Under duress! Thanks to *me*! Me and my shit!'

'No, it was my choice. It's what I wanted to do. And I knew they'd probably send me to Iraq. It's not like anybody lied to me.'

She groans. 'Billy, all those mofos ever do is lie. You think if they halfway told the truth we'd even be in a fucking war? You know what I think, I think we don't *deserve* to have you guys die for us. No country that lets its leaders lie like that deserves a single soldier to die for it.'

She breaks down crying, an awful sound like the scraping of a shovel hitting bedrock. 'Kathryn,' Billy says, and waits a minute. 'Kathryn,' he tries again. 'Kat. It's okay. I'm gonna be fine.'

'I'm sorry,' she says, her voice gone swampy and blear. 'Shit. I told myself I wasn't going to cry on you. It's just that everything's so, whatever. Everything about it sucks.'

'Yeah, pretty much.'

'Listen, don't be mad at me. But I gave those people your number.'

Billy grits his teeth, says nothing. The main thing is not to get her started crying again.

'Just talk to them, Billy, please? Just hear what they have to say. They're good people, they can make it all right for you.'

He doesn't say yes and he doesn't say no. She goes inside to hand the phone off to Denise, and as he waits he tries to imagine how it will be for them if he doesn't come back. He knows Kathryn would survive, a triumph of rage over guilt. Patty also; she has Brian. But his mother? All ego aside, it would be awful for her, possibly fatal, though not right away. He envisions a long slow process of interior numbing-out that takes form in his mind as weather, a plague of bitter-cold days with wind, freezing rain, a pall of daylong dusk fading to black. Days like today, in fact.

But at the moment she's doing okay; halftime got her pumped. 'It was disgraceful,' she tells Billy. 'All those lewd gyrations, they're like something you'd see at the hoochie-coochie show at a county fair. How that mess even gets on TV is beyond me.'

'Not arguing, Mom. It wasn't my idea.'

'Like that woman revealing herself at the Super Bowl, remember? If it keeps going like this people will just stop watching. A lot of folks are fed up. Did you see it? You couldn't even call it dancing . . .'

'Mom, I was there.' She's had a glass or three of wine, apparently. More power to you, Mom, have another. God knows the woman could use a party.

'. . . I remember when Tom Landry was coach you never saw anything like that. They had standards. He kept that team on a tight rein. I don't know if it's since Norman Oglesby bought the team, or that coach he's got or some of those other people he's hired . . .'

340

The longer she talks, the whinier and more righteous she gets, and the less attention she pays to herself. Billy offers small hums of agreement and waits for the momma-logue to wind down.

'I hear you're fixing an awesome feast over there.'

'Well. It's no different from every year.'

'Then it'll be great. Don't wear yourself out.'

'No, I'm fine, the girls are helping out. Did you have Thanksgiving?'

'Sure did, they fed us really well. They took us to a club here in the stadium.'

'Well, that's nice.'

It strikes him again how pitiful her life will be if he gets smoked, all ego aside. Stove-in husband, dead son, piles and piles of medical bills . . . He thinks maybe he should up his GI insurance, then wonders if the hospitals would take it all.

'How's Dad?'

'He's fine. He's in the den watching the game with Pete.'

'Hey, there's a fun couple.'

'Well, they seem to get along.'

Poor Mom, she can't help being the straight man of her own life.

'Where are you now?'

'The concourse. I think they're taking us back to our seats.'

'Are you warm enough?'

'I'm great, mom.'

'Because I saw you weren't wearing any kind of coat.'

'I'm fine. It's pretty warm here inside the stadium.'

'Well, I'm sure you're busy, so I'll let you go.'

'Not really,' he says, exasperated. Maybe the last time they'll ever talk – *not to be dramatic about it!* – and she's giving him the bum's rush, her own son. Not that she means anything by it, he knows. This is simply her lifelong habit of moderation at work, her need to tamp everything down to the routine, the modest, the tepid everyday. He under-stands the whole concept of boundaries, but there's a point where this mania for normalizing turns toxic.

Perhaps this is why he tries something new. 'Okay, Mom, give everybody my love. And I love you too.'

'*Yes bye thanks have a nice day,*' she says in a rush, and he can't help the small laugh that gets loose from him. Let her be, he tells himself. Just let her be. Pressing her for something real seems almost cruel at this point. He clicks off and has a spasm of grief so intense that his knees buckle slightly. His hand finds the wall, and he has to remind himself that it's not absolutely certain he will die in Iraq. Just looking at the odds, he even stands a reasonably good chance of coming through without the proverbial scratch, aside from the laceration and shrapnel wounds he already received from being blown up on Dead Girl Road, and he knows if he makes it back he will *be so good.* Good for Mom, good for the family. And transcendently good for Faison. He can feel it rising in him, this powerful if not quite choate sense of how to live a strong and decent life. Not that you'll actually know except by doing it, by putting in the years – as if there's a salvation specific to combat soldiers, one that comes of learning passion for daily things? So he suspects, at least. That's his sense of it. He would like the chance to find out, anyway.

WILL SLAY VAMPIRES FOR FOOD

Bravo is on the move again. The concourse is thick with fans taking a break from the weather, and more than a few are already heading for the exits. People call out to Bravo, veer over to shake hands, but not as many as before. Major Mac has been holding the fort on row 7, the lone sentinel in their block of ice-spackled seats. Billy ends up on the aisle *per* normal with Mango on his left, and as their post-fight cheerleader buzz wears off Bravo starts to realize how shitty their situation is. Here they sit fully exposed to the sleet and freezing drizzle watching a dull-as-hell 7–7 third-quarter tie two days before they fly back to the war. Sucks! Mango groans and hunches over.

'Dawg,' he says to Billy, 'I just wanna go to sleep.'

'Uh huh. How's your ear?'

'Hurts like a motherfucker.' After a second they both find this extremely funny.

'What'd he do, try to rip it off?'

'He won't doing nothing except weighing about three hundred pounds. I woulda flipped him 'cept his leg was so fat, couldn't get my arm around it. I was like, dude, you never heard of diabetes? You might wanna shed a few, lay off the supersize for a while.'

They try to watch the game, but it's so slow, what's the point. The fans around them are sheltering under blankets, umbrellas, here and there a plastic trash bag; only the Bravos sit there like stock in a pasture, wide open to the weather. Billy pulls out his cell and stares at Faison's number. He is tempted to call just to hear her voice message, which sounds more southern than her real-life voice, the vowels rounder, the hard palate hollowed out, the vox equivalent of a Hill Country feather mattress.

'Dawg, I think I'm in love.'

Mango laughs. 'It'd be gay if you weren't. I saw the way you guys were moshing back there on the field. It means something when they do that shit, you know? They don't touch you unless they dig you.'

Billy stares at his phone.

'You get her digits?'

Billy solemnly nods.

'Well, fuck, she definitely likes you. Kind of sucks it's coming on the back end of the trip.'

Billy moans with the pleasure and pain of it, these violent oppositional forces that are physically molding him into something new. The Jumbotron plays the American Heroes graphic again, then grinds through the deafening commercial cycle, the same ads always playing in the same maddening

345

order. FORD TRUCKS BUILT TOUGH! TOYOTA! nissan! TOYOTA! nissan! FOR ALL YOUR BANKING NEEEEEDS DUM-DEE-DEE-DUMMMMM! Then Sykes sings out in his gruesome falsetto, *If you can't make me say ooo!*, then he pauses to tell the fans fore and aft how much he loves them, how much he loves all Americans everywhere, then he's singing again—

> *WhaaaAAAtttt's love got to do with it, got to do with it,*
> *WhaaaAAAtttt's love but a secondhand emooooo-shun*

Word comes down the row that Dime slipped him a big fat Valium about twenty minutes ago, and now he's the happiest girl in the whole USA.

Billy startles, nearly drops the cell when it rings. He checks the screen.

'Her?' Mango asks.

Billy shakes his head. He doesn't recognize the number. The call rings out, followed a minute later by the chirp of a waiting voice message. Billy stares at the phone. He wishes it would tell him what he wants. He dials up the message and listens, then sits back and closes his eyes. What would Shroom do? Shroom would return to the war, definitely, but that was his destiny in this life cycle, he was fulfilling his warrior incarnation and only by seeing it through would he move on to the next stage. 'So what stage am I?' Billy asked, joking, sort of, but Shroom didn't laugh. You won't know until you work at it, he said. Study, meditate, contemplate, focus. You won't find out just by drifting through your time. So with his eyes still shut Billy tries to envision himself at the ranch. *Very secure and remote,* the voice in the phone message said. *It's a good place. We'll make sure you won't lack for anything.* In the vision Billy is walking down a path. He's wearing jeans, Timbs, a flannel shirt, and a corduroy jacket. The path leads through some woods, and there's a river nearby. He can hear the *shoosh* of rapids, sometimes glimpse the flash of water through the trees, but the vision yaws and stutters until Faison material-izes at his side, and then it all unfolds in gorgeous HD, he and Faison living quiet in their secure location, loving each other, screwing eight or nine times a day, cooking meals and watching movies, going for walks with the dogs. There would be dogs. And lots of books, books piled everywhere. He would apply himself to study in the best Shroom tradition, so he'd know that much more when the shit-hammer came down. And when it did – when the time came to make his stand? He'd have Faison, the lawyers, his Silver Star on his side. He could do it. He'd make statements. Ain't gonna study war no more.

Rrrrraaaaahhhhhxxxx-annnnnn, Sykes is screeching at the top of his lungs, *you don't have to,* then he turns and starts chattering to the fans in row 8 about how much he loves the Bravos, hell yes he loves his boys like brothers, he's just a poor white dumbass from Coon Cove, Florida, but at least he's got the Army, hooah! Down on this end Lodis is slumped in his seat, fast asleep. Dustings of sleet have accumulated on his shoulders and arms as in a comic advertisement for an antidandruff shampoo. A squirt of subcutaneous tissue spills from the cut in his lip. The nice boojee lady in front of them happens to notice the sleeping soldier, such a compelling sight that she turns all the way around for a closer look.

'Ain't he sweet?' Mango says.

'How can he *sleep* in this weather?' she cries.

'Technically he's not asleep, ma'am,' Crack informs her. 'He's passed out.'

The lady laughs. She's a cool boojee lady. Her husband and friends are chuckling too.

'But it's just *miserable* out here,' she protests. 'Shouldn't he at least have a blanket or something? Doesn't the Army give you *coats*?'

'Oh, ma'am, don't worry about him,' Crack assures her. 'We're infantry, that's kind of like being a dog or a mule, we're too dumb to mind the weather. He's fine, believe me, he don't feel a thing.'

'But he could freeze!'

'No ma'am,' Mango chimes in. 'We punch him every once in a while to keep his blood moving. See, like this.' He delivers a sharp whack to Lodis's bicep. Lodis snarls and throws out his arms, but his eyes never open.

'See?' Mango beams. 'He's fine. He's happy. He's like a cockroach, you can't kill him!'

The lady rustles around in her pack, then kneels backward on her seat and drapes a Snuggie over Lodis, one of those personal lounging blankets with built-in sleeves as advertised on late-night dumb-dumb TV. Before long the Bravos have tucked a homemade sign under Lodis's chin. HOMELESS VET – WILL SLAY VAMPIRES FOR FOOD. Below that, HAVE A BLESSED DAY. Then a smiley face. The crowd perks up when a Cowboys lineman boosts an enemy fumble and staggers, slips, and slides all the way to the Bears' three, but then the refs get into it, they convene at the sideline replay machine and discuss, peer, point, and discuss some more, they are a team of Nobel scientists tweaking the breakthrough cure for cancer. At last, a decision is decided. *Upon further review* . . . The fumble is revised to an incomplete pass and that does it for the boojees, they start packing up. Mango reminds the nice lady to take her Snuggie. 'Oh, I can't do that,' she says, smiling down at Lodis, so soundly racked with his eyelashes flocked with sleet, that lip chunk dangling like a squashed bug. 'He looks so cozy. I want him to keep it. You tell him it's my gift to him.'

Bravo erupts: Noooo!

'You're gonna spoil him!'

'He grew up in a ditch, he don't know from being cold!'

'It's like giving a pig a Rolex, ma'am, he's got no appreciation for the finer things in life.'

The lady laughs and waves them off. 'Thank you!' the Bravos cry as she and her group file out of the row. 'Thank you for supporting the troops!'

'Nice lady,' Mango says, settling back in his seat. Billy agrees. They look at Lodis and laugh, then Mango shivers. He hunches over and clasps his hands between his thighs.

'You look like you gotta piss.'

'I sorta do gotta piss.' Mango winces and shivers but stays put. 'You gonna see Faison before we go?'

'Hoping.'

'Dude, gotta be some way you can get with her.'

'I don't think so. I don't know. I don't wanna push it.'

Mango laughs.

'No, I'm serious. I mean, if this was a normal situation all I'd be thinking about right now is where to take her on a date. Trying to nail her, I mean, come on. I've only known her about four hours.'

'Billy, our situation ain't normal, in case you hadn't noticed. You think she's gonna keep on liking you a whole year, and you a million miles away sending her dipshit emails? *Dear Faison how are you I am fine today we busted down a house and killed many bad fuckers as much as we could.* That shit gets old, dawg, shit gets old real quick. Even our moms don't wanna hear it after a while.'

'You are one depressing fuck, you know that?'

'I'm just sayin'! This is your best shot, dawg. This is as close as you're gonna get, so go for it.

If she's a nice girl and she wants to support the troops . . .'

'You're an idiot.'

Mango laughs. Billy's cell is ringing again.

'That her?'

'No,' Billy says, checking the screen. 'My sister.'

'You ain't picking up?'

Billy shrugs. The call rings out. A minute later he gets a text.

> *Dont go pls.*
> *B hero x2.*
> *CALL HIM BACK.*
> *Pls.*
> *Yr sis loves u.*

Billy punches up the phone message again, this time listening not so much to what the man says as to the sound of his voice, whatever information might be coded in timbre and pitch. The voice is white, male, educated, middle-aged; Texan, but with a big-city crispness to his words. Strong. Assertive. Sympathetic. *Son, if you're thinking about taking a new direction in your life, we can sure help with that.* It is a good voice. Billy is tempted to listen again, but here comes Dime barreling down the row, blasting through the obstacle course of Bravo knees and feet. He reaches the aisle and pulls out his cell, crouches by Billy's seat. 'Sykes is driving me fuckin' nuts,' he says, studying his messages.

'Better living through chemistry, eh, Sergeant,' says Mango.

'Yeah, well, it was either meds or ball-gagging the little shit. He'll be fine,' Dime says, though no one has asked. 'He'll be fine once we get him back on post. It's all this other . . .' He falls silent. Billy clears his throat.

'Sergeant, if you had a choice, would you go back? To Iraq, I mean.'

Dime lifts his head; he is not pleased. 'But I don't have a choice, do I? So your question lacks relevance.'

'But if you did have a choice.'

'But I don't.'

'But if you did.'

'But I don't!'

'But if you did!'

'Shut up!'

'I'm just—'

'SHUT!'

Billy shuts. Mango is giving him a WTF? stare. Dime snorts and shakes his head.

'Do you wish we had a choice, is that what you're saying?'

'Well.' Billy understands he's gone too far. 'But we don't.'

'That is correct, Billy, we don't. We're going back, and we all know what we're going back to, and that's why we're gonna have our shit high and tight and look out for each other twenty-four/ seven. But I will say this.' He pauses; his cell is ringing. 'If I'm never in another firefight as long as I live, that'll be okay by me. *Hey.*' He's got the cell to his ear. 'Uh huh. Uh huh. Interesting. How about this, how about if Swank sits on his face, would he do it then?'

Billy and Mango look at each other. The damn movie.

'So it's either that or . . .' Dime looks up at the scoreboard. 'Albert, we're running out of time.'

Mango turns away, hissing something low and hot in Spanish. Down the row Sykes has launched into the old boot camp chant, *Pick up your wounded, pick up your dead . . .*

'He's right here,' Dime says, glancing at Billy. He listens for a moment, then asks Billy: 'Are you available for a meeting?'

Billy laughs. 'Am I *what*? Sure, yeah. When?'

'Now. With Norm. Josh is coming for us.'

Billy's throat knots up. 'Okay.'

'Yes he is available,' Dime says to the cell. 'Anybody else?' Dime listens, then grunts and clicks off. For several moments he just crouches there, staring at the field.

'Sergeant, are you okay?'

Dime snaps out of it. 'I was just thinking, rich people are crazy.' He turns to Billy and adds, with feeling: 'Don't ever forget that.'

'Roger, Sergeant.'

MONEY MAKES US REAL

They come upon Albert in the corridor outside of Norm's suite, head down, back propped against the wall, tapping on his BlackBerry with his silver tapping stick. He beams when they turn the corner.

'Guys! What up?'

'Up, down, all around,' Dime answers.

'Let's hang here a minute, I'll bring you up to speed.' He turns to Josh with a pleasant, pointed look.

'I'll go tell Mr Oglesby we're here,' Josh says.

'Excellent idea.' Albert herds Dime and Billy down the corridor some distance from the suite. 'Looking good at halftime, guys, you did yourselves proud. You meet Beyoncé and the girls?'

'Hell no,' Dime grumps.

'What? No? That's lousy. So what was that about down on the field, after? Looked like a flash mob or something, Black Friday at a Wal-Mart out in North Jersey. We couldn't figure out what was going on.'

'It was nothing,' Dime says. 'Just boys being boys.'

'Somebody giving you a hard time?'

Dime looks to Billy. 'Was somebody giving us a hard time?'

'No, relatively speaking,' Billy answers.

'He'll go far,' Albert says to Dime. 'All right fellas, here's the deal.' He pauses to smile at a passing couple, waits for the swish of their fur and cashmere to recede down the hall. 'Norm's in. He wants to put together an investor group to make our picture, but that's not all. He's *inspired*, shall we say, you guys have inspired him to think big thoughts today. He's decided to form his own production company and start making films.'

'Might as well. His football team sure sucks,' says Dime.

Albert sniggers, glances up and down the hall. 'Apparently he's been mulling it over for quite some time, then we show up and he figures that's God's way of telling him to make his move. And frankly why not, the studios are looking to slough off risk any way they can. A guy who comes in with his own product, his own money, this is a very desirable commodity in Hollywood these days.'

He pauses while several more couples pass. One of the men snaps his fingers at Dime.

'Hey, great job at halftime!'

Dime snaps his fingers back. 'Hey, you too!'

Albert waits until they're gone. 'It helps that he's going all in, we'll have that much more credibility shopping our picture around. With a one-off deal

355

you're sort of a lame duck, but if they know you're sticking around? All the more reason for him to make a statement with this picture. Anyway, as far as our deal goes, as soon as he gets the company formed I'll assign my option over to it, then when we've got the package together the company exercises the option, you guys get some money, and we go into production.'

'Cool,' says Dime.

'I'll need you guys' consent to transfer the option over.'

Dime hesitates. 'But you'll still be our producer.'

'You better believe it.'

'What about the Swank situation?'

'He's still got a blunt up his ass about Hilary, but we can deal with that. All kinds of ways to deal with that. Believe me, having her in the mix is nothing but good for us. But listen.' Albert coughs into his fist. 'You need to know going in, Norm's got somewhat of a problem with the option price.'

'What kind of problem.'

'A size problem. A hundred thousand per Bravo, ten Bravos, that's a tough nut to crack right out of the gate. We're already looking at plunking half a million for the script, then getting a lead on the level of a Hilary, a Clooney, we're talking multiple millions here.'

Dime turns to Billy. 'Here's where we get fucked.'

'No!' Albert cries. 'No, no, no, no, Dave, have some faith! We've come this far together, you think

I'm gonna toss you over the side *now*? Dave, Dave, you guys are *my* guys, either we make it together or we go down together. That's what I told them in there, but I'm not gonna bullshit you, Norm's not Santa Claus, he's not spending one more dime than he has to. He, they, one of his guys – look, these are businessmen, okay? Understand they're very crude in their thinking, just by definition. They floated the idea of dealing with just you two, they see your stories as the principal elements in this and the rest of the guys as, well, ancillary. I said I'd run it by you, but—'

'*No.*'

'—uh huh, total nonstarter, that's what I told them. Bravo lives by the warrior code, I said. They won't ever leave one of their own behind.'

'For them to even—'

'I know! But you have to understand that's the mentality we're dealing with here. Streamlining, return on capital, all that MBA shit, but I think they got the message. It's gotta be all Bravos or no Bravos, nothing in between.'

'Damn straight,' Dime woofs, with volume enough to raise giggles from the busboys down the hall.

'David, relax.'

'I'm totally relaxed. Billy's relaxed too, aren't you Billy?'

'Totally, Sergeant.'

'Hang with me, guys, I'm gonna get you there. Right now what they're offering is, well, what you'd

357

be doing is deferring moneys up front for a net-profits percentage in the movie. You get an advance when the option is exercised, then you get another pop when we go into production—'

'How much?'

'—David, let me finish, please. Look, just ballparking this thing, if it has even decent success on the scale I'm thinking of, you guys will come out considerably better than a hundred thousand, but you'll have to hang in there and be patient. When I set our up-front number two weeks ago I was thinking we'd be playing with studio money, but it's a whole different game when you go independent. The numbers scale back across the board, people usually end up taking a profits percentage in lieu of cash. Even stars take percentage if it's a project near and dear to their hearts.'

'Fine, I hear you. How much.'

'Well, initially it's pretty minimal. Fifty-five hundred against profits when the option's exercised—'

A gurgling commences in Dime's throat.

'—but you'll get that second advance when production starts—'

'Fifty-five fucking *hundred?*'

'I know it's not what you were hoping for—'

'No shit!'

'—but then you'll get that second advance—'

'How much?'

'Well, we're still working on that, but usually it's

tied to production budget. The bigger the budget, the bigger your advance—'

'Not our deal, Albert. You said a hundred thousand up front.'

'I did, because I believe in your story so much, and I still think we're gonna home-run this thing. Look, two weeks ago I thought we had a real chance of taking studio bids, you guys had such outrageous buzz coming in. But we get a couple of no's, and Russell Crowe taking a pass, that really hurt us. It doesn't take much for the buzz to fade, and I admit, maybe I got a little ahead of myself, I jacked up everybody's expectations and now we're all going to have to adjust. Plus the fact that the war's put up some spotty box-office numbers, didn't I say that might be a problem? So we're bucking that too. I know fifty-five hundred sounds pretty lame after the numbers we've been talking about, but for young men like yourselves, young soldiers on Army pay, it's not nothing, right?'

'Albert, don't even talk to me like that.'

'Dave, I'm just trying to get you to think long-term here. This is equity, think of it as stock, stock options, you're deferring a chunk of money up front for a shot at real money down the road. And you guys would be helping to build something, that's what equity's all about. If the company makes money, you make money, you'll be fully vested partners with Legends on this deal—'

'Wait, *who*?'

'Legends. That's the name Norm wants for his company.'

'Jesus Christ, he's already got the fucking *name*?'

'You better believe he's got the name and that's great, I got no interest being partners with a ball scratcher, and neither should you. He's ready to *go*, Norm'll pull a damn trigger – do you not realize the value of that? How freaking *rare* that is in my world? You die by the slow no in this business, *lemme get back to you, lemme get back to you, lemme get back to you*, everybody's so scared of screwing up they'd rather lose a kidney than make an actual business decision. So here we are in Dallas, we meet this guy, he sizes up the situation and wham, he's good to go. I'm not saying you have to love the guy, but you've got to respect the power of that.'

Respect this, Billy can practically hear the Bravos woof. As if in pain Dime swags his head side to side.

'But Albert.'

'What?'

'You said they love us.'

'I did, David, but that was two weeks ago. People move on, they start to focus on other things.'

'So you're saying this is the best offer we're going to get?'

'Dave, I'm saying this is the only offer we've got.'

'Does Norm know?'

Albert shrugs. 'He knows we've been talking to people.'

'So what he's offering is, basically, fifty-five

hundred bucks apiece. And that's all he's on the hook for. No guarantees we'll get anything else.'

'Dave, you want a guarantee, go buy a microwave. No guarantees in my world unless your name is Tom Cruise.'

Dime sighs, and to Billy's profound alarm he turns and asks, 'What do you think?' but before Billy can answer an unmarked door pops open between them and the suite, and Mr Jones leans out.

'Mr Ratner, the third quarter's about to end.'

'Thanks. We'll be right there.'

Mr Jones withdraws but leaves the door ajar. Albert turns to Dime and Billy, lowers his voice. 'Guys, tell me what you want. You wanna go in there and talk, or should I just yell through the door no thanks.'

'No,' Dime says.

'No what?'

'This sucks,' Dime says to Billy.

Albert gives them a big smile. 'Always, guys, always, it's just a question of degree. Be thankful it's not rectal bleeding.'

'What happens to the rest of it if we say no? His big production company, all the movies he wants to make.'

Albert drops the smile. 'I think he's planning to go forward with that. He seems committed.'

'Are you going to be involved?'

Albert's mouth forms a tidy little purse. 'Well, I'd be foolish not to consider every opportunity.'

361

'Albert, you're an asshole.'

The producer doesn't bat an eye. 'Dave, I got you an offer. If you think you can do better, let's go in there and talk to the man.'

'Okay, fuck it. Let's go in there and talk.'

Billy says he'll be fine waiting in the hall, but Dime gives him such a blistering look that he's shamed into coming. Mr Jones is standing just inside the door, which he shuts and locks behind them. They descend a couple of steps into a dim, cramped, low-ceilinged space furnished along the ad hoc lines of a waiting room at a car wash. It's a super-private adjunct to the official owner's suite next door, a man place, ripe with the muzzy smells of sweat, burnt coffee, vestigial cigarette smoke, plus a percolating flatulence that might be stale lunch meat. Everyone turns and smiles for the Bravos. 'Gentlemen! Welcome to the war room!' someone cries, and they are urged forward, offered chairs and refreshments. TVs mounted on wall brackets are tuned to the game, the announcers nattering like parrots in a cage. A bare wet bar occupies one corner of the room. Norm and his sons are seated at a counter that runs the length of the plate-glass front. Scattered about the countertop are laptops, spreadsheets, loose-leaf notebooks, bottles of water and sports drinks; as his eyes adjust to the bad light Billy sees not a drop of alcohol in sight. Two Cowboys executives are moving about, big, burly guys with the trouser-hitching swagger of management who started out on the loading dock. Mr Jones perches on a stool by the wet bar, still with his suit coat buttoned. Everyone else is down to loose ties and rolled sleeves, except for Josh, who's doing his mannequin thing at the back of the room.

Dime asks for coffee. Billy says he'll have the same. Norm has swung his Aeron chair around to face them, and now he rubs his eyes and tips the chair back, giving the scoreboard a last glance as the quarter expires.

'Sorry about the lights,' he says, nodding at the ceiling. 'We keep them off during games, otherwise it's like a fishbowl in here. Damn irritating to look over at the TV and see yourself staring at yourself on the tube.'

'Or dropping the f-bomb,' says one of the execs. 'Not that *that's* ever happened here.'

Norm shakes his head as the others laugh. 'We try to keep at least an R rating up here.'

'Not many people ever see the inside of this room,' says the second executive, who has introduced himself as Jim. 'This is the inner sanctum, boys. A lot of folks would give their left arm to be sitting where you are.'

'You should charge admission,' Dime says, and everyone laughs but him.

'I'm not sure we could get it today,' says Norm. 'Not our most stellar effort, I'm sorry to say. I was really hoping we'd put on a show for you fellas. But maybe we'll turn it around in the fourth.'

'Some pass blocking from Stennhauser would be nice,' says f-bomb, to sour laughs. Norm turns to one of his sons.

'Skip, how many carries does Riddick have?'

Skip consults his laptop. 'Nineteen. For thirty-four yards.'

Groans rise from several sectors of the room. 'He's done, coach,' says Jim. 'Let's give Buckner a go, at least he's got fresh legs.'

'He don't have any holes to hit, what does it matter,' says f-bomb. 'We need to be pushing some bodies around up front.'

Norm frowns and takes a sip of Fiji water. Skip hands him a sheet of paper he's just printed out, from which Norm proceeds to read aloud third-quarter statistics. A waiter enters through a side door, showing a momentary slice of the main suite. Over there it's a pretty good party; over here, a long day at the office. Billy accepts his coffee and takes some sips. He likes it here. The close quarters evoke a sense of primal security, a kind of hunkered-down campfire intimacy that seems specifically masculine. It's that long-sought place of ultimate safety, all the better for its cave-like feel, its air of chummy exclusivity. He would love to wipe the war from his brain, if only for a moment, and indulge in the luxury of pretending that he's permanent here.

'This defense is as tough as any we've faced all year,' Norm says, perhaps rehearsing for the postgame press conference. He sets the printout aside and speaks past the Bravos to Albert, who's chosen to sit where the soldiers can't see his face.

'Albert, did you tell our young friends about our plans for their film?'

'Sure did!' Albert answers, spreading the pep a bit thick.

'Congratulations on your movie company, sir,' says Dime. 'Sounds epic.'

'Thank you, Sergeant, thank you very much. It's something we've been kicking around for a while, and we're excited to get it going, incredibly excited. It's definitely going to be a challenge, but with Albert on the team I like our chances. And I'm especially excited about bringing *your* story to the screen, and let me pledge to you right now, and I can't emphasize this enough, we're going all-out on this. Anyone here will tell you, when I decide to do something, I don't go halfway.'

'Norm loves his work,' says f-bomb.

Everyone laughs, and Norm joins in with a boyish chuckle, he doesn't mind this sly poke at his workaholic rep. Billy is struck by the depths he finds in Norm's watery blue eyes, the sincerity, the evident eagerness to concur and connect. Watching him at close range, it's hard to believe he's as mean as people say.

'I believe in your story,' Norm tells the Bravos, with only the briefest glance at the field, 'and I believe in the good it can do for our country. It's a story of courage, hope, optimism, love of freedom, all the convictions that motivated you young men to do what you did, and I think this film will go a long way toward reinvigorating our commitment to the war. Let's face it, a lot of people are discouraged. The insurgency gets some traction, casualties mount, the price tag keeps going up, it's only natural some people are going to lose their nerve. They forget why we went there in the first place – why are we fighting? They forget some things are actually worth fighting for, and that's where your story comes in, the Bravo story. And if the Hollywood crowd won't step up to the plate, well, I'm happy to pinch-hit, more than happy. This is an obligation I willingly assume.'

Son Skip is absorbed in his computer screen. Norm's other son – Todd? Trey? – has swung his chair around to listen to his father, though at the moment he's tapping out a text on his cell. Jim is pouring himself a soda at the bar. F-bomb executive is leaning against the wall, munching a sandwich and nodding his head to the beat of his boss's speech.

'I have my doubts about Hollywood anyway,' Norm is saying, 'their politics, the whole cultural attitude out there. And some of the concepts they've been throwing around? This whole thing with Hilary Swank – look, I know she's a great actress, I'm sure she'd do a great job. But having a woman in the lead just sends the wrong message, in my view. This is a story about *men,* men defending their *country,* and I'm sorry, that's just what it is.'

'But Hilary's still a prospect,' Albert pipes up, and everybody laughs.

'She is, she is,' Norm concedes, grinning, 'I didn't say she isn't. And if casting her turns out to be the best thing for our movie, that's what we'll do. I'm not interested in making a *good* movie, I want something *great,* something people will be watching a hundred years from now. I want a movie that's going to rank right up there with the best American films of all time.'

And with that everything seems settled and fine, until Dime speaks up and spoils it.

'What makes you think you can?' he asks, taunting, jeering, lifting his chin as if dismissing some object of contempt. Someone gasps, or so it seems when Billy later recalls these moments. Skip turns from his computer, slowly folding down the screen. Todd stares, fingers poised over the keypad of his phone. F-bomb executive has paused in midchew.

'Pardon?' Norm's dazed smile makes a pudding of his face.

'Can you do it, can you deliver. You want to buy our story for fifty-five hundred bucks, that sure sounds like chump change to me. We could sell it to pretty much anybody for that, hell, my granny could swing that deal with a trip to the ATM. With all due respect, Mr Oglesby, sir, show us you're serious. Show us you're a player.'

Still with that knocked-wonky smile, Norm sits back and carefully crosses his arms. He turns to

367

his sons, then to the two executives, and as if cued by some mysterious signal, they all bust up laughing.

'Look around you, son,' Norm says, regarding Dime with a warm, pitying cast to his eyes. 'Look around and think for a moment about everything you see. Then you tell me, am I a *player?*'

Billy knows if it was up to him, he would fold right now. It's too strong, the dark mojo of these rich, powerful men operating in the comfort of their home turf, and Norm above all with his kindly blue eyes, his fatherly patience, the paralytic force field of his mesmerizing narcissism. Billy wishes Albert would speak up and pull them back from the brink, but Dime presses on.

'Sir, may I speak frankly?'

Norm smiles, shows his palms. 'Why stop now?'

More yuks from the cheering section. The small of Billy's back is a peat bog of sweat. Does Dime plan these things or just wing it? *Wings it,* he decides with a fierce burst of pride. He'd follow his sergeant through forty hells.

'I've been told it'll take a budget of around eighty million dollars to get our movie made – am I correct on that, Albert?'

'Ideally,' Albert intones from somewhere south of the Bravos. 'Sixty to eighty million to make a first-class war picture.'

'That's a lot of scratch,' Dime says, turning back to Norm.

'It is,' Norm agrees.

'So where's it coming from?'

'Ah.' Norm chuckles, looks to his son. 'Skip, remind me again, where does the money come from?'

'Capital markets,' Skip says briskly, only slightly condescending as he turns to Dime. 'Banks, insurance companies, hedge funds, pension plans, there's always plenty of money out there looking for deals. Assuming the economy cooperates, we think we can get Legends fully funded in the three-, three-hundred-fifty-million range with a series of private offerings, roll them out over a period of, say, eighteen months. Then with additional funding to come as needed, maybe on a per-project basis.'

'GE Capital's been begging to put some money with us,' says Todd.

'That's right. And that's not counting individual investors. Just with our friends next door' – Skip nods toward the main suite – 'I bet Dad could step over there and have commitments for twenty, thirty million by the end of the game.'

'We have access,' Norm says patiently to Dime. 'We have ample experience raising capital. I think you could even call us' – he pauses and smiles – *'players.'*

'Yes sir, I sure hear you on that, sir. Those are some stout numbers you're talking about, but with all due respect, sir, fifty-five hundred for each of my Bravos just seems kind of . . . small.'

'Albert, they understand how we need to structure this deal?'

'I explained,' Albert answers in a studiously neutral voice.

'So you know' – Norm turns back to the Bravos – 'your fifty-five hundred is just an advance, correct? We could buy you out with a big lump sum, sure, but that makes it harder for us to get your movie made. We need maximum flexibility to put this package together, and what we're asking from you, what we need from you, is in the nature of an in-kind equity contribution. In exchange for the rights to your story you'll have a vested interest in the project, which means you share with us in the upside—'

'And the downside,' says Dime.

'Sure, sure, and the downside. There's going to be risk, just like with any investment. But it won't be any greater for you than it is for any other investor, myself included.'

'Mr Oglesby sir, with all due respect, sir. We're soldiers. We feel like we've already got enough risk in our lives.'

'And I'm certainly sensitive to that, but we're talking about an entirely separate arena here. If we're going to sell this project to potential investors, we've got to show them a solid package. We can't afford to be cutting sweetheart deals here.'

Norm swivels his chair for a look at the field, and Billy realizes that their host was hoping to close the deal before the fourth quarter began. Too late; the players are taking the field. 'You do understand, I trust,' Norm says, turning back to the Bravos, 'this is about a lot more than just money. Our country *needs* this movie, needs it badly. I really don't think you want to be the guys who keep this movie from being made, not with so much at stake. I sure wouldn't want to be that guy.'

'We understand, sir. And I can assure you sir, if anything terrible happens, Bravo is ready to take full responsibility.'

Norm cuts a glance at his execs. He's almost smiling, Billy sees. He's enjoying this. There is a vast asymmetry in the dynamic here that Billy can't quite put his finger on, even though it's the elephant shitting all over the room.

'Sergeant,' Norm says, 'that's our offer. Based on what I'm hearing, it's the only offer you've got, and now, well, you're going back to Iraq. Wouldn't you like to have something before you go? Something to show for all your hard work and sacrifice, the magnificent service you've given the country? Maybe it's not as much as you were hoping for, but I think most people would agree, something is better than nothing.'

'Something would be nice,' Dime says. 'Something would be great. But it's' – he breaks off with a choking gasp – 'it's just, I don't know, it's just so *sad*, sir. We thought you kind of liked us.'

'But I do!' Norm cries, lurching upright in his chair. 'I *do* like you! I think the world of you fine young men!'

Dime clasps his hands to his heart. 'See?' he

gushes to Billy. 'He *does* like us! He likes us so much he's going to fuck us in the face!'

In a second Albert is on his feet, chousing the Bravos out of their chairs with a bright furious smile and asking Norm for a place where he can talk to his 'boys,' and though the Oglesby team takes it all more or less in stride, Dime has offended, clearly. He has crossed the bounds of couth. A very curt Mr Jones leads them down the hall to a small, windowless room with a half bath attached, a kind of massage and decompression chamber, Billy gathers, furnished with a heavily pillowed daybed he would describe as 'French,' a couple of leather and steel-tube chairs, a massage table, and a deep-pile Persian rug. The ubiquitous TV is mounted high in a corner, the first they've seen today that's not switched on. Mr Jones ducks into the bathroom and has a look, then walks a circle around the massage table. He seems to be doing some sort of security sweep.

'Hey, Mr Jones, is this place bugged?' Dime asks. 'It's okay if it is, I'm just asking. Do you think it's bugged?' he continues, turning to Billy and Albert as Mr Jones leaves without saying a word. 'I bet it is, hell, I bet it's wired for video. I bet this is where Norm does his day-shift hookers—'

'David, chill.'

'—um *umph*, check this action out.' He's feeling up the daybed, then testing its bounce with his rump. 'I could definitely jam some high-dollar ass on this. I betcha anything he's got it fixed for video—'

'Settle down, Dave, please—'

'—it's always the billionaires who're the biggest pervs—'

'—would you shut up, Dave, please, please just shut the fuck up? Please? Can you? Yes? Thank you!'

Dime sits on the edge of the daybed and primly crosses his legs, looks over at Billy, and laughs. Albert looks to Billy and rolls his eyes. Billy has taken the leather chair by the bathroom door, as far out of the line of fire as possible.

'You're on his *team?*' Dime snarls.

Albert seems to rear, grizzly-like. 'Hell yes, if that's what it takes to get your picture made.'

'He's an asshole.'

'And that's supposed to mean anything? This is business, there's an asshole every time you pick up the phone. Stop thinking like a twerp and get your head in the game.'

'Oh gee Albert, I'm sorry. I'm really sorry if we're messing up your brand-new partnership.'

'Tell me this, David, do you think *you're* a player? You wanna be a player, you better learn to keep a civil tongue in your head. What you said in there – look, you cannot let emotion escalate into drama, not if you want a deal. You can whine and bitch and argue and everything else, but you *cannot* blow it up just because you're pissed off.'

'Like we haven't heard some rank stuff out of your mouth.'

'That's different, I know how far I can push. And some of these studio guys, they like the abuse, but you're punching way above your weight here. Norm doesn't have to take that kind of shit from you.'

'Norm can lick every pimple on my pretty pink ass.'

'Oh, lovely. Wonderful. I can see how well you're listening. You know what, maybe Billy should represent the squad in there. How about if you stay here, David, stay here and grow some brains. Billy and I'll go represent the squad in there.'

'I'm not going back in there,' Billy says, not that anyone's listening. Dime holds up his hand.

'All right, all right, okay, truce. Okay.' He takes a breath. 'Albert, just tell me this – is Norm just fucking with us? Does he really need to bust us down like this, or is he being a corporate dick just because he can?'

Albert leans against the massage table and sucks his lip, considering. 'Both, probably. I think he could do a lot better by you guys, no question. Fifty-five hundred is pretty thin. But you'll have equity.'

'He'll wanna screw us on that too, that's the vibe I get from this guy. If he's doing us on the front end he'll do us on the back, it's a matter of principle with this guy.'

'He's a pretty tough nut, I'll grant you that. You get in a fight with Norm, you better be wearing a cup, but listen, bottom line? He wants this deal as much as we do. So we just keep him at the table for as long as it takes, when he gets tired enough he'll come around.'

'Not if he runs out the clock on us. You heard him, he knows what we're up against. We don't have unlimited time here.'

'Well, I've always viewed your departure as a somewhat artificial deadline anyway. Signatures can be faxed. They can be e-mailed.'

'Not if we're dead.'

Albert folds his arms and stares glumly at his shoes. A brief, startling vision comes to Billy of big old Albert standing in a rainy field somewhere, head down, shoulders hunched, hands in his pockets, weeping. It has never occurred to him that their producer might be capable of actual tears.

'How about this,' Dime offers, 'how about if we hold a gun to his head?'

'Oh David, don't even talk like that.'

'Hell yeah, vets on the edge, baby! Everybody's got their breaking point.'

'He's just kidding,' Billy tells Albert, looking to Dime to make sure.

'Everybody *supports the troops*,' Dime woofs, '*support the troops, support the troops*, hell yeah we're *so fucking* **PROUD** *of our troops*, but when it comes to actual money? Like somebody might have to come out of pocket *for the troops*? Then all the sudden we're on everybody's tight-ass budget. Talk is cheap, I got that, but gimme a break. Talk is cheap but money screams, this is our country, guys. And I fear for it. I think we should all fear for it.'

Albert blinks, unsure how seriously he should take that last part. 'Dave, all I can tell you is the only way we're going to get a deal is to keep talking to this guy. He made his offer, if you don't like it we'll make a counter and see what comes back, that's how it works. But you keep your emotions out of it and focus on the deal, okay? That's the only way you're going to get some money for your guys.'

'I need to call them,' Dime says, pulling out his cell.

'So call. I gotta take a leak.'

As soon as Albert's in the bathroom Billy moves to the other chair, so that he doesn't have to listen to the movie producer pee. Dime calls Day, and at certain points in the conversation Billy can hear Day's side as plainly as Dime's. *What the fuck?* comes through quite clearly, in addition to *fuck that, fuck that shit,* and *fuck that motherfucking shit.* Dime asks Day to poll the rest of the squad, and their answers boom through like the bellowing of cows in a slaughter chute. Billy pulls out his own cell and clicks on. He's missed calls from Kathryn and the unknown number, and there's a text from Kathryn as well—

Sending car 4 u tx stadium
CALL HIM 4 meet.
JUST GET IN THE CAR.

Dime clicks off. 'They said no.'

'I heard.'

Dime pockets the cell. 'Your thoughts, Billy. What do you think we should do.'

Billy shuts his eyes and tries to have coherent thoughts about everything that has happened today. Into the still of his concentration sails the crash of a flushing toilet.

'He's wrong.'

'Who's wrong?'

Billy opens his eyes. 'Norm. Remember what he said in there, he was like, you guys oughta take the deal because it's all you've got, and something's better than nothing? But I don't think so. I think sometimes nothing is better than something. I mean, I'd rather have nothing than let this guy use me like his bitch. Plus' – Billy glances around and lowers his voice, as though the room in fact is bugged – 'I just sort of hate the son of a bitch.'

For some reason this is suddenly hilarious to them. Albert emerges from the bathroom to find the two Bravos laughing like baboons.

'Sorry, guy,' Dime tells him, 'but fitty-five hundred don't cut it. And Bravo speaks as one on this.'

Albert pulls a poker face. 'Okay, so what cuts it?'

'Hundred thousand up front, then we're out of Norm's hair. And he can keep all that wonderful equity for himself.'

'Guys, I think you're going to have to bend a

little bit. What if we – hang on.' His cell is buzzing. 'Speak of the devil. Lemme just . . . Yes, Norm.'

Billy remains in the chair, Dime on the daybed. They listen.

'You're kidding me.'

'You can't be serious.'

'Can you even do that? On what grounds . . .' Albert laughs, but he's not happy. 'National *what*? Are you serious? I've never heard of . . . Jesus, Norm, at least give us a chance. The least you could do is wait to hear what we come back with.'

'Five minutes?' He turns to the Bravos. 'You guys know of a General Ruthven?' But before the soldiers can answer, he's back to the phone.

'Norm, I really don't think you have to do this. If you'd just . . .'

'Of course I know it's not just about the money. Tell me about it, tell my guys. They put their lives on the line every . . .'

'All right. I guess so. I guess we'll see.'

Albert clicks off and slips the cell into his blazer side pocket. He turns to the Bravos, and the way he looks down at them, it's as if they're in their coffins and he's having a last look before the lid comes down.

'Whut,' Dime says.

Albert squints; he seems surprised to hear Dime speak. 'It's pretty incredible,' he says. 'They've gotten your chain of command involved. Apparently Norm's good buddies with the deputy-deputy secretary of defense or some such crap, he had that guy call your superiors at Fort Hood. He says he talked to a General Ruthven? And the general's supposed to call here in a couple of minutes, to talk to you.' Albert shakes his head; his voice wavers. 'I think they're going to make you do the deal.' He looks at them. 'Can they even do that?'

The Bravos know full well the Army does whatever it wants, and any rights they claim will be shunted into the catch-all category known as 'collateral,' i.e., things to be administered after it's too late. Mr Jones comes to lead them back to the bunker, where the Bravos are greeted civilly, almost warmly. They're offered refreshments. They're shown to the same two seats. 'The wheels came off,' Todd says, indicating the scoreboard, which shows 17–7 in favor of the Bears. 'Interception and fumble, ten points in two minutes.'

F-bomb executive snorts. 'We're gonna send out a search party after the game, help Vinny find his ass.'

This raises a bitter laugh.

'Why the hell does George keep sticking Brandt in the slot? Like he thinks he's gonna block?'

'I haven't seen him throw a block since spring training.'

'Of '01.'

More yuks. Norm sets his headset to the side and swings around to the Bravos. 'Not our day,' he says with a weary smile.

'No sir,' Dime says stiffly.

'I hate to lose, hate it about as much as anything.

My wife says I'm addicted to winning, and I guess it's true, thirty-eight years she's been trying to calm me down. But I can't, I need that rush. I'd rather cut off my little finger than lose.'

'We figured back in June it was going to be a tough season,' Jim says. 'With Emmit gone, Moose, Jay, they left some mighty big shoes to fill. When you lose your core like that . . .' He trails off when he realizes no one is listening.

'I expect you fellas are kind of cross with me right now,' Norm says, and by way of response Dime and Billy say nothing. Norm regards them a long moment; nods. He seems impressed by their wall of silence.

'I don't blame you,' he goes on. 'I know I'm being kind of heavy-handed here, but my instinct tells me to get it done. This is a movie that needs to be made, *now*, for all the reasons we talked about. And if it works out the way I think it's going to, you fellas are set to do very well. Someday before too long I think you'll be thanking me—'

Somewhere in the room a phone rings. Mr Jones answers, speaks briefly, and brings the phone over to Norm. It is the general. Dime stares straight ahead, into the far distance, it seems. Billy can hear him pulling in deep, measured breaths that he holds for several moments, then releases in finely calibrated jets through his nose. Meanwhile Norm is doing big-guy banter with the general, thanking him for his time, wishing him happy Thanksgiving, inviting him to some future unspecified game. You bet, ha ha, we'll do our best to arrange a win for you. Dime rises, as if the general has actually entered the room. Norm looks up, registering the weirdness of the move, and indeed Billy fears that his sergeant is contemplating something extreme, but Dime just stands there exuding waves of soldierly discipline until Norm extends the phone his way.

'Sergeant Dime.' Norm's smile is jacked a couple of clicks beyond mere courtesy. It is triumphant, one might say. Imperial. Magnanimous. 'General Ruthven will speak to you now.'

Dime takes the phone and makes his way to the shadowy back of the room. Josh sidles away to give Dime some space. After a moment Billy leaves his seat and also moves to the back of the room, simply to be near his sergeant and for no other reason. He takes up position near Josh, who shoots him looks of feverish sympathy. The entire room can't help but listen.

'Yes sir,' Dime says crisply.

'Yes sir.'

'No sir.'

'I understand, sir.'

For a full minute Dime says nothing, during which time the Bears score again. Skip and Todd toss their pens, but in deference to the general no one says a word.

'Yes sir,' Dime says presently. 'I didn't know that, sir.'

'Yes sir.'

'I think I do sir, yes sir.'

'Thank you sir. I will, sir. Out.'

Dime pivots and lofts the phone in a high, soft arc toward Mr Jones. 'Come on Billy,' he says, and without another word he's exited the room and goes booming down the corridor at a brisk pace. Billy has to jog to catch up.

'Sergeant, where we going?'

'Back to our seats.'

'What happened? I mean, shouldn't we . . .'

'It's okay, Billy. It's cool.'

'It is?'

Dime nods.

'He said we didn't . . .?'

'Not in so many words.' For several paces Dime is silent. 'Billy, did you know General Ruthven is from Youngstown, Ohio?'

'Uh, no, actually.'

'I didn't either, till just now.' For a moment Dime seems lost in thought. 'It's just over the state line from Pennsylvania.'

Billy begins to think maybe his sergeant has lost it. 'Near Pittsburgh,' Dime continues. 'He's a big Steelers fan. The *Steelers*, Billy, yo? Which just by definition means he hates the Cowboys' guts.'

'Hey guys!' someone calls, and they turn. It's Josh, trotting after them. 'Where're you going?'

'Back to our seats,' Billy answers.

Josh slows for a moment, glances over his shoulder, then gathers speed. 'Wait up, I'll come with you.' He has a sheaf of manila packets under one arm, and with the other he's reaching into his coat pocket. Something white flashes in his palm.

'Billy,' he calls, holding out a small plastic bottle. 'I got your Advil.'

THE PROUD GOOD-BYE

Why make a movie anyway? It seems pointless to go to all that trouble when the original is floating out there for all to see, easily available online by searching 'Al-Ansakar Canal,' 'Bravo snuff movie,' 'America's throbbing cock of justice,' or any one of a couple of dozen similar phrases that summon forth the Fox News footage, three minutes and forty-three seconds of high-intensity warfare as seen through a stumbling you-are-there point of view, the battle sounds backgrounded by a slur of heavy breathing and the bleeped expletives of the daring camera crew. It's so real it looks fake – too showy, too hyped up and cinematic, a B-movie's defiant or defensive flirtation with the referential limits of kitsch. Would a more polished product serve better, one wonders – throw in some story arc, a good dose of character development, artful lighting, and multiple camera angles, plus a soundtrack to tee up the emotive cues. Nothing looks so real as a fake, apparently, though ever since seeing the footage for himself Billy has puzzled over the fact that it doesn't look like any battle he was ever in. Therefore you have

384

the real that looks fake twice over, the real that looks so real it looks fake and the real that looks nothing like the real and thus fake, so maybe you do need all of Hollywood's craft and guile to bring it back to the real.

Then again, everybody always says how much like a movie the Fox footage is. Like *Rambo,* they say. *First Blood.* Like *Independence Day.* Or, as one of their new neighbors in row 6 says, a perky, chatty, twentysomething blonde who's shown up with her husband and another young couple, 'It was just like nina leven all over again. I sat down and cut on the news and got the weirdest feeling I was watching a movie on cable.'

'You guys rock,' says her husband, a handsome, strapping fellow in a Patagonia parka and heirloom-quality cowboy boots. 'It felt damn good to see us finally getting some payback.'

The other young husband and wife echo the sentiment. They aren't much older than Billy, these two young couples who've migrated down from the upper deck for a sampling of the money seats at garbage time. They remind Billy of certain kids he went to high school with, the sons and daughters of the small-town country-club elite who were firmly embedded in the college track, and now here they are in their midtwenties, duly credentialed and married, starting out their grown-up lives on schedule. The young couples are eager to meet the Texas Bravo, but for a moment they don't know what to make of him in the flesh.

385

'You're just a kid!' one of the wives cries, breaking the ice, then they're introducing themselves and thanking him for his service, the two young wives breathy and fond, the husbands racking his arm with welcome-to-the-frat handshakes.

'Awesome,' they say, 'outstanding,' 'an honor to meet you' and so forth, their words sloshing around Billy's brain like soft ice cubes

currj

honor

sacrifice

bravery

proud

and

Kicking Ass!

Billy resumes the aisle seat. Sleet pounds down around them like a spray of fine-grained fertilizer pellets. 'No deal?' Mango asks, and Billy shakes his head.

'So what's that about?'

Lodis and A-bort are leaning in, they want the story too.

'Norm's just a cheap bastard, I guess. What can I say.'

'We thought Day was shitting us when he told us the deal. Fifty-five hundred—'

'—shit's *cold*,' A-bort breaks in, 'all the coin he's got running through his pockets, and that's the best he can do for us? Dude's got millions.'

'Maybe that's why he's got millions,' Mango points out. 'He's careful with his money.'

'I be careful with my money, I had some,' says Lodis, his splotch of lip quivering like a big juicy booger, or a nib of entrails dangling from a gut wound. Josh comes down the row calling their names and handing out manila packets. Inside his packet each soldier finds an assortment of Dallas Cowboys swag: headbands, wristbands, a combination key chain/bottle opener, a set of decals, the cheerleader calendar for the upcoming year, a glossy eight-by-ten photo of the Bravo shaking hands with Norm, signed and personalized by the great man himself, along with several eight-by-tens of the Bravo posing with his trio of cheerleaders in the post-press-conference scrum, signed and personalized by each of the girls. The Bravos sort of shrug once they've gone through their packets. Outright derision is beneath them. Billy's cell buzzes and it's a text from Faison.

Meet after game?

Yes, he answers, love blanketing his heart like a slab of melting cheddar. *Where u be?* he adds, then waits, phone in hand, while the ranch fantasy does a number on his head. Maybe, he thinks, pondering the possibilities. She was into him. She *got off* on him. He and Faison shacked up at the ranch doesn't seem much more extreme than anything else that's happened lately. He scrolls through his call list to the unknown number, intending to see what kind of vibe might come of staring at it, but an incoming call beats him to it. He clicks on.

'Billy.'

'Hey, Albert.'

'Where are you guys?'

'Back at our seats.'

'Is Dime there?'

'Yeah, he's here.'

'He won't pick up. Tell him to pick up for me.'

Billy yells down the row and says Albert wants to talk. Dime shakes his head.

'He says not right now.' For a moment they're silent. 'So did the general . . .'

'You're good, Billy. He's not going to make you guys do anything.'

'What'd Norm say?'

Albert hesitates. 'Well, it's kind of tough on him. Like he said, he's *addicted* to winning.' Albert allows himself the softest of snarky laughs. 'It's okay. He's one of those people who could probably use some humility in his life.'

'He's pissed,' Billy concludes.

'Just a little.'

'Are you?'

'Pissed? No, Billy, I can honestly say I'm not. I love you guys way too much for that.'

'Oh. Well. Thanks.'

Albert chuckles. 'Oh, well, you're welcome.'

'So what happens now?'

'Well, I'm in the main suite right now, Norm's back there in his hideaway. Maybe he'll come out with another offer at some point. We'll just have to see.'

'Okay. Uh, Albert, can I ask you something?'

'Of course, Billy.'

'When you ducked out of Vietnam, I mean, you know, when you got your deferment and everything, how did it feel?'

Albert gives a little yip, the way a coyote might as it dodges a sprung trap. 'How did it *feel*?'

'I mean, like, was it hard. Did it feel like you were doing the right thing. How do you feel about it now, I guess is what I'm asking.'

'Well, it's not something I spend a lot of time thinking about, Billy. I won't say I'm hugely proud of it, but I'm not ashamed of it either. It was a very fucked-up time. A lot of us really struggled about what we had to do.'

'You think it was more fucked up then than it is now?'

'Huh. Well. Good question.' Albert ponders. 'You could probably make a pretty good argument that for the past forty years it never stopped being fucked up. Why do you ask?'

'I don't know. I was just thinking, I guess. About why people do the things they do.'

'Billy, you are a philosopher.'

'Hell no, I'm just a grunt.'

Albert laughs. 'How about both. All right, guy, hang loose. And tell Dime to call me.'

Billy says he will and clicks off. He dry-swallows two more Advil; the first three made no appreciable dent in his armor-plated headache. Mango asks for some, and Billy ends up passing the bottle down the row, never to return. A steady flow of fans is heading up the stairs for the exits, while a smaller contingent makes its way down, looking to squat in the premium seats for as long as the game lasts. A group of five or six guys piles into row 6, friends of the young marrieds it seems; they arrive with much laughing and razzing and immediately pull out pint bottles of Wild Turkey. 'Bro!' one of them caws at Lodis. 'Get some stitches in them dizzles!' They have the clean-cut, mainstream, Anglo looks that Billy imagines must be soothing to bosses and clients, suitable for careers in banking, business, law, wherever it is the money lives. The guy sitting in front of Crack turns all the way around.

'Dude, what happened to your *eye*?'

'It's always like this,' Crack answers. 'But, dude, what happened to your *face*?'

Brrraaaaahhhh, even the guy's own friends send up a howl. 'Hey, these are the Bravos,' one of the young husbands says. 'Don't mess with these guys.'

'The *whos*?' cries Crack's new friend. 'The *what-hoes*? Oh yeah yeah yeah I heard of you guys, yeah, goddamn, you're famous. Hey, tell me something, what do you think about that whole don't-ask-don't-tell deal?'

'Stop it, Travis!' one of the young wives scolds. 'You're being a jerk.'

'I am not either being a jerk, I really wanna know! This guy's a soldier, I'm just curious what he thinks about gays in the military.'

'I think more of them than gays not in the military,' Crack says. 'At least they've got the balls to join.'

The rowdies send up another howl. 'I hear you, dude, hear you,' Travis says, laughing. 'Serving your country and all that, very cool and everything. But I don't know, it just seems kind of wack to me, say you're in your foxhole at night and some queer comes on to you, what're you supposed to do? Guys blowing each other in foxholes, that just doesn't sound right to me. Like maybe it's got something to do with why we're getting our butts kicked over there, you know?'

'Tell you what,' Crack says, 'why don't you join up and find out. You can get in a foxhole with me and see what happens.'

Travis smiles. 'You'd like that, dude?'

Billy wishes Crack would just smack the fool and be done with it, but his fellow Bravo merely stares the guy down. Perhaps one melee is enough for this Thanksgiving Day. Billy checks his cell. Nothing from Faison. Yet. He indulges in another episode of the ranch fantasy, but now while he and Faison are having sex ten times a day he's also thinking about Bravo back at FOB Viper, getting slammed every time they go outside the wire. So he puts that inside the fantasy, how much he'd miss his fellow Bravos, he would *mourn* them even as they live and breathe. They are his boys, his brothers. Bravos would die for one another. They are the truest friends he will ever have, and he'd expire from grief and guilt at not being there with them.

So it seems the war is fucked and his fantasy no less so. He sends another text to Faison. *Wd like to see u and say g-by after game.* She responds almost immediately, *Yes!*, but when he asks where and when, nothing. Dime makes his way down the row and kneels in the aisle by Billy's seat.

'What'd Albert say?'

'Well, he's not mad at us.'

'No, Billy, what'd he say about Ruthven.'

'Oh. He said it's cool. Ruthven did just what you said he'd do.'

Dime smiles. 'We need to send that man some flowers!'

'Albert said Norm might come back with a better offer—'

'Fuck that, we're not doing a deal with that guy, not for any amount of money. Not for a million bucks apiece.'

Billy and Mango look at each other. 'A million bucks—' Mango attempts, but Dime cuts him off.

'Look at it this way, say we do the deal and Norm makes his big-shit Bravo movie, gets everybody all pumped for the war again. What happens then? I think what happens is they'll keep stop-lossing our ass until we're dead or too damn old to carry a pack. Well, fuck that. I got no use for a deal like that.'

Dime turns and bounds up the aisle. The Bears score to make it 31–7, and the game has officially become a rout. One of the rowdies in row 6 drops his bottle, and the sound of shattering glass sends his buddies into hysterics. 'Assholes,' Mango mutters, and Billy agrees. They're too drunk, too loud, too pleased with themselves – more people who could use some humility in their lives?

Billy's cell chirps, signaling a new text. He checks the screen.

'Faison?' Mango asks hopefully.

'Sister.' Billy waits for Mango to turn away before he opens it.

CALL HIM.
They r ready.
They r waiting 4 u.

Oh Jesus. Oh Shroom. What would Shroom do? What would he do if he was Billy, that is the better question, one that turns on the most intimate, pressing issues of soul, self-definition, one's ultimate purpose in life. The two-minute-warning gun fires, which means, great, he has about 120 seconds to figure out what he's doing here on planet Earth. Oh Shroom, Shroom, the Mighty Shroom of Doom who foretold his own death on the battlefield, how would he counsel Billy here at the *Victory Tour*'s end? He needs Shroom to make sense of the situation, to calm the neural scramble of Billy's brain, but now the Jumbotron is playing the American Heroes graphic and the rowdies in row 6 send up a big whoop and holler, clapping, stomping their feet, the young marrieds try to shush their friends but there is just no stopping the fun.

'Brav-ohhhh!'

'Hay-yull yeah!'

'Woooo-hooooo!'

'Army of one, dudes!'

'See?' says Travis, twisting around to grin at Crack. 'We're all kick-ass patriots here, we totally support the troops.'

'Hell yeah,' yells one of his buddies.

'Hell yeah,' Travis woofs. 'Listen, don't-ask-don't-tell, I'm totally down with that. I don't give a shit if you guys are gay or bi or tranny or screw lesbian monkeys for all I care, you're studs in my book. You guys are real American heroes.'

He raises his arm for a high-five, but Crack just stares, lets him dangle. 'No?' Travis flashes a smile. 'No? Whatever, it's cool. I still support the troops.' He laughs and turns away, reaching under his seat for his bottle. When he sits up, Crack leans forward and methodically, almost tenderly it seems, locks his arms around Travis's neck and proceeds to choke him out. All soldiers learn this in basic training, how a forearm applied to the carotid artery cuts off blood flow to the brain, rendering your victim unconscious in seconds. Travis flops a bit, but it's not much of a struggle. He grabs at Crack's arms, kicks at the seat in front of him, then Crack squeezes a little harder and Travis goes limp. Several of the rowdies start to rise, but Crack warns them off with a grunt.

'What's he doing?' hisses one of the young wives. 'Tell him to stop it. Somebody please tell him to stop.'

But Crack just smiles. 'I could break this asshole's neck,' he announces, and shifts his hold, applies some experimental torque. Travis gives a spastic kick; his friends can only watch. They seem to understand he's beyond their help.

'Crack,' says Day, 'enough. Turn the motherfucker loose.'

Crack giggles. 'I'm just having a little fun.' There's a masturbatory aspect in the way he twists Travis one way and then the other, squeezing, relenting, squeezing, relenting, probing the physi-ological point of no return. Travis's face is dark red, shading to purple. A full-on carotid choke results in death in a matter of minutes.

'Damn, Crack,' Mango murmurs. 'Don't kill the son of a bitch.'

'Stop him,' pleads one of the wives. 'Say some-thing to him.'

Billy thinks he might be sick to his stomach, but part of him wants Crack to go ahead and do it, just to show the entire world how fucked the situ-ation is. But finally Crack relents; it's as if he loses interest, the way he turns Travis loose with a casual slap to the head, and Travis sags into his seat like a broken crash dummy. In short order the rowdies decide it's time to leave. They brace up their woozy friend and file out of the row, careful to avoid eye contact with the Bravos. 'You guys are crazy,' one of them mutters as he sidles past, and Sykes shouts Hell yes we're out of our motherfucking *minds!*, and adds a burbling Valium laugh that in fact sounds pretty batty.

Dime returns in time to watch the rowdies hurry up the aisle. He rubs his chin and regards his suspiciously silent squad.

'Something I need to know about?'

The Bravos manage a weak *brah*. 'Mofo kept mouthing off,' Day says. 'So Crack give him some, uh, training guidance.'

Crack shrugs, forces up a smile. He seems chas-tened and at the same time deeply satisfied. 'I didn't hurt him, Sergeant,' he says in all modesty. 'Just messed with his head a little.'

Down on the field, the final two minutes of play have resumed. Dime looks at his watch, looks at the scoreboard, then has a moment's communion with the storming sky. 'Gentlemen,' he says, turning back to Bravo, 'I think our work here is done. Let's blow.'

The squad sends up a lazy or possibly sarcastic cheer. Josh says they're supposed to meet their limo at the west-side limo lane, and he will show them the way. For the final time Bravo trudges up the aisle steps, Billy fighting the tug of all that horrible stadium space. As soon as they reach the concourse he pulls out his cell and texts Faison—

Can u meet west side limo lane?
Look for white hummer limo

Bravo falls into line and follows Josh through the concourse. Sykes and Lodis have managed to hang on to their autographed footballs all this time, while the rest of the Bravos have only their swag packets, precious mainly for the cheerleader calendar and those trophy-cleavage photos. It's going to be a long, lonesome eleven months in Iraq, long and lonesome being best-case scenario. On this final walk through the stadium no one stops to thank the Bravos for their service, to harry them for autographs or cell phone snaps. Cowboys nation is in full retreat; cold, wet, tired, whipped, they are bent on getting home as fast as possible, the hell with geostrategy and defending freedoms.

Oh my people. When they come in sight of the gate Josh leads them over to the side of the concourse, out of the traffic flow. 'We're supposed to wait here,' he tells Bravo. 'Some people are coming down to see you off.'

Who?

Josh laughs. 'I don't know!'

The Bravos look at one another. Whatever. Presently there's a surge of bodies into the already packed concourse, and from this Bravo infers that the game has ended. The fans move in a toilsome mass toward the exit, and in their numbers and necessarily shambling step they seem to take on allegorical weight, as if their gloom, their air of bedraggled wretchedness, is meant to conjure up the ghost of every tribe that ever bestirred itself to leave one place and journey toward another in hopes of a life of lesser evil. Billy thinks, in other words, that they look like refugees. His cell buzzes, and he turns to the wall before daring to look. It is a two-word text from Faison.

Coming. Wait.

His eyes close, and his head tips forward and clunks the wall, his silent thank-you released as a pent-up breath. Then he's nervous. He doesn't know what he's going to do. He's got no training for this, no drill, nothing to fall back on. He can visualize himself and Faison at the ranch, but the transition, the getting there, his mind won't grant him that. Maybe if he actually *rams* his head against the wall? Suddenly Albert and Mr Jones appear, popping out of the crowd in a cartoon sort of spurt.

'Hah,' Dime screeches in his Will Ferrell voice. 'Like a *dog* returning to his *vomit,* here he is!'

Albert grins, he seems perfectly cool with the greeting, though he's careful to keep some distance between himself and Dime. *Albert, Albert, Albert,* the Bravos woof, making a kind of song.

'What about our deal?' Sykes cries.

'Guys, I tried. Believe me, I tried like hell, and I'm going to keep on trying, you can count on that. If there was ever a story that's made for the movies, it's you guys', and I'm fully committed to making that happen.'

'But dude—'

'I know, I know, it's a huge disappointment, I really wanted to nail this thing while you were here. What can I say? We gave it our best shot, but it's not over, hell no. I'm gonna keep working this deal till it happens, I promise you that.'

Monklike murmurings rise from the Bravos, *thankyouthankyouthankyou.* A car is waiting to take Albert to the airport; he's flying back to L.A. tonight. Even though his option extends for an entire two years, this feels like the end of something, with all the nostalgia and melancholy natural to endings. Albert says he'll walk out to their limo with them; evidently Mr Jones is coming too,

399

perhaps to ensure Bravo departs without further insult to the Cowboys brand. They join the weary masses moving toward the exit. A kind of drone, a bottom-register vibraphonic hum emanates from somewhere up ahead, from the threshold, Billy realizes as they draw near. It is the ongoing moan of successions of fans as they step onto the plaza, a windswept barrens of icy concrete with nothing between here and the Arctic Circle but thousands of miles of recumbent plains. The Bravos curse, lower their heads, jam hands in pockets. The sleet gouges micro-divots in their faces and necks. Josh calls the soldiers to him and does a head count, then leads them across the plaza toward the limo lane, limos lined into the murk as far as the eye can see, and, oh Lord, just among these dozen in plain sight Billy counts four in the snow-white Hummer style.

'Billy.' Albert has fallen into step beside him. 'I think your sergeant is mad at me.'

'Well, he's kind of a moody guy.' Billy wishes Albert was on his other side, to block the wind.

'Listen, you've got my e-mail, right? And I've got yours. Let's stay in touch.'

'Sure.' Billy is scanning the line of limos. How Faison is ever going to find him out here . . .

'I admire Dave a lot, but sometimes I wonder how reliable he is. So how about this, whenever I can't get up with him, I'm going to contact you. You'll be my point man for the rest of the squad.'

'Fine.' Billy raises his windward shoulder, digs

his chin into his chest. The wind cuts across the plaza like an unmoored guillotine.

'Listen,' Albert says, lowering his voice, 'you've got the most sense of all these guys, you and Dime. I trust you. You're developing into a real leader. I know I can count on you to keep the communication flowing in a positive way.'

'Sure.' Billy is thinking if Faison hasn't showed by the time Bravo is ready to leave, he'll just bail, go AWOL right then and there. He'll say he's got to take a whiz or something, duck out of the limo; he'll be as good as committed then, more so once he locates Faison and spills his guts at her feet.

'I meant what I said about the deal,' Albert is saying. 'I'm going to keep working it. Sooner or later it has to happen, it's just too good not to.'

Billy looks at him. 'Really?'

'Well, sure. With Hilary basically attached, it's only a matter of time.'

The plaza is lit like a prison exercise yard, all glaring white lights and jabby shadows. Billy turns to scan the area for Faison and almost at once registers a pattern within the crowd, a kind of rippling or cross-current aimed this way. There's a blank moment, then Billy is opening his mouth, he knows what's coming an instant before his mind forms the thought. He's actually shouting as the roadies step from the crowd, then all he knows is that he's down in a fetal curl as a ball-peen sort of thumping pummels his back. He realizes that's himself he hears grunting with every whack, not that it hurts, it's pressure weirdly stripped of pain, and about the time he figures out someone is kicking him here comes Mr Jones stepping into the light. At this point time doesn't slow down so much as congeal into a series of overlapping blocks. Here is Mr Jones standing upright, pulling his gun from his suit jacket, then the massive body slam from behind that sends him flying, and the gun – a Beretta Px4, in the freeze-framed moment Billy sees it quite clearly – launched with great force from Mr Jones's hand. It takes off like a skate across the ice, skittering, spinning just beyond Billy's reach, away it goes and he twists around despite the foot in his ribs because he has to see where it's going—

Straight for Major Mac, as it turns out. With a veteran goalie's timing and economy of effort, the major lifts his toe a couple of inches and traps the weapon under his shoe. He scoops up the Beretta, checks the safety, and chambers a round while holding the weapon down and away from his body, then with the elegance that comes of many hours of practice, he raises his arm and fires straight overhead,

BAM.

In all of tomorrow's exhaustive media coverage of the game – the straight news stories, the human-interest piffle, the brain-draining chatter of the TV and radio jocks – there will be not a word about gunfire after the game. The Bravos will agree this is very strange. Surely thousands heard the roar of the gun; certainly those many hundreds on the plaza who ducked at the report, screamed, cowered, threw themselves on their children, or took off running, and whoever was kicking the shit out of Billy abruptly stopped. For some moments Billy simply lies there, enjoying the profound inner peace that comes of not being kicked. He tips his head to keep the blood from running into his eyes and watches Major Mac, who sets the safety on the Beretta and carefully places it on the ground. Then the major stands tall with his arms T-squared, not crooked at the elbows, not with his hands on his head, postures too suggestive of surrender. No, he stands with his arms straight out to the sides, simply to show the charging cops he is no longer armed.

'Major Mac dah man,' Billy mutters. He says this mainly to hear himself, to see if he's basically all right.

It takes the police some while to sort things out. That there are so many different kinds of police seems to complicate things. Eventually the Bravo limo is located and brought forward, and the soldiers are herded into it while discussion continues on the plaza nearby. Albert and Dime are out there, and Josh, and Mr Jones, all conferring with a cadre of the higher-ranking cops. Major Mac stands slightly apart, not in custody per se but with an officer meaningfully placed on either side. The handful of roadies thus far apprehended stand in a miserable clump, handcuffed, heads down, their backs to the wind.

An officer leans into the limo's open rear door. 'Anybody here need to go to a hospital?'

The soldiers shake their heads. Noooooo.

The officer hesitates. Almost every Bravo is bleeding from the face or head. The roadies came at them with wrenches, pipes, crowbars, God knows what else.

'Just checking,' the officer says, and withdraws.

They find two cold packs in the limo's first-aid kit and pass them around. Mango has a gash over his left eye. Crack lost two teeth. A goose egg of a contusion is rising on Day's forehead. Sykes and Lodis are bleeding from the nose and scalp, respectively. Billy's cheek has been laid open, a two-inch tear along the ridge of the bone – that's the shot that took him down, he guesses. His torso throbs with a muffled, tumbled sort of ache, nothing major, but he's not fooled. He knows tomorrow it's going to hurt like hell.

Dime climbs in and takes a seat. 'Cops want everybody's name and contact info,' he says, passing a clipboard and pen to Day.

'Sergeant, are we going to jail?' Mango asks.

'Nah, we're victims, dawg.'

'How 'bout Major Mac?' Lodis wants to know.

'Major Mac's a goddamn national treasure. Nobody's putting Major Mac in jail.'

'Sergeant,' says A-bort, 'we're thinking conspiracy here. Norm put the roadies on us 'cause we wouldn't take his deal.'

'I'll mention it to the cops,' Dime says, not

smiling. This is a joke. Billy's cell buzzes and it's a text from Faison, *Which white hummer,* and he bolts from the limo even as he's punching in her number. One of the cops huffs, 'Where do you think you're going?' but Billy's focus is such, all his being attuned to the one true thing, that a kind of godly aura repels the officer's challenge.

Her cell barely rings and she's clicking on. 'Hey!'

'See where the cop lights are, all the cops standing around?'

'Uh, yeah?'

'That's ours. I'm standing outside.'

'Stay there,' she says, 'I'm walking that way.' Then, 'I see you! Don't move, I see you, I see you . . .'

He sees her cutting through the crowd, white boots flashing underneath a dark overcoat, and her hair, a muted silver under the horrible prison lights, spilling everywhere, over her shoulders, down her back, across her breasts. She looks so good that he feels himself empty out, no breath, no pain, no thought, no past, his whole life distilled to the sight of Faison striding toward him in all her sleet-spangled glory.

He must have started walking toward her, because they meet with a satisfying crunch. For several moments they can do no more than clutch each other. The crowd parts around them, so many people moving past that a kind of privacy is conjured from the sheer multitudes.

'What happened to your *face*?' she cries, pulling

back, touching his cheek. 'Omigod, you're bleeding.' She glances past him at the cops and emergency lights.

'Those guys from halftime, the stage crew. They jumped us.' He laughs. 'I guess they were still pissed off?'

'Oh God. Oh my God, you're hurt.' She's studying his cheek, fingers brushing the edge of his cut. 'Trouble sure seems to follow you guys around.'

They kiss, hard. It is impossible for them not to be all over each other. 'This sucks,' she soon murmurs, and pulls away just enough to unbutton her coat, a swift downward sweep of her hand and the coat is opening, wrapping around him. She pulls him close and moans as her chest meets his. She's still in her cheerleader uniform. He moves his hands inside the coat and grasps her hips. She shudders, then rises on her toes, her pelvis striving for purchase on that hump in his pants, her mouth clamped so hard that his lips turn numb. 'Go for it,' someone says, brushing past them. Another passerby advises them to 'get a room.' After minutes or possibly hours Faison drops back on her heels and slumps against him.

'Oh God. Why do you have to go?'

'I'll be back on furlough. Probably in the spring.'

She lifts her head. 'Seriously?'

'Seriously.' If I'm still vertical, he thinks.

'Then you better make time for me.'

'Count on it.'

'Seriously, I mean it. How about if you come stay with me?'

He can't speak. He can barely breathe. She's looking from his left eye to his right, back and forth, back and forth, always her two double-teaming his one.

'I know it's crazy, but we're in a war, right? All I know is that it's right, it just feels right. I want every second I can get with you.' She shivers, shakes her head. 'I'm not the type to get bowled over, not like this. I've never felt this way about anybody.'

Billy pulls her close; her head falls against his chest. 'Me either,' he murmurs, the sound of his voice vibrating through their bodies. 'Girl, I'd just about run away with you.'

She lifts her head, and with that one look he knows it's not to be. Her confusion decides it, that flicker of worry in her eyes. *What is he talking about?* Fear of losing her binds him firmly to the hero he has to be.

She touches his cheek. 'Baby, we don't have to run anywhere. You just get yourself home and we'll be fine right here.'

He doesn't resist, because there's just so much to lose. He will forgo the greater risk in favor of the lesser, even though the lesser – and isn't this funny, *funny!* – is the one that might get him killed. He plants his face in her hair and breathes deep, trying to store enough of her smell to last for all time.

YO BRAAAAVOOOOOO booms across the

407

plaza, Sergeant Dime's parade-ground bellow. MOO-HOOOOVING OUT! LET'S GOOOO!

'That's me,' Billy whispers. Faison moans, and they fall into another bruising kiss. There's a violent moment when they try to pull apart – they grab at each other, pick and jab at clothes, body parts, a weird rage burning through them that they can't quite control. Faison's face suddenly crumples and she mashes into him.

BRAAAVOOOOO! **NOW!**

Billy kisses her lips and pulls away, and it feels like the last thing he'll ever do. 'Be careful!' she calls after him, and he raises his fist in acknowledgment. 'I'll pray for you!' she calls louder, and that just makes him feel hopeless. He's dying out here, dying, and that thing in his pants makes it difficult to walk, the rock-hard prong of his virgin member like a flag that refuses to fly at half-mast. He knocks at it with his wrist, the back of his hand, trying to force the creature down without the whole world seeing, and then, oh shit, they're on him, a group of seven or eight fans who want him to sign their game programs. *So grateful,* they say. *So proud. Awesome. Amazing.* This only takes a couple of moments, but while he's scribbling his name it dawns on Billy that these smiling, clueless citizens are the ones who came correct. For the past two weeks he's been feeling so superior and smart because of all the things he knows from the war, but forget it, they are the ones in charge, these saps, these innocents, their homeland dream is the

408

dominant force. His reality is their reality's bitch; what they don't know is more powerful than all the things he knows, and yet he's lived what he's lived and knows what he knows, which means what, something terrible and possibly fatal, he suspects. To learn what you have to learn at the war, to do what you have to do, does this make you the enemy of all that sent you to the war?

Their reality dominates, except for this: It can't save you. It won't stop any bombs or bullets. He wonders if there's a saturation point, a body count that will finally blow the homeland dream to smithereens. How much reality can unreality take? He's in somewhat of a daze as he passes off the last program and starts walking toward the curb, hands fisted in his pockets to hopefully hide his crazed erection. *Thank you!* the nice people call after him. *Thank you for your service!* Sleet pecks at his eyes, but he hardly feels it anymore. The cops step aside as he approaches, revealing Josh and Albert standing by the limo's rear door, and Albert is grinning, waving him on. 'Hurry!' he cries playfully. 'Come on! They're leaving!' As if this was the ride you couldn't miss, the one that would save your life? Albert gives him a quick hug as he slides past. Josh says good luck and squeezes his arm, then Billy is stepping off the curb, half-falling onto the limo's rear banquette.

Albert slams the door behind him and throws out a final wave. 'We're good,' Dime calls to the driver. 'Let's go.'

'Hell yeah, get us the fuck out of here,' says Sykes.

'Before they kill us,' Crack seconds. 'Take us someplace safe. Take us back to the war.'

'Seat belts, everyone,' Dime tells the squad, and Bravo paws around the seats, sorting out their belts. Dime notices the steeple in Billy's lap.

'Looking proud there, soldier,' he murmurs, just between the two of them.

'Some things can't be helped, Sergeant.'

Dime chuckles. 'You say good-bye to your girl?'

Billy nods and turns to the window. He knows he will never see Faison again, but how can he know? How does anyone ever know anything – the past is a fog that breathes out ghost after ghost, the present a freeway thunder run at 90 mph, which makes the future the ultimate black hole of futile speculation. And yet he knows, at least he thinks he knows, he feels it seeded in the purest certainty of his grief as he finds his seat belt and snaps it shut, that *snick* like the final lock of a vast and complex system. He's in. Bound for the war. Good-bye, good-bye, good night, I love you all. He sits back, closes his eyes, and tries to think about nothing as the limo takes them away.